DOWN
GOES
TRUMP

George Thomas Clark

ISBN: 978-1-7332981-1-7 – Trade Paperback
Copyright 2020 by George Thomas Clark

GeorgeThomasClark.com
Bakersfield, California
webmaster@GeorgeThomasClark.com

Books by George Thomas Clark

Paint it Blue
Hitler Here
The Bold Investor
Basketball and Football
Death in the Ring
Echoes from Saddam Hussein
Obama on Edge
Tales of Romance
In Other Hands
King Donald
Down Goes Trump

Introduction

Down Goes Trump is a collection of satirical stories, based on news, about the entertaining but absurd and often quite dangerous events following the election of President Donald J. Trump in November 2016 until shortly after his loss to Joe Biden four years later. In addition to fictionalized first-person entries by Trump and contemporary political and social personalities Nancy Pelosi, Kim Jong Un, Vladimir Putin, James Mattis, Rex Tillerson, John Bolton, Maxine Waters, Meryl Streep, Melania Trump, and many others, the author offers unexpected commentary by historical figures including Martin Luther King, General Robert E. Lee, Babe Ruth, Joseph Stalin, the Ayatollah Khomeini, and General Douglas MacArthur. There are no filters as Trump blunders the nation and world toward a nuclear confrontation with North Korea, a war with Iran, backs out of international agreements, wages psychological war against people of color in the United States, and bungles containment of the coronavirus. Buckle your seatbelts for a turbulent ride.

Contents

2016

2017

2020

2016

ONE

Trump Interviews Romney

Mitt Romney, handsome and trim, marches into Trump Tower and rides high the elevator to the office of President-elect Donald Trump. After security guards strip search the former governor of Massachusetts, a secretary tells him, "Please have a seat. The president will be with you directly."

Romney sits in a soft chair and on an adjacent table beholds dozens of NRA publications. He chooses one, digging in, and reads most of the issue in about an hour before asking, "Pardon me, do you know approximately when the president-elect will be interviewing me?"

"Soon as he can. He's quite busy."

Romney selects a second magazine, glistening with guns on the cover, and reads another hour or so before the secretary says, "President Trump will see you now."

Feeling a little tense Romney rises and practices a few tight smiles as he walks down the hall, and upon seeing The Donald he grins big and says, "Mr. President-elect, this is a great honor."

"I expect so," says Trump.

They move into Trump's office offering a spectacular view of Manhattan, and the host says, "I feel like I can see and understand the whole world from here."

"I've traveled quite widely, too, sir, and have many important foreign contacts."

"That's why I've asked you to interview for secretary of state. Please sit down."

Romney gently descends into a plush chair.

"I'd be honored to serve our country in that capacity, and I'd do a doggone good job."

"You've got the intellect and experience, Mitt, no doubt about that. I do have some concerns, however."

"Please speak frankly, sir."

"I gotta ask about your disgraceful speech calling me a phony and a fraud."

"Aren't we all ashamed of some things we say during the heat of campaigns?"

"You weren't even in the campaign."

"I was kind of hoping to be. But before long, sir, I concluded you were the best and most dynamic candidate, a new breed of candidate unsullied by governmental experience or knowledge of the issues. Furthermore, I now realize I squandered time studying law and business at Harvard and would've been far better served learning from you."

"You also said I was playing Americans for suckers so I'd get a free ride to the White House."

"What an intemperate and utterly indefensible statement that was. In fact, the presidential campaign was long and thorough, and in Darwinian fashion you removed sixteen weak Republican opponents, and I too would've been trampled by the Trumpian juggernaut had I been so foolish as to challenge your candidacy."

"You're right about that. Now, what about saying dishonesty is Donald Trump's hallmark?"

"I didn't mean it literally. Indeed, I was dishonest in making that statement."

"You also criticized me for bullying and greed and showing off and misogyny and absurd third-grade theatrics."

"Wasn't that juvenile of me?" says Romney. "Here in private, sir, I admit that my spleen exploded as I realized that you, rather than I, would become commander in chief of the greatest nation in history."

"Really, Mitt, your cheap shots surprised me since in 2012 you would've dropped to your knees to get my endorsement. You should've won that race and saved us four more years of Barack Obama. But you disappeared."

"I'm profoundly ashamed and ask you to forgive me."

"I may do that. Believe it or not, you're still in the running for secretary of state. I'd prefer General David Petraeus, a real stud, but need someone who can be easily confirmed."

"I can. You know that and so do millions of Americans."

"I'll let you know," Trump says, rising.

Romney also stands, and in storms Kellyanne Conway, the slender blond vixen who guided Trump during his raucous campaign. She says, "How dare you come into this sacred office after the way you betrayed President Trump. You're a vile and disgusting man and a traitor."

"The president-elect and I have been discussing these very concerns."

"We don't even know who you voted for," she says.

"I could lie but I shan't. I wrote in my name, but realize I should've voted for Donald J. Trump."

Bonding with Putin

After aides set up the call, Donald Trump grabs his phone and says, "Thank you so much, Vladimir."

"My pleasure, Donald."

"Don't worry. When I take over, the United States will improve relations with Russia."

"I hope so. The American media persists in portraying me as a bullying dictator determined to resurrect the Soviet Union."

"Much as I admire you, I can't permit any land grabs by Russia, other than the Crimea, or more bad behavior in Ukraine and Chechnya."

Putin laughs.

"Really, what would you do if I want to expand into Baltic States, for example? They were ours and still should be."

"The United States and Western Europe would impose major sanctions. Your people would suffer while the Russian media rips you."

"Most of my journalists know not to push too hard. You should consider getting tougher on your critics."

"I have to be satisfied blasting them on Twitter."

"Once you're in office, you need to come to Russia and establish yourself as a president who understands global dynamics and has the respect of, I must say, the greatest leader in the world today."

"I'll visit within my first couple of months."

"I look forward to meeting Melania, your beautiful Soviet-bloc wife."

"And I'd like to meet whoever you're seeing. You've had some hot ones."

"I don't tolerate invasions of my private life."

"Relax, Vladimir, we're just a couple of guys talking."

"But when you talk, even in private, it makes the news."

Laboring for Andrew Puzder

Most of you still don't know me but soon will since President-elect Trump asked me to be his Secretary of Labor. He knows I'll put America back to work. I'm an expert worker and CEO of the restaurant holding corporation that includes Carl's Jr. and Hardee's. I understand business and money and jobs. Listen to me, not my critics who complain I oppose raising the minimum wage beyond a too-generous nine dollars an hour and pay my employees so little they've got to live in public housing and dine on food stamps while getting health care through Medicaid. I guarantee paying workers too much destroys businesses and jobs. That's the only reason I want to suppress the minimum wage, to help the little workers of America. I don't want to replace people with robots, but I will if the former become too expensive.

Workers must realize I was called in to save Hardee's from a financial grave. I transformed the company into a profitable venture and didn't do so by paying outrageous overtime wages. It's too easy to get overtime which costs me money and will destroy your jobs. Remember, what workers lose in extra overtime pay they more than make up for in pride. Let me show you. I pull into Carl's Jr., park, and walk inside to introduce myself and show everyone how to produce.

"Howdy, I'm Andrew Puzder."

"Mabel, call the cops," says an energetic young lady.

"Relax. I'm the CEO of this corporation."

"What's a CEO?"

"It's the person who guides the corporate ship."

I walk behind the counter and say, "Give me an apron, please."

A nice young man hands me one and I put it on over my suit.

"Where are the fries?" I ask, and go to work cooking them. "I've always wanted to do this. Makes me feel useful. I'm sure you're the same way. A man's got to produce to feel like a man, same for you ladies. Oh, Lord."

The damn grease must've boiled too long before it splattered my face, hands, and arms. I stagger around the kitchen and fall onto a grill full of burgers and fry hell out of my elbow and scream, "Call nine-one-one."

One of the dimwits rubs grease on my wounds and another guides me to a chair where I hold my greasy face in throbbing hands,

"Mr. Puzder, this is Mabel. I want you to know I just googled your name, and I'm shocked."

"Why?"

"This article says more than half of the Department of Labor investigations of Carl's Jr. have uncovered violations."

"Don't believe that hooey. It's just a bunch of bureaucrats who've got nothing to do except cause trouble for working people like us. Besides, most of these joints are independently owned franchises. When I'm in charge, everything will be ideal."

"Mr. Puzder."

"What, Mabel?"

"They say…"

"Who the hell're they?"

"People writing these articles…"

"Liberal nonsense."

"It says you like advertising photos of nearly naked women eating Carl's Jr. hamburgers."

"Damn right I do. Americans love women in bikinis, especially with hamburgers. Where's that damn ambulance?"

Secretary of State Rex Tillerson

Rex Tillerson rides a fast elevator to the world's most vital place, the Trump Tower office of Donald J. Trump.

"Welcome, Rex."

"I'm honored to be here, Mr. President."

"Ever see anything this majestic?"

"Sure, I've been to the Krelim many times, but this place is awful nice, too."

"That's why you're here. We need a secretary of state with the diplomatic chops to carry out my dynamic foreign policy, and I just didn't feel General David Petraeus or Mitt Romney had the necessary experience or insight. My infallible gut tells me only the CEO of ExxonMobil can forge the deals we need to become prosperous and secure."

"You mean I've already got the job?"

"Not yet, but you do have this interview as a result of strong recommendations from distinguished secretaries James Baker and Condoleezza Rice as well as Robert Gates, who did such a good job as secretary of defense for both Bush and Obama."

"You want some oil rights, President Trump, just let me know. I've made deals for billions in more than fifty countries, Russia being my favorite and the most important."

Trump asks, "What's your take on Putin? I doubt he's killed many more dissidents and journalists than lots of leaders we do business with."

"Hell no. And I imagine those who got it deserved it. I like the guy. In 2013 he made sure I got the Order of Friends award in recognition of my efforts to improve the lives of Russians. I did that by profitably drilling for oil we knew about and finding oil no one had discovered. We could've gotten a lot more but President Obama and his clan established sanctions to punish Russia for simply taking care of neighborhood business and reclaiming the Crimea. That cost us billions and hurt our people as well as the Russians. Sanctions usually don't work. I encourage you to use them infrequently, especially against oil-rich nations."

"What would you say to Congress during your confirmation hearing? They may play rough."

"I'll tell them that wherever there's a problem, I'll rush right in, even faster than I did for ExxonMobil, and drill holes that'll fill everyone's pockets with oil."

"What if there's no oil?"

"We'll find something else."

"Your diplomatic IQ's off the charts, Rex. You got the job."

Introducing Michael Flynn

I love public speaking, especially the first night of the Republican convention last summer. I was at the podium and shouting lock her up and clapping with the audience, leading the chants. That's right, I said, if I'd done a tenth what Hillary Clinton did I'd be in jail now. I knew millions at home wondered who I was, and sensed they'd soon learn I'm a retired general who Donald Trump just rejected as a running mate but promised another assignment after his certain victory in November.

What will the president-elect ask me to do? I can do anything. I served thirty-three years in the United States Army, studying hard in many colleges and training programs and earning promotions in peace and war. By 2009 I served as director of intelligence for the United States Central Command in Afghanistan. Everyone, except a few louts, considered me a highly capable intelligence officer, and I felt so confident that without permission I shared with Pakistan our U.S. intelligence capabilities regarding the hostile Haqqani network. Some hidebound officers complained that the Pakistanis' Inter-Service Intelligence was little more trustworthy than Al Qaeda. I alone knew the right Pakistanis.

My critics and their investigations didn't prevent my promotion to director of intelligence for the International Security Assistance Force. In 2010, during war, I shared vital information about the activities of various agencies including the CIA with our comrades the British and Australians. I'm proud of that. Some jealous little men initiated investigations that delayed by a year my inevitable promotion to director of the Defense Intelligence Agency. Trust me, as Donald Trump does; I did a hell of a job.

Tragically, I was soon dealing with another member of the enemy camp, President Barack Obama, a liar who embraced a corrupt U.S. system and feared my powerful statements about the dangers of radical Islam. By 2014 he and his clique forced me out of my job and out of the army altogether. Another enemy, Colin Powell, sent emails saying he'd heard I was canned from the DIA because I abused staff members and didn't listen and ignored policy and managed poorly and frequently spread untruths that became known as Flynn Facts.

Beware, President Obama didn't want to know the truth about the growth of the Islamic State in Syria, and that our NATO ally Turkey was looking the other way. I was happy to get away from all those losers and start an intelligence consulting firm. Last year I was invited to Russia to give a speech and sit with President Vladimir Putin at a party for the RT television network some claim he controls. So what?

I was improving our relations with the largest nation on earth.

President-elect Donald Trump is positive I've made far fewer errors handling classified information than Hillary Clinton, and he knows I'll be a shrewd national security advisor. Ignore those outranked officers who scoff they're going to Las Vegas to wager a year's salary I won't last two years in the White House. .

General Mattis Meets Trump

James Mattis, three years retired after more than four decades as a marine, shakes hands with Donald Trump.

"I'm very pleased to meet you, General."

"A marine's always honored to meet his commander."

"I've heard you own seven thousand books. Is that true?"

"Yes, the longer I study war and history, the more I damage the enemy while limiting our losses," Mattis says.

"I don't read much, General, but I watch a lot of TV, especially Fox News."

"That's wonderful, sir."

"Instead of studying to prepare for this interview, I had one of my aides copy your best quotes from the internet and paste them on this paper. Can we please talk about some of the things you said?"

"Of course."

"You said blowing 'someone away is not an insignificant event' but 'there are some assholes in the world that just need to be shot.' I agree."

Mattis smiles.

"Ultimately, that's the role of our military. To kill as many assholes as possible."

"I assume a man of your wide reading also believes in diplomacy," says Trump.

"I've always required my marines to read about the people they'll be encountering. I want them to understand the foreigners' culture and to smile and communicate with them. 'Be polite, be professional, but have a plan to kill everybody you meet.'"

"I love your quote, 'I'm going to plead with you, do not cross us. Because if you do, the survivors will write about what we do here for ten thousand years.' You mean that literally, don't you?"

"Absolutely. 'There's no better friend, no worse enemy than a U.S. Marine.'"

"I didn't serve in the military, but I know I'd have been a helluva warrior."

"You had some draft deferments, didn't you, President-elect Trump?"

"Yeah, but only four. Now's my time to really kick ass."

"You missed the party. 'Actually it's quite fun to fight… It's a hell of a hoot. It's fun to shoot some people… I like brawling… There's nothing better than getting shot at and missed.'"

Trump says, "I enjoy brawling, too."

"Have you brawled much, Mr. President?"

"Not with guns or even fists, but with words, lots of words and insults like during the campaign. I outslugged all my opponents. Same in business. I'm congenial but when necessary I've always kicked ass."

"That's why you're an extraordinary success."

"General Mattis, I'd be proud if you served as my secretary of defense."

"It's an honor to accept your assignment."

"I know you'll be successful."

"That's guaranteed. Many times I've said, 'I don't lose any sleep at night over the potential for failure. I cannot even spell the word.'"

2017

TWO

Nuclear Trump

I worry about our nuclear triad because I'm a strategic thinker. I knew what the triad was last year even though political enemies tried to use my words to make it sound like I didn't. I did and I do and warn everyone the United States must greatly strengthen and expand its land-based missiles, and submarine-launched missiles, and bombs and missiles dropped and fired from planes. Some cowards say U.S. proliferation might lead to an arms race. Let it. We'll outmatch and outlast them all. Who are they? Russia, China, North Korea, Iran, and everyone else with nuclear weapons or ambitions. We rule this planet and, thank God, I'll soon be commander in chief.

The ninety-nine-plus percent of you who lack my military expertise need to know that fifty years ago we had more than thirty-one thousand nuclear weapons. While it's true Cold Warriors from that era complained about a nonexistent missile gap favoring the Soviet Union, now there really is a gap. We only have four thousand five hundred warheads and less than fifteen hundred are deployed. The Russians have meanwhile deployed more than fifteen hundred. That advantage may encourage them to attack Western Europe or even the United States. I can't imagine my comrade, Vladimir Putin, betraying me and going suicidal, but we've got to make sure he doesn't. We do that by terrifying him.

While we modernize our missiles, submarines, bombs, and planes, I promise to tell Vladimir and the Chinese we're all too smart to really mess with each other. That's big boy deterrence. But I'm not going to say I won't nuke ISIS. I want them to think I might. That's bully boy nuclear strategy.

Bibi the Builder

For thousands of years the Jewish people have had a biblical right to Judea and Samaria, and since our grand defensive victory during the Six Day War in 1967 we've wielded not merely the moral but the political and military right to protect the rest of Israel by administering this land still inhabited by radicals hostile to our Jewish state which extends but ten slender miles from the border of the so called West Bank to the Mediterranean.

Many of our enemies, who are dark skinned and from authoritarian nations, have periodically tried to use the United Nations Security Council to denounce Israel for violations of international law, asserting we have no right to build settlements on occupied West Bank territory. We, however, have insisted upon the fundamental right of self-defense and continued to add housing units as one means of precluding another Holocaust. As prime minister of Israel, I, Benjamin Netanyahu, have embraced this duty above all others.

Until the administration of Barack Hussein Obama, we in Israel depended on our political friends in the United States. But just last week the Americans insulted their closest and only real friend in the Middle East, and the sole democracy, by ignoring their customary duty to veto another U.N. resolution proclaiming us criminals because we've approved plans to build several hundred more homes in East Jerusalem. The Obama-sullied Americans abstained. We don't care. Indeed, we'll build where we must. All of Jerusalem is ours. Palestinians who disagree should move elsewhere, and we may assist in this process.

Thankfully, President-elect Donald Trump denounced the United Nations for condemning our behavior, and we in Israel are most encouraged that a man who so adroitly lies and steals will soon be our guy in the White House and I'll no longer have to address Congress to undermine the leader of the free world.

King Tweeter

every
time
i
tweet
my
balls
get
bigger

Kim Jong Un Tweets Trump

Outraged by the contradictory tweet from President-elect Trump, I snatch my high powered Dear Leader tweeter and fire: It will happen. North Korea will soon have a nuclear-tipped ballistic missile capable of reaching the United States.

In daily telepathic conversations my godlike grandfather and father, who created a paradise that capitalists want to destroy, tell me what I must do. I must always ignore insults from enemies who call me mad and delusional and say I'm fat and fattening. Nonsense, I'm neither mad nor delusional, but Saddam Hussein and Muammar Gaddafi must have been thusly afflicted to believe the Americans wouldn't someday conquer their countries and execute them. I often think about the departed dictators. Wouldn't you?

I guarantee you'll never turn on your TVs and see me with a noose around my neck or North Koreans parading my battered face through the streets prior to shooting me. That worries the Americans. With the probable exception of Donald Trump, they understand my conventional forces are eternally primed and ready to hurl destruction upon Seoul and many other hostile targets, and South Koreans are always uncomfortable during their annual military exercises with the Americans. They'd like to invade my country, they'd like to crush me but know they dare not try.

My enemies claim provocative moves are vital to deter me from attacking South Korea. That's a strange preoccupation. Who have I ever invaded? I'm busy oppressing, starving, and brainwashing my people. I have neither the means nor the desire to conquer. I don't command the United States. I lead a nation determined to ignore the sanctions and threats of imperialists. Their efforts to ruin us have failed. Stronger we grow every day. Shrewder become our scientists. Slimmer are the chances anyone can stop me from developing more nuclear weapons and ballistic missiles.

Here's another tweet for Donald Trump: What are you going to do about my nuclear deterrents? I'll tell you. You're going to accept the fait accompli.

The president-elect enjoys insulting China because it won't "help with North Korea." Does this foreign policy neophyte understand the Chinese don't want my haven to collapse and unleash millions of desperate refugees into their country? Doesn't The Donald realize the Chinese need a buffer zone between themselves and American troops eternally stationed in South Korea? Does he believe the Chinese would tolerate a North Korean collapse opening the gates for Yankee militarism on the Sino-Korean border?

Has Donald Trump read about the Chinese invasion and rout of U.S. troops during the Korean War? I know the Loud One doesn't read but perhaps one of his advisors could tell him. The Chinese are infinitely stronger now and will assure my survival as long as they want.

THREE

Streep Invades Trump Tower

I sense tweeting and TV blasting won't be sufficient so in a radical Hollywood jet I fly to New York and ride a five-limousine caravan to Trump Tower where I exit and announce, "Meryl Streep to see President-elect Trump."

"You aren't really Meryl Streep, are you?" says a secret service agent.

"Indeed I am."

"I didn't realize you were so old."

"I'm three years younger than The Donald. Please notify him I'm here."

"Is he expecting you?"

"I don't need an appointment."

"We'll see." He nods to another agent who by a wireless device in his ear calls into the Manhattan heavens.

"Okay," says the agent, who squints looking for my wrinkles. "Step in the lobby so we can search you."

"A strip search won't be necessary, I hope."

"Not on the ground floor, at least."

I walk through a metal detector, take off my coat, open my purse, and undergo a light pat down before being led into an elevator. After a fast and rather exciting ride up I'm greeted by more agents who are pronouncing the rules when Donald J. Trump steps into the hall and says, "Meryl, frankly, I didn't expect to see your overrated ass around here. But you've got balls to visit me. Come on in."

Melania greets me in the living room and leads me to a sofa and then, along with everyone but her husband, leaves the room.

"Really, Meryl, I'm never supposed to be alone with anyone except my closest family members and advisors, but I trust you'll refrain from physical violence. I'm not being naïve, am I?"

"No. I'm here for rhetorical combat."

"Remember, I always dish out more than I take."

"It's pitiful that you, an amateurish game show host, impugned my unprecedented credentials as a thespian."

"Well, you falsely accused me of publicly making fun of a disabled reporter."

"Your performance is right there on the screen."

"And you failed to understand I was alluding to one of the reporter's very old articles. Now, regarding my assessment of your dramatic short-comings, let's remember that while you've been nominated for nineteen Oscars, you've only won three. That makes you a sixteen-time loser. I run for president once, and I win. I always win. If I'd been your director you might've done a little better and won for *The Deer Hunter*, *Silkwood*, *The Bridges of Madison County*, and some of the others. I guess you were okay in winning for *Sophie's Choice*."

"I urge you to be honest with the American people."

"I will. Their mandate was overwhelming."

"You lost the popular vote by…"

"Yeah, you liberals'll never get over that. I won what counted, and it would've counted for Hillary if she'd won."

"I demand that you quit pretending the Mexicans are going to pay for your wall."

"It's our wall, and I guarantee they'll pay, eventually."

"Your assertion was always that they'd pay immediately."

"I don't recall saying that exactly," he says. "They'll pay, maybe taxes, trade adjustments, or impounded remittances. Whatever."

"Right now Senator Jeff Sessions of Alabama is inevitably meeting serious opposition during his confirmation hearing for attorney general."

"Believe me. He'll be confirmed."

"The man's a racist."

"How do you know?"

"His sympathy for the Ku Klux Klan, his suppression of black voters, the things he's said over the years."

"Those are liberal talking points. He's got the support of some prominent black legal officials in Alabama who know him far better than you. You're used to reciting lines from fictional scripts, and you're doing the same thing in politics."

"You, sir, are the reciter of fables, and unworthy of being our president. It's a fantasy to promise you'll create millions of good jobs by cutting taxes and increasing federal spending. Where's the money coming from?"

"Meryl, I'm going to get a younger and hotter actress. You're fired."

"The American people are going to fire you, and I sense that'll happen in less than four years."

Heart of Trump

For a year and a half I've been disturbed by what Donald Trump's been saying, and since his Electoral College victory over Hillary Clinton I've at times been mortified by his hot pie hole and big tweeter. Only this week have I learned, from Kellyanne Conway, that I shouldn't believe what Donald Trump says, I should instead focus on what is in his heart. Since what most people repeatedly say is a good way to determine what's inside, this comment by his advisor confuses me. However, when charming Kellyanne smiles into a camera I think less about politics and more about what would please her, so I at once call and ask her to please get me an interview with the heart of Donald J. Trump. She agrees, and this evening I meet the ticker.

George Thomas Clark – You're a big heart, as one would expect from a hefty man of limitless ambition. I'd like to begin by asking what your heart really feels about Representative John Lewis, a civil rights hero from the sixties and one of the Freedom Riders, who your mouth said was all talk, talk, talk when he questioned your qualifications to be president.

Heart of Trump – Forty years ago, when I was a young businessman, my father and I declined to rent apartments to blacks. If John Lewis had applied, I'd have turned his ass down, too. Remember, we didn't have to admit any wrongdoing in the lawsuit, we just paid a little dough.

GTC – Do you still feel the United States needs to build a massive wall along its border with Mexico? In his Senate confirmation testimony, your future head of the Department of Homeland Security, General John Kelly, said he doesn't think it would be helpful to build a wall and that economic conditions must improve in Latin America in order to permanently alleviate the need for desperate people to enter the U.S. illegally.

HoT – General Kelly's saying what's necessary to be confirmed. He's also a soldier and understands the chain of command. If I consider a wall necessary, I'll build a wall.

GTC – What if, as seems likely, Congress tells you it doesn't have the money and Mexico continues to tell you to shove it.

HoT – I'll be deporting so many criminals, and frankly many other illegal aliens, like those at businesses I bust, that I'll be able to say, "Look at my toughness and control. We don't need a wall as big as I first thought." I'll get the money to build something, even if it's only symbolic.

GTC – Are you still planning a massive registration of all Muslim immigrants? General Kelly doesn't believe "it's ever appropriate to focus on religion."

HoT – A couple more terrorist attacks here or in Europe will give me the leverage I need to suppress civil liberties. General Kelly will either go along or I'll fire him.

GTC – You've said you plan to use waterboarding and a hell of a lot tougher torture on suspected terrorists. About that, your nominees for attorney general and CIA chief, Sen. Jeff Sessions and Rep. Mike Pompeo, have respectively testified "absolutely illegal" and "absolutely not."

HoT – If I believe I can save American lives by twisting critical information out of terrorists, that's what's gonna happen. Period.

GTC – The United States has a one-China policy that you seemed to undermine when you accepted a congratulatory phone call from the Taiwanese president.

HoT – I take calls from whoever I want. That's none of China's business. It's our business that the Chinese improve their greedy trade policies and aggressive military behavior in the South China Sea.

GTC – You've often praised President Vladimir Putin and don't appear concerned about Russian annexation of Crimea and military incursions in eastern Ukraine.

HoT – I'll keep some sanctions for now, but if our relations improve I'll remove the sanctions. Those who say Putin's a war criminal don't know the man or the difficulties he faces.

GTC – Do you think he's worried about NATO's expansion around western Russian during the last twenty years?

HoT – Of course he is. We wouldn't tolerate that kind of threat looming around us. And I'm tired of Americans paying to maintain that military threat. Let the Europeans pay a fair share of their defense. They've got more money and people than we do.

GTC – General James Mattis, your pick to run the Department of Defense, testified that Putin's trying to break up NATO, and "history proves nations with strong allies thrive and those without them wither."

HoT – We've never had a president who's got the natural feel for Russia and its president that I have. Let's be friends with Russia like we were during World War II. I can make that happen because I sense Vladimir Putin and I are going to understand each other.

GTC – Why haven't you discussed Russia yet with Rex Tillerson, your nominee for secretary of state?

HoT – We haven't had time. I trust Russia and so does Rex Tillerson. That's where we start.

GTC – Tillerson said global warming exists.

HoT – If enough Republicans line up on that side, I'll pivot and say yeah, it exists. Whatever's politically expedient, that's what I'll say.

The Inaugural Speech

I am today honored to stand before the impoverished and miserable people of the United States and take my rightful place as a successor to George Washington and Abraham Lincoln. I too shall be your savior and forever protect you from people like the four failures sitting behind me on this executive stage. President Jimmy Carter left us with high interest rates and hostages in Iran. President Bill Clinton stained the presidency and was impeached for dropping his drawers in the sacred Oval Office. President George W. Bush exhibited a low IQ and reckless nature while luring the nation into an unnecessary and disastrous war in Iraq. And my predecessor, President Barack Obama, talked sweetly as our inner cities rotted and enemies abroad kicked us in the balls. My fellow Americans, I vow this devastation will not continue. We are going to rebuild our pitifully weak nation. And believe me, at this moment we're on life support.

Before I go on, please take a look at my gorgeous and dignified wife Melania, my beautiful eldest daughter Ivanka, and the two blond babes married to my animal-slaying sons from the first of my three holy marriages. I have procreated a great family and many wonderful businesses, and that is why you're so hopeful as I become your president. Every four years we celebrate another orderly and peaceful transfer of power, though during the campaign, when it looked like I'd lose, I threatened to unleash my dim but fanatical supporters.

I understand that many of you, primarily Democrats, view me as a callous billionaire who throughout his life has by money, mansions, and security goons separated himself from the sweaty masses. That's true, but thank God almost half the people in this desperate land want to roll the dice in my casino, betting on the proposition I've somehow become a champion of the poor and the enemy of powerbrokers and thieves in the nation's capital who "reaped the rewards of government while the people have borne the cost."

Our jobs have left and our factories closed. I don't care that unemployment is today lower than it's been in years. It doesn't matter our auto industry has been revived. It's irrelevant the stock market is at record highs. What counts is that you embrace my demagoguery. In return I promise: "This moment is your moment; it belongs to you... This is your day. This is your celebration." You're celebrating that I'm your trusted protector and father of a new America. With my mighty hands guiding us, we will rid ourselves of inner city poverty, shuttered factories, failing schools, and rampant crime, gangs, and drugs. Miraculously, I will stop this carnage right now.

No longer will we defend "other nations' borders while refusing to defend our own." No longer will be spend "trillions of dollars overseas while America's infrastructure" crumbles. No longer will "the wealth of our middle class (be) ripped from their homes and then redistributed across the entire world." Trust me. Many more great developments are imminent. "We will bring back our borders. We will bring back our wealth. And we will bring back our dreams." Before I took the presidential oath minutes ago, you had only chaos, poverty, and nightmares.

Fear not. We're going to "buy American and hire American... We will seek friendship and goodwill" abroad "but we do so with the understanding that it is the right of all nations to put their own interests first." We must cease being so generous and trusting, and I'm going to keep you convinced that you've been a nation of helpless victims until this shining moment as we prepare to "reinforce old alliances and form new ones... and unite the civilized world against Radical Islamic Terrorism, which we will eradicate completely from the face of the earth."

At its essence, "our politics will be a total allegiance to the United States of America, and through our loyalty to our country, we will rediscover our loyalty to each other... When America is united, America is totally unstoppable." Until now, our country has not been so divided since the days of the Civil War. Your agony is over. "We are protected by God," and I know what He wants me to do. Despite what my enemies say, I have always loved God and studied scripture. Indeed, I'm a biblical scholar, and my spiritual beliefs have taught me "that a nation is only living as long as it is striving." We will no longer accept politicians, like the four simpletons on this stage, who are all talk and no action. The time for empty talk is over. It's time for barrages of my tweets to rouse our country to "thrive and prosper again." I may even rent apartments to blacks, and without much regret. We can't worry about the color of our skin. "We all bleed the same red blood of patriots... and we all salute the same great American flag."

I promise "you will never be ignored again.... Together we will make America strong again... wealthy again... proud again... and safe again."

Obama's Letter to Trump

Donald J. Trump is getting ready to have a really great time his first night in the White House and about to hit the sack with the force of an exhausted whale when he notices a paper pinned to the wall above the headboard. He grabs the paper, wondering what the hell it says.

Dear President Trump,

By the time you notice this missive you will indeed be commander in chief of the United States of America. I salute you and promise to not quite so vigorously oppose you, as I otherwise will, if you remember and periodically acknowledge just a few numbers and what they really mean.

When I took office, the unemployment rate was seven-point-eight percent and now it's four-point-seven.

When I took office, fifteen-point-seven percent of the population lacked medical insurance. Now, after several years of the Affordable Care Act – odious Obamacare – only eight-point-six percent are uninsured.

By contrast, you take office two days after agreeing to pay twenty-five million dollars to those you bilked through Trump University. You say you know you would win the case but are settling as a favor to the nation.

That isn't true.

Sincerely,

Barack Obama

FOUR

Off the Wall

I love being the coolest and most powerful man in the world especially as I sit on my throne in the Oval Office and, before the world, sign big my name in thick blue ink unleashing executive orders that implement my campaign promise to save the nation by walling off our southern border not only from Mexico but, by extension, Central America and lots of other bad places. We're under siege from semi-civilized hordes desperate to come here to rape and pillage. Don't listen to liberals who claim one-point-six million illegal aliens invaded in 1986 and the same number in 2000 while only three hundred thousand stormed our borders in 2015. The danger is increasing. I've talked to mothers whose children have been murdered by aliens and we know the statistics are wrong and anyway beside the point. We either have a nation or we don't. In order to have a nation we need a wall that's already being planned. Construction will soon begin. And, yes, Mexico will reimburse us. They're damn lucky I'm not making them pay up front.

After finishing my signature duties, and prior to heading over to Homeland Security and throwing bloody meat at my supporters, I relax a little until a breathless aide runs to my side and says, "Here, Mr. President, you must read this."

"What is it?"

"An article in *Foreign Policy* journal. It's titled, 'Seven Bargaining Chips Mexico Has in Negotiations With Trump.'"

"I've got all the chips, just like in my casinos."

"Some of those casinos went bankrupt, so please take a look."

"Don't be smartass. Is this going to be on TV?"

"It wouldn't be so straightforward in that medium," says the aide.

"Okay, just read me some of the main points."

"Number one, the article says 'six million jobs in the United States depend on trade with Mexico.'"

"What're they going to do? Stop buying our products?"

"They could buy some things elsewhere."

"For more money and less quality."

"Point two says immigrants generate as much as four percent of our gross domestic product and do so without costing this country jobs."

"What's their source?" I ask.

"*Business Insider.*"

"I'm the ultimate insider and guarantee that's bull. Whatever they generate comes out of the pockets of hardworking Americans."

"Or unemployed Americans who don't want to be farmworkers."

"Hold the commentary. Number three."

"They say 'Mexico is the United States' third-largest agricultural export market,' and that earns us almost twenty billion annually."

"Who says?"

My aide monkeys with his phone and says, "It's not in the article but here I see it: the United States Department of Agriculture."

"Twenty billion pesos?"

"Dollars."

"Like I said, if the Mexicans want to buy from someone else, let them."

"Here, Mr. President, I've just found something else from an article in *Forbes* magazine: 'Every major trading partner saw a decline of at least five percent in their imports from the U.S. Only Mexico continued to buy American.'"

"You think President Enrique Peña Nieto knows this?"

"Doubtful, he doesn't like to read, either."

"Anything about my wall?" I ask.

"Point six says our neighbor continues to make it 'very clear it has no intention of reimbursing the United States… for the wall on the border.'"

"We'll find indirect ways to make them pay, taxes, tariffs, lots of stuff."

"Are you going to tell that to President Peña Nieto when he visits you next week?"

"Damn right," I say.

"If he still plans to come."

"Quit playing with your damn phone."

Against the Wall

After his translator puts on headphones and dials about twenty numbers, the dapper man in Los Pinos caresses a phone and waits while the White House phone rings.

"Hello," says a woman.

"This is President Peña Nieto. Who's this?"

"Melania."

"Please let me speak to President Trump."

"What country are you from?"

"Mexico."

"Oh, you're that real cute guy. Let's do a photo shoot sometime."

"I don't care to be photographed with your husband."

"Just the two of us, professional models."

"Perhaps. May I speak to the president?"

Melania extends the phone.

"Enrique, this is President Trump. Don't flirt with my wife."

"Donald, all Mexicans are enraged by your insulting executive order about the wall."

"That's why I canceled our meeting."

"I'm the one who canceled."

"I tweeted for you not to come until you're ready to pay," Trump says.

"No way that ever happens. You have no mandate. Your popularity rating's only about thirty-five percent."

"That's not true. I got forty-six percent, about where I am in the polls. That'll increase now that I'm bringing Mexico under control. And don't tell me about favorability ratings: you're at twelve percent, lowest I've heard of anywhere."

"That'll change as Mexicans gather around me to fight you."

"Listen, Enrique, let's agree to keep our discussions about the wall private. Okay?"

Peña Nieto frowns. "All right, for a while."

"Remember, our trade deficit with Mexico is sixty billion dollars."

"Don't forget that U.S. citizens have much more money and therefore buy more products. Mexico isn't screwing you."

"You're shoving it up our asses, Enrique. Look at the devastation caused by your drug cartels."

"They wouldn't exist if norteamericanos weren't a horde of coke smokers corrupting our young people, who wouldn't otherwise be motivated to sell drugs."

"You've killed sixty thousand of each other along our border," says Trump. "That's why we're going to wall you out."

"Maybe the wall's a good idea if it keeps your gangsters from smuggling automatic weapons used to murder our people."

"There's more trouble coming our way than yours."

"Don't blame Mexico for the murder rates in your inner cities."

"I never exactly said that, Enrique."

"You implied it."

"Maybe I'll cool the rhetoric a little."

Praying for Trump

Everywhere I go people tell me, "I'm praying for you." I appreciate that since I'm a compassionate guy. The world's in big trouble but I'm going to make everything better. That's what I do. I fix things. You should hear what I've been saying on the phone to world leaders.

So many countries are taking advantage of us, practically everyone in the world. I'm going to fix that, but first I'm going to pray for Arnold Schwarzenegger and his disastrous ratings after stepping into my too-big shoes as host of *The Apprentice*.

Some leaders are pretty good guys, especially Vladimir Putin. I talked to him the other day. Maybe a few Russians hacked into our electoral process, but not Vladimir. That's what I told him. It's time to ease sanctions on some of his cyber-security firms. If they did intervene here, at least they helped the right side. We need to be friends with Russia. I don't care some Republicans in the Senate, guys like John McCain and Lindsey Graham, want to keep punishing Russia economically. What have those two ever really accomplished? Nothing.

I know what counts, and am not worried the day after Vladimir and I talked the Russians increased rocket and artillery attacks on Ukrainian military positions. That's not going to force me to sweep away major sanctions the Obama administration imposed after Russia liberated the Crimea and invaded eastern Ukraine. I'll keep those sanctions for the time being so the Europeans don't whine too much. But at some point, maybe when Russia backs off in Ukraine, I'll normalize everything economically.

The people I'm likely to fix first, even before the North Koreans, are the Iranians. They test fired a ballistic missile, and I tweeted they'd been "PUT ON NOTICE" I may do something if they provoke us again. Are they crazy? They've already got the most one-sided nuclear deal in history and should be thankful and peaceful. They'd be starving now if Obama hadn't saved them with a hundred fifty billion dollars. Sure, it was money from their oil, but we should've kept it until forcing them to make a good nuclear deal.

Heil Berkeley

police watch
stormtroopers
march black clad
into uc berkeley
breaking faces
windows and
free speech

Guardian Trump

Our naïve and pitiful nation is as I speak being targeted by terrorists here and abroad, and only I can save you from further carnage. An appellate court of three ultra-liberal and traitorous San Francisco judges has temporarily overturned my order to ban people from seven nations poisoned by Islam. They won't get away with it. I've already tweeted: "SEE YOU IN COURT, THE SECURITY OF OUR NATION IS AT STAKE." When I use all caps I'm pissed and people get scared especially since I've become your president.

I admit, however, that my programs to protect you could be undermined by the gang of judicial and media liars who want to damage me politically and lessen your safety. The Three Stooges in San Francisco claimed they couldn't find any information to verify my assertions that people from those countries had attacked us or threatened to do so. It's far too easy in this country to contradict the president. Someday I may need to write the mother of all executive orders to prohibit the media – and the judiciary – from "hiding incidents of terrorism" instead of trusting me. Believe this: "Bad people are very happy" about this court ruling.

I got rid of a villain a few days ago. Guadalupe Garcia de Rayos snuck from Mexico into our nation when she was fourteen years old. She bore two anchor babies here and was convicted of criminal impersonation after being nabbed during a work-site raid led by the forces of patriot and protector, Sheriff Joe Arpaio of Maricopa County, Arizona. Garcia de Rayos should've been deported at the time but weak authorities allowed her to stay as long as she checked with ICE every six months. That's when we arrested her. There's a new man in charge, and let me assure you this working mother, who lived here twenty years, has already been deported to Nogales, Mexico.

Phoenix Mayor Greg Stanton and Rep. Ruben Gallego are calling my patriotic action a "tragedy" and a "travesty," and accusing me of hounding harmless women and children instead of killers and drug dealers. They're just trying to make Phoenix a sanctuary city, and that wouldn't be smart since I'm going to financially squeeze people around the nation who shield invaders.

FIVE

Empathetic Trump

I know some of you feel I lack empathy and have been calling me a narcissist, and that's really unfair. As your president I'm up every night, tweeting and worrying about your safety and well-being. I also want to help people around the world.

Inevitably, I think a lot about the Syrians. It's impossible to stop a civil war unless you're ready to put several hundred thousand American troops there, and I know you don't want that. Even if we intervened, it would be tough to stop the bloodshed. They've got ISIS on one side, other rebels all over, and they're battling the regime of President Bashar al-Assad that's killed hundreds of thousands. Don't assume I'm immune to this. Long before you read about it, I had reports about an Assad prison where thousands of prisoners are tortured and starved for weeks or months before being hanged. This place is really an extermination camp. But what can I do? You know Russia and President Putin support Assad. Once I meet privately with Vladimir, I think I can convince him that Assad's a bad guy. And after we take care of ISIS we can get rid of Assad and put someone in who may not be as bad. I doubt you'd like to deal with all this.

I can't even relax at Mar-a-Lago with Japanese Prime Minister Shinzo Abe. To insult us, fat little Kim Jong Un of North Korea test fired another ballistic missile. He shot it right into Shinzo Abe's gut and mine. Prime Minister Abe warned him not to endanger Japan. We forgot to mention South Korea, but South Korea knows we're ready to protect it. They also realize we can't stop North Korean conventional missiles and artillery from devastating Seoul and most of South Korea. And we can't really stop nuclear war unless we launch a preemptive strike, but we could annihilate the North Koreans if they start something. I can't let them do that. I empathize with their poor starving people as well as their potential victims.

I care about everyone, and that's what makes me a wonderful father. Ask my five kids. Do you have any? If so, I bet you stand up for them. That's all I was doing when Nordstrom's threw Ivanka's stylish clothes and shoes out of their stores. I tweeted: "My daughter Ivanka has been treated so unfairly by @Nordstrom." The company claims it didn't reveal sales figures for Ivanka's brand. They didn't do it publicly but leaked the thirty percent sales decline from a year earlier to the *Wall Street Journal*. That's a low blow.

Michael Flynn Resigns

The riotous American election had recently concluded and President-elect Donald Trump's strategic guru, and future national security advisor, tough and ambitious General Michael Flynn, lifted a phone to call Russian Ambassador Sergey Kislyak, who told his secretary to open the line.

"General Flynn. I'm delighted."

"Mr. Ambassador, how are you, sir?"

"Please, call me Sergey. May I call you Michael, or Mikhail, perhaps?"

"Mike's fine."

"President Obama just hit us with some more sanctions, Mike."

"Terrible," said Flynn. "You know how that guy is."

"That's why we admire you and Donald Trump and are delighted he won."

"We appreciate your help, Sergey."

"Despite what Obama and his operatives claim, we only offered spiritual assistance rather than technical, I assure you."

"But of course."

"We're most encouraged that President-elect Trump wants better relations with Russia. There's no reason for you to keep squeezing us."

"I think that's how the president-elect feels."

"Did he say so specifically?" asked the ambassador.

"I'd rather not comment on what President-elect Trump said, but I believe our relations will soon be improving."

* * *

Vice President Mike Pence summons national security advisor Michael Flynn into his White House office and, without standing, says, "I'm quite worried, General, about reports we've received from the Justice Department."

"What do they say?"

"That before we took office you inappropriately promised the Russians relief from sanctions."

"Ambassador Kislyak and I discussed many urgent issues, including then-upcoming Christmas celebrations, but I certainly never talked about sanctions."

"You're certain?"

"I am, Mr. Vice President."

"Then I'll publicly and privately defend you as often as necessary."

* * *

Shortly after telling minions to announce he has complete confidence in Michael Flynn, President Donald Trump summons him to the Oval Office and, planted behind his executive desk, says, "Goddamn it, Mike, you're supposed to be an intelligence expert. Didn't you know Ambassador Kislyak's phone is always tapped?"

"Of course."

"Then what the hell were you doing?"

"I was helping you build a new relationship with Russia, Mr. President."

"Frankly, Mike, I can see why Obama removed your hyper ass from the Defense Intelligence Agency. You've already embarrassed me and the vice president and our whole administration."

"I've skillfully served my country for almost forty years, Mr. President."

"You're a patriot but a loose cannon who from now on will be firing blanks from private life."

"I'm so sorry, Mr. President. I just didn't recall discussing sanctions."

"Go tell Mike Pence."

The Deal

hey fbi director
comey whaddya'
say we forget this

thing between russia
and michael flynn

Puzder Laid Off

To hell with it. I'm relieved some Republican senators have sided with moronic fast food workers and forced me to withdraw before I could be confirmed as head of the Department of Labor. They'd have been lucky to have me. I'm a certified business wizard who pulled Hardee's out of the dumpster and made their food edible and the company strong and strengthened Carl's Jr. as well. Who cares my workers were planning to picket our restaurants in twenty states?

Republicans who caved in should have studied my overall record rather than worry I said in fast food we compete for the "best of the worst" and sometimes have to settle for the "worst of the worst." Come on, we're not hiring people who just graduated from Harvard and Yale. And, whatever their merits, they're often gone in a few months. They either don't like or understand the job or complain about the minimum wage, which I've always stressed should be kept low; fifteen bucks an hour would be catastrophic to our bottom line and my sterling entrepreneurial reputation.

"Get the hell out of my way," I say to protestors standing around my limousine. "You got what you wanted."

"We want a living wage," says a fat lady. I'm trim, by the way, and my shiny dome looks kind of hip.

"You've got one."

"We can't rent decent apartments and don't have health insurance even though we work forty or more hours a week, and you and the franchise owners try to stiff us on overtime."

"Paying overtime weakens the company."

"Look, hombre," says a tattooed young man, "you make four million four hundred thousand dollars a year. Do the math. That's eighteen grand a day, about what we make working full-time for a year."

"Aren't you aware I've also complimented many of you? I've said your work is 'meaningful and important.'"

"Then pay us a meaningful wage," says the lady.

"Your wages reflect your contributions."

"You don't give a damn about working people. That's why you want to replace us with robots."

"Robots are always healthy and on time and never protest."

One State or Two

I knew I was going to be a hell of a president but, frankly, I underestimated myself. I've got a great feel for diplomacy and international relations. Did you see me at the news conference last week with Prime Minister Abe after the North Koreans test fired another ballistic missile? I coolly let the Japanese leader denounce the aggressors and, when he finished, simply stepped in and promised to back our ally.

I was just as smooth the other day during my press conference with my good friend Prime Minister Benjamin Netanyahu of Israel. I didn't rant or preach like a lot of presidents. I just said, "I'm looking at two-state and one-state" solutions to the conflict between Israelis and Palestinians, and "I like the one that both parties like… I can live with either one."

Then, before the world, I told Bibi, "I'd like to see you hold back on settlements for a little bit." People assume because my daughter Ivanka converted to the Orthodox Judaism of her husband Jared Kushner, who's also one of my senior advisors, that I won't be fair to the Palestinians. Listen, I understand deals.

"As with any successful negotiation, both sides will have to make comprises," I said, and turned to Bibi. "You know that, right?"

The Palestinians shouldn't worry that Bibi told everyone how long he'd been friends with my family and me and how he knew Jared when he was a kid. I can help them more than their Arab neighbors. Egypt's economy's in the tank, Iraq's been bleeding for decades and Syria for several years, and the Saudis are scared about Iran and terrorists in Yemen. I didn't want to say it to the media, but the Palestinians are getting pretty isolated. Unless someone convinces Bibi and the Israelis to stop building more housing units, they'll soon annex the West Bank. Some say it's really been annexed since the war in 1967.

I'm not going to accept that or any deal unless both sides feel good. I'm going to sit down and find out what they want. Generations of leaders here and in the Middle East have failed to do that. Donald J. Trump is different.

Undercover Trump

Make me a mature Mexican rock star, I tell my makeup lady, hang some long cool black hair on my head and pin a big mustache on my face. I need to blend with families and friends of those being naturalized as U.S. citizens this morning in Fresno. There's already a big crowd in the convention center and about half hold documents that will allow them to officially become part of the nation I'm trying to save. But I can't protect real Americans if some of these folks cheated to get here.

My three Spanish-speaking agents, who don't need disguises, are periodically asked if we're in a band. I focus on hordes of people who keep entering and heading to tables for final documentation.

"Hey," I say to a young lady. "Where're you from?"

"Guadalajara. Why?"

"Just making sure you're not with ISIS."

"Why would you think that?" asks a man I assume is her husband.

"I'm responsible for security. Where're you from?"

"Los Angeles."

"A sanctuary city I'll soon cut off federal funding to. What're you doing in Fresno?"

"I live here. Where do you live?"

"New York, usually. Part-time in the capital."

"Sacramento?"

"D.C."

God, they're still swarming in, countless citizens to be and even more watching from seats in back of the hall. All of them remind me of people filmed darting across the border. Some women are wearing hijabs. You know where they're from, lots of these men, too. And, be honest, most of the time you can't tell the difference between a Mexican and an Arab. Both mean trouble.

My wall's going to keep many people like these from sneaking in. Before I took over they could stay and stay and work the system and sometimes eventually become legal. It's best just to keep them out. Soon, even if they get in, they'll be facing walls I build around convention centers where picture taking and hugs follow dangerous ceremonies.

SIX

Trump Prisons

seventy percent u.s. farmworkers undocumented
many
headed
for
new
private
prisons
owned
big
by
trump
donors

Trump Blasts the Media

The following highlights are from President Donald Trump's recent speech to the Conservative Political Action Committee in Washington, D.C.

What a fantastic standing ovation. You're incredible. And outside people are lined up for six blocks. Please, please sit down. You're embarrassing me with all this love. But you won't read about this tomorrow. The dishonest media will say I didn't get a standing ovation. They're the worst.

Thankfully, you conservatives are the best and like me want border security and a very, very strong military. Some consider that controversial, but you love your country and want to make America great again. The media didn't want that. They didn't think we could win. Every day they quoted consultants who are lousy at politics but great sucking up your money. They underestimated the power of the people.

We all need to understand. Fake news is the enemy of the people. And the media love reporting stories with no sources. They just make them up. They're very dishonest people. They dropped the word "fake" and made my quote, "News is the enemy of the people."

I'd never say that. I'm not against the media and the press. I don't mind bad stories if I deserve them, and I love good stories but don't get many of those. I'm only against the fake news media and the fake press. Fake. Fake. Don't take out that key word.

I'm against people that make up stories and sources. They shouldn't be able to use sources unless they use people's names. If sources say Donald Trump is a horrible human being, let them say it to my face. There'd be no more sources without names. There are some sources as honest as can be. That's great. But some are terrible, dishonest people who do a tremendous disservice to our country. If they had to print the names of sources, you'd see stories dry up like never before.

And remember those polls before the election, all those polls by the Clinton News Network – you'd think they'd fire their pollster. Look at CBS, ABC, NBC – same things. Their polls are so bad, so inaccurate, they create a false narrative that I'm not going to win, so you won't go and vote. We have to fight them. They're smart, cunning, dishonest.

They say we can't criticize their dishonest coverage because of the First Amendment. I love the First Amendment. Nobody loves it more than me. Who uses it more than I do? It gives me the right to criticize fake news. I've got to take them on. Many large media corporations have an agenda that isn't your agenda or the country's. They have a professional obligation to report the truth, but as you've seen in the campaign and up to this minute, they report fake news that doesn't represent the people. We have to be honest.

Speaking to Congress

many think
trump impressive
first time before
congress wash
post says he lied
thirteen times
bet on both

Bull Trump

bear
likely
to
eat
trump
bull
market

SEVEN

Trump Accuses Obama

This is bad, really bad. I just found out President Obama stooped so low he taped my phones at Trump Tower during our sacred election process. That's Nixon and Watergate kind of stuff. Obama's a sick guy.

What are my sources? Where's my proof? Don't worry, I'll provide all that in good time, right along with my tax returns. Right now it's more important for me to blast away on Twitter. It's terrible what Obama did. Presidents aren't supposed to sneak around and wiretap presidential candidates and bring back McCarthyism.

I'm going to get a lawyer, a team of lawyers to prove Obama illegally set A NEW LOW. I'll get him impeached. I know he's out of office, since I'm in his office, but I'll get him impeached retroactively and overturn everything he did after he committed treason.

My political assistants are all good. True, I replaced campaign manager Paul Manafort but not because he had close business and personal ties to Ukrainian leader Viktor Yanukovych who was allied to Vladimir Putin. I let Manafort go because I knew Kellyanne Conway would be even better at standing between the liberal firing squad and my tender body.

And General Michael Flynn, he's a good guy who gave his country three wonderful weeks as my national security advisor. Maybe he had some helpful conversations with Russian ambassador Sergey Kislyak. No big deal. If he'd told me at the time, maybe he'd still be here. Senator Jeff Sessions also talked to Kislyak. That was part of Jeff's job in the Senate. I don't know why during his confirmation hearing he denied talking to the Russians. But who cares? He was doing a great job for this country just as he will as attorney general.

And as the highest ranking legal official in the United States, and therefore the world, Jeff Sessions is going to investigate and prosecute and probably jail Obama for spying on me and undermining our democracy.

Obama Counters Trump

I'm windsurfing like the sleekest of sailboats when an agent on shore radioes a wet-suited agent near my side in the sea that I have to leave heaven and return to reality. Upon arriving at the dock, a new aide rushes up and loudly whispers that President Trump has tweeted I tapped his wires during the campaign.

"That's so ridiculous, I won't even respond," I say. "Let's hit the links."

I hit the ball almost like Tiger Woods in his prime and sink a long par putt to card a hot forty-nine on the front side, and guarantee I'll break a hundred if another assaultive tweet doesn't compel me to shout, "Summon all media members in this beautiful town. I'm going to blast Trump."

"No, be presidential," says my irksome aide. "Let others defend you."

"And who'll promptly do that?"

"Let me check," she says.

I take off my spikes, slip on some tennis shoe loafers, and shadow box like a left-handed panther for a few minutes before she returns and says, "Mr. President, the FBI and numerous intelligence officials have already said Trump's accusations are fallacious."

I like the way she says that, and shake her hand.

"Those folks sabotaged Hillary just like they'll take down The Donald. I can hear it so sweet, 'President Pence.'"

"When do you think that will happen, Mr. President?"

"Less than two years. Republicans won't have his ass around during midterm elections."

Bush Defends Obama

trump says i'm low
iq but tweets obama
cut loose a hundred
twenty-two vicious
gitmo prisoners who're
now fighting us horse

feathers i released
a hundred of those

Headline Trump

sometime in 'eighteen
all enemy media will
report trump battered
by bear market and
failing health plan so
embraces war to make
blubber look like muscle

EIGHT

Trump Pump

first time
since election
i enter democratic
women of kern
meeting in much
larger room with
three times more
people and ask
what's going on
state of the union
says a lady

Trump Stake

if tied
to stake
on pacific
beach would
trump still
proclaim water
ain't risin'

Jill Stein Strikes

An enormous woman, more than six-feet tall and two hundred pounds, stands against the far wall. She's wearing a gunny sack dress and, despite being in her seventies, has long blond hair. I have too much time to examine her as well as look around a small conference room where about twenty people are waiting for Jill Stein to address the state convention of the Green Party. She's late this Saturday night in Bakersfield. Or is she that woman, gray haired and almost frail, talking to people near the entrance? This isn't going to be one of those huge crowds, chanting Donald or Bernie, but people trickle in and forty minutes after the scheduled speaking time some seventy supporters watch slender Stein, in black pants suit and white blouse, step onto a makeshift stage.

In a smooth and pleasant voice she says she's proud of the people here, they're leading the pack and registering Green voters where it most counts: what happens in California will not stay in California. And it's "cosmically" right that this conference is in Bakersfield, one of the reddest and least scenic counties in the state, because Bakersfield is a center for oil, fracking, and chemicals, and a place where agri-business runs free. It's a Donald Trump kind of town where poverty and homelessness are the president's allies because "fascism comes from economic despair. We need to tear down walls, not build them. We also need to cut the military budget." Reactionaries don't always win, she stresses, a Green Party candidate recently beat a fascist in Austria.

Applause rewards many of Stein's statements but I notice the large lady's frowning and clinching her fists as the petite physician declares Trump's numbers are going down; his national security advisor, Michael Flynn, is already out; Attorney General Jeff Sessions has problems; the president quickly backed down on his first immigration order; there are many lawsuits against him; he may be vulnerable to bribery because of his Russian and other international business interests; President Nixon may have been tyrannical but at least during his era the Environmental Protective Agency was started, and now it's under attack from the Trump administration, which ignores there's a problem with climate change.

"Hey, Jill, you say the president's in trouble," shouts the big lady. "Look at your numbers tonight."

"Ma'am, please wait for our question and answer session," says Stein.

The lady rips off her long blond hair, revealing an orange pompadour over the jowls of President Donald J. Trump. People gasp.

"I usually wouldn't go near a fourth-rate meeting like this," says The Donald, "but I'm visiting Kern County to meet with some very important oil people and wanted to see just how bush league you really are."

"Mr. President," Stein says.

"Don't interrupt. We're starting the questions and answers now. I've got your Green Party of California brochure, which is on very cheap paper, and here's the first point – Ecological Wisdom. You advocate restricting resources so our communities and planet can continue to be healthy."

"That's right. We…"

"Our planet's fine but we need to get more resources to grow our economies and rebuild our infrastructure. Next you have Social Justice and Equal Opportunity. Everyone should share in the fruits of our society and all that goody goody nonsense. All great societies are built by their most talented people, and they'll get my tax cuts."

"President Trump…"

"Quiet, Jill. Let's skip the third and go to Nonviolence. You claim you promote peace and advocate nonviolent resolution to conflict. I sometimes advocate nonviolence, too, but don't live in your fairytale world so am adding more than fifty billion to the defense budget."

"We already spend more than the next seven nations combined."

"Not nearly enough. But as a female physician, you wouldn't understand that. This next one is outrageous: Decentralization. You're worried about the concentration of wealth and power in the hands of a few people. Give me a few years and I guarantee the rich will become much richer. But so will everyone else. I'm going to create jobs."

"Are you going to let me respond?"

"Look at this tiny group. You're a bore. Here's Feminism and Gender Equity. You're profoundly inspired by feminism. Well, I'm inspired by hot babes. I shouldn't leave it at that. I'm a pioneer in hiring women for executive positions in my construction empire. And my daughter Ivanka's one of my top advisors. Let's see, going down this list, I notice more silly stuff about Respect for Diversity and Personal & Global Responsibility. You're repeating yourself, Jill."

"I challenge you to a nationally televised debate," she says.

"No way I give you that forum. You've got to earn it in the presidential primaries."

"I should've had you thrown out."

"You would have if you'd had any security."

"After this I'll feel justified when I crash one of your speeches."

"My guys'll toss you in two seconds."

Trump Intelligence

can't believe
comey and fbi
investigating
russia and me
instead of bad
obama

Trump Goals

i'm
gonna
slash
arts
strangle
public
broadcasts
squash
state
dept
and
smother
epa

Trump Care

support
starved
trump
dodges house vote
warning obamacare
soon to explode
on democrats

NINE

Maxine Waters Visits Trump

I know I promised to boycott Donald Trump events wherever they occur including the Capitol and White House. I refuse to dignify the man with my presence because I don't believe anything he says. He's abnormal, dangerous, a male chauvinist pig, an authoritarian racist, and he may be impeached because so many of his aides and advisors past and present have been in bed with Russian oil dealers and probably in collusion with Vladimir Putin and his agents when they hacked our democracy during the presidential election so they can lift our sanctions against Mother Russian oil. I know some of that still has to be proven, but I've got quite a nose for conspiracies and still believe years ago some U.S. intelligence agencies started the crack epidemic on my home turf in Los Angeles. I watch out for stuff like that. And as a strong black woman I say what's necessary, like the other day when I called out Putin for attacking Korea. He won't get away with that as long as Congresswoman Maxine Waters is on patrol.

Late this evening I read another outrageous tweet. He's written so many I can't remember the content but it doesn't matter exactly what he said. Despite my vow to stay away, I call a dependable driver to take me to the White House. I know The Donald will be up. I wish he'd sleep twenty hours a day.

"Maxine Waters, here to see President Trump," I tell the guard at the gate.

He calls someone and returns to say, "The president doesn't wish to see you."

"Maybe he'd rather I post tapes of those Russian prostitutes he hired."

The guard returns to the phone, pointing at me as he speaks, and walks back to report, "The president will give you five minutes."

While one secret service agent searches my purse, another asks, "You carrying any guns, knives, or other weapons?"

"Want me to disrobe and show you?"

"Go on," he says, evidently not anxious to examine someone his grandmother's age.

Four agents usher me into the Oval Office, and two stay as Trump stands, walks around his desk, and says, "Maxine, nice to see you."

"We have urgent business to discuss, Donald."

"President Trump, that's the correct way to address me."

"Fine, if you call me Congresswoman Waters."

"Okay."

"I'm here to urge you to make the most patriotic sacrifice for your country."

The president, who's even porkier in person than on TV, says, "I have no intention of dying, especially while I'm the president."

"I'm asking you to resign to save yourself and the nation a lot of pain and shame."

"I beg your pardon, Congresswoman Waters, but you're half-crazy, at best. The American people love me."

"You follow the polls and know what they say: you're the most unpopular new president since they started modern polling."

"Those polls are rigged. I'm box office everywhere I go. People are crazy about me."

"That support is from a minority."

Wagging a chubby index finger, he says, "No, it's mainly white, but plenty of blacks and Latinos, too."

"I mean a minority of the citizens of this nation. Face it. You couldn't repeal Obamacare. You don't even have the support of your own party. And where's your wall paid for by Mexico?"

"Most Republicans backed me in repealing Obamacare, and we almost got it done. It's probably better to just let it self-destruct, anyway. And believe me, we're gonna build that wall and the Mexicans will pay for it some way."

I tell him, "You ain't gonna build a wall but you're sure working hard to suppress black voters."

"Not true. I'm only cleaning up the electoral process. Millions of fake ballots were cast in the 2016 election and all of them were by Democrats."

"Nonsense, there's no proof of that. Now, why are you so determined to avoid paying people a decent living wage?"

"You don't understand business or you'd know low taxes for the wealthy create jobs that high minimum wages would destroy."

"You mean like the millions paid annually to corporate executives," I say.

"They make business happen. If one corporation doesn't pay what they're worth, another will."

"Listen, Mr. President, you must come clean about your involvement with the Russians."

"I've had no inappropriate contacts with the Russians and plan to have great relations with them."

"Maybe you didn't personally commit treason, but some of those close to you probably did."

"Time's up, Maxine."

"I've said about all I need to, Donald."

"Heard it all before."

"You'll be hearing a lot more."

"Out."

"That's where you're headed, Mr. President."

Immune to Michael Flynn

Yes sir, I know Donald Trump and I said Hillary Clinton and her email coconspirators were inevitably guilty of serious crimes otherwise they wouldn't need immunity, and at attention I still stand by those assertions. Now that I'm hunting for immunity, however, some say I too must be guilty of something. Actually, people have been saying that for a long time, but it's worsening now that I'm doing what all good generals do and that's defend my rear.

Despite my patriotic behavior, I'm the target of a witch hunt. That's what President Trump tweeted. Trust our commander in chief. Some rebellious Republicans in Congress, playing cheap political games, say I shouldn't receive immunity. They want the FBI to investigate my relations with the Russians before the campaign as well as when I advised candidate Trump.

There's really no big deal. I didn't lie. I was just protecting military and political secrets when I told Vice President Mike Pence and other eminent people I hadn't discussed overturning President Obama's sanctions once Donald Trump became president. But why wouldn't I discuss this with the Russian ambassador? We didn't want the Russians to think they'd be facing more hostility from the White House.

I don't think it's at all disturbing I retroactively registered as a foreign agent who did business with the Russians and the Turks. And it's entirely appropriate that in 2015 I sat at a dinner table with Vladimir Putin prior to my speech to the Russia Today television network the Kremlin controls and which paid me thirty-three grand. I needed cash since Obama had trumped up charges when I was General Flynn, forcing me to retire early. None of this made me vulnerable to blackmail. This whole thing is a witch hunt.

Alum Slams Trump University

I just don't know if I'm going to go along with the victorious class action lawsuit against Trump University and, like almost four thousand too-eager complainants, accept no more than ninety cents on the dollar from the man who fleeced us. I paid thirty-five thousand for the elite-level program and expected to turn my financial life around after two bankruptcies. Instead, President Trump gets to send his attorneys into court to proclaim he and they admit no fault while the snake-oil billionaire continues to proclaim if he weren't so busy he'd take this case to trial and win easily. My lawyers and I know I'd win and we could make this a criminal trial and convict The Donald of racketeering and make him pay more and apologize to all of us. Maybe Judge Alonzo Curiel is so accommodating because he wants to show he's impartial despite candidate Trump last year saying Curiel couldn't be fair since he's a Mexican born in Indiana. Besides, how busy really is the president? He's hitting the links more than President Obama did.

Chapo Guzman's Guest

I don't know where I am. Maybe New York. It doesn't matter. I can't see anything but frosted glass and can't talk to other prisoners. I only get out of my cell an hour a day and sometimes am so lonely and depressed I almost enjoy it when guards call me shorty or cabrón or worse. I wish they'd turn off those damn fluorescent lights a little while at night or whenever the hell I'm trying to sleep. I need to escape, if only into dreams.

Oh, that's very funny. The guards open my cell door and just outside wheel a laundry cart like the one I hid in during my first escape from prison.

"You guys gonna give me a ride to freedom?" I ask in Spanish.

"Stand at attention, Chapo," says the guard. I always get at least one or two bilingual bigmouths.

Another guard pulls sheets back from the cart and up stands a guy pretending to be Donald Trump. Guards help him out of the cart and into my cell.

"Hola, actor. You're pretty close but not enough to fool me."

The sheet-lifting guard serves as translator.

"Don't fool around, Chapo. You're lucky as hell I've come to see you, especially after the nasty comments you made about me during the campaign and your threats against my life."

"Okay, I like jokes. What can I do for you, Donaldo?"

"Even though you're right where you belong, your absence from Mexico has created a terrible void. Members of your Sinaloa cartel are killing each other, and many innocent people, as they try to replace you, and other cartels are also moving in. The Mexican murder rate's almost as high as it ever was."

"I'm a man of peace who simply tried to give the gringos the drugs they crave."

"You're a murderer who killed to fatten his wallet," he says.

"Let's see how many people you kill before you leave office. I know what's going on."

"How?"

"Maybe my lawyers tell me, maybe I figure it out myself. You coke-snorting, crack-smoking gringos aren't getting enough to fry your brains, so a lot of you've switched to heroin. We don't need the Colombians or anyone else for that. We grow poppies at home and manufacture the product there, too."

"Heroin's killing thousands in the United States."

"Only the bad stuff. We guarantee quality. Don't forget, junkies are a lot mellower than coke addicts. We're helping you, even though heroin makes us less money."

"Whether it's coke or heroin or illegal aliens coming across, we've got to build my wall," he says.

"That's not going well."

"It will. I'm here to offer an incredible deal."

"And what's that?"

"We'll let you escape again if you return to Sinaloa and supply us with information on your cartel and others. We also expect you to turn over half your sales to us so we can build the wall."

"If I do that, people who love me will kill me, and people who already hate me will torture me to death."

"Given the number of murders in Mexico and heroin overdoses in the United States, we may have to get pretty unpleasant right here in your cell."

"If I agree and go back to Sinaloa, how will you keep me from disappearing?"

"Medical team," Trump shouts.

Four men and two women, all clad in long white lab coats, rush in, wheeling a long silver box.

"We have a new tracking device that can be placed in any large bone," Trump says. "One per person is enough but in your case we'll implant one in each femur and one in each collar bone. If any of these devices are tampered with, or if we're not happy with your efforts, we'll activate explosives in all four."

TEN

Assad Passes Gas

Trust me, as the father of all Syrians, I – President Bashar al-Assad – am more aggrieved than anyone by the cowardly and criminal gas attacks that killed scores of women and children in the town of Khan Sheikhoun. Even though I'm an enormously proud and powerful man, I tell you I wept at reports and newscasts of little ones foaming at the mouth or gasping through poisoned lungs as they suffocated. Seeing their bodies later lined up intensified my agony. What horrible people would commit such atrocities? I'm sure you know it wasn't Bashar al-Assad.

On the contrary, I was attacking the terrorists who've killed more than four hundred thousand in my once-peaceful land. I was bombing the heathens but my freedom explosions detonated a terrorist stockpile of nerve gas. The Russians have already verified this and spoken quite publicly. They know I'm fighting enemies who a few years ago produced their own projectiles to deliver chemical agents to kill our people. ISIS and Al Qaeda and others of their ilk have often launched such attacks.

Only in self-defense did I in August 2013 respond in kind, and grieved in the aftermath of fourteen hundred Syrians perishing from poison gas. The United States appeared poised to attack me but wisely settled down and with the Russians forged a deal wherein I agreed to destroy my chemical weapons. Now, be fair and honest and tell me if, in my position, you would really dismantle every device in a nation under siege by barbarians you very well know would not rid themselves of all weapons of mass destruction. You wouldn't, and I too saved a few gaseous options, which the enemy has on occasion compelled me to use.

Secretary of State Rex Tillerson understands the reality that most foreigners have not: "The long-term status of President Assad will be decided by the Syrian people." President Obama didn't realize that, but what did he ever do about his belligerent red line in regard to limiting my occasional sad but essential use of gas? He did nothing. Now President Trump is saying – about an attack I again swear I did not commit – that I've crossed several red lines with him, and, like Obama, I know he wants to attack me. But the Russians wouldn't like that. And most importantly the Syrian people would disapprove because they know I'd easily win a fair national election.

Trump Strikes Syria

assad doesn't know
what I'm thinking
because i don't
either four years
ago i tweeted obama
don't attack syria
after that i bashed
him for not striking
now i'm firing cruise
missiles and not
worried what's next

Obama Writes to Trump

Dear President Trump,

I have to this point restrained myself from responding to your avalanche of falsehoods and insults but better speak now, in this letter I share with a public likely to suffer from your instability and that should know you're a nonalcoholic version of witch-hunting Senator Joseph McCarthy, whose name still makes free people cringe.

Before leaving office, I refuted your pitiful attempts to deny my birthright as a native of the United States, and from the podium at the 2011 White House correspondents' dinner delivered comedic counterstrokes leaving you speechless as you nodded your head like a bovine bigot. My fellow professional politicians, including the Republicans, could not then have imagined you would someday come to lead this country. Your ascendency – prelude to an inevitable crash – is an insult to those who understand and therefore oppose you but even more to blue collar workers you deluded into believing you care about them and know how to help.

In fact, Mr. President, you know little about working people – how could you, after a lifetime buffered by luxury? – and proved your contempt for them by refusing to pay carpenters and other craftsmen who'd constructed a building to make you more money. Indeed, you despise the workers whose dirty hands and soiled work clothes you'd rather not touch or even look at. You say I let them down. That is nonsense. I helped save the auto industry in America and presided over a range of economic measures that enabled our country to rise from the financial debacle awaiting me in 2009. You, by contrast, have eight years later inherited a steadily growing economy. You say I've left you a world of worries. I say you're full of prune juice.

During the presidential campaign I did not wiretap you, or authorize anyone to do so, and you either know that or are a cable-conspiracy nerd incapable of forging fact-based thoughts. Let me help you understand a few basics about foreign policy. I'll start with Syria, which you say I screwed up by not punishing President Bashar al-Assad for crossing my "red line" after he used chemical weapons. He had already killed two hundred thousand Syrians with conventional bombs and bullets and has since killed that many more. Lobbing a few dozen cruise missiles at him for gassing civilians is not necessarily bad policy – and perhaps I should also have done so – but it assuredly will not prevent Assad from continuing to kill thousands the old fashioned way.

You also berate me for not stopping Kim Jong Un from developing and testing nuclear weapons and ballistic missiles. Okay, you now reside in the White House, and Kim's behavior has become even more provocative. And what have you done? Nothing but talk. If you do much more, you may start or participate in starting a major war on the Korean Peninsula that will rapidly kill tens of thousands of civilians and soldiers.

And regarding Iran and its nuclear programs, you endlessly moan that I made the worst deal you've ever seen. In fact, Russia, France, China, England, Germany and other nations agreed with my administration that we would be safer signing the nuclear deal framework and thereby enabling ourselves to inspect Iranian facilities to ensure compliance. We'll see what you do. I wish you luck. Please restrain yourself. Otherwise, the people of the United States are going to shout, "You're fired." By then, tragically, it will be too late.

Sincerely,
Barack Obama

Kushner and Bannon

"I know you're thrilled the president banished me from National Security Council meetings," says Steve Bannon.

Standing several feet away, Jared Kushner examines the eminent advisor.

"I'm also certain you're very proud to be the son-in-law of the most powerful man in the world. Otherwise, you wouldn't be here. You inherited wealth from your felonious father and political power from your fashionable wife. Congratulations."

"Don't impugn my father or I may trounce a fat old man," says Kushner, tall and slender at age thirty-six. "I'm here on merit. The president wouldn't otherwise give me so much responsibility."

"You're a Democrat temporarily cloaked as a Republican and your presence is a threat to my task of dismantling wasteful governmental agencies."

"You're a reactionary the public will never trust."

"They trust me rather more than you."

"Not true."

"Americans want patriots like those who publish and read Breitbart. com," says Bannon.

"We do need patriots but not conspiracy-loving fanatics who despise non-Anglo-Saxons."

"I don't hate them or you."

"I hope not since *Time* asked if you were the second most powerful man in the world."

"I may have been."

"Certainly not anymore."

"That title's temporarily yours along with Secretary of Everything."

"Jealous?"

"Worried about the consequences."

"The president wants us to get along," Kushner says.

"But we don't want to."

ELEVEN

Trump Confronts Kim Jong Un

Far too busy to be troubled by an inconvenient personal meeting, President Donald Trump, entertaining swells at Mar-a-Lago, and Chairman Kim Jong Un, salivating as soldiers and missiles pass before him in Pyongyang, take a break to offer a little TV time for Battle of the Big Shots.

President Xi Jinping, the referee, prepares to flip a coin in Beijing to determine who will speak first.

"Put that away," Trump says. "I'll start. President Kim, if you test an underground nuclear bomb or fire any more missiles, there will be consequences. One of my naval strike forces is steaming toward you now, and they've got plenty of Tomahawk cruise missiles with your name on them."

"If you attack us, we'll counterstrike with unimaginable viciousness and destroy you and your lackeys with a barrage of nuclear and conventional missiles, bombs, and artillery shells."

"You'd be annihilated."

"You're a naïve bully to believe we'll allow the United States to destroy us like it did Iraq and Libya," says Kim. "Those poor countries couldn't hit back. But we can, and you know it."

"I must warn the United States against taking military action against North Korea," says Xi. "Our nations have been allied for centuries and repulsed such criminal invaders as the Japanese and Americans."

"President Xi, the Chinese must pressure this maniac who's ready to murder millions to save his ass."

"Watch your potty mouth," says Kim. "I'm not trying to kill anyone."

"Only North Koreans so far. I doubt you'd be parading ICBMs and submarine-launched missiles if you didn't plan to use them."

"Actually, these weapons are only a deterrent to save my regime. The right of self-defense is fundamental in all countries."

"I'm already a seasoned foreign policy veteran who generally refuses to tell what I'm going to do," says Trump. "But if it'll help, I'm willing to promise you, President Kim, that we probably won't attack if you do more nuclear testing. But we don't like it."

"We don't like your annual defense exercises with South Korea.

They appear to be a prelude to invasion."

"How do you think we view your belligerent behavior?" Trump asks.

"Stop trying to treat me like Saddam and Gaddafi."

"I suppose we could accept your being able to nuke anyone in your region, but I guarantee we won't tolerate a ballistic missile that can carry a nuclear warhead to the United States."

"We're absolutely committed to developing that capability and progressing rapidly."

"In that case, there's going to be war," says Trump.

"Be careful about hitting our little brother," Xi responds.

"We won't have to, if you control him."

"Don't force President Kim to strike South Korea," says Xi.

"What's South Korea got to do with this?" asks Trump.

First Lady

ri sol ju
please
tell
us
about
your
man
kim jong un

Kim Jong Un to Americans

You Americans are planning to attack me. You're always attacking someone. Look at Iraq and Afghanistan and Libya and Syria and Cuba and Panama and Vietnam. Cry when you look at Vietnam and remember it when scheming against our North Korean homeland. No one believes your lie we invaded the imperialists in the south in 1950. They attacked us and we battered them until you intervened and tried to shove us over the Yalu River into China but our Chinese comrades routed you and forced a massive retreat eventually compelling you to accept another uneasy peace, let's call it a fragile ceasefire, still festering on both sides of the thirty-eighth parallel in the Demilitarized Zone.

I'm warning you. I'm ready to hurl thunderbolts upon South Korea and Japan and even the United States. I will if you and your traitorous allies ever attack my nuclear facilities. I may even strike if you shoot down one of my test missiles. In fact, if I conclude cyber-attacks are destroying some of my missiles soon after launch, I may retaliate.

You're terrified of my military power, and twenty-four million programmed North Koreans know it. We have more than a million soldiers, counting quite a few women, and everyone in the country will attack. I'll personally lead the charge. I'm not afraid. We have thousands of artillery pieces and a thousand short- and medium-range missiles and several hundred warplanes, and you're terrified of all that and more. So are the South Koreans, whose capital Seoul and its twenty-five million depraved souls are only thirty-five miles from my strategic high-ground bristling with artillery and rockets whose fatal assaults would open gates for an invasion and quick victory and reunification of a free and prosperous Korea led by me, Kim Jong Un, godlike as my grandfather and father sleeping but still poised while daily viewed under glass by adoring masses.

We don't care South Korea has twice as many people and a hundred times more money. We're not afraid of cars and TVs and iphones and movies and sports and fancy food. We don't fear American or South Korean troops and their newer tanks and artillery and missiles and missile defense systems and warplanes. You're fighting for consumer goods. We're struggling for something more important, the salvation of my regime and the worldly survival of my sacred ass.

You Americans better quit lying that we're one of the poorest nations on earth and half my people live in extreme poverty. All North Korean citizens are well-fed, not just our soldiers. Don't try to weaken our souls. Quit trying to force China to stop buying our coal and subsidizing most of our oil. We're getting angrier every day. Soon we'll have better missiles and a hundred nuclear warheads. Then what are you going to do?

North Korean Overture to Mexico

Deep in a bunker somewhere in North Korea, Kim Jong Un points to a huge wall map of the world and, aided by his finest Spanish-speaking tutor, says, "President Fox, I feel for the righteous Mexican people who've so long been degraded by the American colossus to the north. Your strategic position and indeed your dignity are now particularly endangered by the madman currently occupying the White House. Let's be frank: Donald Trump hates people of color, especially North Koreans and Mexicans."

"There's no doubt Trump is a racist," says Vicente Fox. "In Mexico we despise him and will never pay for his fucking wall."

"You're quite brave to stand up to this bully. But do you want to forever live under his sword?"

"I don't think we have a choice, President Kim. Geography has dealt us a bad hand."

"We're also suffering from geographic bad lack, and daily face the menace of our belligerent and estranged Korean brothers to the south as well as their nuclear-armed American occupiers."

"At least in Mexico we're safe from an American military attack."

Kim shakes an index finger. "Don't take that for granted, President Fox. Once their economy collapses, the imperialists are certain to invade south and steal your oil and other natural resources. Like drunken cowboys, they'll probably also run off with many of your women."

"I wouldn't put it past Trump. But even if I were still president of Mexico, what could I do?"

"We could work together. I have a plan."

"What is it?" Fox asks.

"You must first stage a coup d'état and establish yourself as the Dear Leader of Mexico."

"I'd certainly be better for our people than smooth-talking shrimp Enrique Peña Nieto."

"I realize you're six-foot-five, the size of an NBA shooting guard, but insist you not demean the stature of anyone who, like me, is a quick and muscular five-seven."

"Agreed. Now, what do you really have in mind?"

"Once you've established control in Mexico, you need to build a powerful nuclear deterrent," says Kim. "I assure you, the United States will never attack once you've targeted ten or twenty of its cities."

"That's a marvelous idea, Chairman Kim. I concede I hadn't been ambitious enough to even consider it."

"My creativity is fired by desperate need. First, we had to build a devastating conventional force to deter the Americans and South Koreans from attacking us. Now we've got nuclear weapons ready to use in this region, and will soon have essential ICBMs capable of destroying Seattle, San Francisco, and Los Angeles."

"I would never endorse such attacks, Chairman Kim."

"Of course not. I'm not building nuclear weapons to use them. Only an unstable and self-deluded man would do so. What I propose is simply this. You and the Mexican people move to South Korea, where our friendship and nuclear might would ensure generations of peace and harmony."

"My status and my height give me great influence, but I don't think I could convince the Mexicans to give up their homes and their culture and move to South Korea. And I doubt South Koreans would accept a hundred million refugees."

"What I envision, President Fox, is a straightforward trade. The South Koreans would at the same time move to Mexico where they'd be close to their American ally, and they too would live peacefully."

"If such a switch can be made, I agree that South Korea would flourish south of the Rio Grande. But I'm a little worried about how we Mexicans would feel living south of your country."

Kim Jong Un, smiling wide in a fat face, says, "Don't worry, President Fox. Our peoples will merge, something I'd never permit with the South Koreans, and we'll form a rich and happy nation."

"A democratic nation?"

"We can hardly permit so many Mexicans to vote me out of office. Given my dynastic experience in Korea, I'd naturally be commander in chief."

"In that case, Chairman Kim, I must decline."

"Very well, sir, but be forewarned that my fourth and fifth ICBMs could target Mexico City and Guadalajara."

TWELVE

Trump Tip

buy
private
prison
stocks
sure
to
rise

Monumental Trump

too many national
monuments federal
land grabs i'll
eliminate till
they put my face
on mt rushmore

Trumpcare in Action

President Donald Trump arrives at a large medical clinic in your state this morning and immediately dons a green surgical gown and cap, scrubs his hands ten minutes, and barges into a packed waiting room.

"Good morning, everybody," he says. "I'm here to accept your thanks for repealing Obamacare and creating much better health care for all of you."

"What about my diabetes?" shouts a woman.

"If your state allows coverage of preexisting conditions, you'll be fine."

"What if this state doesn't?"

"Then you'll have to pay higher premiums."

"But you promised your program will offer much lower premiums than Obamacare."

"It will," says Trump. "Don't worry."

"I hadn't been worried since Obamacare covered all

preexisting conditions."

"Mr. President," says an elderly man, "I need Medicaid to survive. Social security's my only income, and I've got to have heart surgery. I qualify for Medicaid under Obamacare, but under your program a lot fewer will be eligible."

"Sir, why are you only earning a little social security check every month? I make more than that every hour around the clock. In my program, the people who really need Medicaid will qualify for it. But we'll be kicking freeloaders off the gravy train."

"I worked in the fields and as a janitor to qualify for what I've got."

"You should've also gone to college," Trump says.

"In 1950s Alabama?"

"They had Negro colleges."

"Another thing, Mr. President," the old man says. "Under Obamacare they can't charge older people more than three times as much as young people. Under your plan, seniors can be charged five times as much."

"Right, for a better program."

"I like the program I've got and don't want to lose it."

"Believe me, Obama didn't understand the needs of the people," says Trump. "That's why he kept losing the Senate and the House and state governorships and legislatures. People hate Obamacare."

"Most people I know like Obamacare."

"The majority doesn't like it, and proof's in the elections I just referred to. You, and this applies to all of you in this ghetto clinic, need to learn about taxes and especially about tax deductions. I'm proud to tell you, I don't pay taxes."

"When are you going to release your tax returns?" asks a middle-aged man.

"When the IRS completes its audit."

"I get the feeling you never will."

"Get this bum outta here before I bust him up," says Trump.

Three secret service agents respond.

The president fingers and admires his huge pink tie before continuing, "Don't worry about my taxes. Worry about yours. Trumpcare will help. We're offering tax advantages for Health Care

Savings Accounts."

"That doesn't do me any good," says the heart patient. "I've always lived check to check."

"I've got great news. You can deduct the full cost of your health insurance premiums from your federal taxes each year. Obamacare only let you deduct medical expenses when they exceeded ten percent of your gross income."

"I still need Medicaid."

"Not after Trumpcare tax refunds fill you pockets."

Comey Trumped

i did my fbi duty investigating
hillary emails and bellowing
often until i became mildly
nauseated by russia and trump
who now pretends i'm toxic

Nixon Calls Trump

Late at night in the private quarters of the White House, Donald Trump is tweeting about matters foreign and domestic when an aide enters the living room and says, "Richard Nixon's calling again, Mr. President."

Trump grimaces and picks up an old land-line receiver and says, "You've got two minutes, Dick."

"Thanks for taking my call, Mr. President. I want you to know I'm prepared to counsel you about how to avoid this serious threat to your survival as commander in chief."

"What threat? The American people love my strength, intelligence, and glamor."

"Sir, millions of otherwise decent Americans think your dismissal of FBI director James Comey was very much like my firing of Watergate special prosecutor Archibald Cox."

"I don't see any similarities. Cox wanted you to release tapes that incriminated you in the Watergate burglary, so you fired him."

"And Comey wants to prove you colluded with the Russians to defeat Hillary Clinton. Thankfully, your plot worked, but it's put you in danger."

"Listen, I didn't have anything to do with Russian interference in our election, if there was any."

"This call isn't being taped, is it, Mr. President?"

"Of course not."

"Good. Without those tapes, I'd have survived."

"You were stupid to record yourself carrying on like that, and crazy not to destroy the tapes," says Trump.

"In fairness, Mr. President, you've been caught on tape quite a few times."

"When I was a swinging celebrity. I'm not going to tape myself in the Oval Office."

"You tweeted Comey better pray you don't have any tapes of him. If you do, you'll deliver the White House and Congress to the Democrats."

"I appreciate your call, Dick, but I don't need advice about criminal investigations."

"That means I can focus on helping you with foreign policy, a subject I mastered and one in which you're still rather green."

"I have a great sense about what's right and what's needed. I also have top notch advisers like my son-in-law Jared Kushner and Secretary of State Rex Tillerson."

"I'm sure Jared's a fine young businessman, and Rex is a veteran oil executive, but they don't have the knowledge and insight necessary to deal with Iran and North Korea."

"I already know how I'm gonna deal with them," says Trump.

"How?"

"I don't broadcast when I'm gonna attack someone."

"Aren't you going to try diplomacy?" Nixon asks.

"You better not be recording this."

Kevin McCarthy Says

Kevin McCarthy's lucky he'll never lose a congressional election in Kern County because he wouldn't survive as a comedian. Last year he confidentially told GOP leaders, "There are two people I think Putin pays, Dana Rohrabacher and Trump. Swear to God."

"That's absurd," aides of McCarthy and Paul Ryan now say.

"We have the tape," responds the *Washington Post*.

"Just a failed attempt at humor," counter the aides.

McCarthy actually got a few strained laughs but no Republicans are amused today, especially Donald Trump.

The *Post* meanwhile reports Woodward and Bernstein are planning a comeback.

THIRTEEN

Trump Enlightens Middle East

I love the Saudis more every day and they feel the same about me because, unlike President Obama, I understand we share their values of making the rich richer, keeping women in their place, and destroying terrorism. I'm frankly quite surprised that fifteen of the nineteen hijackers on 9/11 were Saudi nationals, and still think the liberal media and even U.S. intelligence are exaggerating continued Saudi financial support of the bad guys.

Today I proudly stand before Saudi and other leaders in the crumbling Middle East and express my confidence in their will and their toughness as I command, "Drive the terrorists out. Drive them out of your places of worship. Drive them out of your communities."

"Where will they go?" a man stands and shouts.

"They'll go to Europe," proclaims a second man.

"Get these bums outta here," I order.

A couple of days later I learn one of the terrorists must have gone to Manchester and blown up twenty-two people and maimed plenty more. But this guy was born in England. So I guess we'll have to drive them out of England and Europe and out of the United States as well as the Holy Land. I'm just not sure where or how we're going to drive them.

Montenegro Counterstrikes

I don't know why but instead of getting mad at outrageous affronts and then cooling off, it's the reverse, and a couple of hours later I start steaming, and that's why there's going to be trouble. Nobody gets away with disrespecting the prime minister of Montenegro. By now I'm sure most of you have seen it online. I'm waiting for a photo session with other European leaders and suddenly feel a hand on my shoulder and then a shove as a fat fellow pries past me and juts his jaw like Mussolini's understudy.

I'd already been repulsed by Donald Trump during his European visit, listening to him lecture us about "reciprocal trade… and you treat us the way we treat you, or we'll treat you the way you treat us." He also spoke to his peers, whom he considers inferiors, as if he alone understands how to stop terrorism. And again he revealed he doesn't comprehend the human component in climate change.

I resolve to punish this baboon. But what can I do as leader of a tiny nation buried in the Balkans across the Adriatic Sea from Italy?

"President Trump, may I please speak to you privately?" I ask as he passes a small room where I stand.

"Very busy now, what's your name?"

"Prime Minister Dusko Markovic."

"And from what country?"

"Montenegro."

"Way too busy, Dusko."

I step into the hall, smile at his security agents, and reach for his right hand with mine, pretending to shake, but actually pull him back into the room.

"We'll just be a moment," I tell his agents.

They look at Trump who nods okay.

Still holding his hand I pull him a few steps along the wall, where we can't be seen from the hall, and release his right hand and with my free right rip an uppercut into his solar plexus and a left hook to his jaw, and hop back so he doesn't land on me as he falls.

Kabul Kills

bombs in kabul
kill more than
ninety civilians
prompting u.s.
commander to
say just several
thousand more
troops will turn
tide but didn't
mention hundred
fifty thousand
hadn't been enough

Trump Paris

climate change isn't hoax
but
donald
trump
is

FOURTEEN

Saint Comey

For more than a year I've been sacrificing as I try to defend the United States of America from people unworthy of leading her. I couldn't allow Hillary Clinton to become president since she was and is a lying, emailing warmonger, and I'm proud that days before the polls opened I altered the presidential election by educating the masses, who didn't know but needed to, that I, James Comey, would again be unleashing my FBI to sniff out criminal behavior by Hillary that, sadly, we hadn't been able to prove. Thankfully, lack of proof mattered not, and by undermining Hillary I delivered Donald Trump to you, the trusting but morally insufficient American people.

I continued my crusade – and it is nothing less – before and after the inauguration of Trump, and he knew that I with bated breath was beginning to corner his national security advisor, Michael Flynn, a loud and unstable lout who couldn't have been trusted with sensitive national secrets, and wouldn't anyway because he knew I could prove he'd had several pre-election meetings with Sergey Kislyak, the Russian ambassador to the United States. President Trump fired Flynn, and then summoned me to the White House.

I'm always honored to visit the world's most important residence. It makes me feel even taller and more important than I already am. It also makes me nervous when the president asks attorney general Jeff Sessions and White House chief of staff Reince Preibus to step out of the Oval House, leaving Trump and me to talk in private.

"I hope you can let him go," he says.

"Who, Mr. President?"

"Michael Flynn. He's really a great guy, a patriotic American. He's just a little hyper."

Despite my stellar intellect, I don't know what to say. I cross my long right leg over the left. Trump stacks his hands on the desk.

"I expect loyalty, Jim. I demand it."

"I'll always be honest, Mr. President."

"That's good, Jim, honest loyalty."

I wish I were wearing a wire. After all, I'm in the FBI. And after the meeting I plan to tell Jeff Sessions what happened but decide he'll alert Trump I haven't been loyal. Instead, I make notes. I carefully write what the president says and what I do and don't say and how uncomfortable I am because I fear Trump "might lie about the nature of our meeting."

Shortly thereafter, President Trump calls me a liar and volunteers to testify before Congress. I'd like that. I hope he does have tapes and people can hear me telling the most powerful man in the world that I'm a champion of justice and decency. If that happens I can see Trump removed from office and a weak President Pence losing to the Democratic challenger in 2020, and I could be that guy if Hillary quits complaining and vigorously backs me.

Trump Tweets Obama

everyone loves my tweets
especially "reason that
president obama did NOTHING
about russia after being notified
by cia of meddling is that he
expected clinton would win"

now democrats keep pressuring
jared kushner great kid who i've
asked to save world this smear
won't work since jared keeps
hiring great lawyers to prove
there's NOTHING to investigate
about his conversations with
russian ambassador and others

Target, Japan

north korea just
fired another ballistic
missile into our sea
of japan we're still

not sure what we're
going to do about this
menace but based on
history we better do
something

Trump Calls Kim Jong Un

Confidential intelligence sources gave us this tape minutes ago.

Donald Trump – Chairman Kim, this is President Trump calling to tell you that it won't happen.

Kim Jong Un – It's already happened.

DT – I'm referring to North Korea actually deploying an ICBM.

KJU – Consider them as good as deployed on quite mobile Chinese-built trucks you'll never be able to track.

DT – I've been leaning on our Chinese friends, but I may have to press harder to get them to keep you in line.

KJU – I've read you're profoundly uninformed and now hear it directly from you. The Chinese aren't your friends. They're my friends, as they were my grandfather's comrades during the Korean War, which for us never really ended. Even if you haven't read the reports yourself, you have aides who did and they've doubtless informed you that many of our rapid advances are based on Chinese missile technology.

DT – The Chinese better not be giving you dangerous technology.

KJU – My scientists are the finest in the world. We don't need to be given anything, just coached a little. Besides, there's nothing you can do about it.

DT – We could annihilate you. And we will, if necessary.

KJU – That's why we're going to maintain many nuclear-tipped ICBMs.

DT – You're still not there.

KJU – We're much closer than you and South Korea and Japan want to believe. We've already fit miniaturized nuclear warheads on intermediate-range missiles that would kill millions of enemies in this region. And unless you're incompetent, you know we'll soon figure out how to similarly arm our long-range missiles.

DT – We'll crush you with sanctions. We'll tighten financial lines to China and force them to cut you off.

KJU – President Trump, I understand you're not a scholar but at least you're quite the cable guy, so I'm confident you've heard accurate news reports that our trade with China grew forty percent during the first quarter this year.

DT – Listen, President Kim, I think our two nations should be friends. We're ready to negotiate the suspension-for-suspension that's been proposed by the peaceful leaders of China and Russia. You quit testing missiles and nuclear weapons, and South Korea and the United States will stop our annual joint military exercises.

KJU – Those issues are quite worth discussing, and soon.

DT – Wonderful. We need to rid the Korean peninsula of nuclear weapons. We took out all our nukes in 1991, you know.

KJU – So? Your missile-firing submarines lurk off our coasts, and you send nuclear-armed aircraft carrier groups into our waters whenever you want. We're ready to discuss the moratorium you mentioned, but you'll never get us to relinquish the nuclear weapons we already have and those we in the future choose to build.

DT – One way or the other, we won't let you have the capability to strike the continental United States.

KJU – Have you discussed this with South Korea and Japan. They're under the gun. So are we. Why shouldn't you also be?

DT – Because we're not you.

KJU – And I'm not Saddam Hussein or Muammar Gaddafi. Good day.

FIFTEEN

Junior Trump

my dad would've loved
damaging info russians
promised about hillary
but their damn female
attorney talked about
adopting kids so i stopped
a wasteful meeting

Trump Weather

don't worry about
south pole ice cube
size of tiny delaware
breaking off big oceans
will drink it while nobody
notices

Trumps Aces Lady Golfers

Can you believe my fake news enemies wanted to steal the women's U.S. Open championship from me and my Trump National Golf Club in New Jersey? They said the president shouldn't benefit by having a major tournament played on his golf course and it would be inappropriate since they claim I'm not always a gentleman with the ladies. Listen, I was voted ladies' man of the year in prep school and have since enjoyed the affection and admiration of countless women. You know they dig confident guys who've got power and money especially if, like me, they're also handsome stars.

I told the liberal bozos I'd sue their asses if they tried to move the tournament and they backed down. It's better this way, giving thousands of people on the course and millions at home the exciting chance to watch me arrive three straight days in my caravan of big beast limousines and step out, wearing a red golf cap, to wave and fist pump and smile and wink at cheering fans. The few protestors have already been sent down the fairway. I casually walk to my elevated box framed by green bulletproof windows. I can still see the players and fans and they can see me well too.

I know it's going to be a hell of a tournament and love the way Sung Hyun Park, a hot lady of twenty-three, shoots five under par sixty-seven the last two days to win her first major. But remember, she got to hit from the ladies tees, and in my prime I could've shot that or better if I'd driven from the same place. Sung is from South Korea, and if this wasn't a good time golf tournament I'd promise her I'm going to protect her country from the lunatic Kim Jong Un and his hordes in North Korea. I can't tell you just how I'm going to do that because I don't want our enemies to know. Just remember, I'll handle it.

I've got everything covered and my presidency is going great. I'm so proud of Don Jr. for explaining why he met with Russians during the campaign last year. He was ready to work with anyone who could help save our nation from a disastrous Hillary Clinton presidency. Look how much better things are with me in command. We've just defeated ISIS in Mosul and Iraq is doing a lot better, though as you know I wouldn't have attacked them in 2003. That was crazy. I'm a dealmaker not a clumsy aggressor.

Pretty soon I'm going to have a great new health care bill for you. It'll be much better and less expensive than Obamacare, and those who say my plan would ruin Medicare and Medicaid are liars. Lots of them are probably among the millions who illegally voted against me. I'm going to clean up our electoral process, and I'm going to keep cracking down on illegal aliens and others who want to ruin our way of life. I'll stop them because I have the support of a majority of Americans who know there's no way my approval rating is only thirty-eight percent like fake news claims.

Trump Mandate

you must at once
repeal obamacare and
forget new reports
seven people joined

don jr to discuss how
russians could help
beat hillary

Bad Ass

i've told gop senators people are hurting and they better
repeal
obamacare
or
they
won't
be
senators
much
longer

Russian Love

my daily white
house email just
announced i'll make
america safer stronger
and more prosperous
but didn't mention
i may have to squeeze
and eventually fire
special prosecutor
robert mueller who
won't be missed any
more than james comey

Free Trump

pardon me
you

know
i
can

The Savior

i must repeal
obamacare and
save its victims

i must fire
beleaguered
attorney general
jeff sessions and
save my ass

GOP Warns Trump

republican
senator
cornyn
says
don't fire jeff sessions
or
you'll
foul this chamber

Food for Trump

house
gop
feeds
trump
new
russian
sanctions

Anthony Scaramucci Speaks

I bet last week ninety-nine percent of you hadn't heard of me but already you consider me a box office stud. *The New Yorker, The Atlantic,* CNN, and lots of other important news organizations are publicizing my fight to identify and squash White House leakers who don't care my friend, President Donald Trump, is trying to save the United States from getting fucked over. He knows I've got his back. I don't backstab, I front-stab. If necessary, I'll cut a guy's balls off.

That's probably what I'll do to chief of staff Reince Preibus, the paranoid schizophrenic who spent six months cock-blocking my efforts to work in the White House and leaking my financial information. Now he squeals when the president and I break bread together. You know The Donald would rather be with a smooth operator than a dorky little bastard like Preibus. By the way, if Preibus hasn't been leaking, I invite him to say so. I also encourage Steve Bannon to swear he hasn't been sucking his own cock. I guarantee I haven't been blowing mine.

I've got perfect instincts and training to be communications director in the White House. I think like a gangster and studied law at Harvard University the same time as Barack Obama who's aware twenty years later I overcame his Wall-Street bashing and managed billions of dollars. People don't forget Anthony Scaramucci. I'm the Mooch operating in a cesspool called Washington and know how to get things done fast like removing Sean Spicer as press secretary. We've got too many fish who stink from the head down.

I don't mind when people take a look at my political record. I first backed Scott Walker in the Republican primary and then switched to Jeb Bush and on TV said tell Donald "he'll be President of the Queen's County Bully Association." That's front-stabbing. The president likes guys ballsy enough for that. So what if I opposed walling off Mexico? That shit's not going to happen anyway. Yeah, I said Islam's a religion of peace, a position I can alter as quickly as my presidential candidates. I supported gun control but be careful. Don't I look like a guy who could be packin'? All right, I said humans may be affecting the climate. But maybe it's just cyclical, like the president says. Things change. I'm proud to have been a hardliner on Russia because I think The Donald's going to start getting really tough on them, too.

Preibus Removed

trump and scaramucci
brag they cut my balls
off while ousting me
as white house chief of
staff but I'll stand front
row when they're mounted
backward on jackasses
and run out of town

SIXTEEN

Kim's Second ICBM

After my Fourth of July ICBM present to the United States I decided, little more than three weeks later, to air mail you another test, "a powerful sword for keeping peace," and this one flew higher and longer than the last and, I'm confident, terrified those who live not only on the West Coast but deep in the American hinterlands as well as warmongers on the East Coast. Our Russian and Chinese friends continue to do little but issue plaintive press releases to discourage us. Likewise, your hastily arranged firing, with South Korea, of live nonnuclear missiles into the nearby ocean is merely a pitiful expression of your inability to control our dynamic nuclear weapons program.

For those who want to scientifically chart our progress, please note that our Hwasong-14 missile, which can carry a "large-sized heavy nuclear warhead," soared two thousand three hundred miles into the heavens and landed six hundred and twenty miles away, landing pretty near Japan which can do nothing but quake every time I send fire into the sky. As you know, when we change the trajectory of the missile, its warhead would land somewhere in your neighborhood. Even you imperialist Americans, who killed two million of us during the Korean War and leveled our nation, have already conceded I'll have an operational nuclear ICBM by next year. But don't worry. That's not so much a threat as deterrence.

Nuclear Bull

people who enflame
my horns in spain and
enjoy suicidal head butt
against stake may soon
be lit by nukes i watch
from heaven

General Kelly Takes Command

I've been sworn into many positions of command, led marines all over the world, including in combat in Iraq, and am currently head of the of Department of Homeland Security in a capacity that compels me to warn that terrorism "is everywhere. It's constant. It's nonstop." And it will continue, probably for generations. "If some people knew the truth they'd never leave home." We've got to secure our borders and a major part of that process is building a vast wall on our border with Mexico. I expected completion within two years of President Trump taking office but progress has been hijacked by ignorant people. Today in the Oval Office I'm emphasizing threats, and President Trump's even more worried and intense than usual.

"General Kelly, I need you to take over as my White House chief of staff," he says.

"You do indeed, Mr. President, but I'm not going to involve myself in your quagmire of loud and undisciplined recruits. Furthermore, I still have much work to improve our security."

"I'll give you whatever you need in the White House."

"I'd insist on complete control."

"I'm still commander in chief, General Kelly."

"Correct, and as such you need one person, and one alone, patrolling the entrance to the Oval Office."

"Fine," Trump says. "Why don't we swear you in today?"

"Let's make sure you understand my terms. The new communications director can't stay."

"I agree."

"Even Ivanka and Jared Kushner, like all other GIs, would have to go through me to access you."

"No problem."

"This edict also applies to Steve Bannon."

"Sure, it applies to everyone."

We stand and I say, "Very well, sir. I'm ready."

At the ceremony I proudly raise my right hand and later use it to shake the president's before I lean over Anthony Scaramucci's ear and say, "Meet me in my office within two minutes."

When he arrives I tell him, "Sit down."

"General," he says, "I'm so sorry about my comments last week, many of which were taken out of context or fabricated, but no matter, I swear I'll keep my mouth zipped."

Standing in front of him, I say, "Your comments have certainly been intolerable, Private Scaramucci, and are sufficient for me to court-martial you, but I'm even more concerned by your public boasts that you report directly to the president rather than his chief of staff."

"I was only referring to Reince Preibus."

"Whom you insulted and schemed against and were instrumental in removing."

"I'd never do that to you."

"Quite right you are." I motion to rise.

The little fellow stands, and I pick up my phone and say, "Guards…

"I'm relieving you of your White House duties, Private Scaramucci, and you're to leave the premises at once. Two of our finest former marines will march you out of here. Thank you for ten days of inspired duty."

"You're welcome, General Kelly. It's been an honor."

Scaramucci Confronts Kelly

you wanna my job
anthony scaramucci
shouts at general john
kelly you gonna suffer
charging by trump and
cameras to stab general
with toy knife

Japan Watches

we japanese would be
fascinated by tests of
north korean offensive
and american defensive
missiles except we're
in middle of lunacy

SEVENTEEN

President Pence

i'm not running for president
in twenty-twenty i'm focused
on the donald's agenda and
getting him reelected but if
for some unimaginable reason
he doesn't run i've formed a
fundraising committee that
collected a million bucks
last month

Robert E. Lee Rides Again

i
general robert e lee
statuesque astride my
stallion order you not to
remove me from charlottesville
or complain i shattered families
selling my slaves and petitioned
to overturn five year limit on those
i inherited alas i lost in court and
on battlefield but war continues
as confederate car attacks enemies
of our privileged life

Trump Unglued

sad our great statues
celebrating slavery
and bloody civil war
are being ripped apart
by liberals bad as
charlottesville nazis
who defend our values

which early twentieth
century required us to
dip bullets in pigs blood
to kill muslim terrorists
who didn't understand
they were our prisoners
in their philippines

Bye Bannon

i leaked all
over white
house fools
and sailed
back to
breitbart.com

Free Arpaio

ignoring families
who roasted in
desert tents on
arizona border
trump says you're
pardoned sheriff
joe

EIGHTEEN

Kim Says Mellow Out

Hey, come on. Chill, it's me, your rock-n-roll roundball buddy on top here in the righteous Democratic People's Republic of Korea saying everything's okay and the only reason you're panicking is because you lack precise and trustworthy news organizations. I don't allow such things in my country but you should because right now your outlets are feeding you surgically distorted quotes wherein I ostensibly guarantee I'm going to unleash nuclear weapons to destroy you and South Korea and Japan and, inevitably, myself. That's not so.

Here, let me refer you to a straight shooter called 38North.org. Read a few of its articles and you'll wonder why your media is deceiving you across the political spectrum.

We didn't say under no circumstances would we put the nukes and ballistic rockets on the negotiating table. We said essentially the opposite: "Unless the hostile policy and nuclear threat of the U.S. against the D.P.R.K. are fundamentally eliminated, we, under no circumstances, will put the nukes and ballistic rockets on the nego-tiating table and will not flinch even an inch away from our path of strengthening of the nuclear forces, which is chosen by ourselves."

We didn't say we were planning to strike a merciless blow. We said something quite different: "Should the U.S. dare to show even the slightest sign of attempt to remove our supreme leadership, we will strike a merciless blow."

If you want us to consider dismantling our nuclear weapons program, quit threatening us with nuclear-armed planes and submarines and aircraft carriers. Stop trying to undermine my regime. Cease strangling us with sanctions. Don't stage military exercises, with our Korean brothers, that look like preludes to invasion. Remove your arrogant precondition that bilateral talks can't take place unless we beforehand cede what you most want, removing the only deterrent that will spare my country from being trampled like Iraq and Libya.

And clean up your reporting about what my comrades and I are really saying.

Kim's Big Bomb

You tell me not to make ballistic missiles, I create them. You tell me not to test them, I fire whenever I want. You tell me not to make nuclear warheads, I produce them. You tell me not to test them, this morning I tested one eight times more powerful than the bomb you dropped on Hiroshima. You tell me not to threaten you, I spit in your eye.

You told my grandfather what to do, he ignored you. You told my father what to do, he defied you. You mess with me, I'll hurl thermonuclear war in your face. You say you're going to rain fire on me, I'm betting you won't. You'll instead blather about how the Chinese must strangle us economically, but since our friends and neighbors generate ninety percent of our foreign commerce they're not going to help you. They don't want your foul breath near the Yalu River. You then say you'll wage a trade war against China and cripple its economy. And that'll damage yours. I doubt you'll do that, and even if you do, our nuclear program will continue to grow apace.

Your president, the tweeter, accuses South Korea and China and his own country and others of bribing us to behave, and he's right: we accept your money and then do what we want. We have to. Otherwise, you'd attack us.

Nuclearizing East Asia

During a break at an economic summit Prime Minister Shinzo Abe of Japan motions for Korean President Moon Jae-in to join him in a conference room where President Vladimir Putin arises and says, through several interpreters, "Please sit down. Let's talk."

They sit at a small dark wooden table.

"North Korea's headed toward a very bad place," Abe says.

"And we'd be there, too," says Moon.

"Gentlemen, North Korea's recent underground nuclear explosion is definitely a provocation, but we must control our emotions," Putin says.

"I doubt, President Putin, that you'd be so calm if the threat had been aimed at you,"

Abe says.

"We need to acknowledge that sanctions aren't working and strive for a political solution," says Putin.

"In that regard, President Putin," Moon says, "we have for you a copy in Russian of the new Japanese and South Korean position regarding the renegade kingdom and our future defensive steps. You're free to release it when we leave this room, for as we speak it's now being disseminated worldwide."

Putin pushes both palms on the table and raises his voice, "Why have you done this without consulting me?"

"As Prime Minister Abe indicated, your nation isn't in the crosshairs. Please read."

In the six official languages of the United Nations, this document proclaims: "After long and quite difficult consultations about the strategic and technical shortcomings of our two nations relative to the growing nuclear might of the Hermit Kingdom, Japan and South Korea have decided to develop forthwith our own independent nuclear arsenals to deter Kim Jong Un, an unqualified inheritor of power whom we, and most of the world, view as egotistical and unstable. We reluctantly take this bold step since our conventional weapons, though formidable, are capable only of destroying surface structures and insufficient for busting the bunkers, caves, and other subterranean orifices where North Koreans hide not merely nuclear weapons but vast inventories of chemical and biological weapons. Furthermore, we assume this grave responsibility, which with hindsight we should have earlier undertaken, because we cannot forever depend on the United States to extend its nuclear umbrella over our vulnerable lands. The U.S. is itself daily more susceptible to North Korean nuclear terror, and we can help them and at the same time help ourselves, and we must.

"In an accelerated first phase we each plan to develop, test, and deploy at least thirty (primarily mobile) ballistic missiles carrying warheads more powerful than the one-hundred-twenty kiloton device that recently precipitated an earthquake in North Korea. Furthermore, we shall independently, but in full coordination, build fleets of submarines that fire precise nuclear-tipped ballistic missiles. We will also arm our jets with bombs and air to surface missiles of comparable formidability. We take these urgent and mandatory steps not to threaten any nation but to deter a hidebound and politically deformed nation from being tempted to hurl itself, East Asia, and indeed the world into Armageddon."

"Haven't you first discussed this with China?" Putin asks.

President Abe stands and says, "We don't think China could change North Korea's behavior, and we're certain it hasn't really been trying to."

Donald Trump v. Kim Jong Un

Let's see, in 1950 North Korean soldiers, materially aided by China and Russia, attacked and mauled South Korean troops, which then received massive aid from American and other United Nations forces to repulse the invaders but the rescuers themselves became invaders and, despite many warnings from the Chinese, continued to charge further north, bombing and shooting hundreds of thousands of civilians and threatening to cross the Yalu River into China. While General Douglas MacArthur puffed his foot-long pipe and pontificated about using nuclear weapons to annihilate the communists, a few hundred thousand Chinese soldiers slipped undetected into North Korea and battered the Americans into a massive military retreat. Forces in the south eventually recovered and drove Chinese and North Korean soldiers back onto their side of what we now call the DMZ, and that's about where we are today, except the North has nuclear bombs and continues to develop and test fire missiles, twenty-one since February.

Last week Kim Jong Un and his cowed commanders launched a Hwasong-12 intermediate range ballistic missile over Japan, an appalling affront to the only nation ever struck by atomic weapons. The Hiroshima and Nagasaki attacks were carried out by the United States, which has often bombed civilians, as in Viet Nam and Iraq, to name but two. Americans shouldn't be singled out for barbarism since it's heretofore an incurable human characteristic – imagine if Tojo or Hitler had possessed the bomb. And soon, what might immature and reckless Kim Jong Un do with his missiles when they're nuclear tipped and operational?

In the United States we have our own unstable leader. His name is Donald J. Trump. He responded to North Korea's provocation of Japan, which above all was a warning to the United States, by saying, "The U.S. has been talking to North Korea and paying them extortion money for twenty-five years. Talking is not the answer."

If talking, which hasn't been tried at a high level, isn't the answer, what is it, Mr. Tough Guy? Is it putting you and your family on the front lines in a war with North Korea? Will the other blowhard, Kim Jong Un, and his brood, be on the other side of the battlefield, facing you and yours? Those who order the slaughter of millions shouldn't be permitted to cower in bomb shelters.

If Kim Jong Un and Donald Trump refuse to negotiate, or if they prove as diplomatically inept as one fears, this could appear in a future news report: "Helmeted and bold at dawn this morning, Donald J. Trump and Kim Jong Un simultaneously shout, 'Attack,' and thus unleash nuclear and conventional missiles, artillery shells, and bombs as well as hundreds of thousands grim and determined soldiers. The Dear Leaders, teeth clenched, are thrilled to start World War III, but missile technicians don't push their launch buttons, artillery officers fail to shout fire, and troops on both sides put down their arms and say, 'Let's gather in the DMZ and watch the fight.' Trump and Kim keep demanding fire, but soldiers simply grasp their elbows and say, 'This way.'

"In a few hours countless troops march, drive, and fly to a huge natural amphitheater around which they intermingle and talk as they order hot dogs and beer and other delicacies. The two leaders are meanwhile relieved of their uniforms and attired in boxing trunks. No other garments, undergarments, or gloves are permitted. The referee summons them to the epicenter and says, 'Okay, gentlemen, I don't have to go over the rules since there are no rules. You each have the full complement of limbs and natural weapons and are free to use them in any way you please. Are you ready? Attack.'

"At last a martial order is obeyed, and young Kim, a relative babe at age thirty-three, grunts, lowers his head as a battering ram, and hurls his five-foot-seven and three-hundred-pound frame at The Donald, who's seventy-one and listed at six-two and two thirty-six. He's quite modest about his weight, focused in his belly and hips, which appears to be at least two-seventy. And Kim, I believe, isn't really three bills but only ten pounds heavier than his opponent, who braces and absorbs the young man's face in his Trumpian belly and with both arms reaches under the Korean's chin and locks in a chokehold. Short arms flapping at his sides, a distressed bird, Kim is in great danger until, like a pro, he shoots each hand up into Trump's groin, grabbing a testicle in each hand and pulling. Trump shrieks but he's a warrior and joins both hands to form a mighty hammer he brings down on the back of Kim's neck, breaking the grip and knocking the young leader face down on hard Korean earth. He pounces on Kim, facing the same way, and tries to reattach his chokehold but this time Kim bites deep into his tormenter's right wrist.

"Trump screams, and both men roll onto their backs, Kim holding his neck and Trump sucking his wounded wrist, and breathe like buffalos, disinclined to move.

"'Let's call it a draw,' shouts a soldier.

"'A draw it is,' says the referee, a Korean woman barely twenty.

"One tank arrives and the Dear Leaders are loaded inside, and the tank moves away."

Rocket

trump
joins
nuclear
rocket
man
one
way
to
mars

Trump at United Nations

It's a great honor to be at the United Nations right here in my hometown of New York. I do think the building's a little shabby and would've been a lot prettier if I'd built it but that's okay. We're here today to celebrate the fact that because of my leadership the stock market is at an all-time high, unemployment is the lowest it's been in years, and our military will soon be stronger than ever. All that is critical since terrorists are gaining momentum and spreading to every corner of the planet while rogue nations support them and threaten international peace with the most destructive weapons in history.

To overcome the perils posed by these loser nations and terrorists, we need to form coalitions of strong and independent nations. I don't expect them to share the same traditions but want them to respect their people and other nations. We don't seek to impose our American way of life on anyone. If you're thinking about places like Vietnam, Iraq, and Libya, don't forget how much better off they would be if we'd better handled their Americanization. Let the United States shine as an example for everyone.

Right now, the scourge of our planet is a small group of rogue regimes who violate every principle on which the United Nations is founded. Iran and Venezuela are terrible, but no one has shown more contempt for other nations, as well as their own people, than the depraved regime in North Korea that oppresses, imprisons, tortures, and murders. And every day they're recklessly pursuing nuclear weapons and ballistic missiles to deliver death. It's an outrage some nations trade with North Korea and arm and supply and support them.

The American people, and I in particular, have great strength and patience, but if we are forced to defend ourselves or our allies, we will have no choice but to totally destroy North Korea. Rocket Man is on a suicide mission for himself and his regime. It's time for North Korea to realize denuclearization is its only acceptable future. The U.N Security Council twice voted fifteen to nothing to adopt hard-hitting resolutions – but not as hard-hitting as I wanted. I'd like to thank Russia and China for joining to vote for sanctions. All nations must work together to isolate the Kim regime until it ceases its hostile behavior.

I'm not talking regime change but you know I'm thinking about it and so are plenty of others, some inside North Korea.

Notes – President Kim Jong Un responded by calling Donald Trump "deranged." Kim is likely even more unstable. I propose these two egomaniacs undergo mandatory psychiatric examinations, and appropriate treatment, before they contaminate the world.

NINETEEN

Taliban Responds to Trump

We fighters in the Taliban never rest long and this morning some of our highest ranking members arise quite early and form a semicircle around our color TV to watch President Trump rail about Afghanistan. One of our English speakers conveys the highlights, though we'll later get an official translation. Trump starts by declaring there can be no tolerance for bigotry or hate in his country, and that's quite amusing since he campaigned on bigotry and hate. He then laments that the United States has been fighting in Afghanistan for sixteen years, the longest war in U.S. history (not counting three centuries of genocide against the Native Americans.)

Trump says he's saddened his country's been wasting its time, money, and lives to try to build nations rather than focus on U.S. security. He says his first executive instinct was to leave Afghanistan but his analytical generals talked him out of it. He should've talked to some now-departed Russian and British generals about what happens to foreign fighters in our mountainous land bristling with fighters. If he knew a little history – and he doesn't – he'd leave. Instead, he states there must an honorable and endurable solution only possible if he gives his forces the tools to win. The consequences of a rapid withdrawal, he says, would be terrible and predictable, creating a vacuum for ISIS and Al Qaeda. In fact, the consequences of eternal war here are predictably terrible.

Trump laments that twenty terrorist organizations lurk in Afghanistan and he's been dealt a horrible hand. But he's a problem solver and his team will win by stripping us of our assets and territory – we now control about forty percent of the country, the most since 2001. He also wants to keep us from getting ahold of nuclear weapons. I understand how he feels. I wish he didn't have them, either.

It seems Trump thinks the magical strategy is to end "time-based programs" and let conditions on the ground determine his actions. He won't say when they'll attack, but attack they will. And he won't micromanage from the White House; instead, his fighting commanders will improvise. Regarding Pakistan, he laments it's a sanctuary for terrorists. He forgets it may have been an American who reminded comrades that "one man's terrorist is another's freedom fighter." Most of our friends and neighbors in Pakistan aren't going to help the Americans "deal" with us, and many who tried are dead.

Trump believes the stronger the security forces of the Afghan government the less his troops will have to fight against the Taliban. At the same time he undercuts himself by noting "military power alone will not bring peace to Afghanistan." He's certainly correct about the latter point. During the regime of George W. Bush and the first part of Barack Obama's, the Americans poured troops into Afghanistan and peaked at a hundred thousand in 2010. Were we in the Taliban close to being defeated? Absolutely not. Yet Trump's big announcement calls for adding a paltry four thousand troops to the nine thousand here today. He thinks they can train government forces well enough to prevent us from killing eleven thousand bad Afghans a year.

We nod when Trump says elements of the Taliban have to be part of the solution. I'd say we are the solution, but we'll talk to the Americans, knowing they'll someday have to leave. We could hasten their departure by promising not to be a staging ground for any more 9/11 attacks and the like. I believe that's what a small but growing number in the Taliban want. We rebuke reactionaries who, among other barbarities, pretend polio workers are spies and murder them and then ban the vaccine in parts of the country. We don't want people like that to prevail, otherwise the invaders may stay for decades.

DACA

trump doesn't favor punishing
children for actions of illegal
alien parents but stresses kids
now law abiding adults may have
to leave since we're nation of laws

McCain Care

draft dodging
trump demeaned

my imprisonment
in vietnam but
that's not why i'm
thumbs downing his
health care plan

Fake Launch

trump tweets iran
test fired missile
designed to reach
israel but there
was no launch and
one wonders why
president is forever
permitted to lie

Market Value

real wages
stagnate while
dreary houses
soar and stocks
climb on high
limb

Puerto Rican Tweet

hurricane devours puerto
rican food water and
electricity and san juan
mayor begs u.s. to save
people from dying at one
of his golf courses trump
tweets such poor leadership
from mayor and others who

can't get their workers to
help

Armed in Texas

Thank God I escape from that godless pansy state California where you have to struggle to get a concealed weapon permit and then keep the dang weapon hidden in public. I can't live like that so quit my job and sell everything and move to Texas where I keep my holstered handgun on one hip and a Bowie knife or sword on the other. Unfortunately, I can't take my protection into sporting events, schools, churches, or lots of other dangerous places. I bet that changes when people accept good guys always have to be ready to stop bad guys.

TWENTY

Hot Tweet

from erect tweeter
trump declares secretary
of state tillerson
wasting time talking
to little rocket man
in north korea where
the donald will do what
has to be done

Viva Vegas

gunman kills dozens at concert
is
that
really
a
surprise

Please Explain

how can a man carry so many rifles
to
thirty
second
floor
of
any
hotel

You Know It

twenty five times more murdered with guns
in
united

states
than
in
other
wealthy
nations

NRA in Hiding

freedom's
safest
place
nra website
still
hasn't
mentioned
las
vegas
slaughter

Trump Towels

hurricane victims
huddled in puerto
rico get paper towels
thrown by trump who
has lovely touch

TWENTY-ONE

Trump Backs Tillerson

it's
totally
phony
that
rex
tillerson
called
me
a
moron

Buy Your Bump Stocks

las vegas firearms just fine
because they weren't illegal
automatic weapons but legal
semi automatics souped up by
bump stocks which are also
legal and make good sense

NRA Logic

nra swallowed tongue
until suddenly denouncing
obama administration for
twice approving sales of
bump stocks which nra
believes should be subject
to additional regulations

Tillerson Reassures

listen to me
trump's smart
and loves his
country and i
hope won't fire
my ass

Tillerson Confronts Trump

Walking fast Rex Tillerson enters the office of White House chief of staff John Kelly and says, "Tell the president I'm here and we need to talk."

"You don't have an appointment," says the retired four-star general, rising to attention.

The secretary of state pivots, marches out, and turns toward the Oval Office.

Kelly from behind grabs Tillerson's left elbow and pulls, and the stocky former oil executive whirls and right-hand slaps Kelly's face.

Dazed, Kelly raises his left hand to console his cheek and does not reply. Tillerson moves through Trump's open door.

"Please excuse us," Tillerson says to Trump's son-in-law Jared Kushner.

"Jared needs to watch and learn. He could be the man who brings peace to Asia and the Middle East while he solves the opioid crisis."

"He's a busy boy. Close the door on the way out, Jared."

Glancing at Trump, the young man rises and departs.

"I told you to let me know when you're coming."

"Listen, Mr. President, I'm sorry for questioning your foreign policy intelligence during that meeting at the Pentagon, but I won't tolerate what you've just been quoted as saying, that your IQ is higher than mine."

"Nothing personal. Mine's higher than just about anyone's."

"Let's settle it right here," says Tillerson.

"Go ahead."

"What's the capital of Vietnam?"

"Saigon."

"Wrong."

"No trick questions. My turn. How much per square foot is office real estate in Manhattan right now?"

"Irrelevant. How much was a barrel of oil the day you took office before that sparse crowd?" Tillerson asks.

"You don't answer my questions, I won't answer yours."

"Here's one you can't avoid: what the hell were you alluding to when you said 'only one thing will work' when trying to convince the North Koreans to stop testing nuclear weapons?"

"What's it sound like?"

"Like you're conceding nuclear war is inevitable."

"We either fight them now, before they can hit us, or we wait till they can," says Trump.

"I'd get better diplomatic results if you'd quit tweeting 'I'm wasting my time trying to talk to North Korea.'"

"They lie, they intimidate, they murder Americans and others, and they never keep their promises. It doesn't matter if you've established direct contacts with North Korea to probe its willingness to negotiate.'"

"Surely you're not going to just give up on diplomacy," says Tillerson.

"Talking won't stop them from developing and deploying missiles that can soon destroy our cities."

"With the help of the Chinese and the Russians, I think our sanctions will influence the North Koreans."

"Sanctions haven't worked and never will. There's only one solution…"

"Mr. President, you're worse than a moron."

TWENTY-TWO

Iran Trumped

the donald
decertifies
iran nuclear
deal as well
as persian gulf
he calls arabian

Trump Assesses The Donald

I knew I was going to be a great president but, frankly, I'm far surpassing my own expectations and am rebuilding the nation and the world in ways I know are necessary. Let's start with disastrous Obamacare, the Affordable Care Act I cut back last week because its author had lied to the American people and told them they could keep their own doctors and pay lower premiums. We know that was never true. My plan, and I guarantee I've got one, will really make health care affordable for all Americans. Fake news hounds want you to believe six million will suffer when I eliminate cost-sharing subsidies paid to insurers by the federal government. And in particular it's a lie that seventy percent of those who benefit most from Obamacare live in states I won in 2016. My enemies won't be able to weaken my already excellent chances for reelection.

I'm also ensuring American strength by ignoring wild claims that human activity is causing the world to heat up and lash us with hurricanes and other disasters. Listen, the world has always had extreme changes in weather and there's nothing we can do about it. Pumping billions of tons of carbon dioxide and coal smoke into the atmosphere won't hurt us a bit, and only wimps and hypocrites fear efforts that lead to economic growth. Let me ask the solar and wind loonies a simple question: do you usually travel in private or public vehicles powered by fossil fuels? You damn well do unless you ride a bicycle or hang-glide to work.

I'm as strong on women's rights as I am the environment and understand that crude and unattractive women should keep their mouths shut so powerful men don't get turned off by their barking. I like beautiful young babes who're great pieces of ass and very deferential, especially in public. Melania's hot as they come but obedient most of the time. Look, I've got five kids so I understand women, including pregnant women, and babies. Trust me, we can't force God-fearing companies to pay for birth control if they believe it's wrong. Those who say "restricting birth control will likely increase the rate of abortions" are wrong. I admit I used to be pro-choice but can't continue that while building a Supreme Court, and a society, that during my first term may overturn Roe v. Wade. We need more babies but we have to be careful about too much maternity leave since we've got to keep the country competitive. If women want equal pay, they've got to work and produce like men.

I'm protecting American jobs by continuing to strengthen our borders. The Great Wall of Trump is coming, a little slower than I planned but it's on the way. Meanwhile, I'm preparing to send millions of those Dream Act babies back where they came from. I know their parents brought them here when they were minors, or even babies, but a nation must have laws and enforce them. Now we need a new national law to protect the flag and fire all those blacks in the National Football League who kneel during the National Anthem. I also plan to enact criminal and civil laws to prevent fake news from polluting your minds. They're so pitiful they often publish lists of what they claim are my lies. I don't lie or I'd have never gotten elected by a landslide.

I'm really strong in the field of foreign policy. No, not because the Russians tutored me during the campaign. I'll soon be suing people who say things like that. Right now, though, I'm focusing on our most dangerous enemies, and will keep denouncing the nuclear deal with Iran which isn't following the terms of the agreement. I don't care what biased inspectors say. Our European allies – are they really our friends? – as well as the Russians and Chinese also maintain the terms are being adhered to. I disagree, and my call for Congress to reinstate tough sanctions is the first step in getting rid of this deal and writing a better one. If the Iranians don't shape up, they may end up like North Korea.

Senatorial Blast

about those two gop
senators who claim
i'm debasing our
nation bob corker's
a flake and jeff
flake's incompetent
neither could get
elected dogcatcher

The Culprit

fake investigation none of my guys
colluded
but
hillary
sure
did

TWENTY-THREE

An Honorable Man

In the mid eighteen fifties, near the grand columns of Arlington House in Virginia, about seventy of us stand before our master George Parke Custis and feel great joy as he says, "When I pass from this earth, you shall all be free."

"Did Master write his instructions so his heirs would understand?" I stun myself by asking the adopted son of George Washington.

"I have, indeed, Wesley Norris. I believe it's God's will. Now, return to your duties."

We comply, and in a little while a friend says, "I wonder how long he'll live."

"He's too fat and old to bother our women anymore. I expect we'll soon be free."

In October of eighteen fifty-seven, at age seventy-six, George Parke Custis stops breathing, and in the privacy of our shacks we dance and sing. A few weeks later his son-in-law, Colonel Robert E. Lee, husband of Mr. Custis' only surviving child, rides in from Texas and dismounts his fine stallion. An aide orders us to assemble. Colonel Lee, wearing a beautiful blue uniform, looks quite serious as he announces, "My duties here at the plantation are such that I must leave my command and devote myself to reorganizing this unproductive and debt-ridden enterprise. I therefore demand that all of you follow orders and improve yourselves as I bring profitability back to this splendid estate."

"We're supposed to be free now," someone shouts.

"That's right," adds another.

"It's what Master Custis wanted," I say.

"Quiet," says Colonel Lee. "If I read you his will you'd understand your master decreed that only after his debts are paid can you be freed. Don't worry. He stipulated this process take no longer than five years."

We're quite unhappy, since we've already been slaves all our lives, and after about a year and a half, in eighteen fifty-nine, I tell my sister and cousin we'll never be free unless we escape which we do by running and hiding and horseback riding until we're almost to Pennsylvania when they capture us.

"We'll get paid a lot for this," says one of the slave catchers, smiling at me.

After getting little food, water, or sleep for two weeks in jail, we're tied up and sent back to Arlington House. When we arrive, the overseer runs inside, and Colonel Lee soon marches out.

"Why have you betrayed me?" he asks.

"We should be free," says my sister.

"We're already free," I say.

"It's God's will," says my cousin.

"Don't speak to me of God. You're property, and that I'll teach you in a manner impossible to forget."

Colonel Lee turns to his overseer and orders, "Take them to the barn, remove their filthy shirts, and bind each of them to a post."

The overseer and his helpers tie our hands tightly. Colonel Lee stands close to observe, and then hands a whip to the overseer and says, "Lay on fifty lashes each."

"Even the woman?"

"Twenty will suffice for her."

"I'm sorry, Colonel, but I can't do this. Maybe you could do it."

"That's beneath me. Get the constable."

Robert E. Lee retires to his mansion while we wait. It's a long wait and I envision them ripping our flesh. When the constable arrives, Lee returns to duty and says, "Get started."

The constable begins with me, and after several lacerations Lee shouts, "Harder."

Afterward, unbound, I slump to the dirt floor of the barn and two men drag me to the side. My cousin's next and Lee continues to demand the hardest lashing. He's quiet while my sister gets her twenty.

"Bring out the brine," says Lee.

The following day we're sent away to work, my cousin and I one place, and my sister another. A couple of years later, in eighteen sixty-one, I'm not surprised Lee joins the Confederacy and in fact becomes leader of its army. At the Battle of Gettysburg he orders free black farmers kidnapped and sold into slavery. When I escape to the north I try to avoid anywhere he might be. After the war I'd have expected a traitor like him to be punished. Instead, he becomes president of a university and opposes political rights for former slaves.

I know he was a good general who looked great in a uniform on his horse, but I don't see how anyone can call him an honorable man. Will General John Kelly please explain that to me?

Texas Church

twenty
six
dead
in
texas
church
more guns won't help
more mental health care might

Kim Jong Un in Iran

Just so you understand, I have a hot line to Iran and can contact Supreme Leader Ali Khamenei any time I want but I won't need a phone today. After a secret trip by means that must remain mysterious, I'm meeting Khamenei in Tehran where I've been invited to discuss how we can save our two countries from the nuclear arsenal wielded by Donald Trump and his warmongering Americans. I know what Trump's up to. He's in Asia right now, conniving with imperialists in South Korea, Japan, and, yes, even China. They no doubt plan to tighten sanctions and call me a terrorist.

I nod at our two translators and tell Khamenei, "I'd like to expand our military aid for your great nation."

"We'll need your help if the Americans violate our nuclear deal."

"I hope they do. Then you'll be free to develop your deterrent, which is the right and duty of all sovereign nations."

"But Trump says he won't permit 'Iran to become another North Korea,'" says Khamenei.

"We've already given you important information about our ICBMs, and I'm today prepared to offer insights that, within a couple of years, can make your missiles and warheads as formidable as mine."

"Our ballistic missile tests have been encouraging. And our academic research of nuclear weapons is accelerating, but we're essentially abiding by the terms of the treaty."

"That's a mistake," I say. "You'll always be a hostage until you can destroy some of their cities."

"We really don't plan to attack Israel or the United States."

"We won't be attacking anyone, either. But they'll destroy us if we don't have nuclear weapons."

"I'm not convinced Iran will ever have that option without fighting. We might benefit from war, as long as the Americans keep it conventional."

Economic Delights

trump celebrates stock market that could top
annual
record
set
in
nineteen
twenty
eight
but not clear he knows what happened next

Roy Moore for Senate

maybe i chased
some teenage skirts
years ago in alabama
but never without
first meetin their
mommas

TWENTY-FOUR

Golfing with Shinzo and Donald

I've caddied for many of the greatest golfers in history, packing Tiger Woods' bag the day he shot sixty-two in an exhibition with Japanese legend Jumbo Ozaki who, despite being almost sixty, fired a hot sixty-seven. Today, I won't be carrying clubs because our distinguished guests here at Kasumigaseki Country Club – Hideki Matsuyama, fourth ranked pro in the world, President Donald Trump, and Prime Minister Shinzo Abe, the host – will be riding in carts. My crew and I will walk and replace all divots, rake every sand trap, and repair ball marks on greens.

On the first tee Matsuyama drills a mammoth drive down the middle, at least three hundred thirty yards. Trump follows with a duck hook into the left rough and quickly pulls another ball out of his pocket and says, "Mulligans on the first tee," and hits his second drive about two-twenty down the left side of the fairway. Abe swings and misses his first shot and screams a bad word I won't translate. He then slices one about a hundred thirty yards into the right rough. Trump and Abe ride together in their cart, a two-seater with translators in back, and seem very friendly.

I already know Hideki Matsuyama's going to break par, Trump's going to score in the low forties for nine holes, all these hotshots have time for, and Abe'll struggle to break sixty, but I'm more focused on what they're saying. After the first hole, a birdie for Hideki, a bogey for Trump, not counting the retry, and a triple bogey for Abe, I hear Trump speak and the translator tell the prime minister, "I'd like to get Kim Jong Un on a golf course."

"Better be careful, if he plays like his father."

"Kim Jong Il played golf?" Trump asks.

"Just once, at North Korea's only course. Regulation layout, par seventy-two."

"What'd he shoot?"

"Thirty-four with five holes in one."

"Who the hell would believe that?"

On the third hole, after Hideki and Trump nail their drives, Abe duffs his about a hundred yards. At his ball he proclaims, "Watch this.

My three wood's a rocket launcher," and slices a worm killer into the fairway trap. He wades into the sandy crater, examines a ball buried and only half visible, and grunts as he swings, moving his target less than a foot. On the next attempt he thrashes even harder and nails a hook into the trees on the other side of the fairway. "Get that damn ball," he orders, and one of my crewmen dashes into the forest. Meanwhile, instead of exiting through the rear of the trap, as dictated by etiquette and common sense, Abe tries to take a giant step from the bunker up to the turf, raises high his right foot, planting it not entirely on the fairway and, as he lifts himself, loses momentum and falls back into the trap. Two secret service agents run toward him but he waves go away and crawls out of the hazard, leaving foot, hand, and body images I have to rake away.

On the sixth green Donald Trump, like Hideki Matsuyama, is putting for birdie. Trump's ball is about two feet further from the hole and on the same line. After Hideki marks his ball, the president says, "Tell you what, pro. I've got five hundred bucks that says I beat you right here."

"You're on," he says.

Trump strikes a bold putt that misses the hole by an inch and skids twelve feet by. "Don't you guys water these damn greens," he says, and stomps in Hideki's line all the way to the cup before moving to mark his ball.

A split second before Hideki strokes his ball, Trump drops his putter and Hideki, flinching inside, I believe, leaves his approach three feet short. Trump, after studying green contours from every angle, drains his putt and, in a celebratory jump, lifts his fleshy frame an inch off the ground. "Don't swallow the olive, Hideki."

"Please don't disturb me this time, Mr. President."

"What're you talking about?"

The fourth ranked golfer in the world pulls his putt which hits the left side of the hole, circumnavigates it, and pops out.

"Don't worry, you can pay me in the clubhouse."

"This is supposed to be a friendly round of golf, Donald," Abe says.

"Before China started screwing us in trade, Japan reamed us. Today I'm doing something about the imbalance."

Prime Minister Abe tells me, "Take my clubs and put them in Hideki's cart."

I comply, and President Trump chauffeurs two interpreters the final three holes.

Japan and the United States have critical security concerns and I'm relieved the two leaders shake hands after the round. Hideki Matsuyama stomps off without saying goodbye.

"My five hundred," hollers The Donald.

Hideki keeps walking.

"Americans just keep getting ripped off."

"Let's have lunch," says Abe. "We've got what you asked for."

"Thank you. I don't hate Japanese beef but, frankly, it ain't as good as American prime."

"We could've acquired American beef. It wasn't necessary for you to bring your own."

"I'm sure your security's okay but I can't risk eating hamburgers not made from a homegrown steer. Besides, I shot it myself, three rounds between the eyes."

My Guy Putin

i believe putin's sincere
he didn't interfere in my
election or know cia
political hacks are trying
to sabotage my relations
with russia

Donald Duterte

Bearing a big smile Donald Trump for a hefty man strides rapidly into Malacañang Palace and extends a hand to his host, President Rodrigo Duterte, who says, "No, bro, like this," and holds out his right fist, evidently a more macho version of the Nazi salute, which after all was open-handed, and nods for Trump to do the same. Both leaders brandish knuckles, and only afterward do they shake hands, smile for photos, and make a few perfunctory remarks before retreating to a private chamber for discussion.

"Go ahead, President Trump, I know you have to talk about it?"

"About what? Call me Donald, by the way."

"You know, that human rights stuff liberals in our countries are complaining about."

"I saw that on TV. Terrible. All those criminals in your streets, protesting that I plan to expand U.S. military bases in the Philippines and push you into our war with North Korea. It's not true. I still hope there won't be a nuclear war. Maybe Japan and South Korea should have nuclear weapons, and if they do then you should, too."

"We're not really planning to develop nuclear weapons, Donald."

"Look, if you'd had nukes in 1941, the Japanese never would've attacked you."

"No one had nukes in 1941."

"Exactly my point."

"I was earlier referring to my war on drugs," says Duterte.

"Great job. I've already praised you publicly and by phone and am happy to tell you today that I admire what you're doing. How many of the bad guys have you gotten so far?"

"My police have killed at least four thousand dealers and addicts in the year and a half I've been president, and a few thousand others are missing, and I think, really, there are a lot more than that."

"We should bring you to the United States for a while," Trump says.

"I'm glad you aren't going to lecture me about due process and the rule of law and all that crap. I am the law, and if my police or vigilantes think people have been using or selling drugs, then who the hell needs a trial? Shoot the bastards. Some are shooting at us, anyway. You understand this problem, unlike that black son of a whore Barack Obama."

"Obama was a terrible man and worse president."

"I can't imagine a president letting his town, Chicago, be inundated by drugs and murder. When I was mayor of Davao City I used to speed around on my motorbike, looking for criminals to shoot, and told my police, 'If I can do it, why can't you?'"

"Maybe I should get a motorbike, too," says Trump.

"I've got an extra in the garage. We could go riding and shooting right now."

Encouraging Mass Murder

Let me understand. Kevin Janson Neal often fires gunshots from his home and neighbors complain when police come, knock on his door, and leave when Neal doesn't answer, except the time he stabs a neighbor and is arrested and soon out on bail and barred from having firearms police allegedly know he still has. So it's not surprising Kevin Janson Neal shoots his wife and the neighbor he stabbed and tries to shoot his way into an elementary school but is locked out so drives other places, killing five wounding ten, and to angry citizens police say they don't have a crystal ball, but I wonder why they think they needed one.

Trumpenstein

imagine senator al frankenstein lecturing others about sexual
harassment
until
we
learn
he
behaves
about
like
me

Trump Scorches Balls

I'm sure you all read my vital presidential tweets and know I worried those three shoplifters from the UCLA basketball team were going to show me up and not tell everyone how much they appreciated that I intervened with President Xi and saved their asses from ten years in a Chinese prison. They should've said so immediately. Don't they have tweeters? Okay, maybe they were flying home and then were ordered to wait for someone to write their apologies for the press conference. But at least they did finally thank me for my efforts, and I tweeted for them to have a great life, and everything should've been wonderful. But bigmouth LaVar Ball, father of DiAngenlo, has been very insulting so I tweeted he's "unaccepting of what I did for his son… (and) I should have left them in jail."

That's right. Disrespect me and I'll scorch your ass. You know how I called Rosie O'Donnell a pig and more and said the same about lots of women and started calling my opponents Lyin' Ted Cruz and Little Marco Rubio and Crooked Hillary Clinton and now short and fat Kim Jong Un is the Rocket Man. If LaVar Ball keeps implying that moves by UCLA and Chinese billionaires, who aren't that much richer than I am, were what got those guys out of jail, I'm going to come up with a devastating nickname and tweet about him. But my media people warn that's just what he wants.

TWENTY-FIVE

Meet John Larson

The ruddy face of Representative John Larson moves through our Facebook news holes this afternoon, and, shortly after wondering who the hell's he, we click the video and watch as in strong voice he addresses Republican opponents on the floor of the House, saying it's time to "expose a lot of (their) myths, like this notion that social security and Medicare are entitlements."

Right index finger jabbing, he states, "News flash – it's the insurance that the American people have paid for. News Flash – ten thousand baby boomers become eligible for social security every day. News Flash – the average woman when she retires gets fourteen thousand dollars annually from social security, and for more than half that's all they've got to live on. Yet, these bastions of courage on the other side would like to cut these programs."

The Republicans don't want this process to be decided in Congress, Larson explains. They plan to introduce "an amendment where they'll never have to face a vote on what their constituents actually have to face day in and day out… If you want to take away people's benefits, have the courage to vote on it."

I conclude he'd make a good president and Google him to learn he's from Connecticut and age sixty-nine, two years younger and much more lucid than Donald Trump, but supports energy independence, clean renewable fuels, reducing greenhouse gases, protecting consumers, and increasing efficiency of products, buildings, and vehicles. Those positions, along with preserving social security and Medicare, make him unelectable.

Blooming Charlie Rose

felt i pursued
shared feelings as
i pranced naked
before female
coworkers decades
my junior only

now do i realize
i was mistaken

Manson Confesses

glad i checked
out or these days
my girls coulda
accused me of
some wild shit

Moore Voters

trump finally says
go get 'em roy but
unclear if he refers
to teenage skirts or
alabama voters

Sunday Morning Conyers

I've fought for civil rights in the streets of Detroit, through the media, and in the House of Representatives more than half a century. A bunch of attention-seeking female employees can't take that away from me. My legacy is secure because their claims are absurd. I touched no legs or fannies, though I'm sure many wanted precisely that from the most important Democrat on the House Judiciary Committee. Just look at the latest lady to throw garbage at me. She claims we were sitting in church, in the front pew of God's house, and I eased my hand under her skirt and stroked her thighs. Isn't that ridiculous? Someone on her side or mine would surely have seen this sacrilegious act. The pastor, high in front of us, would have had the most revealing view of all. No, these fantasies won't destroy my legacy. That's indestructible, but my eighty-eight-year old body and soul are tired, and I've resigned. I don't need this. My children will carry on my good work.

Franken Out

ok i'm resigning
from senate but in
that spirit demand
pussy grabber in chief
leave office and girl
groping roy moore drop
from alabama senate
race

Roy Moore Says

loving sweet girls
the ten commandments
the confederate flag
and stepping on gays
i'm shocked alabamans
betrayed me electing
liberal doug jones
i demand a recount

TWENTY-SIX

Nuclear Role Reversal

Frankly and without self-pity I tell you that I have a dangerous and therefore stressful job as president of South Mexico, which for years, with the help of our Chinese allies, has been holding off communist hordes in North Mexico and the United States. To help you understand, let me briefly review essential events after World War II. In 1950 our belligerent brothers to the North, backed materially by the United States and Canada, attacked and battered us and would have plowed us into the sea if not for the quick return of Chinese troops who, with peaceful intent, had withdrawn to their military facilities in Hawaii.

Our able warriors and the Chinese counterattacked the North Mexicans, knocking them back north toward the Rio Grande River. The Americans repeatedly warned us to stay away from the Rio Grande and never consider crossing it. I confess my South Mexican forefathers and our Chinese comrades wanted to crush North Mexico and unify the nation. Their goals were noble but, alas, they lacked reconnaissance, and a few hundred thousand gringo soldiers first slipped and then charged south across the Rio Grande, forcing us to retreat and again almost pushing us into the sea. We did recover, of course, and counterattacked and mauled the invaders back onto their side of the internationally recognized border, the DMZ, and that's where everyone is today, bristling on each side of the most dangerous line in the world.

And now, as surely everyone in the world is aware, the North Mexicans have developed a nuclear weapons program no one has dared try to stop, lest they obliterate Mexico City with fifteen thousand artillery pieces and rocket launchers positioned nearby in hardened places. We and the Chinese must also consider what the United States would do if we either bombed or invaded their tyrannical and oft-starving ally. We believe, though are by no means certain, that any military action by South Mexico would, at minimum, trigger massive artillery barrages onto our capital city, and quite possibly frighten the North into initiating a nuclear conflagration.

The Chinese have often stated they will destroy North Mexico if it strikes us, and would of course do so if the North, using its rapidly developing ICBMs, launched a suicidal attack against China, as the

North often threatens to do. Would the United States risk annihilation to save North Mexico if the latter started the war? We're not sure, and neither are you. Therefore, we tell – and I should more accurately say entreat – our Chinese allies to respect our dictate that "no military action in Mexico shall be taken without the prior consent of the government of South Mexico."

We in South Mexico are weekly more concerned by Chinese statements that destruction of Mexican cities, North and South, would be preferable to the loss of a single Chinese city.

Bibi's New Home

In my beautiful brown fortress on Balfour Street, cleverly named after the Balfour Declaration, in our eternal capital of Jerusalem, I'm dreaming about ever-expanding settlements when awakened by shouts and thundering footsteps that crush my bedroom door and leave my imperial bed surrounded by armed men speaking Arabic.

"Guards, kill them at once," I order.

"I'm afraid your guards are no more," says a young man I assume is in command.

"Impossible."

"Get dressed at once."

"I demand privacy."

He raises his revolver and fires a shot into the mattress on each side of me. Thank God Mrs. Netanyahu's out of town. I arise, naked and rather fat, and slip on clothes men throw at me.

"You won't need a suitcase," says the commander.

"You're going to prison or worse," I say.

"You – and therefore all of us – have only a few more minutes to evacuate this condemned site."

"What the hell are you talking about?"

Two large men one on each side grab my arms, burying knuckles into armpits, and lead me out of the bedroom, down the hall, and quickly out of my home. A dozen bulldozers are lined up facing the front and side walls of my compound.

"Is everyone out?" shouts the commander.

"Probably," someone answers.

"Then get started," he says.

The bulldozers begin to batter and chip the stone walls.

"You're animals," I shout.

"Didn't know you objected to bulldozers, Bibi."

"This is a cowardly crime."

"No, here, read our paperwork. The second part's in Hebrew. I'll just tell you the essence. You didn't have a proper building permit when this house was constructed. It must therefore be destroyed."

"Of course I had an official building permit. Jerusalem's our capital."

"It's not all yours," the commander says.

"West Jerusalem's officially ours according to international law."

"Perhaps, but as this ancient map proves, this property is owned by Arabs."

"Your bulldozers aren't having much effect."

"Naturally, this isn't a shack under occupation. We'll let you watch a few more minutes, then blow the place up. Everyone in this neighborhood's got to go. I expect we'll live in all these homes, except yours."

I start cursing in basic Arabic I learned years ago as an elite member of the armed forces but one of the goons shoves a handkerchief in my mouth while another blindfolds me, and together they pull me into a windowless van, jump inside, and I'm driven away.

In less an hour the van stops and the men jerk me outside, remove the blindfold, and the commander, who's driven us, says, "Here's your new home."

"This is your home," I say, gesturing toward hovels in a parched and broken land. "My home's in the beautiful condominiums in hills around you."

"Now the hills surround you. That shack's yours."

The commander and the two men leave. In less than an hour I hotwire and borrow a car and drive to the checkpoint where not Jews but Arabs stand armed and at attention.

"Your papers," says a guard.

I show my ID and say, "I'm the prime minister of Israel."

"Better keep that quiet."

"Everyone knows."

"Where's the registration for this car?"

They take me to jail where I say, "I want my lawyer."

"There'll be no lawyer," says another officious Arab.

"I demand a trial."

"There'll be no trial."

"I demand to know what the hell's happening."

"Simple. You're going to prison."

Six months later, most in solitary, I'm released and taken back to the shack I'd been assigned. It's dirty and bug-infested and there's no damn electricity or water. It's winter and cold as hell especially when I have to go to the bathroom, which is hardpan outside. I'm not going to live like this. I organize my new neighbors, who're other confused Jews. We save money from our jobs as laborers and, after futile waiting for bureaucratic permission, we hire carpenters, plumbers, and electricians to build decent houses. I soon feel stronger in mind and body and tell my neighbors, "We must expand our organization to the adjoining communities."

"Good idea, but we still can't drive directly to the village over there," says a bearded man I won't identify.

"We'll change that."

In the morning bulldozers and armed men surround our shacks.

"Where are your building permits?" says the commander.

"The right question," I say, "is where the hell are the permits we applied for?"

"These houses are illegal structures on land you don't own and will be destroyed in five minutes, once you've removed your belongings."

"We'd rather die," I say.

"Be careful talking like that."

"Where do you expect us to go?"

Jerusalem 2117

Who was that American president, the minor figure who blabbed a lot? Donald Trump, that's right. He acknowledged seventy years of reality and proclaimed Jerusalem the capital of Israel, and promised the United States would move its embassy from Tel Aviv, as soon as

GEORGE THOMAS CLARK

his architects and engineers could build and secure a big beautiful building. As it developed, the Americans didn't give this project priority and, as I recall from junior high textbooks, it took three or four years to complete. A far more important proclamation came too many years later when President Blank proclaimed that Jerusalem was also the capital of the Palestinian people. I mean, where else would their capital be?

I don't worry too much about what's Jewish or Palestinian because I'm both, pretty much right down the middle, and bet a majority of people in Israel are quite mixed up, biologically speaking. It doesn't matter much since I often mistake one for the other no matter the origin. What certainly counts is that the two-state solution didn't work in such a compressed area and, when the Israelis officially annexed the West Bank, after decades of slow and painful bites, so much strife ensued that our forebearers reluctantly acknowledged that in order to survive they had to form one nation, a diverse and democratic place of unqualified personal and religious freedom.

To those mired in the enmity and violence of a century and more ago, this would sound naïve. Very well, to us in modern Israel, the old violence and repression are difficult to comprehend. I'm glad our ancestors studied world history, and eventually learned that slavery, holocausts, and segregation could be overcome. Today, it all seems relatively simple, or at least straightforward. We have fine homes, schools, businesses, medical facilities, and social and cultural options, and I think we'll maintain these as long as we offer them to everyone.

What About Predatory Women?

Envision those male politicians, corporate bosses, and college administrators who enjoy flagellating themselves and other men while females of all ages and stations help them lay on the whip. Right now, that's the self-righteous, politically essential, and cool thing to do. Make believe that most men are beasts and most women aren't. Pretend the fair sex is helpless and blameless and never predatory. Pontificate that female accusers are always honest and accused males forever dishonest. Shred men's lives and careers based solely on accusations that must

151

be believed since women leveled them. Some of this groundswell is inevitably founded on lies. And if you pretend falsehoods are sacred truth, that makes you a liar.

Trump Taxes

working poor know
my
tax
cuts
don't
favor
rich

Trump Health

obamacare
is
dead
long
live
trumpcare

2018

TWENTY-SEVEN

Proud Putin

Alexei Navalny is evil man who lied and insulted me during fake campaign for president he won't win because he's felon convicted of corruption and our noble election commission kicked him out of race I'll dominate since few believe Navalny's charge his popularity is surging because Russians know struggling economy's my fault along with problems in Crimea, Ukraine, and Syria. In three months Russians will announce the truth: I've beaten worthy opponents to win my fourth presidency and can do what I want.

Rocket Man Ready

our nuclear forces are complete
the
magic
button
is
on
my
desk
happy new year

Trump Button

my
nuclear
button's
bigger
than
yours

Admiral Yamamoto in Korea

We'll talk about North Korea in a minute but first you should know I love the sea and more Kawai especially when I'm in Tokyo out of uniform in her arms. I tell her about studying at Harvard two happy years, and likewise two incisive years as naval attaché in Washington, D. C. I like baseball, you know. I've seen the Yankees of Babe Ruth in the early twenties, and with friends from school and work I play cards and chess and learn English, and my second two years I rent a car to drive around the United States, and without much money I stay in modest places fine for me. I see a vast country of empty plains and vibrant cities getting stronger and decide Japan must not confront this industrial giant. In a few years I also state we shouldn't attack Manchuria and China or sign the Tripartite Pact with fascist Germany and Italy. Groups of young right-wing officers are enraged and threaten to kill me. I try not to worry.

I'm a specialist in naval aviation and the best strategic planner in the Japanese Navy but can't overcome politicians and diplomats who're bumbling with aggressive elements in the U.S. Roosevelt's the most powerful among a belligerent group that demands we surrender our conquests in China and Southeast Asia. If our nation wants to fight, it must do so my way or I'll resign. Ultimately, our high command understands when I explain we must use planes from aircraft carriers to strike undetected and swiftly at the heart of the enemy. At Pearl Harbor we sink and damage a number of ships including battleships and kill about two thousand in the attack but their aircraft carriers and submarines are out of port and the commander responsible under me ceases operations prematurely, after only a second wave of warplanes, and leaves enemy storage and supply depots untouched.

It's still a great victory and I'm a hero. For the moment, we're all heroes in Japan. But we've got to batter the giant near Midway Island and make him quit in the Pacific. I think we'll get him when we find him. I'm stunned he often spots us first and sinks four aircraft carriers. We get one of his but this is a disaster. Instead of my wife I tell Kawai, loveliest of all geishas, that we won't be able to stop the enemy from plowing across the Pacific. Inside the Navy, I speak of victory at

Guadalcanal. We fight several months, trying to lure Americans into a decisive battle they ignore while slowly crushing us. In early 1943 I tell some officers the truth, we can't win this war. No one listens long. They want me to rouse discouraged men in the Solomon Islands. It's not a trap, I tell worried aides. I'll be fine in one of two bombers escorted by six fighters. I try to enjoy the flight. We're already over Bougainville. I think I hear something. Maybe it's my nerves. No, I'm hearing other engines, much louder now, and look out the window and see more than twice as many attackers firing machineguns. Then I hear something I also feel – a shot into my left shoulder. I don't feel the next one, a machinegun bullet to the head and my plane crashing in the jungle.

Some in the Navy and Army gloat that my demise is good for Japan since I'm to blame for Midway and Guadalcanal. Feel that if you please. Every commander makes blunders. I'm more interested in avoiding future disasters and therefore enthused to join Kim Jong Un for a conservation at one of his palaces near Pyongyang.

"I'll never submit to the Americans," he tells me.

"You wouldn't be submitting. You'd be cooperating."

"People our color who cooperate with the United States don't end up well."

"Those who resist end up worse."

"I'm not going to concede my inalienable right to possess nuclear weapons ready to strike my tormenter."

"Be careful," I tell Kim. "Listen to Secretary of Defense James Mattis when, on Korean soil recently, he warns U.S. Soldiers, 'There's very little reason for optimism, storm clouds are gathering.' They must be 'ready to go' to war so his 'diplomats can speak with authority and be believed.' He says he wants tough new sanctions that'll compel nations to cut off sales of oil and other essentials to your country. That reminds me of what the United States did to Japan before World War II."

"Precisely," says Kim. "The Americans aim to strangle us while they threaten us with joint military exercises, spy on us, pollute the minds of my people, and most of all maneuver to destroy my regime. If I surrender my nuclear weapons, how do I deter the Americans from attacking me?"

"I don't have any guarantees for you in that regard but suggest working with the Chinese, South Koreans, Americans, and Japanese to establish the framework for a peaceful and independent state in the north."

"Do you think my regime can survive another twenty years."

"I doubt you'll last that long, President Kim," I say.

TWENTY-EIGHT

Trump Immigration

the donald says he's not racist but wonders why u.s. brings
in
haitians
and
people
from
shitholes in africa

Trump Clarifies

I'm not the person the media's portraying me to be and am as far from being a racist as you can get. Okay, in private I did talk a little tough about immigration, but I didn't say what reporters of fake news claim. In fact, the whole meeting was really about love. I want to grant amnesty to all the Dreamers whose parents brought them here when they were children. As long as they're not rapists or murderers, and are working their asses off or serving in the military, I think they should stay.

I love more people than you can imagine and may eventually grant amnesty to all eleven million illegal aliens in the United States. But I'm going to get my border wall as part of the deal. That wall's a powerful symbol of our commitment to security as well as my most memorable campaign promise. I don't believe those who say border security would be better enhanced by upgrading radar technology and adding more agents. Nope. What we need is a giant stationary wall that won't be nearly as easy to go over, under, around, or through as critics claim.

As part of this deal I'm also insisting we get rid of chain migration which allows one legal immigrant to petition to bring over his family and then they bring over other relatives and pretty soon one immigrant has brought over a village of people who may have been living in huts and won't be educated enough to support themselves here and American taxpayers will have to pay the bills. I'm just as worried about the visa lottery which doesn't let us select the best educated and most socially appropriate individuals to live here. Instead we get too many terrorists and bums and if we're not careful they're liable to turn our great nation into a shithole.

Martin Luther King Visits Trump

Speeding in a golf court on a splendid golf course not far from presidential palace Mar-a-Lago, Martin Luther King steers toward the executive foursome and brakes hard, skidding along the grass behind the fifth tee just as President Donald Trump begins his downswing. Trump dribbles the ball about twenty yards and spins to scream, "Hey, moron, can't you see I'm hitting?"

King steps from the cart, removes his blue golf cap, and says, "Is that how you address a man on his national birthday?"

"Oh, I beg your pardon, Dr. King. I wasn't expecting you."

"I had to come at once after hearing your latest outrageous comments."

"What could that be? I only tell the truth as I rebuild this once great nation."

"I'm referring to your unkind characterization of some African nations."

"I've already said I didn't say what they say I said."

"So, Mr. President, you didn't refer to certain African nations as shitholes?"

"No, but they aren't too sweet, either. I hope you'll admit that."

"I'm concerned about your lack of goodwill and empathy for people of color."

"Don't worry. I'm further from being a racist than any man on earth."

King puts his cap back on, covers his mouth with a fist, and coughs. "I forgive whatever you said and concede I once privately commented that white Americans were worse than German Nazis. But most of the time I championed peace and equality. I therefore note with chagrin that you're pushing the world toward the nuclear abyss."

"Actually, I'm trying to stop the most dangerous people from starting nuclear wars. That's why I've threatened North Korea with fire and destruction and also why I'm modernizing our nuclear weapons that one of your guys, Obama, let get old."

"He was trying to deemphasize nuclear weapons as a means of maintaining international peace."

"And he was wrong to do that. We've got to worry about crazy Iran and aggressive China and a Russia that keeps attacking former Soviet Republics and may be planning to use small nuclear weapons to blackmail us on the battlefields of Europe."

"There should be no battlefields in Europe just as there never should've been an American invasion of Vietnam."

"Agreed. It's my job to keep the peace."

"I pray, President Trump, that you're a man of sound judgment."

"I'm the Rock of Gibraltar, Dr. King."

"God bless you. And I hope your recent physical revealed you're in fine health."

"Tests proved my brain is working great, and I'm still the healthiest president in history."

"You're seventy-one and obese."

"I need to drop a few pounds, but I'm only two-thirty-nine."

"I'd say two-seventy is a rather more accurate figure."

"You can bank on my figure. I'm the most honest man you'll ever meet."

King smiles.

"Come on and join our group," Trump says.

"Sorry, I must go. But I'll be watching."

State of Trump

Look at Paul Ryan trying so hard not to smile, in his seat behind me, as he thanks heaven he no longer has to frown throughout a State of the Union speech by Barack Obama. Like all true citizens, Ryan knows under my leadership our country is enjoying a "new tide of optimism... incredible progress and... extraordinary success." I can't take all the credit, though. "No people on Earth are so fearless or daring or determined as Americans... And together we're building a safe, strong, and proud America." Before I moved into the White House, we were pitiful and weak.

Since my election only one year ago, "we have created two point four million new jobs… Unemployment claims have hit a forty-five-year low. African-American unemployment stands at the lowest rate ever recorded, and Hispanic American employment has also reached the lowest levels in history." Gentlemen, and ladies, even my enemies must admit I keep leading us to unprecedented achievements. "Small business confidence is at an all-time high. The stock market has smashed one record after another, gaining eight trillion dollars in value… And as I promised… we enacted the biggest tax cuts and reforms in American history." These changes do not favor the rich. "We eliminated an especially cruel tax that fell mostly on Americans making less than fifty thousand dollars a year – forcing them to pay tremendous penalties simply because they could not afford government-ordered health plans." Furthermore, "we repealed the core of disastrous Obamacare."

My tax cuts will be incredibly helpful for a long time. "Apple has just announced it plans to invest a total of three hundred fifty billion dollars in America, and hire another twenty thousand workers… There has never been a better time to start living the American Dream." If you work hard and do as I say, we can achieve anything. "Together, we are rediscovering the American way… faith and family, not government and bureaucracy, are the center of the American life. Our motto is 'In God We Trust.'" That almost brings me to tears since I've always been among the most devout men.

How is it that my approval rating is still less than forty percent? Liberals in the media lie about me every day, but I return fire with devastating tweets. Our foreign enemies can expect no less since I demand "trading relationships to be fair and reciprocal… The era of economic surrender is over."

The era of immigration surrender has also ended. I love immigrants but "for decades open borders have allowed drugs and gangs to pour into our most vulnerable communities. They have allowed millions of low-wage workers to compete for jobs and wages against the poorest Americans. Most tragically," these illegal aliens have done a lot of murdering and raping. "Right here tonight are two fathers and two mothers" whose daughters were butchered by savage members of the MS-13 gang. Many of these criminals "took advantage of glaring loopholes in our laws to enter the country as unaccompanied alien minors."

As we recover at home from damage inflicted by the meek and incompetent president who preceded me, we must at the same time teach enemies abroad that we're no longer a nation of whiners and losers. Rogue regimes and terrorist groups will be our first students. Russia and China, who challenge "our interests (and) our values," must also learn that I "know weakness is the surest path to conflict and unmatched power is the surest means of our defense."

Clearly, we must spend much more than six hundred billion dollars a year on defense. We now outspend the next several countries combined, but that just isn't enough. We must build more and better nuclear weapons. We must crush ISIS. We must everywhere imprison terrorists and those suspected of terrorism. We must expand our navy to prevent China from dominating its territorial waters. We must renege on our terrible nuclear deal with Iran. We must understand that concessions will only make the criminals in North Korea more aggressive. Look at the grieving parents of Otto Warmbier here tonight. For months he was tortured in North Korea and then released just before he died. Look at Ji Seong-ho holding high the crutches he must use because the North Koreans starved and maimed him. In order to defend ourselves, we must remember the sacrifices of our forefathers. We must be "proud of who we are and what we're fighting for." We must rejoice there is nothing we cannot achieve. And we must trust in our God who blesses America.

Trump Justice

There's no need for you or me to get confused by legal mumbo jumbo liberals throw at us. It's all very simple. I did not hire Russian hookers, while visiting their great country, to pee on the bed African Obama once slept in. I did not sleep with Vladimir Putin or Stormy Daniels or anyone else but my lovely young wife who loves my powerful physique. I did not collude with the Russians. I did what I did with the Department of Justice because I had every right to. I did what I did with the FBI – including firing director James Comey – because I had every right to. And what I did is none of your business. Liberals and even some others don't understand I'm the CEO and majority owner of the United States and this is how business works. If the DOJ and FBI don't shield me from vicious attacks and strike those I tell them to, they're going to have trouble.

Trump Tweets Rob Porter

I'm tweeting and shouting that lives and careers are being shattered by mere allegations, some true, some false, some new, some old, and I want to know what happened to due process. Doesn't Rob Porter deserve to be innocent until proven guilty?

Sure, I'm the big boss but retired general John Kelly, my chief of staff, is the immediate supervisor of my bright young assistant secretary Rob Porter, and Kelly says he has "full confidence" in our impressive graduate of Harvard and Oxford and is "not actively searching for replacements." That's because John Kelly believes Porter's a "man of true integrity and honor" and he "can't say enough good things about him" because he's "a friend, a confidante, and a trusted professional" and Kelly's "proud to serve alongside him."

I'm also proud to have Rob Porter close to me in a White House office where he decides which documents I should read. I generally don't read much of them but Rob advises me about the content. Look, the FBI gave Porter "interim clearance" the same way other administrations have handled things. He probably would've had full clearance except for allegations by two former wives. My first wife, Ivana, wrote in a book that I once raped her. You know that's gotta be a lie.

So I wonder about these two wives of Rob Porter. The first, Colbie Holderness, a hottie, claims he abused her before marriage. Then why'd she marry him? And she says on their honeymoon in the Canary Islands during an argument he kicked her in the thigh. A couple of years later on an Italian vacation – he took her to real nice places – she claims he threw her down on the bed and punched her face. She says that's the only time he ever punched her but he sometimes yelled and choked her and pushed his limbs into her body. Who really knows about that stuff unless they were there? Rob Porter told me he didn't do it. And he told you, "These outrageous allegations are simply false" and he's "been transparent and truthful about these vile claims" and refuses to "further engage publicly with a coordinated smear campaign."

I guess his second wife, Jennie Willoughby, another babe, is part of this smear campaign. She claims on their honeymoon in Myrtle Beach he called her a "fucking bitch" and shouted it was "fucking ridiculous" she wasn't giving him as much sex as he wanted on their romantic vacation. She also says she later on walked away from an argument and took a shower until Rob reached in, grabbed her shoulders, and pulled her out of the shower. She says her horrified look shocked Rob into apologizing.

This gossip might have been the end of the matter but first wife Colbie posted a photo of the black eye she says Rob gave her during that expensive Italian vacation. Okay, where'd that picture come from? Rob took it, Colbie says. So you tell me. Why would Rob photograph evidence of an assault he swears he didn't commit?

That's why I'm tweeting about due process. I'm catching a lot of heat now, and you better believe chief of staff John Kelly is catching hell from me because I'm not sure he really "took immediate and direct action" about Porter. I'm the one who said he's gotta go. In business, sometimes you gotta let good people go. I imagine we'll be in touch, though, since Rob's dating Hope Hicks, a nice piece of ass who's one of my closest advisers.

TWENTY-NINE

We Love Guns

another massacre proves
every school
must have
metal detectors
armed security guards
armed teachers
armed students
anyone caught
without gun
will be shot

Help Us, NRA

nra
still
hasn't
updated
its
website
wonder
why

Open Season

republicans quickly aim and fire
gun
control
wouldn't
have
prevented
slaughter
at florida school

Holy Mitch

mitch mcconnell prays for florida gun victims
and
swears
he
always
wears
pants
when
nra
mounts
him

Trump Arms Mentally Ill

why did trump overturn obama era regulation
that
made
it
more
difficult
for
mentally
ill
to
get
guns

Stimulation

impotent
old
shooters
stroke
their
guns

NRA Praises AR-15 Rifle

As I write this on Sunday afternoon, four days after deranged Nikolas Cruz used an AR-15 semi-automatic rifle to massacre seventeen former high school classmates in Parkland, Florida, I again check the National Rifle Association website – NRA.org – and still predictably find nothing about another national tragedy. Instead, the NRA has reposted an article from July 2016: "10 Reasons to Own An AR-15 Rifle," an insipid but quite dangerous rant written by the site's editor, Mark Chesnut.

I know that many readers, before proceeding, have already clicked the link above to verify this isn't a hoax. No, it's true, for as people say, "You couldn't make this stuff up."

Chesnut starts by bemoaning that the "AR-15 rifle is once again under fire by gun banners—who ignore the fact that rifles of any kind are seldom used in crime, and seem to despise anyone who dares to own one. Many who are ignorant on (sic) firearms even consider the gun a 'weapon of war,' suitable for nothing but murder and mayhem."

That's preposterous, the editor notes, and "in no particular order" he offers his "Top 10 reasons to own" this splendid weapon.

First, self-defense. Mark Chesnut works with people who believe "there is no better firearm to defend their homes against realistic threats than" this rifle. "It's accurate. It's reliable." It's all that and more.

Second, Fun/Recreation. There's no "rifle out there that's more fun than the AR-15 to take to the range and punch some holes in paper." One cannot doubt this rifle's ability to puncture targets.

Third, Teaching/Learning. "There's no better rifle to teach youngsters the skill of accurate rifle shooting," Chesnut notes. This baby "is easy and tons of fun and also makes it great for starting out new shooters, regardless of age." Throw out those baby rattlers, baseballs, footballs, basketballs, and bicycles, and go buy something great for the kids: an armful of AR-15's.

Fourth, Hunting. This rifle is "perfect for varmints and predator hunting, and with the proper ammunition can make a great deer rifle." Chesnut gushes, "Don't buy the gun-banner lie that the AR-15 can't be a good hunting rifle." As for me, sir, I'm not trying to ban all guns, and I never said or implied this gun isn't a consummate killer.

Fifth, Tinkering. "If you like to tinker, the AR-15 is the rifle for you," Chesnut writes. "If you can't build one of these rifles on your kitchen table with just a few specialized tools (legally, of course), you probably skipped shop class in high school." I wish to hell I'd skipped woodshop as a freshman because I screwed around and cut off the tips of two fingers. But I believe Mark Chesnut. Most of you can build your own. I guess that means you can build one a week, if you want.

Sixth, Farm/Ranch Use. Chesnut gives hope to all food producers: "Excellent accuracy combined with good magazine capacity is enough to put the hurt on a pack of coyotes preying on calves or lambs – or on wild hogs tearing up your alfalfa or wheat field." If you're a city slicker, fret not. Blast away at any obnoxious cats and dogs who trespass on your lawn.

Seventh, Competitive Shooting. Chesnut is a "3-gun competitor (who sees) hundreds of people shoot AR-15s safely and accurately on a regular basis. Banning ownership… would be devastating to 3-gun – the fastest growing shooting sport in the country." Human hunting is also a popular shooting sport in this land.

Eighth, Disaster Preparedness. Keep in mind that Mark Chesnut is "not someone who believes in an impending doomsday scenario." But he's also "not one who thinks that couldn't happen." He knows "any survival situation" is improved "by having an AK-15 or two on hand." Indeed, "the AR-15 might just be the perfect SHTF firearm." I confess, as the wimpy owner of but a single pistol, I didn't know what SHTF is. It's "shit hits the fan." Okay.

Ninth, Bringing Women Into Shooting. Women are "the fastest-growing demographic in the shooting sports… (and they) "love the 'cool factor' of the AR just as much as men do." I'm sure most red-blooded Americans agree there's nothing cooler than firing a "soft-recoiling" AR-15.

Tenth, America's Rifle. "Owning an AR-15 is as uniquely American as baseball, apple pie, and the Second Amendment," states Mark Chesnut. "It's the musket of our day – everyman's rifle…" Mass murder of children and adults is also as American as apple pie.

When I finish desert I'll for the twentieth time check NRA.org to see how long the world's most powerful gun lobbyists are going to wait before commenting about the latest slaughter, this one wrought by a lunatic armed with the beloved AR-15.

Trump Victimized

trump
tweets
fbi so busy framing me for colluding with russia
it
failed
to
follow
up
signals
from
florida school shooter

Fortifying Schools

I'm dynamic General Jones on my way to becoming Chairman of the Joint Chiefs of Staff. Before I get there, I'm going to unveil my blueprint for fortifying our schools, arming educators, and protecting our children from the insanity and violence of those who misuse some of the most wonderful firearms yet created by man.

First, we must build impenetrable defensive perimeters around every school. That means the chain-link fences surrounding most soft targets must be either electrified or extended from eight feet to twenty feet into the heavens. But that's only for now. Those cheap fences can be cut through by pruning shears and just won't get it done. Frankly, we're going to have to build walls around every school. Once that's done, we're in business. Parking lots obviously must be outside the walls so we won't have to worry about checking cars, which could be wired with bombs. Agents and electronic devices will scrutinize students as they arrive, and we'll limit every school to two entrances in the wall, and at these points we'll install weapons detectors, and we'll check all backpacks and purses, and in fact we'll handle things the same way they do in airports and at ball games and concerts. Take everything out of your pockets and get out of those shoes. You build a damn wall and control and check who passes, and you've probably solved the problem right there.

However, if some lunatic does get in – and I don't know how he could, especially if he's armed – we must be prepared and rid ourselves of this namby-pamby notion that teachers and other employees on campus should not be armed. They must be armed and they will be. I know we'll soon have a national law mandating that all school employees carry guns. If you can't handle that, you can't be in our new army of educators. We only want warriors leading our students because, goddamn it, we're at war. And I guarantee that good classroom soldiers, administrators, security guards, secretaries, cooks, and custodians will start blowing away the bad guys before they even get off a shot.

Yes, I've heard naysayers, like Ms. Smith, who wrote: "I never liked guns but after my divorce I heard many eerie sounds at night and decided to buy a pistol. The gun dealer who sold me the arm also sold me a gun safety course that included plenty of shooting at the store's big indoor shooting range. I dreaded the explosion of that big gun and still do and refuse to fire it and sure can't holster a big thing like that inside my thigh. Where would I keep it at school? Probably in my purse. Students would know where it is. And that lunatic who couldn't get in armed could easily get in unarmed and grab my purse and open fire. Don't tell me that can't happen. Tell me why it wouldn't happen."

Ms. Smith, you're not the kind of soldier we're looking for. I suggest you try domestic work but, unless you're armed, your libidinous male employer could lock his office or house and have his way with you.

We can't worry about the Ms. Smiths of the world. We must concentrate on the lunatics we know are coming. I'm flexible. Before we arm all school employees, let's train the security guards, which many campuses already have and all must promptly deploy, and transform them into certified sharpshooters. You know damn well their firepower would deter even a crazy man. And, like I said, few if any bad guys will even get through our walls and airport-style checkpoints.

Marco Rubio Embraces NRA

I care about my constituents. They're hurting and angry after tragic losses at a Florida high school and unhappy the NRA gave me a hundred percent approval rating and three million dollars for my Senate reelection campaign. I'm proud the NRA appreciates my defense of all guns and my commitment to God. That usually plays well with supporters. I don't have many of those tonight, though. These kids who survived the mass shooting and their parents are interrogating and hissing me almost as if I'd pulled the trigger.

Please understand, if I believed an assault weapons ban would've prevented this bloodshed, I would support it. I am at least proposing we require people to be sane and twenty-one, instead of eighteen and disturbed, when they start buying assault weapons. And about the money I receive from the NRA, it's insignificant compared to the fact they back my agenda and we're philosophically in tune. So, no, I'll never sever my commitment to Second Amendment comrades. However, I do concede that magazines on assault rifles may be a little too big. Smaller magazines wouldn't have prevented the recent slaughter but they would have reduced the casualties, and I pray the NRA won't punish me for saying so.

Wayne LaPierre Visits Trump

America's protector in chief, Wayne LaPierre, enters the White House and, as a secret service agent approaches, waves go away. "It's okay, I'm only packing a pistol."

"Excuse me, sir, but no one's permitted to bear a firearm when entering the Oval Office."

"Listen, son, I'm head of the NRA that donated more than thirty million bucks that got your boss elected."

"Sorry, but no exceptions."

"Then tell President Trump our meeting's off."

The agent speaks into a small device clipped to his collar and, in seconds, big Donald Trump walks fast as he can out of his office and says, "Wayne, hold on. Please don't leave."

"I'll have to if you try to take my gun."

Trump points at the secret service agent, and three others who've appeared, and says, "Don't worry, Wayne, they'll protect you."

"I believe in protecting myself, and I might have to since I know those guys are armed. How about you?"

"I have a concealed weapons permit, and this is my house."

"I've got more concealed weapons permits than anyone."

Trump looks at each of the four agents and says, "It'll be all right."

"No way, sir," says the original agent.

"You guys relax. Come on, Wayne." The two warriors, who somehow missed their opportunity in Vietnam, walk toward the Oval Office.

Trump extends a hand toward a chair and after LaPierre sits, Trump, standing at attention, tells him, "You know how much I love guns and the NRA but sometimes we need brass balls. Like I've just told the nation, I believe I would've stormed into that high school in Florida even if I didn't have a weapon. Those four armed and trained cops who stayed outside are a disgrace."

"I would've charged in, too, Mr. President. But I damn sure wouldn't have been unarmed. Why the hell would anyone be unarmed in this violent country that's been ruined by The Obama Decade of European-style socialists seizing control? None of them believe in freedom or capitalism or assault rifles in every home. It's terrifying.

"The intellectual elites think they're smarter and better than all of us, but they're too arrogant to understand socialism is feeding racism and sexism and xenophobia. What socialists really want is to ban guns."

Trump, still standing, says, "Wayne, as long as I'm president, no one will ever ban guns in the United States. I love the Second Amendment, and you know it."

"I sure do, Mr. President. We're law-abiding citizens who support guns so we can fight illegal aliens and gangs and opioids."

"Above all, we've got to protect our kids," Trump says. "And that means we're going to have to raise the legal age to twenty-one for buying assault weapons."

Shooting straight up, LaPierre aims an index finger at the president and says, "No sir. We can't tell people old enough to serve and die in the armed forces that they can't buy an assault rifle to protect their homes. You know what would be next. There'd be universal background checks, then universal gun registry, and then the socialists would start knocking on our doors in the middle of the night and taking away our guns and our liberties."

"You may be a little hyper, Wayne, but that's understandable since you're really under fire from the left."

"As usual, the lefties are trying to exploit a national tragedy," says LaPierre. "They're smearing the NRA because they hate the Second Amendment and despise personal freedom. Instead of blaming us, they should admit failures of the family and the mental health system and the FBI."

"Don't worry. We're going to make our schools hardened targets."

LaPierre tries to smile but can't complete the maneuver. "God bless you, President Trump. We're fortunate to have a commander in chief who understands it's lunacy to secure our many public places while we leave our schools wide open and the most inviting of targets."

Nodding, Trump says, "Listen, Wayne, we gotta give the left something and get rid of those bump stocks that basically turn an automatic rifle into a machine gun."

"I agree, Mr. President. The NRA doesn't want any more automatic weapons. Semi-automatic arms are good enough to maintain our freedom."

Swiftly reaching inside his coat Trump pulls out a revolver, points it at the ceiling, smiles, and says, "Pretty slow there, Wayne."

"I didn't expect that from you, sir."

"Next time, be ready."

Gun Checklist

Most citizens have already formulated and memorized their gun checklists. I'm writing mine down.

1. No one under age twenty-one can buy any gun. Nikolas Cruz, the deranged school shooter in Parkland, Florida, was nineteen. End of discussion. If you can't support this sane law, Senator Marco Rubio, resign your seat.

2. Establish a universal database containing the names of everyone who owns a gun. If you own a motor vehicle, it is universally registered. If you have a driver's license, it's officially registered. The same standard must apply to guns, which, even for NRA members, aren't as essential as cars.

3. Establish a nationwide database containing the names of all who have concealed weapons permits. This would be part of the universal database identifying all who own guns.

4. Establish a related database containing the names of all people who have made threats of violence. Many of these people are mentally disturbed. This law encompasses all threats especially those issued verbally, in writing, or through social media. People like Nikolas Cruz will be flagged if this system is properly monitored and acted upon. Early intervention and treatment of mental illness must also be expanded.

5. Ban assault weapons. Gun enthusiasts don't need them to shoot deer or hit targets at the shooting range.

6. Ban bump stocks. Las Vegas concert shooter Stephen Paddock killed fifty-nine people, riddling them with bump-stock-enhanced fire similar to that of machine guns.

7. Ban extra-capacity magazines. They can't be justified. Even the most ardent hunters aren't going to shoot a deer a hundred times.

8. No nationwide reciprocity for concealed weapons permits. It's ghoulish enough to know that millions of citizens are legally packing in their states. They can't be allowed to randomly roam the nation with guns shoved in their pants and concealed by shirts.

9. Improve school security by implementing procedures already in effect at airports, athletic events, and concerts.

10. Work to diminish the importance of fanatical gun organizations like the NRA, and dedicate yourselves to defeating gutless politicians who jeopardize public safety in order to bring in gun dollars.

11. Improve education, jobs programs, and community relations with law enforcement in low income areas where most murders take place.

According to recent polls, the overwhelming majority of Americans support most of the measures above. People have had enough.

Reform McConnell

mitch mcconnell
hot
on
banking
reform
cold on guns

THIRTY

Trump Surge

hey
hope you've noticed
my approval's back
over forty percent
and people like my
economy and jobs
and tax cuts so you
tell me which dem
can beat me in three
years

President Forever

congratulations xi jinping
upon
becoming
president
for
life
usa can't complain much
because
it
needs
chinese
help
dealing
with another president for life

William F. Buckley Remembered

William F. Buckley
National Review

Dear Mr. Buckley,

Despite being a liberal who never met you, except through *Firing Line* and your columns, I still miss your wit and charm and, let us not fail to mention, your convoluted but entertaining proclamations about conservative rectitude.

As noted by many, you're not really gone, the energy you created is eternal.

Regarding the passage of time, I remember a 1975 *Firing Line* show when your guest asked, "How old are you?"

"Fifty," you said.

"He's getting up there," I said to stoned friends, convinced we'd always be twenty-two.

Yesterday, unaware of the tenth anniversary of your passing I would read about today in your *National Review* online, I recalled that innocent evening, and reminded myself, "I'm now fifteen years older than Buckley was then."

And daily I try to convince myself I'll age no more.

I should like to close with a more realistic fantasy: you'll be backing Mitt Romney in 2020.

Wishing you the best,

GTC

Trade Warrior

republicans extremely worried about tariffs
trump
relaxed
because
trade
wars
easy
to
win

Confirmation 1991

on college stage in red bakersfield
anita hill says she wasn't filing
sexual harassment suit against clarence
thomas she was stating that character
does matter and today she worries the
current president glorifies predation

Jeff Sessions Invades California

Jefferson Beauregard Sessions, the Alabama-bred former judge and senator who's now attorney general of the United States, gallops his white steed to the Capitol steps in Sacramento, dismounts, and, bugle in hand, blows a sound that compels local dogs to howl and political workers to cover their ears.

Charging out the door and down the steps, Governor Jerry Brown unsheathes his sword and says, "Don't come into the Golden State filing lawsuits against our commitments to civil rights."

"How dare you, sir," says Sessions, drawing his saber. "You and this corrupt state of hippies and illegal aliens have passed countless unconstitutional laws, and I order you to cease disobeying United States law which supersedes that of any self-righteous state."

Pointing his sharp tip at the nose of Sessions, energetic-octogenarian Brown says, "We're a state of innovators who've built the sixth largest economic entity in the world. We'll continue to welcome immigrants."

"They're not immigrants, they're gangsters and drug dealers, and your sanctuary cities are an affront to Abraham Lincoln and all those who died to defend our union."

"You'd have been wearing a gray uniform during the Civil War."

"I'm wearing blue today while you're attired in gray. I therefore warn you, sir, that the federal government may force you to obey existing laws and those to come in this new era of Donald Trump, who vows to end lawlessness wherever it exists."

"I demand that you apologize to the people of California for your lies. We don't disobey laws. We simply decline to enforce those we disagree with and that are at any rate the responsibility of the federal government."

"Fine, Governor Brown, we'll be happy to ensure it's a felony to use fraudulent documents."

"And we'll continue to ignore you and Donald Trump."

"In that case, sir, we shall send in federal troops, just as President Eisenhower did in Arkansas to enforce school desegregation."

"I'd expect the Trump administration to send in troops to reestablish segregation."

"En garde, Governor Brown."

Maxine Trump

maxine waters wants to impeach me
for nothing because she's a low iq
individual says the president

donald trump's a con man been one
all his life and loves dictators
and repression counters maxine

THIRTY-ONE

Big Boys to Meet

The following are transcripts of recent, and quite separate, private utterances by the world's two most feared warriors.

Donald Trump – Other presidents didn't have the guts to negotiate with Kim Jong Un or his father or grandfather but I've got big balls, and my threats to completely destroy his country have scared Little Rocket Man. And all this time I've been strangling his sick economy with sanctions that get tougher every day.

Kim Jong Un – I knew Trump would meet me. His predecessors thought they were too powerful and rich to meet us at the executive level, but Trump is different, he might be crazy. I better calm him down and, in effect, put his aging body and mind in the freezer.

DT – I'm always ready for the *Art of the Deal* but think this deal's almost done even before we sit down to negotiate. Kim knows he's not dealing with Barack Obama, George W. Bush, Bill Clinton or any other weaklings who did everything by the book and therefore did nothing.

KJU – All I had to do to lure the big fish was tell him I'm committed to denuclearization. I didn't say I guaranteed it.

DT – Kim has promised to get rid of his nukes. I've even forced him to stop testing bombs and missiles. Otherwise, I wouldn't honor him with my presence.

KJU – It's irrelevant I'm not going to test for a while. My scientists and military officers will privately be working even harder than usual.

DT – We're still gonna have our great annual exercises with South Korea. Kim knows he can't stop that.

KJU – The excited puppy's wagging his tail because I invited him to talk on the grandest stage. I know joint military exercises are not, for the time being, a prelude to invading my nation.

DT – When Kim starts destroying his nuclear weapons, I'll slowly start easing the sanctions. The guy's gotta get something in this deal. And a few years after all his nukes are gone, we'll meet again to talk about normalizing relations and withdrawing American troops from South Korea.

KJU – I'm not going to deactivate a single nuclear weapon until all sanctions have been removed. If our economy collapses that would be as dangerous to me as war. Trump will also have to get his troops out of here if he expects me to dismantle the only things that deter him from invading.

DT – I'm going over there in good faith, ready to accept Kim Jong Un's offer to denuclearize. But if he lies to me like his family lied to other diplomats from other administrations, you already know what I'll do, and so does Kim.

KJU – You see what happens to American adversaries when they voluntarily give up their nuclear programs. I not only have a program, I've got the weapons and am making more all the time, and no matter how many I might someday dismantle, I'm too shrewd not to keep some.

Trump Shock

hold it
i thought south korea said kim jong un promised to denuclearize
but
maybe
he
just
wants
to
talk
about
it
and i'd look dumb

Trump Interviews John Bolton

I like saying, "You're fired," to people who aren't on board with my views and I'm probably going to say that to my national security advisor, H.R. McMaster. He's still an active general but no way does he understand war the way I do. And I also think John Bolton knows a lot more about combat and strategic matters than any military man.

"John, thanks for coming," I say, shaking his hand in the Oval Office. "Please have a seat."

"Thank you, Mr. President," Bolton says through his droopy gray mustache. "I've been here many times, you know. I was President George W. Bush's most aggressive policy maker in the Middle East, and I directly advised Vice President Dick Cheney."

I step behind my executive desk and before sitting say, "That's why you're here."

"Have you read my seminal 2017 essay: 'How to Get Out of the Iran Nuclear Deal'?"

"Not yet, but I see you a lot on Fox News and know you understand we have to do something about the worst deal in history."

"If the Iranians don't cooperate, I'd be ready to respond," Bolton says. "'Facing Reality on Iran' is my 2015 blueprint for destroying nuclear facilities and, in general, kicking their asses."

"Haven't read that one, either, but I've been briefed. I see you supported the war in Vietnam but didn't fight there. I didn't have time, either."

"I wasn't afraid to fight, Mr. President. I wanted to and would have if the United States had been trying to win. I just didn't want to go over there in 1970, right after I graduated summa cum laude from Yale, and get killed before guys like Ted Kennedy lost the war."

I nod and say, "I guess you know I opposed our invasion of Iraq in 2003."

"That was a brave position, Mr. President, since you were very much in the minority."

"I'll always take on a majority."

"May I be frank?" Bolton asks.

"Of course."

"You made a mistake. I served as undersecretary for arms control and every day ensured the right intelligence moved up the chain of command. Sometimes my subordinates said I was ignoring intelligence that indicated the Iraqis didn't have weapons of mass destruction. I lectured those people. If they tried to argue, I'd say, 'Shut the hell up.' No one was going to prevent me from proving the Iraqis were arming to destroy us.

"I was just as tough a couple of years later as our ambassador to the United Nations, a building I'd like to slice ten floors off of and then eliminate many of the strange nonwhite people trying to ruin us. I'm proud I was an undiplomatic diplomat. I shouted at and insulted our enemies, and that includes enemies on my staff. Anyone who crossed me got her door pounded and a severe lecture and if she didn't open up the next time I'd shove blistering notes under the door.

"I appreciate President Bush getting me the UN job on a temporary basis. But I had to leave the following year because the Senate wouldn't have confirmed me. I imagine you know all that."

"No problem, John, we wouldn't have to worry about a confirmation for this job. I've got a tough management style, too. People have to respect the man in charge."

"You're the strongest leader we've had in my lifetime," Bolton says. "Thank God, since you're dealing with North Korea and Iraq."

"What should we do about Kim Jong Un and his nuclear weapons?"

"We need to launch a preemptive strike. And soon."

"What about Iran?"

"We need to hit them with a preemptive strike, too, but we have a little more time there. Let me explain."

"Thanks, but not right now, John."

I stand and walk around my executive desk and shake the hand of John Bolton. He thinks like I do, but I'm trying to figure if I want to look at that damn mustache every day.

"Don't worry, if I have to strike, it won't be limited. And if I hire you as national security advisor, I'll study your details in dealing with North Korea and Iran. Just give me a shorter version, please."

"Of course, Mr. President."

Presidential Fire

yeah that's right
i told some republican politicians they were scared of the nra
but i'm not
i just had a couple of meetings and decided it's better we
keep letting kids buy assault weapons

Clean GOP Election

intelligent republicans on house committee declare trump team
didn't
collude
with
russians
intelligent democrats say republicans refused to subpoena bank
phone
and
other
relevant
records

Calling Rex Tillerson

Listen, I already told you all I'm not going to let anyone damage this smooth-running administration by forcing me to admit I called Donald Trump a moron. I have great respect and affection for the president, and hope he feels the same about me.

It's my duty to tell him the Iran nuclear deal is pretty damn good since it prevents the Iranians from advancing their weapons program rapidly and forcing us to either accept it or attack. The president always says it's a terrible deal, an Obama blunder, and he's going to do something about it.

"What are you actually going to do?" I ask.

I can't really tell you his answer because he starts talking and confuses himself and his listeners and doesn't actually say anything except he'll handle it and everything will be great.

I guess the president's also confident about the Middle East and Mexico because Jared Kushner, his dimwit son-in-law, is mishandling things in places where this Texan spent decades making deals with leaders and pumping trillions of dollars of oil.

The president sure gets irritated when I publicly state what everyone knows: the Russians interfered in our presidential election. CIA chief Mike Pompeo also understands this, but I guess he says so in a pleasing way, and Trump likes having him around.

More than once I've said what almost any reasonable secretary of state should: we're a long way from summit negotiations with North Korea. Last week on assignment in Africa, I was mad as hell Trump didn't bother telling me he'd decided to meet with Kim Jong Un. In the middle of the night White House chief of staff John Kelly woke me with a call: "Rex, as a courtesy, I'm telling you the president just tweeted he's replacing you with Mike Pompeo."

The Right Walls

i don't like california but it's great
to be here at the border where
i'm looking at prototypes of eight
wonderful walls i'll chose from to
save countless lives and hundreds
of billions of dollars and that's how
mexico's really paying for our wall

THIRTY-TWO

Gun Safety in the Classroom

I love living and going to high school in a beautiful California town by the sea where my favorite teacher is Mr. Smith. He's also got eleven years of experience as a reserve police officer and knows a lot about guns. This morning, in his administration of justice class, he's showing us how to use them safely.

"Always assume a gun is loaded and then make sure that it isn't," he says.

Mr. Smith points his gun at the ceiling. I'm enjoying this lesson very much until we hear, "Bang," and I almost jump from my desk and consider diving under it. Other students look as scared as I feel.

"Oh, sorry about that," says Mr. Smith.

I assume Mr. Smith's going to call one of his buddies at the police station or at least let the principal know, but he keeps teaching us about gun safety, and I sure hope there aren't any more bullets in his gun.

I notice one of the students has blood on his shirt, and watch as he rubs a wound on his neck. "Mr. Smith, I think I just pulled a bullet fragment from my neck."

"I'm very sorry, Johnny."

Mr. Smith continues the lesson and we pay attention because we all respect him.

We finish class and have lunch, and about three hours after the gun safety lesson the police arrive and talk to Mr. Smith and us. As far as I know, no nurse or doctor has been called for Johnny. He goes home where his shocked parents take him to the emergency center. Fortunately, he's okay. So are a couple of other students hit by falling debris.

Like many students I probably didn't know all the school district's rules about guns, but right away I make sure to learn. The policy is that "only active law enforcement employed as armed security at schools can carry guns." I guess that means even a reserve cop and firearms expert like Mr. Smith shouldn't have had a gun, loaded or not, in the classroom.

By coincidence, the next day many high school students around the nation, as well as at our school, walk out of class to protest gun violence on campuses. Quite a few students are also telling administrators and

police what a fine man Mr. Smith is. He sure is, but he should obey
the rules and be more careful.

Poison Putin

it's shocking and inexcusable england accuses me
of
sending
agents
to
poison
ex
russian
spy
and
daughter

Counter Tweet

About Trump, former CIA director John Brennan tweets: "When
the full extent of your venality, moral turpitude, and political corruption
becomes known, you will take your rightful place as a disgraced
demagogue in the dustbin of history... America will triumph over you."

McCabe in Retirement

the donald says
get
it
straight
fbi wanted deputy director andrew mccabe fired and attorney
general complied
not
my
fault
lying mccabe cut off two days short of full pension

GOP Supports Mueller

trump
panting
to
fire
special
prosecutor
robert
mueller
republicans warn he better not
mueller's
just
following
the
facts

THIRTY-THREE

China Pressures North Korea

These secret communiques between President Kim Jong Un and President Xi Jinping were intercepted and assembled in March 2018 by the intelligence agencies of the United States and South Korea, and released early this morning.

Kim Jong Un – Mr. President, you've slashed imports of our products by eighty percent so far this year. And you've cut exports to our country by a third.

Xi Jinping – These are necessary steps.

KJU – So you can side with our mutual enemy?

XJ – China can't afford to have the United States as an existential foe now or in the future. Neither can you.

KJU – Within a year I'll be able to destroy American cities.

XJ – It's alarming you say that, even in private. And shouting it publicly, as you have been, is intolerable.

KJU – We don't want war. The Americans do.

XJ – I doubt they want a war with your country, either. You can hit back. And unless they're fools who've forgotten history, they also know China would intervene, as long as you haven't started the hostilities.

KJU – Trump and his new national security advisor John Bolton would be the aggressors.

XJ – They're bullies who look for the least dangerous targets. If they attack anyone, it'll probably be Iran. Trump needs war to divert the American public from his many problems.

KJU – In the meantime, I'm going to continue to develop, test, and display my burgeoning nuclear forces.

XJ – You'll do quite the opposite. I've already eliminated almost all our petroleum and steel exports, and if necessary I'll cut you off completely.

KJU – What do you want?

XJ – It's quite straightforward, Chairman Kim. I want the Korean Peninsula to be denuclearized.

KJU – I'll consider it.

XJ – You'll follow my advice, unless you want to starve.

KJU – But the Americans…

XJ – I'd like you to come to China later this month.

Kim Jong Un in China

I have always admired President Xi Jinping and warmly congratulated him last year when he won reelection as general secretary of the central committee, and this year I again send my regards after he is reelected president in a way that means president for life. Even these overtures seem insufficient, so I convey to President Xi my desire, and indeed my obligation, to congratulate him in person and at the same time discuss not merely our personal comradeship but the special relationship between our two nations. He promptly invites me to visit and confer with him in Beijing.

It is outrageous that a distant enemy presents such a threat that I dare not fly. Instead, I secretly escort my lovely wife Ri Sol Ju and my diplomatic team onto my dark green armored train, blackened by thick windows, and for the first time move toward the vast and mysterious land to our north. President Xi and the Chinese delegation greet us affectionately before we're taken to our quarters to rest prior to essential talks in the morning.

Flanked by his closest associates, President Xi sits across a long table from me, and my dedicated advisors, and says, "The visit of Chairman Kim comes at a special time and is of great significance because it embodies the importance that he and his nation attach to the relations between our two countries."

"I'm most honored to be here," I say. "This is a critical period since the situation in the Korean Peninsula is developing rapidly, many important changes have taken place, and I feel I should personally inform President Xi out of respect and moral responsibility."

"Thank you," says Xi. "Our traditional friendship, established and cultivated meticulously by the elder generations of leaders of both countries, is precious and continues to be based on sharing common ideals and beliefs as well as profound revolutionary respect. For several generations the leaders of our two countries have trusted and supported each other, and written a fine story in the history of international relations. Instead of not staying in touch, as has been the case in recent years, we need to resume close exchanges and pay frequent calls on each other like relatives. We've long supported each other and coordinated practices that made great contributions to the development of the socialist cause.

"Both Chairman Kim and I have personally experienced and witnessed the development of the China-North Korea relationship. Both sides have repeatedly stated that our traditional friendship should be passed on continuously and improved."

Exhaling in relief, I smile at President Xi and his advisors, and say, "I'm greatly encouraged and inspired by the president's view that the North Korea-China friendship is unshakable. It is a strategic choice of North Korea to pass on and develop our relationship with China, even under the new situation. We now believe that our commitments to each other will remain unchanged under any circumstances.

"On this current visit I plan to establish a permanent bridge to meet Chinese comrades, enhance strategic communication, and deepen traditional friendship. I hope to have opportunities to meet with President Xi often, and keep close contacts through special envoys and personal letters to each other. In this way we can promote a new level of relations between our two countries."

President Xi nods and says, "In China we've drawn a grand blueprint for building the nation into a great modern socialist country in all respects – building a moderately prosperous society by 2020, and achieving modernization by 2035, and building a great modern socialist country that is prosperous, strong, democratic, culturally advanced, harmonious and beautiful by the middle of the century.

"I've noted that Chairman Kim has led the people of his nation in a series of active measures that generated achievements in developing the economy and improving people's wellbeing. We Chinese expect North Korea to maintain political stability, economic development, and people's happiness. We support Chairman Kim in leading the people of his nation to advance along the path of socialism as well as endeavors that develop the economy and improve people's livelihood."

On this greatest day of my life I am no longer seeing fireballs envelop our nation. I'm saying, "I sincerely hope China will continuously make new great achievements in the course of building a prosperous society and great socialist nation."

President Xi pauses, studies me in a concerned way, and says, "Regarding the Korean Peninsula issue, China sticks to the goal of denuclearization of the peninsula, safeguarding peace and stability on the peninsula, and solving problems through dialogue and consultation. In that regard, China calls on all parties to support the improvement of inter-Korean ties, and take concrete efforts to facilitate peace talks. China will continue to play a constructive role on the issue and work with all parties toward the thaw of the situation on the peninsula."

"The situation on the Korean Peninsula is starting to get better," I say. "My nation has taken the initiative to ease tensions and put forward proposals for peace talks. It is our consistent stand to be committed to denuclearization on the peninsula, in accordance with the will of the late President Kim Il Sung and the late President Kim Jong Il. We are determined to transform the inter-Korean ties into a relationship of reconciliation and cooperation and hold summit meetings between the heads of the two sides. North Korea is also willing to have a dialogue with the United States and hold a summit meeting between the heads of the two sides.

"The issue of denuclearization of the Korean Peninsula can be resolved if South Korea and the United States respond to our efforts with goodwill, create an atmosphere of peace and stability while taking progressive and synchronous measures for the realization of peace. North Korea hopes to enhance strategic communication with China during the process and jointly safeguard the trend of consultation and dialogue as well as peace and stability on the peninsula."

President Xi rises and walks around the table and I stand to shake his hand. That afternoon my wife and I tour the Chinese Academy of Sciences, and in the evening President Xi and his pretty wife Peng Liyan host us for a banquet at the magnificent Great Hall of the People. Aided by an interpreter, we happily talk and toast and later watch an artistic performance as we anticipate a peaceful future.

Notes: Many of the sentences and sentiments quoted or paraphrased above came from Chinese and North Korean news releases after the summit meeting.

Trump and Biden Brawl

Joe Biden, former vice president and still a slender six-footer at age seventy-five, stands at the microphone in an elegant Washington, D.C. hotel and, before Democratic governors and their staffs, begins hammering President Donald Trump for cutting taxes for the wealthy, risking a trade war with Europe and Asia, risking nuclear war with North Korea and China, doing the same with Iran, behaving like a deranged despot as he handles his White House staff, and in all dealings demonstrating a lack of honesty and moral character.

A symphony of gasps and loud voices erupts at the rear of the large room, and uninvited Donald Trump, surrounded by secret service agents and assorted sycophants, pushes toward the podium, shouting, "I heard your lies but that's not why I'm here. You said if we'd gone to the same high school you'd have taken me out back and beaten me up because of that secretly-recorded conversation I had about women a long time ago with Billy Bush, who, by the way, was in awe of me."

"We're a bit beyond high school, aren't we, Donald?" says Biden.

"You brought it up. Was it typical liberal pansy talk or you wanna back it up?"

Biden takes off his suit coat, hands it to an aide, unties and removes his tie, unbuttons his top three shirt buttons, and exits stage right. Trump also removes his coat and tie but leaves all shirt buttons secure. From my table in the California delegation, sitting next to Jerry Brown, perhaps the nation's most qualified person to be commander in chief, I estimate Biden weighs one-sixty max, and rotund Trump has to go about a hundred more. They're about the same height.

"Okay, Joe, Marquis of Queensbury rules?" says the president.

"Limit yourself to boxing if you want, Donald. I'm fighting however I want."

Almost everyone in the room's now standing and exhilarated by the buzz of a title fight.

"Be careful. I have experience in the World Wrestling Enterprise."

"You were in greater danger on *Celebrity Apprentice*," says Biden.

The president crouches, holding high both hands, and eases toward Biden who lowers his head, lunges, and butts Trump's forehead, knocking him on his executive ass. Biden jumps onto Trump and fires hooks to each side of his head until the president, a noted badass on the streets of Queens before he conquered Manhattan, hooks his right index and middle fingers into Biden's nose and jerks, sending him onto the floor. Trump bounds up.

"Come on, Joe, it's like Scranton," shouts a septuagenarian from the Pennsylvania table.

Though Biden and his indigent family left that hardscrabble town when he was about ten, he remembers the ways of the streets, and from his back on the deck, as Trump dives at him, he raises his left foot into Trump's belly. The president grunts like a wounded elephant and lands on the floor next to Biden who rolls toward Trump who rolls toward him and, immobilized on their sides, they butt foreheads until Governor Jerry Brown, a delicate man of eighty, sticks his foot between their colliding brains and says, "Gentlemen, you're behaving as children."

"You never were man enough to become president, and neither were you, Joe," says Trump, staggering as he rises.

Biden, breathing hard as Trump, also gets up, and says, "Let's finish this outside, buddy."

Secret service agents, who'd evidently been too fascinated to intercede, finally step between the combatants.

"They saved your ass," Trump says.

"I'll be at the White House at ten tonight."

"Fine. This time it'll be just the two of us."

Guns and War

When a few million citizens, many quite young, gather to protest gun violence in scores of cities and towns from Washington, D.C. to Los Angeles, I advertise links to stories on my website I've written about guns and war, and hope to attract liberal and educated readers. Regrettably, the tactic doesn't work. Many people on the right seem supernaturally aware of every contrary opinion about firearms and state aggression.

In a recent story titled "NRA Praises AR-15 Rifle," I criticize the National Rifle Association for saying not a word about the slaughter at a high school in Parkland, Florida, and instead re-posting an old and oafish article about what a wonderful creation is the AR-15.

Reader A comments these rifles "are awesome."

But they're too "powerful," I respond.

"Powerful, are you kidding? It's a hopped up .22."

It's hopped up enough to kill seventeen and wound fourteen during six minutes and twenty seconds survivor Emma Gonzalez riveted with silence during the D.C. demonstration.

"The founding fathers would have the citizens have exactly the same arms as the standing army, nothing less," types B.

"Tanks, bazookas, artillery, jets, and nuclear weapons in the hands of the militia," I reply.

"You are a media-manipulated 'citizen' who doesn't realize the danger he is putting us all in," C proclaims.

I'm not putting anyone in danger. I simply stated AR-15s are designed to kill, and military-style weapons don't belong in the unsure hands of citizens.

"Anyone who blames an inanimate object for what a human does is an idiot," D opines. "I stand with the NRA always."

Let's concede almost everyone is sometimes an idiot. It's therefore reasonable to ban the most destructive weapons.

The macho gunners also pounce on my satirical story "Trump Interviews John Bolton." The latter is a warmonger who advocates preemptive strikes in North Korea and Iran, and helped manufacture "fake" evidence that Iraq had weapons of mass destruction, and therefore should be attacked. Apart from Donald Trump and Kim Jong Un, Bolton, the president's new national security adviser, is the most dangerous man on earth.

"You sound like a chicken shit," E charges. And, checking back in, he adds, "Those who fear all war or conflict are doomed to experience it! That's chicken shit."

I finally receive rhetorical help from F who writes, "There is a difference in being chicken shit and stupid, sadly we have a president who is both."

Guns and war guys keep unloading tough words.

"The North Korean regime is a hazard but because now we have a president who isn't taking (Kim's) shit, the left is crying," G explains.

Reader H also readies for battle, writing, "Trump would never attack, only defend. Stop being whiny ass pussies. Obama took it up the ass. Guess liberals like that. We got a president with balls. That puts fear in our enemy."

I'd like to thank assault-weapons lovers and preemptive strikers for their profound insights.

Easter Egg Hunt

no more daca deal
too many dreamers
need wall
happy easter
love donald

Fox Counters Trump

Lights glow, TV cameras roll, and Donald Trump says, "I want you to remember my remarks at Trump Tower the day I started my campaign for president. I used the word rape, and people said I was too tough. Now they're saying I'm right. On the journey coming up here, from Central America through Mexico, women are being raped and murdered at levels nobody's ever seen, and caravans of criminals are coming right into our country."

Vicente Fox, tall and mustachioed, rises to announce, "High rates of homicide in Mexico are related to drug violence that's driven by the consumer market in the United States. The drug cartels are based right here, and they hire Mexicans to bring narcotics to addicts here."

"Those are some bad dudes, Vicente. We're definitely not getting your good ones. Too many aren't coming here on merit. They're either sneaking in or winning a lottery and being pulled in by chain migration. It's crazy. A guy can come in and eventually bring his brothers and sisters, and mother and father and grandparents, and then his cousins, aunts, and uncles. One guy eventually brought in twenty-two people, and one afternoon he just pulled off the road along the Hudson River where people run to stay in shape, and ran over and killed eight and maimed several others.

"We've got a crisis with illegal immigration. They're not only committing violent crimes, they're voting illegally. Don't let the Democrats deny that. They're voting illegally and they're voting against Republicans. I'm doing something about it. I've already got about two billion dollars for the wall, and we're building it, and pretty soon I'm going to send a few thousand National Guard troops to the border and keep them there until my wall is finished. Construction will move a lot faster once Mexico starts paying us for the wall."

"Like I told you, Donald, we're not going to pay for your fucking wall," says Fox. "Mexicans in the United States work and make you money here, and our citizens at home buy your products. You better not forget that every year Mexican farmers buy forty billion dollars of corn from the United States. Now, because of your tariffs and trade war, they've started buying in Central America. Your prices for food are going to go up, and because of your steel tariffs a lot of people in the United States aren't going to be able to afford cars."

"We need a better neighbor, Vicente."

"Perhaps you'd prefer Afghanistan, Iraq, Syria, Russia, China, North Korea, or Iran on your southern border."

"We'd like Canada on either side of us."

"So would we," says Fox.

Border Politics

since arrests
at border continue
declining to lowest
in forty-six years
why is trump banging
immigration drum

THIRTY-FOUR

Trump Tweets Assad

my first message says
assad you're a sick animal
and i'm gonna punish you
for poison gassing
mothers and children
my second says
we're getting out of
your shithole country
before midterm elections
in november

Mighty Morals

I accept your passionate call to step in and stop the investigative nonsense that's enveloping this nuclear nation of bluenose hypocrites. First, we don't need to know if Donald Trump twelve years ago had a quick roll in the sack with stripper and porn star Stormy Daniels. We also don't need to know if, during that period, he rendezvoused with Playboy centerfold Karen McDougal several times a month in hotel rooms. The ostensibly important issue here is whether Trump authorized personal attorney Michael Cohen to wire Daniels a hundred-thirty grand and the *National Enquirer* to pay McDougal a hundred-fifty thousand for exclusive rights to her story the publication then buried.

None of that matters. Donald Trump likely pursued romantic opportunities that would have delighted a majority of men if they had the same options. Sadly, most married men deny they'd behave in such a way, and maintain straight faces as they preach about morality and restraint and the devil and more. Equally relevant, numerous married women would, and do, stray when they meet men who attract them. That's how hypersexual humans behave, and it's unfortunate all presidential candidates must pretend to have been monogamous since their wedding nights.

Trump knew his 2016 presidential chances would disappear if there'd been last-minute allegations of marital infidelity. As a man who reveres money and its many uses, he likely authorized the two nondisclosure agreements now incessantly in the news, but he shouldn't have had to worry about public revelations of private passions, and therefore he shouldn't have had to pay for silence. Additionally, it doesn't matter if he did pay. The only relevant concern is if people acting in his behalf, with or without Trump's knowledge, threatened Stormy Daniels, as she alleges.

The preceding three paragraphs mean that special counsel Robert Mueller, a Republican, shouldn't have felt compelled to ask Deputy Attorney General Rod Rosenstein, a Republican, for a search warrant, and the latter shouldn't have needed to refer Mueller to Geoffrey Berman, United States attorney for the southern district of New York and a Republican, and the FBI shouldn't have raided the office of Trump's attorney Michael Cohen and seized, probably at random, boxes of business records, emails, and other documents. A separate group of federal investigators known as the "taint team" will determine which documents are relevant to the sex case and/or Robert Mueller's eternal investigation of possible Trump collusion with Russian operatives seeking to influence him and subvert the presidential election.

I hereby order the immediate cessation of all investigations and legal proceedings regarding the intimate life of President Donald Trump. I hope he'd do the same for us, though I doubt he would. The day after the raid, Trump fired some strong points he should remember when others are under siege, calling the raid "a disgrace... a witch hunt... an attack on the country... a whole new level of unfairness... ridiculous (since) there was no collusion with Russia..." and stating "attorney-client privilege is dead."

Don't worry about The Donald's hormonal moments. Focus instead on the Russian investigation, tariffs, trade wars, preemptive wars, nuclear weapons, health care, and the environment.

Au Revoir, Paul Ryan

i'm tired of riding trump titanic
and snoozing on capitol couch
but

may
someday
return
if i can sleep in white house and keep
attacking social security and medicare

Saint James Comey

hillary the satanic emailer
i had to take down
donald the prevaricating mobster
i'm going to take down
while in heaven i loom
atop bestseller list

Stalin Assesses Syria

I love my giant TV in sky and hotlines to hell where you still dwell. No longer do I have to worry about deadly schemes of millions of enemies internal and external and my stressful duty of arresting, torturing, and slaughtering them. Those tasks now fall to others, in many nations, and I'm retired and handsomely paid pundit who appears on your favorite news outlet, proffering opinions and analyses unique to body and soul of Joseph Stalin, five-foot-five giant who crushed Hitler and dominated Soviet Union for quarter century.

All my fancy gadgets from twenty-first century were alight yesterday when President Trump launched cruise missile strikes against chemical weapons facilities in Syria. Before further addressing this matter, I'd like to reference CIA operation Timber Sycamore wherein callow President Obama ordered his agents to train and agitate opponents of President Bashar al-Assad, many of whom were jihadists, and almost knocked out awkward eye doctor and would have but for intervention of Russians and President Putin, who forever strives but fails to match my stature. As result of foreign provocateurs and Assad, obsessed with maintaining power inherited from his inept father, six hundred thousand Syrians have died and fourteen million are displaced, often starving and homeless in nations that generally don't want them and can't offer much help.

I'm still utterly untroubled by anyone's suffering except my own but this catastrophe compels me to point to American inconsistencies. Why didn't they punish Saddam Hussein and Iraq for using chemical weapons during Iraq's war with Iran in eighties? Why didn't Barack Obama ignore congressional threats of impeachment and attack Assad for gassing civilians? Why did Donald Trump criticize Obama for publicly discussing strike? Don't tell enemy our military plans, said man who, after Assad may have gassed about seventy women and children near Damascus last week, maniacally tweeted, "Get ready, Russia, because (the missiles) will be coming nice and new and 'smart.'" There's no such weapon as smart bomb when used by dumbass.

Putin, who might have qualified as one of my commissars, then prudently ordered all personnel out of air force bases likely to be targeted. After launch of hundred and five slow and low-flying cruise missiles by the U.S., France, and England, Syria claimed it shot down thirteen, and Russians later asserted they destroyed an astounding seventy-one missiles. As we wait for evidence to confirm or refute, I wager no one hits seventy percent of incoming targets.

Russia proclaimed attack act of "barbaric aggression" and said there would be "consequences" for anyone "insulting President Putin." Furthermore, U.S.-led operation is "militarily a strike against Syria. Politically, it's a strike against Russia." That's true, and American aircraft carrier group is steaming toward Syria while Russian attack submarines wait, but I doubt they'll exchange anything but hot words. Even I feared nuclear weapons.

Representing Sean Hannity

it's private but now you know michael cohen's
given
me
legal
tips
but he never sent invoices
and
i
swear
none of this had to do with third party

THIRTY-FIVE

Mattis Moderates Bolton

Dr. Harrison doesn't get drunk on fine wines at the party for powerbrokers in Washington, D.C. but consumes enough to hand the keys to his wife, after only brief debate, and rides shotgun, singing his alma mater's fight song. At home he again accedes in gentlemanly fashion and, still clothed except for shoes, retires to the guest bedroom about two a.m. and thus has only three hours of fitful rest when his wife dashes in to announce, "President Trump needs you at the White House immediately."

"Where's Dr. Dillard? He's supposed to be on duty."

"There's trouble and your medical services are urgently needed."

"What the hell?"

"Get up. I'll drive."

In less than twenty minutes, somewhat disheveled, Dr. Harrison stumbles into the Oval Office, carrying his medical bag. He at once notices Trump is exhausted and says, "Please sit on the sofa so I can examine you. You've got to start getting more sleep and exercise."

"I'm the healthiest man in White House history. You're here to serve as ring doctor."

"I beg your pardon."

"Ring doctor, octagon doctor. Whatever you want to call it."

Dr. Harrison looks at several stern men wearing uniforms or suits, recognizes most of them, and asks, "What's going on?"

"Real simple," says the president. "I'm tired of having my ears blistered by these two blowhards, James Mattis and John Bolton."

The secretary of defense, a retired four-star general, steps within a couple feet of the new national security advisor, who retreats a few inches.

"You two settle it quick with words or some other way," says Trump.

"You're an academic runt who loves to advocate wars while cowering far away," says Mattis. "The United States can't just go in and start bombing Syria."

"That's the kind of timid response that caused several years of civil war and hundreds of thousands of deaths," Bolton says.

"You don't care about lives. You want to strike Iran, with whom we and other nations have an internationally recognized nuclear deal. You want to bomb North Korea and had no interest in even talking to them until President Trump agreed to do so. Now you want to bomb a nation that's devastated and bleeding."

"Last week the Syrian government used chlorine, and perhaps sarin, to kill civilians. We've got to punish Bashar al-Assad."

"We need to respond with a limited and focused strike on three of his chemical weapons facilities."

Bolton glances at Trump before saying to Mattis, "That didn't work last year and won't this year. No more weak responses. We need to devastate Assad's air force and war-making ability."

"You goddamn fool, don't you know there are Russians at lots of Syrian government bases?"

"They shouldn't be there."

"They are there," Mattis shouts, jumping closer and rising on toes to level his eyeballs at Bolton's.

"We'll force them out," Bolton says.

"How?"

"I've already told you ten times: by destroying Assad's air force and other military facilities."

"That would be logistically difficult and unbelievably risky."

"You don't have the guts for battle," says Bolton, turning red as his mustache bristles.

"Listen real good, you cowardly son of a bitch. You've never been near combat. I've fought in wars and led men in lots of battles and been decorated for it. I know what combat's about."

"Yeah, and you say you like it."

"Not against Russia," says Mattis. "Against fucking chicken-hawks like you."

Bolton steps back, removes his glasses, and, before he can set them on Trump's desk, Mattis kicks him in the knee and left hooks Bolton's forehead, cutting it. The verbal warrior pushes out both palms chest high.

"What's a matter," says Mattis. "This is sissy stuff. Imagine if my strikes were bombs."

"Mad Dog, Mad Dog," chant the uniforms and suits.

After using his tie to dab a bloody forehead, Bolton says, "The president hired me as national security advisor because he admires my experience and intellect. He doesn't expect me to actually fight."

"You saying you quit?" Mattis asks.

"Maybe I'll kick your ass next time."

Trump points at Dr. Harrison and moves finger toward Bolton.

"Mr. Bolton, please have a seat," says the doctor. "I better give you a few stitches so you'll be ready for the big debates about Iran and North Korea."

Nikki Next Time

trump
confused
about
nikki
haley's
plans
in
twenty
twenty

Korean Melody

k pop pretty singers travel north
after
concert
lips
tight
for
kim
jong
un

At the Border

kim jong un
walks south
across the border
kim jae in
walks north
across the border
and both return
south to discuss
making korea
nuclear free
and they live
quite happily
until
real
negotiations
begin

Nobel Trump

people ask what i had to with north korea's improved behavior and
offer
to
meet
at
summit
my answer's simple
everything
it's almost cinch i'll win nobel peace prize and if i don't
blame
kim
jong
un

THIRTY-SIX

My NRA

trump enters nra bordello and says
elect
more
republicans
to
protect
sacred
gun
rights

Trump Nuclear Strategy

we need more long and intermediate range nukes
so
what
russia
will
also
make
more
we'll make more than their more and be on top

Bolton Advises Trump

This conversation was recorded by trusted contacts in the National Security Agency

"I alone have made this historical decision," says Donald Trump.

"Please remember, Mr. President, we do need excuses."

He moves behind his desk in the Oval Office and plants himself. "What excuses could we use?"

"The same ones I recommended in my *National Review* essay last year. I sent you a copy at the time, and again last month."

"I'll check it out later. Just tell me."

I pick up my annotated original manuscript and say, "First, Iran is in significant violation of the Joint Comprehensive Plan of Action."

"Haven't the inspectors said Iran's in compliance?"

"Yes, but inspectors are either liars or incompetents."

"Probably both," says the president.

"Also, Iran's behavior is everywhere unacceptable. Look how repressive they are at home, and consider the disasters they're exacerbating in Syria."

"They're a rogue regime, for sure."

"George W. Bush abrogated the Anti-Ballistic Missile treaty and nobody could do anything because we're the United States," I say. "They won't do anything now."

"They better not try."

"The treaty itself is gravely flawed, as you've often said, Mr. President. The Iranians are allowed to continue to enrich uranium. And there's nothing to prevent them from developing and advancing their centrifuges. We need adequate verification."

"This is the worst deal ever."

"It certainly is. President Obama wouldn't have dared submit his flawed agreement to the Senate."

The president says, "Right."

"This deal doesn't even take Israel's interests into consideration. The other signatories don't have the special relationship we have with the Israelis."

"Prime Minister Netanyahu's a big fan of mine, and he told me he likes you, too."

I smile, which I don't often since my mustache droops against my teeth.

"Anything else?" the president asks.

"Absolutely. We've got to consider the nuclear linkage between Iran and North Korea, two dangerous peas in a pod."

"I'll artfully deal with both of them."

I point through the wall and say, "We need devastating sanctions against Iran, not the current sanctions relief. Iran's nothing less than a central banker for international terrorism. They control Hezbollah and will continue to destabilize Iraq and Lebanon as well as Syria."

"They're bad dudes."

"We need to quietly tell the other signatories, except Iran, that we're going to abrogate this agreement. I'll give you several more reasons…"

The president extends his right palm toward my mouth and says, "That's fine, John."

Trumping Iran

No, wise guy, I'm not sitting on the can but an executive chair at a presidential table in the White House and am appropriately stern but proud as I sign the Presidential Memorandum announcing the United States will violate the Joint Comprehensive Plan of Action in order to prevent Iran, the most terroristic nation on earth, from continuing its rapid development of nuclear weapons. I don't care the International Atomic Energy Agency and its inspectors have ten times said Iran is in compliance with the agreement. The agreement is defective to its core. It doesn't matter I haven't had a chance to read it. My instincts tell me other signatories, all pipsqueak nations compared to us, made a huge mistake.

I'm not against the Iranian people. I'm for them. Maybe by resuming tight-ass sanctions we'll be able to topple the theocracy that oppresses them. England, France, and Germany don't understand that by "staying committed" to this dangerous deal they're helping our enemies acquire the most destructive weapons, which they're philosophically and racially unqualified to handle. I'm ready to negotiate a new and much better deal, one that more tightly restricts nuclear activities and also forces the Iranians to limit or eliminate ballistic missiles, which would carry nuclear weapons, and tie future sanctions relief to their stopping terrorism. I've got to compel them to behave. I'm a patient man, despite what political adversaries shout, and am ready to give sanctions and diplomacy a reasonable shot. I'd rather not attack, but John Bolton says we could fairly easily destroy key nuclear facilities in Iran and there wouldn't be that many consequences. I know, he and George W. Bush and Dick Cheney and others said the same thing about Iraq in 2003. But this is 2018 and I, Donald J. Trump, am president of the United States.

People fear and respect me. They know I'll kick 'em in the balls. Just listen to Barack Obama now calling me "misguided" and claiming that my "flouting of agreements… erodes American credibility… (and) puts us at odds" with other major powers. What a wuss. We're the ultimate power. Russia and China don't have our economy or military. Neither do tiny European nations who still want to appease Iran. Sometimes you've got to be tough. I beat all my opponents because I pounded them. You all saw it. I do what's needed and don't care if we lose some business in Iran because of this. Let Russia and China have it. They also signed the devil's deal. I'm tearing it up.

Nobel Delay

I'd never say it, but almost everyone else is: President Trump's a lock for the Nobel Peace Prize. Obviously, I agree. None of my timid predecessors could have brought Kim Jong Un running to the peace table. Only my threats of unprecedented death and destruction have made peace possible. I'm not worried Kim threatened to pull out of talks because we still held our annual joint military exercises with South Korea. Kim knew our plans long ago, and recently said he understood the need for the exercises, which are only designed to deter him from attacking south across the DMZ. He also made a mistake in cancelling a high-level talk with South Korea. They need to talk. We all need to.

I ordered our diplomats to continue preparing for my grand summit with Kim Jong Un in June in Singapore. I assume he's just sending a message he plans to be difficult at the bargaining table, but he better be receptive and quit saying he's not interested in discussing "unilateral nuclear abandonment." He should be thankful. I'll offer him business and infrastructure investments as well as our unequalled brainpower. We can make his country almost as rich as South Korea. All he's got to do is hand over his nuclear weapons and ballistic missiles and chemical and biological weapons. He won't get any help until he does that. And if he tries to delay disarming due to a bunch of technicalities, I may give him fire and fury instead of opportunities for economic growth. I guess in that case I wouldn't get the Nobel right away, at least for Korea, but maybe I can get it because of my toughness in dealing with Iran and forcing that hellish country to get rid of its nuclear weapons and ballistic missiles and start acting better. But if Iran behaves like North Korea, I may have to attack, and wait a year or two before officially becoming the world's greatest man of peace.

Trump Animals

i'm talking about ms 13 gang
members it's crazy because of
weak laws these people come in
fast we get them we send them
away we get them again we're
taking them out of the country
at a rate that's never happened
before it's so ridiculous they
aren't people they're animals

THIRTY-SEVEN

Trump Investigates

i demand dept of justice look into possible fbi doj surveillance
of
my
trump
campaign
and
find
out
if
crime was ordered by obama administration

Trump Cancels Kim

kim said he understood our around his neck nuclear exercises with
south korea
and i explained
john bolton's
gaddafi model
gaffe applied
to kim's nukes
not his head he's got to settle down so someday we can actually meet

Khomeini and the Shah of Iran

I'm writing this commentary in French, the most sublime language, from my Parisian penthouse where I've been ruminating almost forty years. I assure you I remain a most formidable leader and lover, and am primed to educate you about what is happening to Iran. Don't you wish I, instead of radical and incompetent theocrats, still led the great Persian kingdom? I'm not blaming the United States for my ouster nor am I ungrateful for decades of financial, political, and military backing. I simply recall what you surely know. I, the Shah of Iran, was and will always be your friend despite your betrayal.

"The satanic Americans didn't betray you," says a most unwelcome intruder, my neighbor the Ayatollah Khomeini. "They betrayed the Islamic people of Iran by installing and protecting a heathen and spendthrift dedicated only to eternal power."

I put my pen down and say, "My moves to maintain domestic tranquility were infinitely less severe than yours. I was civilized. In fact, I gave women the right to vote."

"Yes, and for that alone you should've been flogged."

"Perhaps I should be thankful you're here, polishing my image and besmirching yours. I sought not to conquer, unlike your successors who're bloodying the Middle East and squandering our treasure while financing Hezbollah in Syria and Lebanon, Hamas in Palestine, the Houthis in Yemen, hosting Al Qaeda, and terrorizing the world."

"The Iranian people have already rendered their judgment of you," says Khomeini. "Let us examine contemporary matters, specifically the latest American outrage, a list of degradations pronounced by Secretary of State Mike Pompeo."

I pick up my Pompeo paper and use it to point to Khomeini's copy in his hand. "Very well."

"Pompeo accused us of marching 'across the Middle East,' during the nuclear deal they violated, and nourishing ourselves with 'blood money... wealth created by the West.' I think Mr. Pompeo is confused and in fact thinking about white men rampaging across the North American continent and enriching themselves while they abused their slaves and slaughtered Indians. He also seems unaware the money comes from our oil, and foreign payments that should've gone directly to us have instead been hijacked and banked by the West. And why would Americans object to our establishing a 'corridor' from Afghanistan to the shores of the Mediterranean? Our enemy has a corridor from sea to shining sea."

"That's in their country," I say.

"Taken by force."

"The way things are usually taken."

"The Yankees and their European lackeys also have a corridor from the Atlantic to the Baltic Sea."

"Shall we examine the Americans' twelve points?" I ask.

"Pompeo first threatens to apply 'unprecedented financial pressure on the Iranian regime,' and support our enemies in the Middle East, and 'advocate tirelessly for the Iranian people' to force us to 'improve how it treats its citizens.' It's unfortunate, isn't it, my dear Shah, that the United States didn't compel you to improve your treatment of Iranians?"

"Under my enlightened leadership Iran was but ten or twenty years from living as well as Europeans and Americans. That's hardly the case in your sanctions-strangled and medieval state."

"Point one," says Khomeini. "We 'must declare to the International Atomic Energy Agency a full account' of our nuclear weapons program and 'permanently and verifiably abandon such work in perpetuity.'"

"In perpetuity's a long time," I say. "I'd ignore the future requirement and give an incomplete accounting of our history in regard to nuclear weapons."

The Ayatollah Khomeini almost smiles, frightening me.

"Second, the Americans – I assume Trump's too dense to have written this – demand 'Iran must stop enrichment' and close our 'heavy water reactor.' We'd already done the latter, as part of the abrogated nuclear deal, but we shall certainly continue to enrich at peaceful levels. That's our sovereign right, especially as a signatory of the Non-Proliferation Treaty."

I don't respond.

"Point three," says Khomeini, "I assume they're joking: 'Iran must also provide the IAEA with unqualified access to all sites throughout the entire country.' We'll do that when the Americans allow us to inspect their nuclear installations."

"Have you something to conceal?" I ask.

"Has Israel something to conceal? More than a hundred nuclear weapons, perhaps."

"Israel has proven, at least at the nuclear level, that it won't strike unless existentially threatened, and that hasn't happened."

"Before it does, we must destroy the Zionist pseudo state," he says.

"That attitude's quite dangerous for any Iranian leader and precisely why Israel developed nuclear weapons and, in concert with the United States, is determined to prevent Iran from developing its own."

"I always considered you a lover of Jews."

"I'm proud I was. During my reign, Jews in Iran flourished and contributed in many ways to our country. Your fanatical regime excludes so many."

Khomeini's eyes become more unpleasant.

"Point four," he says. "'Iran must end its proliferation of ballistic missiles and halt further launching or development of nuclear-capable missiles.'"

"I don't think we need nuclear weapons but we must have ballistic missiles carrying conventional warheads for national defense."

Khomeini's slightly eases his hostile manner before turning to point five. "Iran must release all U.S. citizens" and other allies "detained on spurious charges."

"Do so. That's a reasonable point."

"I may, indeed. But what are the Americans to give me in return?"

"Perhaps an exchange of prisoners," I say.

"Point six. 'Iran must' – all their points start with 'must,' which means these are ultimatums – 'end support to Middle East terrorist groups.' No deal. The Americans have their allies. We have ours."

"Please proceed," I say.

"Point seven. 'Iran must respect the sovereignty of the Iraqi government and permit the disarming, demobilization, and reintegration of Shia militias.' You'll recall what happened when the Americans disarmed and demobilized the troops of Saddam Hussein. Our help for Shia militias saved them from ISIS, which America swears it despises. We still await a signal of U.S. appreciation."

Pointing at the heavens, I say, "It's a better world without Saddam, who killed hundreds of thousands of our people."

"I don't require your reminder of a tragic conflict I led us through. In contemporary Iraq we haven't been bleeding in order to retreat and let a chaotic and hostile regime again threaten us."

"I won't dispute that point."

"Point eight. 'Iran must end its military support for the Houthi militia and work toward a peaceful settlement in Yemen.'"

"That's reasonable," I say.

"Not when Saudi Arabia, armed with some of the finest American jets and other weapons, slaughters Houthi civilians," says Khomeini. "Point nine. 'Iran must withdraw all forces under Iranian command throughout the entirety of Syria.' That's absurd. Iranian and Russian forces have bled, with those of President Assad in Syria, to defeat ISIS and other terrorists and traitors. We'll certainly stay as long as our allies need us. We must also be there to breathe hot air on the Zionists."

"If so, my dear Ayatollah, the Israelis and Americans will surely breathe hotter air on us."

"Not with impunity. Point ten. 'Iran must end support' for the Taliban and Al Qaeda in Afghanistan and the region."

"You're going to have to yield some points. Break with the Taliban and Al Qaeda in Afghanistan."

"Impossible. Americans in Afghanistan continue to aid terrorist operations inside Iran. The Taliban was once the enemy of both Iran and the United States. Now the Taliban's fighting a giant who plans to stay forever.

"Point eleven, 'Iran must end the Iranian Revolutionary Guard Quds Force's support for terrorists' around the world. I hope the United States is sincere about stopping support for terrorists. If so, it will at once tell Israel and Saudi Arabia they 'must' stop murdering civilians in Gaza and Yemen."

I gaze at Khomeini.

He exhales and says, "There's so much these Americans say we must do. In point twelve, the final one, for today, 'Iran must end its threatening behavior against its neighbors,' including such bad actors as Israel, Saudi Arabia and the United Arab Emirates.

"Will you please help me draft our response, my dear Shah?"

"But of course."

"The United States must forevermore cease terroristic and genocidal attacks against the people of countries such as North Korea, Vietnam and other Southeast Asian victims, the people of Iraq, Afghanistan, and…"

"Just a minute. Let me get more paper."

Kim Yong Chol in New York

In a Chinese airliner I fly to New York where atop a beautiful skyscraper my aide and I are dining with Secretary of State Mike Pompeo and Andrew Kim, America's purported expert in all matters North Korean and a man whose real name isn't Andrew Kim. As my nation's preeminent intelligence and security expert, and to date a wily survivor of three generations of leadership by the Korean Kims, I distrust hawkish Pompeo and devious Andrew Kim as much as they doubt me, but those feelings don't matter. I'm here to prepare Pompeo, and by extension Donald Trump, to meet Kim Jong Un and me sometime this month in Singapore.

This is a wonderful place to talk. I can see Central Park and the Statue of Liberty and, I confess, feel the power of the United States. I think that's why this location was chosen but my hosts won't find me in awe. I'm having a very good time. Pompeo and Andrew Kim are fine dinner companions. And the food is delicious: spring pea salad with cheese and shaved crudité followed by filet mignon and fancy corn and spinach and topped off by chocolate soufflé with homemade vanilla ice cream.

I'm so glad President Trump realized he made a mistake in cancelling the summit. He no doubt listened to the bellowing of John Bolton. We responded to Trump with kindness and he promptly announced the meeting was back on and said, "I truly believe North Korea has brilliant potential and will be a great economic and financial nation one day. Kim Jong Un agrees with me. It will happen."

In order for the United States to make it happen, assuming our adversary really wants it to and is able to deliver our great future, we in North Korea are expected to forget seventy years of hostility and threats and sanctions, and surrender nuclear weapons essential to our survival. In frankness, I do not believe the Americans would keep their promises once we buried our deterrent. I think they'd decapitate us.

So you're wondering what I'm saying to Mike Pompeo. And you're hoping Kim Jong Un has already agreed to denuclearize and won't ask much of the United States in return, such as withdrawing all its soldiers from the Korean Peninsula and keeping its planes and warships away from our borders and our skies. We won't dare move too fast. Whatever happens will happen in stages. If the Americans leave and quit threatening us, we may be able to work something out. But everyone must be patient.

THIRTY-EIGHT

Trey Gowdy Clears FBI

i'm hard head of house
oversight committee and
support trump but gotta
tell you fbi planted no
spies in his campaign and
investigated properly to
determine russians tried
to help elect trump and
if president didn't know
he should act like it

Roseanne Barred

donald trump and roseanne barr tweet about race and ethnicity
one
becomes
president
other
loses
tv
show

What's a Samantha Bee

from around the nation
conservative pundits call
to ask why i haven't
denounced samantha bee

who's she

the unfunny comedian who
c worded ivanka trump

four letters

right

then that's what samantha
bee is

Absolute Trump

robert mueller can't interrogate me because i
have
absolute
authority
over
all
federal
investigators
and may fire mueller to prove it

Dangerous Ally

hated
weak and dishonest justin trudeau
at g7
honored
will meet powerful kim jong un
in singapore

Attorney General at the Border

Astride a beautiful large gray horse and wearing an elegant suit gray
as Robert E. Lee's uniform, Jefferson Beauregard Sessions patrols the
border, looking for intruders. I pity his prey. Sessions appears warrior
enough to slay any foe.

In each hand I wave a white paper overhead and shout, "Don't
shoot, sir. I just want to ask a few questions."

"Are you a U.S. citizen?"

"Of course," I say, retrieving my blue passport from a front pocket of my pants.

"Is it legitimate or did you get it from a dirty immigration lawyer?"

"I've got just as much Anglo Saxon blood as you, sir."

"Very well. What do you want?"

"Is it true our government is separating parents from children at our southern border?"

Sessions points an index finger down at me, drilling my nose, and says, "We aren't separating children from parents, we're liberating them from criminals who've tried to illegally enter the United States."

"But the parents are going into custody and the kids are either sent to relatives or, if none are available, into social services."

"We take a lot better care of kids in facilities and foster homes than parents who smuggle children. People must obey our laws. What do you think the Mexicans do to illegal aliens? They're a lot tougher than we are."

I pause and examine Sessions who as a young man had a sweet face and sort of still does.

"Nations need laws," he says. "Like President Trump often reminds everyone, 'We either have a nation or we don't.'"

"We've got a great nation, sir. That's why millions want to come and live here."

"Hundreds of millions, and none of them can come here unless they do it legally, like my ancestors did."

"Are you sure your ancestors had immigration documents before sailing from Europe?"

"I don't know all the details but I know they came here legally."

I point at the border a few yards to our south, and say, "Many are trying to come here legally. They aren't avoiding official ports of entry. They're going right to them. And many say they're turned back. U.S. officials tell them they don't have room to house them."

"That's a lie," Sessions says, again targeting my nose with a martial finger. "Those who come to official ports of entry are taken into custody and treated very well. We try to adjudicate their cases fast as we can. You bleeding hearts have got to accept the truth. Most people coming in are sneaking in."

"Let's concede that's true."

"It is true."

"Okay," I say. "But what about a couple of thousand kids currently separated from parents who are in detention?"

"Like I told you, the kids are being well taken care of. And we'll find most of their parents, and they'll be happy to return home together."

"Home is why they need asylum, which is their right under international law. Home is places like Honduras and El Salvador where they have the two highest murder rates in the world."

"You're making my point, son," says Sessions. "We don't want those kinds of folks in our nations of laws."

"Do you think your attitude may have been formed by your Southern heritage?"

"No sir. Folks all over agree with me. The president's from New York, you know."

Digging spurs into each side of his horse, Jeff Sessions shouts, "Giddy-up, Traveller."

THIRTY-NINE

Trump Gets Ready

don't really need to prepare much for kim jong un
just
gonna
keep
massaging
my
balls

Trump Arrives in Singapore

It's a great honor to participate in the summit meeting with Kim Jong Un, and I'm proud to be the man who made this happen. I really feel like a statesman now. I'm more mature and modest as a leader responsible for the lives of countless millions of people not only in the United States but in Asia and around the world. Arriving in Singapore Sunday night I'm inspired but quite tired as I exit Air Force Once, take the rail in my left hand, and slowly walk down the steps, waving a little. On the tarmac I only shake a couple of hands before getting into my limousine. I'm pretty worn out but have the energy of two young men and will be ready to go at nine a.m. Tuesday when Kim and I publicly shake hands and have our photos taken before meeting privately for two hours. Only our translators will join us.

I hope Kim likes me. I love to be liked. Doesn't everyone? He undoubtedly wants me to like him, too. And I think I will. I'll certainly like him if he likes me, and if we like each other I know we can make a great deal. I've already told everyone what I'm going to tell Kim. If he agrees to begin taking verifiable steps toward denuclearization, we will help transform his country into an incredible place. This will be his only chance. I think he'll agree. That's why I've been calling Kim a very smart and honorable man who's warm and gracious. He's all of those things, and so am I.

We can work things out. I don't want to strangle his isolated and backward land with more sanctions. Sanctions haven't slowed down his nuclear weapons development at all. We need to make a deal. We need to make America safe again, and we need to make North Korea great. If we can't do those things, my advisors who want maximum pressure may convince me war is the only way. I don't want that and neither do you.

Kim Jong Un in Singapore

This evening as I stroll through beautiful grounds of a Singaporean resort people are cheering and squealing like I'm a rock star. This is certainly a good sign for my meeting tomorrow with President Donald Trump. I know he loves stars and winners.

The summit begins when the president and I march to each other and shake hands, and he pats my shoulder and taps my back before pointing with the other hand to guide me to the next place. He's acting like the host. I don't mind. The president of the United States is happy to see a fellow commander in chief, and the whole world is hoping we're successful. We go to a private room briefly open to all and sit next to each other in soft chairs. I feel great as Trump again shakes my hand and gives me a thumbs up. I'm sure you've also had the feeling: I should've done this long ago. I'm leader of a top country in the world and belong on the biggest stage.

When doors close President Trump and I are alone with our translators. My English isn't bad but not good enough for this. We've earlier almost agreed on the main points. I'm ready to denuclearize my country as long as the whole Korean Peninsula has no nuclear weapons and the United States guarantees it won't try to destabilize or conquer my country. If we can maintain peace without nuclear weapons, then I think we'll be fine, like Japan and Germany. I'm most interested in improving the health and prosperity of my nation. At home I rarely talk about it even in private, and never in public, but we need more non-military technology and business and money. We can't have those things when we're spending so much on defense and at the same time fighting tough sanctions by the United States and many other countries, even China. Thankfully, our great protector to the north has resumed doing a little more business with us.

"Chairman Kim, you've got an incredible location between China and South Korea," says President Trump. "I know real estate. You can soon have the best hotels in the world, and your country can be really rich."

"We'd like that," I say.

After forty-five productive minutes we walk to a little larger room with a long table. My staff and I sit across from President Trump, Secretary of State Mike Pompeo, John Kelly, their translator, and to my far right warmonger John Bolton, who I don't even look at. We're here for peace. We reaffirm that for almost two hours before moving to a beautiful dining room for lunch. I love to eat and know President Trump does, too. Today we have prawn's cocktail, avocado salad, Korean stuffed cucumber, beef short ribs, spicy potatoes and steamed broccoli, sweet and sour crispy pork, fried rice, cod fish, ice cream, and more. I don't eat as much as I want because I'm trying to lose weight but keep gaining.

Following lunch President Trump and I walk outside together, smiling and joking, and I bet he's impressed with my English and my Swiss education.

"Great, fantastic meeting, better than anyone could have imagined," Trump tells reporters. We're going to celebrate our new relationship by signing an agreement in an hour or so.

After relaxing with our respective staffs, President Trump and I enter a large room where a table offers two chairs backed by twelve beautiful flags, six representing the Democratic People's Republic of Korea and six the United States. We sit, and I thank the president for making this meeting happen. Secretary of State Mike Pompeo, who also enjoys fine food, presents a copy of the agreement to President Trump, and my sister, Kim Yo Jong, opens my agreement and gives me one of our pens in case the one provided isn't safe. Trump looks at me, and we move to sign at the same time.

The agreement is short but extremely important. We not only agree that I have a "firm and unwavering commitment to complete denuclearization of the Korean Peninsula," we affirm that "President Trump committed to provide security guarantees to the DPRK." We also promise to "establish new U.S.-DPRK relations in accordance with the desire of the peoples of the two countries for peace and prosperity" and to "build a lasting and stable peace regime on the Korean Peninsula." Naturally, we also reaffirm the Panmunjom Declaration, between South Korean President Moon Jae-in and myself two months ago, in which we agree "to work together on ending the Korean War and the Korean conflict."

As we leave the room I gently place my hand on President Trump's back. He and I walk to another place backed by flags, under the hallway roof of a massive patio, and shake hands again. We're very happy. Soon we shake hands a couple more times. President Trump has already promised me he'll stop the provocative joint military exercises of his country and South Korea, and I've assured him I'm already dismantling a rocket testing facility.

This meeting has been as successful as President Trump said. I think he'd like to have dinner with me tonight but I've got to get home. No, I'm not rushing back because I think the military might stage a coup. I'm not worried about that after firing three of my highest ranking generals last month. They were old and belligerent and didn't understand my new and dynamic thinking. I replaced them with younger generals who want to avoid military confrontation. They'll help me decide how much we really can concede.

Fat Kim

ignore lies
forty percent
north koreans
malnourished
they all love
my big belly

Trump after Singapore

You'd think everyone would be congratulating me about the most extraordinary diplomatic breakthrough in decades, but some aren't. They're complaining I conferred legitimacy on a murderous dictator. In fact, I got off my presidential ass, unlike all my predecessors, and traveled thousands of miles to talk to a guy who has lots of nuclear weapons and the missiles to deliver them. But critics whine that by cancelling the joint military exercises with South Korea I weakened our alliance and emboldened Kim Jong Un. Wrong. Kim was already too bold and would've become more radical if we'd kept waving our swords in his face. You want China and Mexico to start holding joint military exercises?

I'm also tired of hearing I shouldn't have talked to Kim because he violates human rights and imprisons critics in North Korea. I know more about atrocities there than most of you and plan to help those political prisoners but can't do anything now. They'll end up winners when I take care of the first priority and denuclearize the Korean Peninsula. We removed our nuclear weapons from South Korea long ago. The North Koreans have a lot of work to do. We'll be monitoring them.

If we want Kim Jong Un to completely change the nature of his military, and maybe his country, we've got to be nicer. I related well to him and right away noted he was smart and talented and understood why his people love him. It's an honor to meet a man who at age twenty-seven was strong enough to inherit a dictatorship and secure it by inspiring friends and eliminating enemies. That doesn't mean I like everything he does. North Korea's a rough place but in only a year and a half I've been able to scare hell out of Kim and his generals and then charm him so he sees what he has to do and I can tweet, "There is no longer a Nuclear Threat from North Korea."

I didn't give up anything by diplomatically forcing Kim to promise to denuclearize. If he doesn't make satisfactory progress, I'll just pick up the phone and tell my generals, "Start planning the biggest joint military exercises in the history of our alliance with South Korea." Prior exercises didn't prevent the North Koreans from developing their missiles and warheads and behaving recklessly. That's why I'm trying something else. If it doesn't work, and I pray it will, I'll have to send cruise missiles and bombers to strike vast North Korean artillery sites, which would destroy Seoul if I don't take them out, and direct other missiles and bombers to hit known nuclear facilities in the north. That's all pretty risky, especially for South Korea and Japan, but better than Kim Jong Un firing nukes at us.

Kim Debates Himself

Three days after his triumphant return from Singapore, Kim Jong Un visits his dentist's office for cleaning and a checkup. Under the glare of three security agents the dentist lifts a syringe, smiles, and says, "Just a little Novocain."

"Why Novocain for cleaning?" says one of the tough guys.

"The Dear Leader usually has some rather deep pockets of plaque. They'll have to be removed or he may lose a few teeth."

"Make sure he doesn't," says another rough guy.

"Get started," says Kim.

"Yes sir." The dentist gently inserts the needle into his gum. "This should take effect very soon."

Two hidden cameras with sensitive microphones are recording this session.

"Congratulations on your marvelous agreement with Donald Trump," says the dentist. "I hope the Korean Peninsula will soon be denuclearized."

"We've spent seventy years and more than all our money to deter the United States from crushing us. Nothing will happen soon. I know President Trump thinks I'm going to start dismantling ballistic missiles and nuclear weapons in a couple of months, and maybe I should. I want the Americans to think we're cooperating. I really do want to cooperate but not how they want. They expect me to surrender and hand over all my nuclear weapons. I suppose I'll have to give them some but never all. I must be able to strike at least a few U.S. cities or they'll march me through the streets of Pyongyang first chance they get."

"Our people would never permit that," the dentist says.

"Look how Italy turned on Mussolini and Libya on Gaddafi. People back whoever's got them by the throat. I don't like choking them but I can't let people say bad things. I can't even let them think that way. If they do, their families also suffer. Imagine what they'll do if I ever weaken? But I'm not conceding I ever will. I'm confident we can build a paradise. President Trump's right. We can be rich like South Korea and Singapore. But people with money and knowledge don't like dictators. They'll complain and agitate and overthrow me if they can. And the

Americans will help. So will the South Koreans and Japanese. I might not even be able to depend on the Chinese if they think I'm a pain in the ass. I'm really trying to help my people. I don't like seeing them malnourished. I don't like having to imprison them. What if they get out? They won't escape as long as I have nuclear weapons. Trump may not be bluffing, though. I may have to fight or turn over my sword.

"Or maybe I won't have to do either. I'm going to negotiate and make promises and stall and continue moving slowly, and when the Americans start threatening me again, and holding joint military exercises with our dangerous brothers to the south, I'll make some concessions. In fact, I'll already have made concessions. I'll have destroyed old bombs and equipment and test sites irrelevant for the future. And I'll plan a huge new ceremony and invite President Trump to stand beside me as I blow up more junk. Trump will love it. He'll give me thumbs up and salute my generals and I'll pat his back and, this time, I'll even embrace him."

"Get to work," a tough guy tells the dentist.

He nods and says, "Open wide, Chairman Kim."

"Don't interrupt…"

As Kim Jong Un continues talking with increasing intensity and diminishing coherence, security agents call a special emergency medical team and arrest the dentist. Chemists determine Kim has been given a massive dose of methamphetamine. The dentist's name is removed from the door and his whereabouts are unknown. Cameras continue transmitting an empty office to the National Security Agency.

FORTY

Sessions Heads South

No longer will I tolerate renegades calling me a racist divider of families along the southern border of these United States. I'm already astride Traveller, my galloping gray steed, and arriving at what I'm confident is a humane detention facility for those who tried to illegally enter our sacred land.

"Mr. Attorney General, thank you for coming," says a border patrol officer to whom I hand the reins before I step onto hot Texas earth.

"You're quite welcome, sir. Let us begin the tour."

We enter a large warehouse appointed with chain-link cages atop a hard polished floor. I smile and say, "Good morning, kids. How y'all doing?"

The border patrol officer is Hispanic, like so many of our finest guardians, and he translates my message.

There's a chorus of responses. "Not very good. We're locked up. We're bored. Where's my mother? Who the hell are you?"

"I'm Jeff Sessions and I'm here to help you. I want all of you to know that you won't be here long. You'll be back with your parents just as soon as they get out of jail or when we find them."

I turn to the officer and whisper, "How many kids are in this place?"

"About two hundred without parents. And over there we've got several hundred kids with parents. And beyond that we've got adults with no children."

"Lots of these kids are real young. Are you sure they're safe?"

"Absolutely," says the officer.

"And well-fed?"

"Yes."

"And well-bathed?"

"Not bad at all."

"You're very organized," I say. "Are the other facilities with children this good?"

"I haven't been to the others, but I hear they're pretty decent."

"Nationally, how many kids are separated from their parents?"

"About two thousand."

"I admit this isn't pleasant for the kids but see no reason why critics claim we're 'traumatizing' them. We're teaching them and especially their parents that no tolerance means you can no longer illegally enter our country and get away with it. I pray the message spreads."

I turn to the caged kids and wave. "Goodbye, y'all."

"I can't understand what they're saying, but I didn't hear 'adios.'"

The border patrol officer smiles. "That's more or less what they said."

"Their parents shouldn't put them in such dangerous positions."

"Their countries are much worse. Have you been to El Salvador and Honduras?"

"Not yet," I say.

"Check them out."

"I'll do that right away."

First, I call my aide and make arrangements to fly to San Salvador aboard a United States military transport, which is neither comfortable nor quiet. I leave Traveller in a spacious stable connected to a big corral where professionals will exercise him every day.

In San Salvador it's hotter and more humid than Alabama. I can handle it.

"Take me where the action is," I order my hosts, a U.S. diplomat and a Salvadorian police officer.

"Please put on this bulletproof vest," says the officer.

"No need for that. Besides, you're not wearing one."

In an armored SUV we drive into the dirtiest, toughest-looking neighborhood I've seen. I jump out, breathe deeply, and say, "Maybe it's not as bad as it seems. I think I'll take a little stroll. Y'all just wait here."

"No sir, we can't do that," says the diplomat.

"You sure can. Be right back."

I walk fast down the street and around the corner and right away two young men run up, stick guns under my nose, and say something I can't understand.

"Hold your horses," I say.

One of them hits my cheek with his gun, knocking me onto a dirty, broken road. They remove my wallet and everything else on my person and before walking away the other guy kicks me in the groin.

"Oh my God," I shout. In a little while the diplomat and the police officer charge around the corner. The policeman aims his gun at an empty horizon.

Two faces appear behind a barred window, and the officer motions for them to come outside. A mother and her teenage daughter, I surmise, open a heavy metal door and walk over to me – I'm standing now – and the mother applies a wet rag to the gash on my cheek.

"Pretty tough around here," I say. The diplomat translates.

"You're lucky it's daytime," says the mother. "Otherwise, we'd be burying you. Lots of people die around here, especially after the gangs break in and take over their homes. Look at all the stores. Most are closed. Owners either pay the criminals or die."

"Don't you call the police?" I ask, holding the rag to my swelling cheek.

The diplomat looks at the officer, who in English says, "Tell him."

"The police do what they can. They're obviously very busy. And, frankly, sometimes they make sure they're too busy to respond to calls likely to get them killed."

"I have a wife, four kids," says the officer. "The gangs, they know where I live."

"These problems get bigger every day," says the diplomat. "Gangs confront teenagers on the street and tell them they're new members. 'You'll love it,' they say. 'See that pretty muchacha over there. Want her to be your novia? We'll arrange it. She'll cooperate. And so will you. Or else…'"

"I admit this is terrible, and I've never denied it," I say. "But that doesn't mean people from all over the world who have problems can enter the United States illegally."

"Many are legally applying for asylum for reasons we've seen and discussed today," says the elder diplomat.

"I feel awfully sorry for these folks, I really do," I say. "If I could help them here, I would. Maybe we should invest more in this region. Back in the United States I can only make sure the aliens are housed comfortably until their cases are promptly adjudicated. We're working hard to expand housing. You suppose these ladies have any ice?"

Campaign Mexico

i was running for mexican office in unnamed place but dropped out
after
cartels
killed
more
than
hundred
politicians
and
many
journalists

Trump Tough in Minnesota

I've come to Minnesota to get away from this border hassle. Don't
lecture me about kids. I've got five and they're all really great, especially
Ivanka. I'm concerned about kids everywhere. That's my job as the most
powerful hombre in the world. All along I've been worried about kids
getting split up from their parents on our southern border. That isn't
our fault. We've got to have zero tolerance for illegally entering the
United States. Finally, with me in office, we're securing the border and
promoting law and order, and I wanted Congress to fix the problem
with the kids. But you know how slow and inept Congress is. On
TV I kept seeing all the suffering at the border, and hearing about it
from Ivanka and Melania, so decided to step in. My executive order
now prevents families from being torn apart. They'll be housed in the
same place. We'll still be tough defending the border. We're building
my wall in lots of places. Must be liberals who say we're only repairing
existing structures near San Diego. These fat and poorly educated
Minnesotans before me tonight know my wall is a symbol: if people
come from shithole countries, the United States isn't obligated to solve
their problems. We'd like to but can't really solve our own problems.
My weak predecessors left piles of them. We'll be fine if people vote
right in November.

Melania's Jacket

I'm a model who understands the power of clothes and nudity, and know the latter pays better. Still, I must wear clothes to the border. After thinking about it quite a while, I select a green jacket showing white words in back, "I don't care. Do u?" Of course I wasn't referring to children I visited in cages at the border. They're separated from their parents because of stupid policies by my husband's opponents. I was talking about the fake media who always insult our family. You don't think my fashion selection was poorly timed, do u?

Trump Infested

i'm a big man with a big belly and write large my name
on
executive
order
before
tweeting
democrats are the problem and want illegal immigrants
no
matter
how
bad
to infest our country and become potential voters

FORTY-ONE

Trump Meets Lopez Obrador

After sundown at the White House, President Donald Trump climbs into a laundry truck and in utmost secrecy rides to an undisclosed airport where he boards Air Force One and flies to an unnamed airstrip near the Rio Grande. He then overrules agents and drives his armored beast to the shores of the eternal river, steps into black hip waders, and plows to the middle where Andres Manuel Lopez Obrador, also attired in waders, awaits him. Newscaster Jorge Ramos, sleek in a gold wet suit, stands to their side, ready to translate.

"On July first I shall be elected president of Mexico for six years," says Lopez Orbador.

"That'll be a helluva sad time for Mexico," Trump says.

"You continue to be frightened by your neighbor to the south."

"I wouldn't say frightened. I'm mad as hell about all your illegal aliens and those from Central America you permit to use Mexico as a pipeline to the United States. That's going to stop and so are the massive trade surpluses in your favor, seventy billion dollars last year alone."

"There's nothing sinister about our trade," says Lopez Obrador. "You buy more because you have immeasurably more money. The deficit is economically irrelevant but a political weapon for you."

"You're ripping us off just like the Chinese and the Europeans and pretty much everyone else."

Lopez Obrador frowns as Jorge Ramos finishes the sentence.

"You seem to have a persecution complex that's likely to worsen when I, as president, continue to urge Mexicans to move to the United States. That's their inherent right, and we'll defend it."

"Listen, Manuel, we're going to build a wall and add many more border agents and maybe even use our military to secure the border. You're not going to be able to defend anything."

Pointing an index finger at Trump, Lopez Obrador says, "You can't even get your Congress to pay for the wall. And I don't hear any more absurd claims that Mexico will pay. What we'll do is continue to reap our geopolitical inheritance and populate the United States with residents first, and then citizens, who like me are socialists, or at least anti-Republican, and that means anti-fascist."

Trump slaps his finger away and says, "Don't give me sob stories of being mistreated, and forget about being entitled to live in the United States. We're a sovereign nation. Why don't you absorb most of the Central American refugees? They live right next door to the south and speak the same language. You're a hell of a lot tougher on them than we are on you. But that's changing, Manuel, that's definitely changing."

"I'm sure you realize that many things I say are campaign rhetoric."

"I used plenty of campaign rhetoric, too, but I'm still saying the same things now, and doing them. Soon we're going to start taxing your damn remittances from the U.S. to Mexico that drain thirty billion dollars from our economy every year."

"Mexicans work very hard and cheaply for that money and in so doing they build the wealth of the United States. It's strange that a rich man in such a wealthy nation feels so oppressed."

"You and Mexico aren't used to dealing with a president who defends American rights."

Andres Manuel Lopez Obrador smiles, hands a paper to Jorge Ramos, and asks him to read these points recently in the news: "Your most influential enemies are in the United States, not Mexico. Leaders in California farming, and I mean white leaders, are calling for an 'agricultural visa program large enough to accommodate California farmworker needs, and recognize current high skilled immigrant employees and help them gain documentation.' Owners of agribusinesses are tiring of rising business costs that resulted from your immigration crackdown."

"We're going to give those farmworker jobs to American citizens."

Laughing, Lopez Obrador says, "Yes, and I'm a Bostonian. Listen, Donald, the Republicans just lost a bill that would've slashed legal immigration, increased border security, and forced employers to use electronic systems to verify if workers are legal. You're on the wrong side of history."

"It gets down to this, Manuel. We have to do something to build Mexico's economy."

Lopez Obrador nods. "Don't you know?"

"Know what?"

"Please tell your aides to pass along the good news already widely reported in the United States. I have the most ambitious economic program in Mexican history. Most immigrants now come from southern Mexico and Central America. My economic team is every day planning to manifestly increase agricultural production in our southeast, and we're going to do the same in forestry, planting millions of trees, and I'm going to link our grand economic development, which will encourage Mexicans to stay and work in their country, with high-speed railroads to the Gulf of Mexico, and then from the Gulf to the Pacific Ocean. I'm amazed you hadn't heard."

"All I'd heard was the America bashing of your campaign," Trump says.

"I hope this gives us some common goals."

"It sure does. In a business climate like that, you'd have great tourism, and I'll help with special deals on Trump hotels, casinos, and golf courses. We'll turn that region into paradise."

"I'm a socialist but accept your farsighted offers."

Trump Travel Ban

patriots in republican senate blocked obama radical merrick garland from
joining
supreme
court
and
my guy neil gorsuch provided victory margin in banning most terrorists from
iran
libya
somalia
syria
yemen
and don't forget non muslim north korea and venezuela

Honduran Heat Revisited

Honduran money's in a few hands closed to the rusty prison where every cell's sealed and the sole set of keys is dropped by a guard fleeing fire. Outside, guards block firefighters and shoot at a few prisoners not trapped in cells. Most scream as fried or suffocated but quit carrying on when they're charred in stacks totaling three hundred fifty-five stinking so bad survivors put on masks. I wonder if during the next fire guards, prison officials, and politicians will be locked in remaining crypts.

Today, several years later, I note Honduras leads the world in homicides and pours refugees north into Mexico and the United States.

Trump Embraces White Europeans

Have you heard? I hope you have. Lots of European leaders feel just like I do about immigration from the south. They can't build a wall like mine, but they'd like to. Austrian Chancellor Sebastian Kurz, a bright young guy who's only thirty-one, wants a Rome-Berlin-Vienna "axis of the willing against illegal immigration." Okay, maybe he shouldn't have said axis, but at least he wasn't talking about Rome-Berlin-Tokyo. Hungarian Prime Minister Viktor Orbon's already doing something I may have to do here. He's jailing "individuals and nongovernmental organizations for assisting undocumented migrants." Lock illegal employers up and fewer illegal aliens will come. Matteo Salvini, Italy's interior minister, is also a very tough guy who says, "We need a mass cleansing, street by street, piazza by piazza, neighborhood by neighborhood." I better invite them and other nationalists to the White House for a summit meeting on international immigration.

Latin Presidente

harvard harris poll reveals hispanic support
for
trump
up
ten

percent

Babes Block Trump

trump says he's gonna select supreme court justice
who'll
help
overturn
roe
v
wade
plenty of gop women say that ain't gonna happen

Trump in Newsroom

today's violence at capital gazette was tragic and evil
and
i
hope
you
understand
killer
was
mentally
ill and not motivated by my attacks on media

FORTY-TWO

Xi to Trump

Dear President Trump,

Rather than burden you with a long list of complaints, I will simply state that you chose to violate the Iran nuclear deal signed by that country as well as the United States, China, Japan, Russia, the United Kingdom, Germany, and France. Not only that, you initiated a series of arrogant and heavy-handed sanctions designed to make the Iranian people suffer prior to overthrowing a government you don't like because forty years ago it ousted the authoritarian Shah.

I'm going to make this clear: China and Iran are friendly countries and will "maintain normal exchange and cooperation conforming to our obligations under international law, economy, trade, and energy. This is beyond reproach." I don't care that you want every nation currently buying Iranian oil to cease doing so. Surely, you don't believe we're going to salute you and thereby forfeit the six hundred fifty thousand barrels of oil we daily purchase from Iran. Crunch the numbers. That's two hundred thirty-seven million barrels a year we're going to continue to buy. In fact, President Rouhani is my special guest here in Qingdao, for the annual meeting of the Shanghai Cooperation Organization, and he and I have agreed to expand our economic cooperation. It is in our national interest to do so.

You have started a trade war with China, in particular, and also appear determined to wage economic battles with Europe, Mexico, Canada, and, of course, Iran and North Korea. I concede you may have some concerns about Chinese piracy of American intellectual property, and I expect you to understand we will not long tolerate the imperial aggression of your navy in international waters too close to our shores.

I suppose bullying the whole world is an essential part of being a superpower. There are two of us now, and I'm betting on the one that builds a high-speed train in Africa before the other even makes a modern train at home.

Sincerely,

President Xi Jinping

Scott Pruitt Pollutes EPA

As attorney general of Oklahoma I shoved environmental fanatics out of my office, buried them somewhere else, and established a special unit to destroy the jobs-suppressing policies of Barack Hussein Obama. Oil and gas companies knew I was right and contributed more than three hundred grand to my campaigns and applauded each of the fourteen times I sued the Environmental Protection Agency.

President Donald Trump understood I was his guy to ride into Washington and rein in and hopefully dismantle the EPA, which keeps moaning about the myth the world's getting hotter and forest fires more frequent and storms more deadly. All that liberal anguish just means that weather fluctuates. It sure doesn't mean human activity has anything to do with it. It's just God shuffling the meteorological deck once in a while.

Once I got in the EPA saddle I began helping businesses, which help everyone, but some of the college scientists who never worked a day in private enterprise started squalling that my policies would kill scores of thousands of Americans per decade. In fact, I was trying to take a sledgehammer to Obama's environmental excesses and help our country recover from his catastrophic presidency. Our new leader, President Trump, agreed with my vision, and we were making progress. We hadn't annihilated the Obama regulations but we'd made enforcing them more difficult.

Damn right I was worried about security. Look how wild liberals are these days. I put together a security detail as large as twenty agents and installed a big bubble to descend over me in my office when I made secret calls and at minimum I flew first class and hated that since I should've been traveling in private and government aircrafts and did so as often as possible. In a top notch operation like this I naturally had to pay people good salaries and resent enemies charging I overpaid energy-connected friends and wasted taxpayer money sending employees to pick up my dry cleaning. Those expenditures were designed to protect your jobs and not ruin everything by pretending we've got a bunch of environmental problems.

The liberal minority colluded to accuse me of being corrupt and incompetent, and they're a bunch of liars, so I quit.

Misperceptions in North Korea

mike pompeo says
wish i'd met with kim jong un this trip
but north koreans still negotiated in
good faith and we made significant
progress toward denuclearization

north korea says
u.s. betrayed singapore spirit making
unilateral and gangster-like demands
for denuclearization just like trump's
cancerous predecessors

Trump Interviews Brett Kavanaugh

My White House bed is very lonely. Fortunately, I'm asleep and dreaming about one of my most profound duties as president: nominating a Supreme Court justice. In eight years Clinton, Bush, and Obama each only got to select two. In my year and a half I'm already considering my second pick, and I really like Brett Kavanaugh, a great appellate judge, legal scholar, professor, family man, and youth basketball leader, known as Coach K, who appears in my room, standing at attention.

"Tell me your basic legal philosophy in a brief way that won't bore or confuse me," I say.

"Mr. President, a judge's job is to interpret the law, not to make law or make policy."

"I agree. And I like the fact you've gone after both Clintons. My followers love to chant, 'Lock her up.' Maybe we can still do that."

"I tried to get rid of President Clinton when I worked as an associate counsel for independent Counsel Ken Starr."

I give a thumbs up to Brett and say, "Ken Starr's a patriot."

"He certainly is, and in his behalf I was one of the key writers of the Starr Report that emphasized going easy on Clinton would be 'abhorrent' and that he should either 'resign or confess perjury and issue a public apology to Ken Starr.'

"Clinton 'disgraced his office and the American people by having sex with' a ripe intern only twenty-two years of age. His behavior was 'callous and disgusting.' Can you imagine a president behaving like that?"

I hold a palm in front of each breast and say, "Certainly not in the Oval Office."

"I wanted to pin Clinton's libidinous corpse to the wall by asking if he 'twice ejaculated into Monica Lewinsky's mouth' and on another occasion climaxed into a bathroom sink beside the Oval Office and on another if he masturbated into a trash can in his secretary's office."

I throw off the covers and stand on my bed to say, "Brett Kavanaugh, you're the greatest American since Sean Hannity. What did you do next?"

"After Clinton escaped the noose, I worked to elect George W. Bush and served on his legal team during the Florida Recount of 2000. Thank God, we won. The whole world won. Imagine the catastrophes that would've resulted from an Al Gore presidency. Once President Bush took office, I worked first as his associate counsel and then as his staff secretary, helping to nominate conservative judges, publicize Iraqi weapons of mass destruction, and downplay U.S. torture."

"I hear you don't like Obamacare," I say.

"That's true, Mr. President. In fact, as an appellate judge I wrote, 'Under the Constitution the president may decline to ensure a statute that regulates private individuals when the president deems the statute unconstitutional, even if a court has held or would hold the statute constitutional.'"

"What's the hell's that mean?"

"It means you may someday declare Obamacare unconstitutional and our conservative court will agree with you, or, rather, the Constitution, and we'll be rid of that mess. Quite a few people, millions, will lose their health care coverage, though."

"Only temporarily. I'll have Trumpcare ready to take over."

I step off my bed and take a seat at a table and motion for Brett Kavanaugh to join me.

"It's terrible how these collusion loonies are trying to frame me about Russia. I have to worry every day."

Brett nods before saying, "It sounds like you know I wrote, 'Congress should establish the president can only be indicted after he leaves office or is impeached by the House of Representatives and removed from office.' And I also believe 'the president should appoint the independent counsel and the independent counsel should be approved by Congress, not by a panel of judges.'"

"The Congress will protect me from Robert Mueller and his hounds."

"As long as the majority of its members are Republicans."

"I've got no problem there, Brett. My approval rating's soared to forty-five percent."

"That's most impressive, Mr. President. No commander in chief should be burdened by criminal prosecution or civil suits."

"You have an extraordinary legal mind, and I think you've got the job. But I've got to make sure you'll satisfy my base and work to overturn Roe v. Wade."

"I don't like Roe v. Wade but consider it established law, Mr. President."

"Maybe it's unconstitutional," I say.

"That presupposes a fetus has more constitutional rights than the mother."

"They should have equal rights."

"I agree, but that'll be difficult to sell."

I pick up a paper on my table and say, "Here we have a brief summary of Garza v. Hargan from last year. You wrote, 'The government has permissible interests in favoring fetal life, protecting the best interest of a minor, and refraining from facilitating abortion.'"

"I certainly feel that way, Mr. President, but during arguments I also stated that the seventeen-year-old girl should be released from custody, 'presumably a good thing,' and allowed to obtain an abortion if she so chooses."

"Seems like you sometimes take both sides of an issue," I say.

"Politics are essential in every profession."

Notes: *Politico* and *Vox* reported some of Brett Kavanaugh's legal quotes above.

FORTY-THREE

Senate to The Donald

after
trump
lands
in
brussels
u.s. senate votes ninety-seven
two
saying
nato's
friend
and
ally
while putin and russia are not

Trump Warns Europeans

Seated at a large table during the summit meeting in Brussels, President Donald Trump crosses his arms in a tight jacket, eyes leaders of NATO nations, and says, "I love Europeans and they love me. My wife is from Slovenia, my mother from Scotland, and my father was conceived in Germany before his parents, no doubt legally, immigrated to the United States. I own a spectacular golf course in Scotland and property in Ireland. I own property all over Europe and the world. More than anything I want international peace. You only get that when you're really strong. That's why I'm telling you you're paying far less than you should for NATO and defense. You also expect us to do most of the fighting and dying in an increasingly nonwhite world.

"I look at Germany, and Chancellor Angela Merkel over there, and I think, 'What the hell are you doing?' You're paying the Russians billions of dollars to pump natural gas into your country, and at the same time you're making us pay billions of dollars to defend you against the Russians. You're treating us very shabbily and we're not going to take it anymore. We're tired of protecting the French and the British, we're tired of protecting everybody."

Frowning, Merkel says, "Mr. President, you don't understand many of the benefits the United States receives from its NATO membership. You pay more because you're using our military bases to project your power into Central Europe, the Middle East, and North Africa. Without us, you really wouldn't have any strong allies."

"Don't interrupt, Angela. Your days of paying less than two percent of your gross domestic product on defense are history. All of you should be paying four percent, but I'll let you slide for a few years as long as you get up to two percent as soon as possible.

"It's a disgrace you aren't prepared to spend much more. Your great continent's being infested by hordes from the Middle East and Africa, and they're changing your societies and bringing terrorism to what won't be a decent place much longer. Many in Europe agree with me. Look at political trends in Hungary, Poland, and Italy. You've got to defend yourselves against mass immigration. I wouldn't have won if I hadn't understood and emphasized the dangers of immigration."

"We feel that immigrants are adding new energy and experiences to our country and making us better," says British Prime Minister Theresa May.

"Quit dreaming, Theresa. London's a major center for drugs and your murder rate's higher than in New York. Londoners are being stabbed and shot by stoned immigrants riding mopeds while you and London's Arab mayor, Sadiq Khan, do nothing."

"Mr. President," May says, "London's murder rate is lower than that of every major American city. Only briefly did London's rate edge fractionally higher than that of your native city."

Trump stands and points at the ceiling as he says, "Europeans are headed for the dumpster unless you're ready to defend your way of life. I hope you get my message and respond quickly. If you don't, I'm ready to go it alone."

"Auf wiedersehen," says Angela Merkel.

"What's that mean?" Trump asks.

"Goodbye," she says, prompting a standing ovation.

Trump Turnberry

I love playing beautiful golf courses especially when they bear my name. Today I'm by the sea at Trump Turnberry in Scotland and ignoring orange-faced weirdos who're jealous I'm the most powerful man in the world and just roughed up some of their European leaders in Brussels. Today, I'm really having a great time. Turnberry's a magical place I've made more incredible by investing millions to build the finest sand traps and dunes and fairways and greens as well as a lavish hotel where Melania and I are staying before we fly to Helsinki for my private meeting with President Vladimir Putin of Russia.

I really think I could've been a professional golfer if I'd concentrated on that instead of becoming a billionaire playboy. I'm not playing quite as well today as usual. I'm seventy-two and a bit overweight and on these tough and beautiful courses I order the rough deep and thick and right now I'm looking for my drive. There it is. I'll just improve the lie a little – this isn't the British Open – and chip back in the fairway. Nicely done. Now I'll hit an iron and probably get the ball close enough to sink a putt and save par. You can bet it would've taken Obama three or four whacks to get out of this stuff.

I guess you've already heard the good news I'd received several days earlier. The Mueller investigation, which should've finished long ago, announced there's no evidence my campaign people were "knowingly in touch" with the twelve Russian intelligence officers just indicted for hacking into Crooked Hillary's campaign computers and spreading tens of thousands of emails. It was just a coincidence in August 2016 I joked the Russians should find Hillary's missing emails. I have no idea who is Gucifer 2.0, a Russian agent who the same month and year supposedly contacted a "person in touch with the Trump campaign" and offered to help. I didn't need Russian help. The mistreated blue collar workers of America pushed me forward.

Putin's Puppy

Smiling big and happy Vladimir Putin, leash in hand, leads Donald Trump, tongue wagging, onto the small stage in Helsinki, bends to unhook the choke chain around his neck, puts a treat in his mouth, and says, "Go stand behind podium, Donald."

Trump complies, panting, and looks at his master, who says, "Good boy. Speak."

"Until four hours ago and my great conversation with President Putin, Russian-American relations were never worse and that includes during the Soviet blockade of Berlin in 1948 and the 1962 Cuban Missile Crisis," says The Donald. "I knew he was a great man and believed him with all my heart when he told me 'that the Russian state has never interfered and is not going to interfere' in internal American affairs. Why would the Russians do that? We talked about this a great deal, and he may want to address it because he feels very strongly and has a fascinating idea."

Putin speaks about a variety of issues before reporter Jeff Mason of Reuters says, "President Trump, you tweeted this morning that it's U.S. foolishness, stupidity, and the Mueller probe that is responsible for the decline in U.S. relations with Russia. Do you hold Russia at all accountable for anything in particular? And if so, what would you consider them responsible for?"

"I hold both countries responsible. I think the United States has been foolish. We've all been foolish. We should've had this dialogue long ago, years before I got to office. Now that President Putin and I have talked, our countries have a chance to do some great things, like stopping nuclear proliferation. That's why the Mueller probe is a disaster. The United States and Russia control ninety percent of the nuclear weapons in the world. We don't want that critical issue undermined by some silly, unproven allegations about collusion. There was no collusion. We ran a brilliant campaign and that's why I'm in office."

Putin, who's been smiling most of the time, suppresses his grin to say, "We should be guided by facts. You can't name single fact that definitively proves there was collusion. This is utter nonsense. It would've been even more nonsensical if I hadn't hoped that Donald Trump would defeat Hillary Clinton. Candidate Trump repeatedly said he wanted to restore U.S.-Russian relations. I was naturally sympathetic toward one who wanted to work with us rather than Crooked Hillary.

"I have nothing to conceal. As former head of KGB, I always advocate transparency. In fact, I'd like to permit official representatives of United States, including members of Mueller probe, to come to Russia and be present when our legal experts question our twelve intelligence officers recently charged with interfering in U.S. presidential election. But there would be another condition, one of mutuality. We would expect Americans to reciprocate by questioning law enforcement officials and intelligence services of their country, whom we suspect have been responsible for illegal activities in Russia. Naturally, we request presence of our law enforcement."

"Great idea."

"Thank you, Donald. For instance, we want to ask you about Bill Browder and his business associates who earned over billion and half dollars in Russia and didn't pay any taxes."

"I never pay any taxes, either."

"Not now, Donald. Browder and his gang never paid their taxes anywhere, yet they escaped and later contributed four hundred million dollars to campaign of Hillary Clinton. We have solid reason to believe some U.S. intelligence officers accompanied and guided these transactions."

An AP reporter stands and says, "President Trump, just now, President Putin denied having anything to do with the election interference in 2016. Every U.S. intelligence agency has concluded that Russia did interfere. I'd like to ask, who do you believe? And with the whole world watching, would you denounce President Putin for what happened in 2016 and ask him not to do it again?"

"I just wonder why the FBI never took Crooked Hillary's server. Why hasn't someone taken the server? I've been tweeting that for months. Where is the server? I want to know where is the server and what is the server saying? Where the hell are Hillary's thirty-three thousand emails? I'm not worried about President Putin. He isn't after my ass, but the FBI and Robert Mueller sure are."

Stalin Summons Trump

This is entirely unfair. While I had to fight that ruthless bastard Adolf Hitler and form alliance with shrewd but treacherous capitalists Franklin Roosevelt and Winston Churchill, my most celebrated successor, Vladimir Putin, is blessed with world in which his strongest adversary, Donald Trump, isn't really enemy but most ardent admirer. Hitler tried to grind Soviet Union and me into rubble and almost succeeded while Roosevelt and Churchill dawdled about opening a meaningful second front on European continent. In realm of today's politics, I gather that Trump would sacrifice himself, or at least United States, in order to make life more congenial for his hero.

I shall watch no longer. I order Putin to my dacha, personally arrest him, and send him where he's sent many opponents, and I've assigned millions, whether or not they were foes. Henceforth, President Trump will be dealing with me.

"Get him on phone," I order, delighted with all this fancy new technology.

"Vladimir, I guess it's you, sir," says Trump. "Who else would claim to be Stalin?"

"This is Stalin, Donald, and you're to meet me in Kremlin in two weeks."

"Where's Vladimir?"

"Don't worry. Unlike you and me, Putin was leader of second tier nation."

"He's got plenty of nukes."

"They're mine now, and we really must discuss those and other urgent issues."

"Maybe I should let Russia cool off a little. The liberals are claiming Vladimir took me to the woodshed in Helsinki."

"Nonsense. If anything, opposite is true."

"You really think so?"

"I do. See you in two weeks."

On time – I'd sent word not to keep me waiting – Donald Trump marches into my office with his matronly interpreter. I receive him with my new interpreter who says, "I was in your Miss Universe contest here in Moscow."

"You must've won," he says.

"No, I didn't even place."

"The judges were fools."

"You had option to overrule them."

"Sorry, I just didn't see you."

"All right," I say. "Let's reshape world."

"I'd love to," he says.

I motion for Trump to sit before my desk and for his interpreter to sit several feet to his left where mine sits in relation to me.

"Crimea should not have had to be annexed because it's intrinsically part of my Russia," I say. "I don't want any more sniveling from West."

"You won't hear strong complaints from me. I assume the people are happy."

"Ukraine is next."

"For what?"

"For return to its Soviet father."

"There'll be a lot of trouble about that," says Trump.

"You'll complain?"

"More than that."

"What?"

"I'll send Ukraine more defensive military equipment and really lay on the sanctions."

"You think Man of Steel would be bothered by economic inconvenience?"

"You won't like it."

"I survived Nazis killing twenty-five million of us and destroying thousands of our cities and towns. I endured certainty Hitler would torture and execute me if I lost greatest war in history. And you speak to me about not liking puny effects of sanctions. Levy all sanctions you want. We'll cut off oil and gas to Germany and Western Europe. That'll wreck their economies. Yours, too."

"I guess a lot of Ukrainians speak Russian."

"More than half in cities are ethnic Russians. And Russian is preferred language of those who know what's coming. It would be official language of Ukraine if traitors hadn't banished commercial imports of Russian language books. Tolstoy and Dostoevsky wrote in Russian. Have you read *War and Peace*?"

"Not yet, but I will if it's not too long."

"Never mind," I say, lighting my pipe, leaning back, and examining Trump. "You were imprudent to violate nuclear deal with Iran."

"I'll get a far better deal soon," says Trump. "In the meantime, I'm smothering the Iranian government with sanctions. People are rioting all over the country. I doubt their crazy Islamic leaders will last much longer."

"Iran is good friend of my country and China."

"The United States won't let the Iranians acquire nuclear weapons."

I blow smoke in Trump's direction and say, "I commend United States, particularly your predecessor, Barack Obama, for establishing international framework that was in fact preventing what most concerns you."

"The Iranians better stick to the terms of the agreement, or else."

"Or else what?"

"They'll regret it."

"You better not attack them," I say.

"They're not in a position to stop us and neither are you."

"They're prepared to strike you in Middle East and all over world. West will call it terrorism, but Iranian counterattacks will be self-defense."

"That won't last long. When we strike the government and military, the Iranian people will receive us as liberators."

"Sure, like Ukrainians received Nazis as heroes and Iraqis greeted Americans. You'll face massive shit storm far worse than Iraqi debacle, which you swear you opposed in 2003 and thereafter. And while all that's hitting you in face, North Korea will continue developing its nuclear program and be ready to use it, if necessary."

"Kim Jong Un and I established a great relationship. He's quit testing missiles and bombs. The danger of nuclear war has virtually disappeared."

I cough and put down my pipe. "Would you like to share bottle of Georgian wine?"

"I've never had a drink in my life."

I try to smile but don't think I succeed. "You'd have been far better off keeping Iranian deal you had and then trying to get something that good with North Koreans."

"North Korea and Iran will either denuclearize or suffer the consequences."

"We won't tolerate you destroying our neighbors."

"Respectfully, Premier Stalin, you don't have the economic or conventional military strength to stop us."

"We have as many strategic nuclear weapons as you."

"You're not going to nuclear war to save the asses of Kim Jong Un or the Ayatollah Khameini."

"And you're not going to attack when I liberate Baltic States and Ukraine and Belarus and all our other wayward Soviet Republics."

"Go ahead and take them," Trump says. "They'll be burdens more than anything else. That's why they splintered in your face thirty years ago."

I finish my glass of wine and relight my pipe.

"President Trump, I think we're going to get along very well."

"What about Vladimir?"

"He sends his regards."

Trump's Astonishing Offer

I hope you heard when I recently referred to myself as a genius. You know I am or I wouldn't have gotten elected and then created millions of jobs and eliminated the danger of nuclear war and done many other great things. But many of you, especially Democrats, are having trouble following my recent moves so I'll take your hand and lead you.

Last week, I hammered our so-called allies in NATO for being cheapskates and making us pay seventy to ninety percent of the annual costs of the alliance, which is probably outdated and unnecessary due to the peaceful nature of President Vladimir Putin and my special relationship with that extraordinary leader who's on pace to be in power even longer than Stalin.

Don't you understand psychology and friendship and dealmaking?

Obviously I couldn't have stood next to Vladimir this Monday in Helsinki and accused him of interfering in our 2016 presidential election. A shrewd leader doesn't publicly kick another in the balls. Besides, I wasn't giving him a pass. As I explained the following day, I didn't mean to say, "I don't see why Russia would" be involved in undermining our election. I meant to say, "I don't see why Russia wouldn't" be involved. Double negatives are easier to understand, don't you think?

During the press conference I wanted to emphasize that I'd just privately told Putin face to face to stay out of America's elections. I let him know we can't have this, and we're not going to have it. I know I scared him. And I told you about this a couple of days later. Then, sure, I did say I don't think Russia is currently interfering in our political system. I doubt Vladimir would allow that. Still, he'll be responsible if it happens again. He's the president and should know but some of his secret agents are probably operating without his knowledge.

I wish you would understand that no president in our history's been tougher on Vladimir than I have. I've hit him with sanctions and expelled Russian spies and warned him to behave himself in Syria. That's plenty. Our relationship with Russia, and my bond with Vladimir, is more important because the two of us can save the world from nuclear war, which is closer than you think. Take Montenegro, a tiny nation full of very aggressive people. Now that they're a NATO member they could attack someone and start World War III.

I'm not going to let that happen. At this moment I'm offering the greatest peace initiative in the history of the human race. I'm inviting Russia to become a member of NATO.

Tough Trump

if
diplomacy
fails
i'll be putin's worst nightmare
unlike
russian

patsy
obama

Kim Calls Putin

Today, in my secret laboratory, I'm listening in stereophonic sound as Kim Jong Un speaks into a phone and says, "Congratulations on your meeting with Donald Trump."

"Thank you, Chairman Kim," says Vladimir Putin. "Trump and I communicated quite well, and he's already invited me to visit him."

"He's quite eager to be to be friends with the toughest leaders. He had me in a corner, threatening to blow me up as he convinced the world to cut off my economic lifelines. I couldn't imagine he'd agree to meet. And based on my country's history of ignoring agreements while continuing to develop nuclear weapons and ballistic missiles, I doubted he'd believe I really intended to denuclearize the Korean Peninsula."

"That wouldn't be bad idea."

"I'll destroy my nuclear weapons the same day as you and the United States and China."

"We can't give up our nuclear deterrent."

"Neither can we," Kim says. "At any rate, I've got Trump backpedalling. When Mike Pompeo was in Pyongyang recently he thought I was going to meet with him but I didn't have time for a mere secretary of state. Let Pompeo meet with his counterpart Kim Yong Chol. I'll probably talk to Trump once in a while. I'm in demand. I just visited President Xi Jinping the third time this year. He's going to continue to ease sanctions against my country."

"Yes, I know."

"May I ask who told you?"

"I have so many sources, I can't remember. We'll also continue helping you, especially with oil."

"Trump's sanctions will soon be a pile of rubble."

"That may be unfortunate metaphor, Chairman Kim."

"I don't think so. Deterrence works. That's why, as you doubtless know, since meeting Trump I've been upgrading nuclear enrichment sites and building more and better solid fuel engines for my missiles.

Before long I'll simply present the Americans with a fait accompli."

Putin says, "Be careful about double crossing them."

"They know what I can already do to South Korea and Japan and will soon be able to do to them."

"On latter point, Chairman Kim, I believe Americans would strike when they believe you'll imminently have operational ICBM and warhead."

"Maybe I already do."

"I think not," says Putin. "And you better not test them when you think they're ready."

"What would Russia do in the event of a preemptive strike by the Americans?"

"We'd lend political support."

Trump Caps Rouhani

President Trump's not afraid. He's just under a lot of stress but starts to relax until Iranian President Rouhani tweets, "Don't play with my lion's tail or you'll profoundly regret it."

Trump reads the message and fires capital letters, "NEVER EVER THREATEN THE UNITED STATES AGAIN OR YOU WILL SUFFER CONSEQUENCES THE LIKES OF WHICH FEW THROUGHOUT HISTORY HAVE EVER SUFFERED. WE ARE NO LONGER A COUNTRY THAT WILL STAND FOR YOUR DEMENTED WORDS OF VIOLENCE AND DEATH. BE CAUTIOUS!"

Rouhani tweets back, "You fool, so violent and demented, 'twas you who violated our nuclear agreement which is still upheld by everyone else. YOU BE CAUTIOUS."

Trump responds, "We'll completely destroy your country."

"Isn't that what you told Little Rocket Man of North Korea?"

"Damn right, and my warnings brought him to the peace table."

Rouhani tweets, "A thousand laughs. Kim Jong Un's treating you like a buffoon."

"He better not or he'll face fire and fury."

"I doubt he'll ever behave as well as Iran verifiably has since our nuclear agreement."

"You'll soon call and beg me for a deal I dictate," Trump tweets.

"We've already got a deal. Try getting a better one with North Korea. BLEEP YOU."

Trump Logic

trump claims in midterms russians
will
push
hard
for
dems
they definitely don't want trump

FORTY-FOUR

Wild Trump Video

As Russian intelligence agent and aficionado of good educational TV, I'm at first intrigued by excited commentators on CNN and MSNBC who proclaim they have audio tape that offers stunning conversation between Donald Trump and his legal consigliore Michael Cohen. They instead broadcast barely audible and utterly boring conversation about best way to pay former Playboy playmate Karen McDougal to keep silent about her affair years earlier with Trump. I wait several minutes for narrative to improve, squirming as hosts and lawyerly guests talk about nothing. I also worry viewers will nod off or change channels so decide to activate some nonpareil Russian technology and surveillance footage.

In minutes most television networks based in United States are broadcasting blockbuster video that begins with Trump charming Stormy Daniels in hotel room. Stormy disrobes as does her suitor and they begin to make love and doubtless would continue unless Karen McDougal, red-faced and screaming, doesn't storm into room and tackle Trump with such force he's uncoupled from Stormy. Despite her televised testimony to contrary, porn star has been ablaze under real estate baron and curses McDougal whom she springs on and tackles and pins to bed.

"Ladies, please," he says.

He shouldn't fret. Stormy's soon kissing Karen even more vigorously than she had Trump who watches with interest until passion overcomes him and he pounces on both ladies and alternately lies on one while other spanks him with her panties. They all make much noise until someone raps door, and from hallway one of our agents opens it for aroused and cowboy-hatted Vladimir Putin who strides into room, administers rear naked chokehold on Trump to pull him off Stormy whom he mounts and then orders billionaire, "Tend to other one until further notice."

Michael Cohen Explains

trump asks

what kind of lawyer
records his client

cohen responds
a lawyer you plan
to sacrifice

Confronting Michael Cohen

Betrayed by his friend and employer Donald Trump, besieged by the media, and hounded by prosecutors, attorney Michael Cohen silently escaped and now endures another solitary night in his New York hideaway, studying mounds of documents he prays the feds won't discover and listening to explosive tapes only he and Trump know about. Many unpleasant people consider Cohen a mortal threat to the president, and he seldom finds sleep anymore. Thankfully, no one knows where he is. He rents and pays bills under a pseudonym. He enters and leaves his home incognito. He sends encoded messages to loved ones who haven't seen him in weeks. So who could be pounding his iron door?

Cohen grabs his big pistol and tiptoes to a peephole invisible from outside.

"Go away," he shouts.

"Let me in."

"What for?"

"We need to talk."

Cohen cracks blinds over dark tinted windows on each side of the door and, seeing no one else, unlocks the doorknob and two deadbolts and pulls the door open. "You alone?"

"Yes."

He unlocks the doorknob and deadbolt on a heavy black security screen. "Come in."

"I can't believe you plan to testify Donald knew that Don Jr. and others were going to meet the Russians to talk about Hillary."

"I don't have a choice." Cohen puts his pistol in a cabinet.

"You could be faithful."

"At what cost? People are laughing I claimed he didn't know about my payment to Karen McDougal before the election."

"He appreciates that but still needs your help. He's worn out."

"Look how I've aged since he became president."

"You look a lot better than him."

Cohen smiles sadly. "I'm twenty years younger."

"You have a lot of time left."

"I'm not spending it in prison."

"Quit worrying about those files the FBI took."

"I know what's in them," says Cohen.

"You know he'll pardon you."

"He told me he wouldn't."

"He would now."

"Too late," says Cohen.

"This is a president who's creating jobs and defending our borders."

"He shouldn't need my carcass to do those things."

"Please come to the White House and talk to him."

Cohen shakes his head. "I don't like his deals anymore."

"He's done so much for you."

"He made me his legal garbage collector."

"I won't let you keep hurting him."

Cohen points to the door and says, "Time for you to leave."

Reaching into her purse she grabs a cell phone, dials nine-one-one, and screams, "Please help me."

Joe Six Pack Reports

I'm excited looking at an email from Team Trump. They need our participation "because we're close enough to change everything." And we have to. "Illegal voting in the United States wreaks havoc with elections. Every election… it seems we rarely get our candidates elected." Damn right "it's time we do something about this." Team Trump will be "Defending Your Vote (with) radio and TV ads (that) warn illegal aliens, in their own language, of the dangers they face if they vote as a noncitizen." They'll go to prison.

There are links patriots can use to contribute by credit card and

PayPal. I don't make much, because President Trump hasn't had time to get rid of all the Democrat anti-business policies, but I'm going to chip in a hundred bucks. Every real American must stop millions of aliens from casting votes against Donald Trump and other Republican candidates. There's no way Hillary Clinton legitimately got three million more votes than Trump. Now we're going to make sure all elections are fair and Republicans win.

President Trump is also protecting our democracy and way of life by walling off the border and sending invaders back south to their dirty and violent countries. Have you seen the latest polls? A historical high twenty-two percent of Americans, and thirty-five percent of Republicans, consider immigration the country's number one problem. From his great campaign speech that special 2015 day in Trump Tower, I knew Donald Trump was determined to protect us from aliens. Many European countries are just as worried about immigration. We need an American-European alliance to keep ourselves pure.

I know a lot of Democrats are influenced by fake news, instead of learning what's true from "fair and balanced" Fox News, and don't understand economic growth is very high and unemployment really low and black unemployment's the lowest ever. Yeah, I know what Democrats say, that George W. Bush left an economic disaster for Barack Obama and over eight years he turned things around and brought unemployment down from a high of ten percent in October 2009 to under five percent when he left office several years later. Okay, bottom line, President Trump's now got unemployment down around four percent or even less.

We're doing just as well overseas because countries fear and respect us again. North Koreans swear they're going to denuclearize and they better or Donald Trump will fry their asses. I get the feeling that's what he's going to do to Iranians whether or not they develop nuclear weapons. They're terrorists and anti-Israel and Israel's the greatest and only democracy in the Middle East so we must attack their enemies. I'm ready. You know damn well Joe Six Pack's always packin'.

Trump Pumps White Fertility

Worried and nervous but with hope I turn on my television to watch President Donald Trump, wearing pajamas in the White House presidential bedroom, speak about our national crisis.

"Sometimes I wish I had a way to address an all-white audience," he says. "If you're nonwhite I can't prevent you from listening but be forewarned that I'm unabashedly addressing the pure European Americans who dominate my base and have created most that is worthwhile and wonderful in the world. To these extraordinary people, my biological brothers and sisters, I sound the most urgent alarm. Our birthrate continues to decline and more whites are dying than being born in about half the states, including California, New York, and Florida, and in a generation we will be a minority in this great nation.

"What should we do? You're probably baffled, but I'm your president and know precisely what has to be done. We must produce more babies. Whites don't want to have more than two children, many will respond, if they want any at all. That must change, and I will provide leadership. Despite being seventy-two and having five wonderful kids, I will return to the fertility factory and start cranking out more. This sacrifice may not be good for my current marriage, as similar exertions hurt previous marriages, but I must think about what's best for the United States of America.

"Starting this evening I will five nights a week host one, two, or even three young Aryan ladies and in them implant my marvelous Anglo-Germanic seeds that generate beautiful and brilliant children. How will a man my age sustain such a Herculean pace? The answer is quite simple. I will gorge myself with testosterone and other drugs that enhance sexual performance. I encourage all other white men of my generation to do the same. Either do so voluntarily or I may have to someday order you to participate in order to protect our bloodlines. Don't worry about access to medical specialists or the cost of drugs. All that will be paid for by a special new tax cut. If you're a young white man, you are of course encouraged, and may soon be required, to sire at least three children. You will also be paid a fertility bonus of fifty thousand dollars for each child you produce after the fifth.

"I know you're wondering: what about white women of childbearing age? They, too, will be given tax cuts and bonuses for prolific results, and may be required to participate in this program. No longer can we afford to have millions of childless and one-child career women. You can have lots of kids along with a rewarding career. I realize that American women alone will not be sufficient to sustain the vital population boost. We must recruit women from all over Europe, particularly in the East where they are poor and uneducated and anxious to better themselves and should not be walking the streets in places like Madrid and Amsterdam. They need to be in the beds of America, safe and affluent as they conceive millions of nation-saving babies."

From somewhere off camera a woman shouts, "Never," and President Trump orders, "Lock her in her bedroom."

Pastors Visit White House

Thank you inner city pastors for being black and brown in my White House so I can tell you I've cut taxes, reduced regulations, increased American industry, and promoted manufacturing to create almost four million jobs since I was elected, lowering black and Hispanic unemployment rates to lowest levels ever.

FORTY-FIVE

The Booming Economy

These are highlights from my conversation with an economist who graduated from an elite university, served on public policy staffs during the administrations of Richard Nixon and Gerald Ford, and later consulted international businesses.

George Thomas Clark – Okay, I read your recent newspaper columns about economics and foreign policy, respectively. You emphasize what President Donald Trump daily brags about: the economy is growing, unemployment continues to decline, black and Hispanic unemployment are at historic lows, and the stock market remains robust. That's great. But Trump inherited a healthy economy from the Barack Obama administration that had to deal with the domestic and foreign policy catastrophes of the George W. Bush presidency.

Economist – I quibble a little with your assessment that Bush is to blame for the colossal house of cards of 2008. Congressman Barney Frank, a Democrat, was head of the House Banking Committee that allowed a Fannie Mae Ponzi scheme that strangled lending institutions. During that period some government employees were making millions of dollars a year based on their sales of mortgage backed securities. How did a public employee make that kind of money?

GTC – That's outrageous. I hadn't heard. Who were the government employees getting that kind of compensation?

E – I don't have the names at hand. That's something you could easily look up online.

GTC – I've looked at unemployment figures for every month of the Obama administration. After recovering from the avalanche he inherited from Bush, Obama presided over steady decreases in unemployment that led to a rate of about four-point-nine when he left office.

E – Unemployment's at about four percent now. And the latest growth rate, four-point-one percent, is much more sustainable than under Obama.

GTC – Obama had two quarters of four-point-six percent growth and another at five-point-two.

E – Growth now is attributable to tax cuts that create good jobs.

Corporations had parked two trillion dollars overseas to avoid high taxes, and that money's come home and is helping the economy. Under Obama there was a massive increase in spending. The national debt rose from four to seventeen trillion dollars. The Federal Reserve Bank was pushing free money out the door. The Fed is tightening a little now and that's healthy.

Tax cuts are a much better way to generate revenue. That's the Faustian bargain. If you cut taxes, the economy improves and wages go up. Many say it's unfair that the rich get richer. But, if you tax the rich, the poor get poorer, and that's not an option. Remember, John F. Kennedy cut taxes. That's how you grow the economy.

GTC – The George W. Bush administration slashed taxes, and look at the results.

E – One of the key reasons Bush drove up the debt was because of spending for Medicare Part D. It was a lot more expensive than they'd projected.

GTC – Money spent on Medicare Part D is vital. I know because I just got my Medicare card several months ago. I earned it. Conservatives always want more money for defense and less for social programs.

E – Trump has made the country stronger by increasing the defense budget. He's forced NATO to spend more, and the United States and the European Union appear to be ready to cooperate on lower tariffs. Russia's less dangerous than when Obama was president. Trump told Putin he was going to increase the defense budget because of new Russian cruise missiles that violated an agreement. China's also less dangerous. If you can move past Trump's rhetoric and style, the results aren't bad. Strength leads to peace.

GTC – The United States spends more on defense than the next seven countries combined. That makes military spending more of an economic issue than one of defense.

I wanted to ask you about the phrase you used regarding the path this country must choose: "America or Venezuela?" Venezuela's a failed state.

E – That's an extreme comparison I made because Venezuela sold the notion of soaking the rich. Socialism just doesn't work. Look at Spain, Italy, and Greece and their unemployment and economic issues.

Meanwhile, in northern Europe, Germany, specifically, they're working more hours and becoming more conservative.

GTC – In one column you write, "The Democrats' open-border policy is a knife in the heart of the economic prospects" of minorities, women, and young people. I taught English as a Second Language for adults for twenty-four years, and I guarantee that the people coming to this country are working hard and contributing to society. I was always impressed by their high rate of home ownership. More than ten years ago I debated this subject several times with right-wing bloggers and made the point that people come here from Latin America to work. Millions have become farmworkers. Who owns the big agribusinesses that hire them? The wealthy. The Republicans.

E – At this stage almost as many people are coming in from Asia as Latin America. I think immigration is a great thing when it's controlled but problematic when it's uncontrolled and too many unskilled workers come in. We need to manage the economy and manage immigration. Otherwise, minorities and the poor will be the ones who get hurt.

GTC – Thank you very much for your time.

Donald in the Dark

fake news lies i'm worried my wonderful son met
with
russians
to
get
information
on
crooked
hillary
this is done all the time but i didn't know

Trump Reimposes Sanctions

Good morning, America. I stand tall and tough before you to announce I'm reimposing nuclear-related sanctions against Iran. These sanctions had been lifted by the Obama administration and other misguided leaders in Russia, China, Germany, France, Great Britain, and the European Union. Unlike me, they did not realize the Joint Comprehensive Plan of Action is horrible and one-sided and gives the Iranians a clear path toward building nuclear weapons and at the same time allows these international terrorists to retrieve oil revenues they earned but that had been withheld by peace-loving nations of the world.

The United States is determined to enforce our sanctions, and we expect other nations to obey us. I don't like hearing, even as I speak, that our European allies are announcing they deeply regret the reimposition of sanctions and will today issue a blocking statute to protect their investments. I don't care what they do. I'm going to figure out how to destroy Iran's nuclear weapons, which the International Atomic Energy Agency and the rest of the world don't realize they have, and rescue the long-suffering Iranian people who will deserve prosperity and peace certain to come once we stop bombing them.

Melania Defends LeBron James

Soaring through the heavens in mighty Air Force One, President Donald Trump grabs his tweeter and writes, "LeBron James was just interviewed by the dumbest man on television, Don Lemon. He made LeBron look smart, which isn't easy to do. I like Mike!"

Two minutes later, grim and squeezing her pink tweeter, Melania Trump rushes into the presidential suite and says, "I told you to stop making trouble for me and the rest of our family."

"I only tell the truth. The fake media lies."

"Here's the truth," says Melania, who types and then tweets the following, "LeBron James is doing good work on behalf of our next generation."

"What did you write?"

She turns and leaves the room.

Trump follows her into the main cabin, reading his legendary communication device.

"Don't ever betray me again."

"I beg your pardon," she says.

"This'll be all over the world."

"And I'll see it on CNN."

"I told you to quit watching those scumbags. All your news should come from Fox News, where they offer the truth."

"I'm watching CNN," she says, reaching for the remote control.

Trump grabs her right wrist. She shoves her left palm under his nose, forcing him to release her.

"Come on, Melania. The school district in Akron's paying for the school. LeBron's just a figurehead."

"Stephanie, please come here," Melania says. Her spokeswoman Stephanie Grisham rushes up. "Please get me some information about the I Promise School."

"It'll be lies," says Trump.

"Shut up and sit down."

Trump sits on the edge of a sofa, frowning and leaning forward, an elbow on each knee.

Grisham returns with two pages, printed from the internet, and hands them to Melania.

"Listen, Donald," she says. "The LeBron James Family Foundation is committed to pay two million dollars a year, twenty percent or more of the budget of eight million."

"Okay, that means taxpayers are getting screwed for the other six million."

"No, the 'money will come from the district's regular budget, covered mostly by shifting students, teachers, and money from other schools.'"

"And what the hell are taxpayers going to get for their money."

He stands.

"I told you to sit down and listen."

After her pouting husband returns to the sofa, Melania reads, "Students get free tuition, free uniforms, free breakfast, lunch, and snacks, free transportation within two miles, a free bicycle and helmet, access to a food pantry for their family, guaranteed tuition for all graduates to the University of Akron, and parents of students will receive help with job placement and getting their GEDs."

Trump frowns. "These kids are being taught that everything's a government giveaway."

Melania picks up her device and tweets.

"What'd you write?"

"You'll know in a minute," she says.

Omarosa Manigault Writes a Book

I love being on *The Apprentice* with Donald Trump. We have great chemistry. My beauty and charm energize him and he helps me become rich and famous on TV and later hires me to attract blacks during the presidential campaign and then as Director of African American Outreach in the White House. I've got so many good ideas. I can't keep them to myself all day. I've got to share with President Trump.

I'm not going to let all these White House gofers slow me down. They know I've already blown by them. I'm the highest ranking black aide on the premises. They're jealous I'm so good praising the president in public. He's strong and brilliant and helping all workers especially blacks. I'm not loud and controversial except to those I make invisible like John Kelly, White House chief of staff who ignores me for a year before he finally summons me to talk in a secure room. He brings three other men. Why the precautions? I know this is serious and resolve to electronically protect myself against a dreary man my sources reveal has called me a "loser and nothing but problems." That's what envious people said when I worked for Al Gore in the nineties. They lied then and they're lying now.

"There are significant integrity violations concerning you," Kelly tells me.

"Have you talked to the president?"

"We can discuss that some other time. I'm in charge of all personnel at the White House, not the president."

"Are you terminating me?"

"A friendly departure will enable you to land without much damage to your reputation."

"I'd like to talk to President Trump."

"These gentlemen will escort you off the premises," says Kelly.

"I have many personal effects to gather in my office."

"This isn't the time for that. Good afternoon."

Frankly, I'm a lot more athletic and about twenty years younger than John Kelly and pretty sure I can kick his ass. That's why he brought his henchmen. In a few hours President Trump calls and says, "Omarosa, what's this? What's going on? I had no idea."

I wake angrily the next morning, knowing Trump told Kelly to fire me. He's always been a liar. He's publicly lied thousands of times since he's been president and he lied just as much on *The Apprentice* and used a lot of racially offensive language. This time, he's disrespected the wrong lady. I'm smart and I'm a writer soon at work on *Unhinged*, a revelation of what's really happening inside the White House. I guarantee Donald Trump is mentally waning and paranoid as hell and takes extreme measures to keep ex-employees quiet. That won't work with me. My book's already a best seller, even before it's published, and I'm being interviewed all over television and promise my work is accurate and backed up by plenty of tapes.

You know our obsessive tweeter is already attacking me. Now I'm "Wacky Omarosa... Not smart."

It's sad, really. Here's the president of the United States, who should be busy, taking the time to insult me. This is his pattern with everyone, especially African Americans. I knew he degraded people but, once *Unhinged* was already in production, I heard a tape of Donald Trump using the n-word. I wish I'd known before press time. Someone's going to make plenty. That doesn't bother me. My book's already number two on Amazon en route to number one.

FORTY-SIX

General MacArthur Revisits Korea

I saved the Korean people, you're no doubt aware. Communists from the north, materially aided by the Chinese and Russians, invaded south and almost swept our disorganized allies into the sea. From my imperial perch in Japan I decided United Nations forces, principally comprised of Americans, must counterattack and crush the heathens. I then planned the inspired amphibious landing behind enemy lines at Inchon and we soon had the communists retreating as we charged toward the Yalu River.

Our reconnaissance then failed to detect Chinese hordes sneaking in to rout us. I demanded that President Truman allow me to wage total war and seal the Chinese border with dozens of nuclear blasts. Alas, Truman did not understand limited war is for cowards and second rate nations. I publicly rebuked him and he fired me, and I came home to deliver my eloquent Old Soldiers speech to Congress. What I said has proven correct. Don't fight wars unless you seek absolute victory. Look what we have now in North Korea: a bulbous midget is threatening to fire nuclear warheads at American cities.

President Trump, who should have continued to perform on reality TV, believes he made a great deal by forcing Kim Jong Un to promise, in an unenforceable way, that he plans to denuclearize the Korean Peninsula. Based on this farce, Trump boasts he and his special diplomatic friend ended the North Korean nuclear threat. Additionally, and with gruesome fanfare, he's celebrating the return of American soldiers who died sixty-five years ago. Meanwhile, the devious North Koreans continue improving their nuclear weapons.

Think of leaders like Roosevelt, Churchill, Stalin, even Truman, and then consider Trump. This appalling comparison rockets me back to full vigor and into a Pyongyang meeting room with Kim Jong Un.

"You're not adhering to the spirit and terms of our agreement to denuclearize the Korean Peninsula," I tell Kim.

"We have no reason to trust Americans who under your leadership slaughtered so many of our citizens."

"We really don't have anything to negotiate, Chairman Kim. Either begin full and verifiable nuclear disarmament now or the following will take place. South Korea and Japan will begin building nuclear forces far more prodigious than yours. And the United States, at the propitious moment, will destroy your nuclear program."

"You won't get all our weapons."

"We'll get the majority."

"We'll strike South Korea and Japan with nuclear weapons. We'll also devastate you. American cities will look like Hiroshima and Nagasaki."

"You still can't strike the sacred American homeland."

"We'll soon be able to."

"I agree and therefore warn you that our existential moment is at hand."

Trump Hosts Manafort and Cohen

Arriving in separate helicopters, two consiglieres shake hands and enter a van that rushes through dark streets and delivers them to the rear of the White House. Four secret service agents escort them inside and up to the private quarters of President Donald Trump.

"We gonna have any privacy here?" asks former Trump lawyer and handyman Michael Cohen.

"Don't worry. My family's asleep. Come on in the living room."

Trump nods as two agents each search Cohen and Paul Manafort for listening devices.

"I trust you guys and am sorry as hell you were both convicted of eight felonies today," Trump says. "Let's have a seat."

Neither guest moves, and the three men stand and wait for the next shot.

"I'll die in prison unless something happens," says Manafort.

"You should've told me you didn't pay your taxes."

"Did you pay yours?" Manafort asks.

"I'm not the one on trial."

"Only because you're president," says Cohen.

Paul Manafort, seemingly calm as he daily walked to court and smiled for TV, looks haggard and ready to cry. "They'll really nail my ass at the next trial. They can prove Russian oligarchs paid me sixty million for unregistered lobbying. All those guys are buddies of Putin."

"You never told me any of that."

"I sure as hell did," Manafort says.

Trump says, "Relax, Paul."

"I've been saving the next trial as my bargaining chip. If I talk to the feds, they may conclude you broke laws and colluded with the Russians."

"I never colluded with them," Trump says.

Manafort draws a sharp hand across his throat.

"Paul, even though you advised my campaign only a short while, and even though your past and future trials deal with crimes you committed long before I ran for president, you know I'll take care of you."

"What's that mean?"

"I'll pardon you."

"Put that in writing," Manafort says.

"Paul, you've got to handle stress. Just a little longer. Wait until they convict you at the next trial, then I'll pardon you."

Michael Cohen, looking balefully at the president, says, "What about me, Donald?"

"You? The guy who taped our conversations."

"I'm the guy who knows you broke campaign finance laws I was just convicted for. The guy who paid for your screwing Stormy Daniels and Karen McDougal. The guy who's going to tell the southern district of New York, and the feds, everything I know about you. I do that and the five years I'm looking at will be reduced to a few months."

Trump smiles in grimacing fashion. "That's not long at all, kiddo. I'll always have a great job for you."

"After all the shit I did for you, you'd let them put me away?"

"Of course not."

"What are you gonna do?" Cohen asks.

"I'm gonna pardon you, too."

"If you don't, it'll be your ass, for a change."

"Thanks for stopping by, guys," Trump says and walks from the room.

Refuting Cohen

Can you believe that bum Michael Cohen? I virtually pulled him off the streets and hired him as my personal attorney and made him an important part of the Trump organization, the best in the world. He learned how I operated and I trusted him with confidential information for more than ten years. Now he's acting like he was in the mafia. I had no idea he paid two broads to stay quiet and not accuse me of screwing around. I only found out about those payments later. So what's the problem? The money didn't come from my campaign. It's my money. There's no campaign violation.

If you're looking for a good lawyer, stay away from Michael Cohen. He's incompetent and a liar. People now ask how come I didn't notice long ago. I guess he started off loyal before he got greedy. Now he's breaking down like a weakling and making up wild stories about me. I consider loyalty more important than anything. I'm a loyal guy. Ask people who've known me throughout my life. They'll tell you. Donald Trump's loyal as hell. I thought Michael Cohen would repay my loyalty. Instead, this dumbass is pleading guilty to two campaign violations that aren't even close to crimes. Obama had to pay big bucks because of his campaign violations and that was easily settled. This smelly deal with Michael Cohen should be made to go away so I can keep making our country great.

Does Donald Always Pay?

From his desk in the Oval Office, President Trump hollers, "Ivanka, that bastard published the same article again."

She hurries into the room. "Which one?"

"The guy from *USA Today* who says I don't pay lots of people who worked for me."

"Here, Dad, let's print out a copy and review the accusations."

Trump reclines in his chair and sticks both feet on his desk. "We shouldn't have given him an interview."

"We had to respond," she says.

"Just highlight what I need to read."

In a half hour, after The Donald knocks down two cheeseburgers and an order of fries, Ivanka hands him several papers marred red by ink.

Tapping his temple, Trump says, "This great mind already knows how to respond. Just keep tweeting till I'm finished: 'To those lying incompetents who claim I didn't pay them what we contracted, you're damn right. Many of you didn't do a good job. Many didn't even finish the job or were way late. I deducted from your contracts, absolutely. And I'd do the same today. I still dock lousy workers. Your scheming lawyers have a long list of complainers. I remember all of you. The plumbers fixed toilets that still overflowed. Carpet installers put in mildewed carpets that stopped two inches short of the wall. Painters splattered the carpets. Dishwashers supposedly washed dishes that were still dirty the next time I served really important guests. Bartenders served short drinks, pocketed payments, and often got drunk on the job. Real estate brokers failed to close many deals that should've been easy. Lawyers I paid a fortune to defend me against these crooks started padding their invoices. I hired more lawyers to punish them, and then the latest lawyers tried to rip me off. Nobody gets over on me. I'm the mastermind of Trump University.'"

Call from Above

Pushing the telephone at her husband, she says, "Donald, John McCain wants to speak to you."

"Knock it off, Melania."

She puts the phone to her ear and listens again.

"He insists, Donald."

"I don't like pranks," he says, taking the phone. "Who the hell's this? You want the secret service on your tail."

"Look into the heavens and watch my thumb hammering down on you."

Smirking, Trump says, "Even though you've been brain dead a long time, I hear you've seen my bigger thumbs down reminding supporters there was a sick senator who didn't help me get rid of Obamacare. I didn't even have to say your name. They know you're a traitor."

"You can fire up the crazies but you're unqualified to be president. I didn't think you'd win but knew if you did you'd struggle to actually govern the country."

"John, in 2008, you begged me for support and I offered plenty. Then you dropped me because of a few recorded jokes about the ladies. More people should know you screwed around as much as I did and cussed a lot more."

"I should've stressed the real reasons I abandoned you. You'd rather spread hate than make lives better, and you're a phony patriot who could've served in Vietnam but preferred to keep getting student deferments."

Trump turns red. "You calling me a coward?"

"I certainly am."

"You talk a lot for a guy who got shot down because he ignored his control panel alert that enemy radar just locked onto his plane."

"I grant that I was a better prisoner of war and senator than pilot."

"I like guys who weren't captured," Trump says.

"I hope you also admire the dedicated Americans who more every day are wiping your face in the garbage you leave everywhere you've been."

"I won't be missing you, John."

"That's why I ordered you barred from my funeral."

"I wouldn't have come, anyway."

"At last we agree on something."

FORTY-SEVEN

Google Trump

Standing next to his computer in the Oval Office, Donald Trump declares, "It's a disgrace Google rigs search results to show bad stories about me when users search Trump News. You know that can't be right. Liberal fake news organizations like the *Washington Post* and CNN always pop onscreen while the fair conservative news media are blacked out. Google's gagging us. Step on around here with your TV cameras, zoom in, and I'll show you what I mean."

Trump motions for Ivanka to come over and says, "Type: Trump News."

He grins as she obeys. Then he becomes solemn. "Look at all this propaganda. Terrible. 'Trump may be impeached. Trump is getting screwed by Kim Jong Un who's still building missiles and nuclear weapons. Trump is planning to start a war in Iran. Iran nuclear deal was better than anything Trump will ever get with North Korea. Trump's tax cuts may soon cause a budgetary crisis. Credit for jobs boom should go to Obama administration for more than seven straight years of economic expansion. Trump's a narcissist. Trump's an egomaniac. Trump's a swinger. Trump bribes bimbos.'

"All those are lies, of course. That's my point."

The president walks around in front of his desk and motions for cameras to prepare for the next shot. "All right, goofy Google founders, Little Sergey Brin and Invisible Larry Page, either make Google a fair search engine and media outlet or the Republican Congress and I will pass antitrust and other legislation that'll cost you billions. We'll also start promoting other search engines. Yahoo and Bing are far more honest and their revenues will pick up immediately."

Sergey Brin and Larry Page receive this warning in separate yachts. It's unclear who's where but certain they're connected.

"Sergey, what should we do?" Larry asks.

"We better respond before we end up broke as a Trump casino."

"Let's tickle our algorithms and satisfy Trump until he forgets about us and steps in a hole somewhere."

"We'll need to work on this twenty hours a day along with our thousand finest computer engineers around the world," says Sergey.

A few weeks later, Donald Trump stands by his computer in the Oval Office and says, "Sergey Brin, who used to be a Russian, and Larry Page are two of the greatest Americans I've ever met. They're patriots and geniuses and we owe them our truth today and our prosperity tomorrow.

"Bring those cameras around here and zoom in. Ivanka, please come on over and type in: Trump News."

Ivanka, attired in a long low-cut pink dress, smiles at the cameras.

"Okay," says Trump. "Let's see what Google offers. 'Trump is an economic wizard. Trump is better for jobs and production than any president in any country ever. Trump's economic expansion will virtually eliminate poverty in two years. Blacks love Trump for brightening their future. Hispanic citizens of the United States idolize Trump for protecting their homes and jobs from hordes of illegal aliens. Satellite evidence indicates Kim Jong Un is rapidly destroying nuclear and ballistic missile facilities and will soon be unarmed and vulnerable to a joint U.S.-South Korean invasion. China is terrified of Trump and will quadruple its purchase of American products and rush half its navy into mothballs. Stormy Daniels says it never happened. Robert Mueller says the independent investigation has gone too far and must end right away. Trump will win two Nobel Peace Prizes. Trump likely to receive at least sixty percent of popular vote in the next election.'

"I could go on but am too humble for that."

Trump Swings in Kern County

Donald Trump is visiting Republican hotbed Bakersfield where native son and House majority leader Kevin McCarthy hosts him.

After thrilling a crowd of believers downtown, Trump says, "Kevin, it's hotter than hell. Is it any better up in those hills I can barely see?"

"Sure, Tehachapi's a lot cooler and you can breathe."

"Let's go."

A secret service agent says, "Mr. President, we haven't done any advance security."

"Don't worry. No one knows we're coming."

A caravan of fortified beasts cruises up Highway 58, gaining elevation and passing oak trees, and after thirty miles moves by Keene where McCarthy points. "Right over there Cesar Chavez lived and had his United Farm Workers offices."

"Where's he living now?" asks Trump.

"He died twenty-five years ago."

"He hated businessmen, I know that."

In ten more minutes, rolling by an occasional thirsty pine, they enter Tehachapi and cruise down the main street.

"Don't quote me, Kevin, but this is a hick town. Do they even have a golf course?"

"Horse Thief Country Club's about ten miles from here. It's surrounded by little mountains and real pretty."

"We've got time for nine holes. Let's do it."

"I played there all the time as a kid," says McCarthy. "It's an exciting course, lots of boulders and elevated tees."

"I hit massive tee shots from elevated tees. You're twenty years younger, Kevin, but I'll beat you by five strokes today."

After cruising through the tiny community of Stallion Springs, McCarthy says, "Okay, we're just about there. Look to your right."

Trump turns his full face to the window and says, "I get excited every time I see a beautiful layout."

"Coming right up."

"Where?"

"I thought it was there. It's got to be around the next turn."

"All I see is brown weeds high as my ass."

"I know there's a long par five around here," says McCarthy.

"You sure we're on the right road?"

"Positive. This is it. Oh..."

Pointing, Trump says, "They've stopped watering. The place is a cow pasture. Why didn't you know they'd closed the course?"

"I'm sorry, Mr. President."

"Where was the clubhouse?"

McCarthy replies and the caravan turns right and then right again into a parking lot sprouting weeds. The clubhouse and restaurant are shuttered.

"This is a shithole, Kevin. I may have to back someone else as the next speaker."

"Please don't overreact, Mr. President. I'll take you to lunch at the beautiful motel on the hill overlooking the course."

They go back the same road about a half mile and turn off to climb a steep hill leading around trees and rocks to the motel and a parking lot.

"There are a few cars here, but the place looks abandoned."

"No, there's a young man," McCarthy says, powering down the window. "Hi, there. That great restaurant's still open, isn't it?"

"No," the fellow says, "this is just a dorm for the extreme sports academy down the road."

Trump frowns.

"That dining room had the greatest view in Kern County," McCarthy says. "You could see the whole valley as well as the golf course. We can walk around the building and I'll show you the patio.

"Okay, Kevin, get my clubs in the trunk. I'm gonna hit some bombs over the road and into the weeds."

Trump Investigates Op-Ed Leaker

Like a water buffalo President Trump marches back and forth in front of his top aides in the White House ballroom, waits till he senses fear, and roars, "I'm going to give lie detector tests to every one of you then have you strip searched, whatever it takes to find out who wrote that lying op-ed column in the failing *New York Times*. You've all sworn a personal oath to me. Breaking that oath is treason. I demand the *New York Times* and its loser editors identify the criminal. Who'd write that many of you are working to frustrate my worst inclinations? I've given us the greatest economy and should be celebrated. Raise your hands if you agree."

Using cameras and electronic tablets, several secret service agents verify everyone raises a hand.

"The op-ed traitor also claims I'm anti-trade and a bully. I'm just defending us. I love great trade. But we've been treated unfairly for decades, and I'm finally doing something about it. Who understands I'm a brilliant backer of fair trade? Hold up your hands."

Trump studies the group.

"The op-ed coward says I'm against democracy. Some of you supposedly feel the same way. I don't believe that. I love freedom more than anyone and am ready to sacrifice lives, millions if necessary, to protect our liberty. How many understand I'm the most pro-democracy man in the world?"

Everyone raises at least one hand.

"Who the hell would think I'm acting in ways detrimental to the health of our republic? I'm saving the country from immigrants and liberals and nuclear madmen. Go ahead. Let me know if you think I'm making America great again."

No one fails to raise a hand.

An agent hands Trump a piece of paper he reads. "Our op-ed enemy doesn't like my leadership style and uses a lot of big words to describe it – 'impetuous, adversarial, petty, ineffective.' Only idiots believe that nonsense. In fact, I'm bold, tough, and effective. If you agree, let me see your hands."

Referring to the same paper, Trump says, "Our traitor claims I 'rant' and often make 'half-baked and reckless decisions.' Didn't you see the Republican debates in the primary? I was the only cool cookie in the bunch. If you know I'm not an unstable blabbermouth, put your hands in the air."

Trump smiles, and tries to look at everyone in the room before he says, "The press is the enemy of the nation. Raise your hands if that's true."

Several high-tech agents surround Trump and tell him he's unanimously confirmed as great.

"Ladies and gentlemen, rest assured, I'm going to preserve our freedom by sending federal troops to occupy that cave of traitors called the *New York Times*."

Hurricane Donald

I'm always on duty so I can squeeze tweets that provide the most important opinion in the world. Right now as Hurricane Florence batters the Carolinas you need to know I "got A pluses for our recent hurricane work in Texas and Florida" and should have gotten the same in Puerto Rico but the island was inaccessible and had "very poor electricity and a totally incompetent Mayor of San Juan."

When I went down there and threw paper towels to grateful Puerto Ricans they told me at most eighteen people had died. But, in the following months, I started to hear rising death tolls that eventually reached three thousand. Turns out my enemies were adding those who died for any reason, like old age, murder, and alcoholism. Everyone should instead be talking about billions of dollars I've raised for rebuilding the island and making sure everyone has electricity.

I'm ready to battle Hurricane Florence and save the Carolinas, too, and am positive no one will ever accuse me of not doing enough. I've got the National Guard ready to move in along with all the local police and firefighters and politicians. Once the wind stops blowing, I'll be down there, too, making sure everyone's all right and understands who made sure fatalities were limited. Don't blame me for buildings being damaged or destroyed. Even I can't prevent that.

FORTY-EIGHT

Trump Defends Kavanaugh

I have to tell you that Brett Kavanaugh is such an outstanding man it's very hard for me to believe as a drunk teenager he pulled a girl into a bedroom, locked the door, turned up the music, threw her on the bed and jumped on her and tried to pull her clothes off, and put his hand over her mouth when she screamed. I'd believe that about Bill Clinton. And, yeah, except for the drinking, I guess plenty of you'd believe that about me. But Justice Kavanaugh doesn't seem like that kind of guy. In thirty-six years since, no other woman has accused him of grabbing her or doing anything else inappropriate.

Some are demanding an FBI investigation so we can learn more, but we don't have time to wait on Justice Kavanaugh's Senate confirmation. The mid-term elections are coming in early November. I don't trust the FBI, anyway, and neither should you. They're a phony, incompetent, and biased group. Besides, this kind of thing isn't what they do unless I tell them to.

I take this whole thing seriously, though. I'm a high morals guy and think Christine Blasey Ford should have an opportunity to testify under oath before the Senate, and if she's convincing, I'll have to make a decision. Justice Kavanaugh has to defend himself, and I'm sure he'll do a great job. I think his friend Mark Judge, who was also in that party bedroom, should step up and testify what he's already said: he never saw Brett behave like that.

It's not a big deal Mark Judge wrote a Noel Coward quote in someone's high school yearbook: "Women are like gongs and should be struck regularly." Come on, that was a joke. Noel Coward was a funny guy. So is Mark Judge. I know Judge had a problem with alcohol, and maybe Brett and Christine were also out of it that night and none of them really remember exactly what happened. Maybe Brett Kavanaugh wasn't even at that party. Who knows?

Party Time

young
brett

kavanaugh
shoulda
avoided
keggers

Donald the Defender

Oh, Jesus, here comes another one. First, Christine Blasey Ford says when she was a drunken chick of fifteen Brett Kavanaugh groped her at a high school party in a year and house she can't remember. You know damn well that's political. And it's totally political that Deborah Ramirez, another hard-drinker, needed more than thirty years, and six additional days last week, to get it straight in her scheming head that it was Kavanaugh who shoved his penis in her face during a drinking game in a dorm at Yale. Brett Kavanaugh probably wasn't even there. Ramirez is just upset some fellow drunks taunted her, "Kiss it, come on, kiss it." It had to be some other guy pulling up his pants and laughing at her.

Even the *New York Times,* which is always hostile to me, wouldn't touch this story after contacting dozens of classmates about the allegation. Most didn't respond to requests for interviews and those who did declined to comment or said they weren't even there or didn't remember. If you saw something like that at a party or anywhere else, you'd never forget. Shame on the *New Yorker,* supposedly a classy publication, for printing gutter gossip to try to ruin a man's life and keep me from building the right kind of Supreme Court.

The Kavanaugh Defense

Yeah, I liked beer in high school and college. Didn't you, Senator? No, I never passed out. I just went to sleep. That's not blacking out. How about you, Senator, do you black out when drinking. Okay, you don't have a drinking problem and neither do I and I never did. It doesn't matter that people who knew me in those days say I was often drunk and belligerent. They're lying or maybe mistaken. I still love beer and always will because I handle it so well. I've got a hundred percent rating as a federal judge from the American Bar Association.

In high school I was captain of the basketball team and a cornerback and wide receiver on the football team. I worked my tail off. I lifted weights in the summer for football and also played basketball to get ready for the regular season. On Sundays I always went to church. For me that was a matter of faith. Academically, I was number one in my class, along with a couple other guys. At Yale I played junior varsity basketball and studied in the library every night and got exceptional grades. I've always had great discipline.

I want you senators to quit asking me if the FBI should investigate allegations I assaulted Christine Blasey Ford and a couple of other girls. The FBI's already investigated my background six times. Isn't that enough? I'm telling you today it's too much. Of course I'm speaking loudly and at times choking up and crying. I didn't see Dr. Ford's testimony but I hear she was emotional too. I don't bear her any malice. She's got some problems, but they don't have anything to do with me. One of my daughters prayed for her.

Are you praying for me? You should be. You senators and liberals and the vengeful Clintons have permanently damaged my life with your lies and attacks. We don't need the FBI to investigate the latest allegations. I'm right here. Ask me. All four people Dr. Ford said she remembers from the party have said they didn't remember anything unusual or even remember the get-together at all. Under penalty of felony they signed their names on statements certifying my innocence. I'm not going to say I want an FBI investigation of Mark Judge. We were good friends but I haven't seen him in several years. He developed serious problems with drinking and drugs and almost died a couple of times. Mark Judge has already said I never did anything to Christine Ford, who I don't even remember, and not because I was too drunk.

It's a disgrace what you Democrats are doing to me. Advice and consent have been replaced with search and destroy. One of you called me "evil" and another said I was "a nightmare." I'd say the same about you. My family and I have been receiving physical threats and people are sending vicious emails to my wife. We've already had plenty of Judicial Committee hearings. You couldn't take me out on the merits, so there's a last-minute smear campaign, a calculated political hit. This is a circus and the character assassination is grotesque. The consequences will last for decades. In my fifty-three years and seven months of life I'd never been accused of anything, especially assaulting a woman, until a little over a week ago. This onslaught of last-minute allegations doesn't ring true. Give me a second, here, I'm breaking down.

I've been under scrutiny for twenty-six years because I've had jobs at the highest level. I was part of Ken Starr's team that tried to destroy Bill Clinton. Now there's a sexual predator. Donald Trump isn't a predator and neither is Brett Kavanaugh. We don't need more than the six FBI background investigations we've already had. I'm innocent. I'm innocent. Look at these calendars I've kept like a diary most of my life. Right here, in the summer of 1982, you can see I wrote I was out of town on the weekends of August 1982 when Dr. Ford says I assaulted her. I couldn't have. You're destroying my family and me. Just a minute, I'm choking up.

I was a virgin in high school and many years after that. I've never been in a room with Christine Ford. You don't need to ask Mark Judge again. He's already signed a paper, under penalty of felony, that none of this ever happened. I never ground my genitals into her. I've never been sexual with her. The police have never contacted me about this. They know I haven't done anything wrong. There's no reason to listen to the American Bar Association's demand for FBI investigations of last-minute allegations that are lies designed to destroy me. I'm already ruined. For the rest of my life my name will be associated with this. It's time to ignore my accusers and move on and vote to confirm me as a Supreme Court justice.

Trump Thrills Mississippi

I love traveling around this huge country and speaking to the honest working people who love me and wait hours to get into my rallies. They know I'm one of them even though I'm really rich and have spent most of my life in luxurious places around other wealthy people and plenty of babes. I know it's amazing but I'm the guy working whites and evangelicals trust.

It's great visiting here in the Bible Belt, in Southaven, Mississippi, a suburb of Memphis. Folks in Southaven, where the average house costs about a hundred forty grand, are thrilled to be around a guy who spends that much a month on hairdressing and makeup. I love their energy and now I'm really going to excite them.

Can you believe what the Democrats are doing to poor Judge Brett Kavanaugh during the Senate confirmation hearings for the Supreme Court? These days you're guilty until proven innocent and that's very dangerous for our country. The Democrats have nothing. Dr. Christine Blasey Ford says she had one beer some night long ago. One beer. I hold up a powerful index finger. Okay, how did you get home? I don't remember. How'd you get there? I don't remember. Where was the place? I don't remember. How many years ago was it? I don't remember. I don't know, I don't know, that's about all she knows. And for that, a man's life is shattered.

These simple workers are cheering and filling me with love. I'll fill them with something else. If the Democrats get control in November, they will raise your taxes, flood your streets with criminal aliens, weaken our military, outlaw private health insurance, and replace freedom with socialism.

These folks won't let that happen. They'll do what I say because they know I represent strength and winning and freedom and truth. Look what a few posted on YouTube after my sermon.

"Greatest president in American History BY FAR & Gold Bless America."

"That's one of the best rallies I've seen. Love the way he got stuck into lying Dems and the lying Dr."

"Missed rally working OT… Production UP BIGLY over past year… Thank you Mr. President."

"Remember to vote. Republicans vote on November 6th. Democrats vote on April 1st (April Fools Day)."

Come on now, you Democrats. With my great economy and fanatical support and my star power, which one of you can beat me in 2020? Looks like none of you can.

Senator Kennedy Bongs Democrats

Democrats who've been smoking bongs sometimes ask if I'm President John Kennedy. No, I say, I'm Senator John Kennedy of Louisiana, a righteous and God-fearing Republican, and I want you Dems to sober up and admit that no amount of FBI investigation of Judge Brett Kavanaugh will ever satisfy you. I don't think some of you were even breast fed, you just started eating raw meat.

Open your eyes, the FBI's supplementary investigation is in. Right now we're not going to confuse people by showing them the full report but I guarantee you that Kavanaugh's buddy Mark Judge and Christine Blasey Ford's friend Leland Keyser still say they don't know anything about the party where Kavanaugh allegedly assaulted Ford while Judge watched and laughed. Meanwhile, Keyser supposedly sat downstairs.

At this point I'm sure the three fence-sitting Republicans are going to vote to confirm. Flaky Jeff Flake of Arizona says no new corroborative information came out, and Susan Collins of Maine says the FBI appears to have provided a very helpful investigation. Lisa Murkowski must be roaming the Alaskan wilderness and still hasn't read the report but when she does she'll come around.

The chairman of the Judiciary Committee, Chuck Grassley of Iowa, says what everyone surely understands: "There's nothing in the report we didn't already know. These uncorroborated accusations have been unequivocally and repeatedly rejected by Judge Kavanaugh, and the FBI could not locate any third parties who can attest to any of the allegations."

Democrats are alleging the latest investigation was shallow and hurried. Put down your bongs. It's time to vote.

Kavanaugh Confirmed

God, I'm a rock star like there's never been and so happy to be your incredible president here in excited Topeka. Hello, Kansas. I know you're thrilled this afternoon the Senate confirmed Brett Kavanaugh to the United States Supreme Court and I already signed his commission. He's a great man and will sit proudly alongside Justice Neil Gorsuch, another guy I picked. Together they and the conservative majority on the court will uphold your sacred rights and defend your God-given freedom.

I'd like to thank Republicans for refusing to back down in the face of the Democrats' shameless campaign of political and personal destruction. Radical Democrats tried to delay, destruct, and demolish Brett Kavanaugh, a man of great character and intellect. What he and his family have endured at the hands of Democrats is unthinkable. In their quest for power they have turned into an angry mob that threw away due process.

In just four weeks you'll have a chance at the ballot box to render your verdict about the Democrats' conduct. We must stop radical Democrats – that's what they've become – and increase our majorities in the Senate and the House. We need more Republicans. Every American has a profound stake in the upcoming election. If the Democrats are willing to cause such destruction in pursuit of power, just imagine the destruction they'd cause if they ever obtained the power they so desperately crave. You don't give matches to an arsonist and you don't give power to an angry left-wing mob.

Kavanaugh Begins

I just got sworn onto the Supreme Court and vowed to seek to be a force for stability and unity. The Supreme Court is an institution of law. It is not a partisan or political institution. The Justices do not sit on opposite sides of an aisle. Ken Starr and Donald Trump and my guys will caucus with the Clintons and that gang as long as they're morally pure.

FORTY-NINE

U.N. Comedian

Standing hefty and happy before the United Nations General Assembly, President Trump says his administration accomplished more in two years than almost any other in our history, evoking much laughter Trump says he didn't expect. But that's okay, he's proud to be an engaging fellow who warns that Iran is a brutal and corrupt regime that sows chaos, death, and destruction across the Middle East. The Donald won't let that continue since he cancelled the nuclear deal Iran was and is adhering to and has levied many sanctions and will impose many more because he cannot allow the world's leading sponsor of terrorism to possess the most dangerous weapons. One senses that even if Iran never tries to build and deploy nuclear arms Trump will attack anyway. The most accomplished administration in history needs a war and is banging the drum.

Jim Brown Endures

i'm still toughest running back on earth or
couldn't
have
survived
kanye west blowing trump in oval office

Brian Kemp Defends Democracy

Patriotic Georgians are going to elect this good old boy governor because I'm so conservative I run ads (explosion in background) to blow up government spending. I own lots of guns (see all those behind me and the one I'm cocking) that no one's taking away. My chain saw's ready (it starts right away) to rip up some regulations. I got a big truck (I'm driving) in case I need to round up criminal illegals and take 'em home myself. Yep, I just said that. If you want a politically incorrect conservative, that's me, the current secretary of state who'll be moving up in November after fair and square beating Stacey Abrams, a tax and spend liberal even more dangerous than Barack Obama.

I strongly support President Trump, our troops, and ironclad borders, and (putting a hot right hand on my heart) I stand for our national anthem. If any of this offends you, I'm not your guy. I'm the tough secretary of state who's cancelled one point four million voter registrations the last six years, and during this campaign I've put fifty-three thousand voter registrations on hold because they aren't "exact matches" with information at the Georgia Department of Driver Services or the Social Security Administration. Sometimes there's a missing hyphen or transposed numbers and sometimes the deceptions are more outrageous than that.

It doesn't matter that seventy percent of those registrants are black and as secretary of state I'm overseeing an election where I'm running against a black candidate. Like I've told my campaign people to repeatedly tell you, I'm "fighting to protect the integrity of our elections and ensure only legal citizens can cast votes." I'm not worried about losing, anyway. Yeah, the polls say Abrams and I are in a statistical dead heat right now, but only thirty-two percent of the voters are black and I'll find some more who cheated to register and keep 'em away from the voting booths. No one's getting over on me. My guns and explosives and big truck are ready to rock.

Fair and Balanced

A little after one p.m. today Fox News is offering the following headlines:

Elizabeth Warren's DNA test mocked… average Native-American link could be stronger

Dems poised for historic, post mid-term push to oust Trump if House retaken

Democrats prove they are the party of exploiting women

Robert De Niro offended by behavior of Trump and Republicans in general

Alec Baldwin wants to overthrow President Trump

FIFTY

Calling Donald Trump

"Is it really him?" asks Donald Trump.

"It certainly sounds like the man I've often spoken to," says an unnamed advisor.

"Hand me the phone. This is President Trump. Is this really Jamal Khashoggi?"

"It is," says the caller.

"Are you all right?"

"No, President Trump, I am not."

"There've been some pretty bad stories going around, and I don't like hearing them. Where are you? Still in the Saudi consulate in Istanbul?"

"They tortured and dismembered me there, sealed my remains in boxes, and in a darkened van rushed me to the airport. I'm back in the nation I wouldn't otherwise have returned to."

"You shouldn't have gone to the consulate," says Trump.

"They lured me there as the only way I could get immigration papers for my fiancé. U.S. citizens can go to their embassies around the world without being set upon by hit squads. Three of those guys in Istanbul were bodyguards of Crown Prince Mohammed bin Salman."

"I'm not happy about what happened."

"What are you going to do? At least punish them economically."

Trump rises behind his Oval Office desk. "I don't like stopping massive amounts of money pouring into our country. If I don't sell the Saudis a hundred ten billion dollars of military equipment, they'll just buy from the Russians and Chinese. What do you expect me to do?"

"Don't you understand what kind of men the prince and his henchmen are?"

"I hear things," says Trump.

"Now hear this. They've killed ten thousand civilians in Yemen."

"They're protecting the Yemenis from the Iranians."

"The Saudis are the problem in Yemen. And in Saudi Arabia – did you hear my BBC interview in England several weeks ago?"

"No."

"Here are the key points. Those in power arrest people who do nothing more than say something critical at a dinner party. This has happened to some of my friends. They aren't even dissidents. I'm a writer who just wants to express his opinion in the *Washington Post*. Saudi Arabia would be a better country if we had freedom of expression. Every couple of months the prince surprises us with a multi-billion-dollar project that wasn't discussed in a parliament or newspapers. People just clap and say, 'Let's have more of those.' They're making other critics like me disappear, and they're still publicly beheading people."

Trump drums his desk. "Don't forget, Crown Prince Mohammed bin Salman is finally giving Saudi women the right to drive cars… Hello, Jamal… Mr. Khashoggi…"

Looking at his advisor, Trump says, "I think we got disconnected."

Saudi Explanation

All right, everybody, I just got off the phone with the King of Saudi Arabia and he flatly denied he has any knowledge of whatever may have happened to his "Saudi Arabian citizen." He's trying to help, though, and said he thinks Jamal Khashoggi may have been a victim of fifteen "rogue killers" who flew in from Riyadh and nabbed Khashoggi after he got immigration documents for his fiancé and left the Saudi consulate in Istanbul.

We'll get to the bottom of this. We'll leave nothing uncovered. But the king's a good guy who's buying arms and selling us lots of oil and standing up to Iran and he really likes me and the United States so maybe the killers weren't really bodyguards of Crown Prince Mohammed bin Salman.

Smiles in Saudi Arabia

I love being Mike Pompeo because, as secretary of state, I get lots of exciting jobs. Today I'm in Saudi Arabia with young Crown Prince Mohammed bin Salman. We're two husky fellows – don't call us fat – and we're very happy and smiling big. We really like each other and we love each other's countries. That's why I'm here. I want to help Saudi Arabia, our best friend in the oil-producing Arab world and a bulwark against Iran.

The Saudis are in a tight spot because Jamal Khashoggi, a trusted insider until he moved to the United States and became a liberal journalist writing newspaper columns critical of the reform-minded prince. Khashoggi complained about many things he shouldn't have like the roundup of rich Saudis and their detainment in a luxury hotel. How many potential traitors get the five-star treatment? It was an accident one detainee died and about twenty others had to be hospitalized. About those public beheadings, Khashoggi perhaps made too big a deal. Prince Salman could've hidden those falling heads, but he's an upfront guy. Sure, he imprisons his critics but lots of leaders do that, and my boss, President Trump, would lock up plenty of his defamers if he could. Maybe someday he'll be able to.

Jamal Khashoggi should not have been so strident in criticizing Saudi mass murder in Yemen. We want our friends to combat Iran there. I know there aren't many Iranians in Yemen but plenty of Houthi rebels are threatening to turn the country into an Iranian domino and we can't have that and we also want our allies to get plenty of war practice, using great weapons purchased from us, because we'll need their help when President Trump decides to attack Iran for being an international terrorist seeking nuclear weapons.

"Secretary Pompeo, we'll cooperate in every way," says Crown Prince Mohammed bin Salman.

"I know you will," I say, "and so much appreciate that you've 'agreed on the importance of a thorough, transparent, and timely investigation that provides answers.'"

"Beautifully stated," says the prince.

"I must tell you, Prince Salman, that it didn't look good yesterday when, in front of journalists outside your consulate in Istanbul, you sent in a cleaning crew armed with mops, trash bags, and bottles of bleach. That kind of clean up usually takes place after the forensics team does its work."

"The Turks were a little slow sending them in."

"You wouldn't let them in."

"That may also have been a factor."

"You know, lots of times there's evidence even after a seemingly thorough cleanup."

"We have nothing to hide," says the prince.

"So you swear you didn't plan the murder and dismemberment of Jamal Khashoggi."

Prince Mohammed bin Salman pumps his fist. "I certainly did not."

"I believe you."

"I may have approved Mr. Khashoggi being interrogated in the gentlest manner. Only the blunders of a tragically incompetent intelligence official have caused this problem."

"The official was no doubt derelict, Prince Salman, but it arouses suspicions when you send to Istanbul fifteen agents accompanied by a forensics expert carrying a bone saw. The Turks also say they have eleven minutes of audio of the interrogation you approved."

"And that was mishandled by the tragically incompetent intelligence official."

I place two big hands palms down on the prince's vast desk and say, "There'll have to be consequences for this. Even Republicans in the Senate are outraged."

"Don't threaten us, Secretary Pompeo. Don't test out patience. We'll turn off the spigot and drive oil to a hundred a barrel and ruin President Trump's wonderful economy, and then the Democrats will start winning elections."

"Relax, Prince Salman. We'll more or less back your version because we know we have a historic mission in Iran."

We rise, smiling and husky, and shake hands before calling in the photographers.

Trump Update on Khashoggi

I'm just being very fair and careful by not allowing any more of this guilty until proven innocent garbage like happened to Brett Kavanaugh. But don't forget, I already said we're going to get to the bottom of this. And we are. The Saudis aren't going to make a jackass out of me, and liberals aren't going to force me ruin an alliance with the best-armed and most loyal Arab nation.

Don't preach to me. I knew before you that some bad guys, rogue killers or maybe even agents of Crown Prince Mohammed bin Salman, jumped on poor Jamal Khashoggi, and I'm anxious as you to hear whatever audio recording may have come from surveillance devices the Turks had planted in the consulate.

The whole thing is pretty gruesome. Can you imagine that forensics doctor putting on headphones and telling his helpers, "Listen to music. It'll relax you."

Letter to Mohammed bin Salman

Dear Mohammed,

I'm not going to address you as Crown Prince since, like many, I don't recognize the legitimacy of those who inherit political power unless, as in the case of Kim Jong Un, they're armed with nuclear weapons.

You, Mohammed, have doubtless been quite busy lately, planning or at least overseeing an operation during which your agents lured Jamal Khashoggi to a gruesome death. His criticism you evidently could not endure.

I wonder how long it took to realize you'd made a serious mistake. You can jail your critics in Saudi Arabia, you can behead many of them, and you can kill thousands of Yemeni civilians, using weapons from the United States paid for with oil money that represents most of what your country can produce. You can also collude with Donald Trump, Mike Pompeo, and John Bolton about the best way to continue framing Iran as a nuclear threat and push American leaders to do what they at any rate crave: attack Iran in an attempt to destroy nuclear facilities and remove that nation's leaders. This criminal act of war, which appears almost inevitable, is crude and misguided since informed people realize the International Atomic Energy Agency has ten times certified Iran is in compliance of the Joint Comprehensive Plan of Action guidelines restricting development of nuclear weapons.

You're aware of all this, and you also know people around the world are enraged about your barbarism. You've blundered so badly even some Republicans in the United States Senate are denouncing you. And you know where this is leading. Your inherited position, consecrated in the blood of those who opposed such a young and unstable man running

Saudi Arabia, is very much in peril. Donald Trump will back you, if he can. He'll back anyone who agrees with him.

Unfortunately, Mohammed, many other princes in Saudi Arabia would offer the same support and are already maneuvering to replace you. This doesn't mean you're certifiably doomed. Unlike Jamal Khashoggi and other critics, your heart yet beats and you may be able to survive. But you can't kill all those who oppose you, and you won't be able to terrorize the Middle East for the next half century, as you plan. Other forensic pathologists have been contacted about the biggest job yet.

Sincerely,

GTC

Mohammed bin Salman Writes

I'm mad as can be at some of my generals, advisers, security agents, consular secretaries, and others. Their recent incompetence has temporarily tarnished my exemplary reputation. I would've cleared up this whole mess two weeks ago if these rogues hadn't deceived me.

First they told me Jamal Khashoggi rapidly took care of his fiancé-related paperwork at our consulate in Istanbul and left a happy man. But his fiancé was waiting out front and said he never emerged and security cameras confirmed her version. Then I was told Khashoggi, who I considered a friend, left through the rear entrance. I don't know why he'd do that, but I trusted my experts.

I became worried upon learning that a team of agents and others had been dispatched to Istanbul in two private planes. They planned to wait at the consulate in order to talk to Khashoggi and persuade him to return to his Saudi Arabian homeland. Somehow this unauthorized order got mangled as it bounced from one imbecile to the next and by the time Jamal Khashoggi arrived at the consulate several agents greeted him. Khashoggi unwisely attacked the agents who tried to gently subdue him but, alas, one overzealous fellow applied a chokehold too vigorously and the *Washington Post* columnist expired.

I don't know where the body is. Some of our contacts in Istanbul disposed of it. Who are the contacts? Their names are confidential. Even I don't know their identities. I also can't imagine why Turkish authorities are spreading wild stories about Saudi agents and a forensic pathologist torturing Khashoggi and cutting off his fingers before dismembering his body.

The Turks claim they have an audio tape verifying their version of events. I've even heard the Turks have some video footage. I'm betting that's not the case. So is President Donald Trump, our greatest ally, who said my explanation is "credible" and a "good first step." I know President Trump is also pleased that I've already fired an important adviser as well as my deputy intelligence director and arrested many rogue agents and others.

FIFTY-ONE

Stop That Caravan

Last night I visited the White House to talk to President Trump about immigration. He offered ten minutes and demanded I not ask him about Saudi Arabia. I agreed.

Donald Trump – You've read my tweets. Everybody reads them. There's a caravan of four thousand migrant criminals from Honduras, El Salvador, and Guatemala headed this way right now. They're killing and raping each other, and they'll kill and rape Americans when they get here. And you liberals keep demanding open borders.

George Thomas Clark – Only a very small and radical group of U.S. citizens are advocating open borders. That doesn't mean other citizens who oppose your wall somehow support open borders. Don't forget, President Obama was known as the Deporter in Chief because on his watch more undocumented immigrants were arrested and returned than during any previous administration and almost more than in all administrations combined.

DT – He didn't have the balls to build a wall. I do. The wall isn't ready now because of the Democrats' opposition, so in the strongest terms I'm telling Mexico to stop this onslaught. If they can't get it done, I'll call up the U.S. armed forces and close the whole southern border. I'll also stop all payment to those countries. They've got to learn to control their populations.

GTC – First, you should keep in mind that many Republicans haven't been anxious to waste billions on your wall. Its effectiveness is in question. And the political message insults people on both sides of the border. Having stated that, I do concede it's a concern that a large number of people are vowing to bulldoze their way into the United States. A few days ago I read about four thousand people. Now I'm seeing figures like sixteen hundred to two thousand. Authorities along the way are dispersing some of the group and others are breaking away and going home. Your threat to mobilize the U.S. military to close the border is a rant designed to bring out more Republican voters for the midterm elections.

DT – I have the support of my base. They elected me because I oppose illegal immigration.

GTC – You won't have much support when this caravan turns into a trickle. The would-be immigrants…

DT – Migrant criminals…

GTC – The people heading this way just got out of Guatemala and are in southernmost Mexico. They've still got to walk and survive for almost two thousand miles.

DT – They'll invade us if they can.

GTC – They can't.

DT – Because they know Donald J. Trump is ready to mobilize the greatest army in the world.

GTC – I imagine your blustering will be worth a few House seats on November sixth. But you'll lose more than that the way you've been kissing Saudi ass.

DT – You broke your promise. (He points to two secret service agents, jerking his thumb.) Get him outta here.

Lopez Obrador Calls Trump

This morning President-elect Lopez Obrador of Mexico called President Trump. On a third line I served as translator.

Andres Manuel Lopez Obrador – President Trump, please don't do anything rash before we've had time to meet.

Donald Trump – Thanks for calling but let's keep in mind you're not the president yet and won't be until December first.

AMLO – The impoverished Central American immigrants still have to walk more than a thousand miles.

DT – A few days ago there were about four thousand in their caravan. Now there are seven thousand.

AMLO – It'll take them months to walk to the United States.

DT – They won't be walking long. They'll be riding buses and jumping on trains.

AMLO – Most can't afford transportation.

DT – I'm talking about freight trains. And I know people save thousands for coyotes at our border so they've certainly got bus fare.

You've got to stop them or I'll send in the army, and I don't mean the reserves.

AMLO – That's contrary to U.S. law, which forbids using the army to act as a police force. Please also acknowledge that we're offering the immigrants applications for refugee status. At least a thousand have so far accepted.

DT – Too many Mexicans are giving them food and water and rides in pickup trucks.

AMLO – You can't possibly object to basic human decency.

DT – I understand that. But Mexico's attitude is part of the problem. You just want to push them up to and through our border as fast as you can.

AMLO – In that regard, President Trump, you're quite mistaken. I'm calling you today so we can begin focusing on economic development in Central America and southern Mexico. That's where poverty and crime are worst and most of the people in the caravan come from.

DT – The United States has been quite generous to Latin America over the years.

AMLO – Your country has also enriched itself greatly. But we don't need to debate history. We need to focus on investments that generate jobs and economic growth. Agriculture, transportation, technology, and infrastructure are all areas we can improve if we focus our attention and our resources.

DT – We can take a look at that.

AMLO – Keep in mind, President Trump, that as these regions become wealthier, they'll buy many more products from the United States.

DT – That should decrease our trade deficit with Mexico.

AMLO – It definitely would.

DT – We don't have to wait till you're sworn in, Andres. Let's get together as soon as possible.

Democracy in Georgia

voter-suppressing brian kemp worried gubernatorial foe
stacey abrams
may win if
everybody
exercises
right to
vote

Patriotic Trump

i'm nationalist who loves all americans
how
can
you
call
me
white
nationalist

Trump Money

my
economy
helps
everyone
especially
blacks hispanics and women

FIFTY-TWO

Midterms

b
   o
      m
        b
          s
  b
    r
      a
        w
         l
           s
  b
   l
     o
       w
         h
           a
             r
               d
              s

Everyone's Crazy

We're all lucky Trump enters politics and tells us Barack Obama was born in Kenya and is quite different and ruining the country with Obamacare and debt and Bill Clinton's a sexual predator and we should lock up Crooked Hillary and that CNN and others are fake news, look right over there he points at enemies we jeer, and John Brennan's an erratic communist whose security clearance he has to take away and George Soros is a socialist who hired cranky women to oppose Brett Kavanaugh and Maxine Waters is a crazy low-IQ broad.

It's not Trump's fault someone sends yellow manila envelopes containing pipe bombs to his verbal targets and he immediately denounces these despicable acts and promises we'll spare no resources to stamp out threats of violence that have no place in America. He also reminds us "the media has a responsibility to set a civil tone and stop the endless hostility and constant negative and often fake attacks and stories."

The president knows Mitch McConnell is stalked and insulted when he walks through an airport and he and his wife can't eat in a restaurant unless a man pounds their table and tells them to get out and a woman screams he's a traitor and flips him off. And he remembers Maxine Waters only believes in civil rights for some since she says, "If you see anybody from Trump's cabinet in a restaurant, a department store, a gas station, you get out and you create a crowd and you push back on them and you tell them they're not welcome anymore, anywhere."

Some people wear black hoods and others wear white hoods while thousands of migrants from Central America march toward a wall of hostility and our good friend Mohammed bin Salman lurks at home and abroad and we battle Chinese in trade and plan for wars on land at sea and in space as we joust with Russians about which missiles the other has and we lie about Iranians who lie about almost everything but their compliance with the nuclear deal and the air's getting pretty dirty but we can ignore it and be happy everything's swell here compared to most places.

Rush Limbaugh Speaks

I love being fat and famous and talking out of my ass. Listen. We just don't do this. Republicans don't make bombs and mail them to enemies of freedom like Obama and the Clintons and CNN. That's the low-rent style of liberal conspirators desperate to smear conservatives before the midterms.

Meet Cesar Sayoc

Uufff. Just one more set. Got to keep my muscles big and bigger so I can be a stripper or, more likely in my fifties, a bouncer. I'm a tough guy. I know about wrestling and mixed martial arts. I haven't been using those skills recently, though, because I'm a witty guy and been working four nights a week as a DJ in a strip club. The girls there think I'm cool but I guess they like the younger guys more because they never invite me home. I can't invite them home because I live in my van. My mom kicked me out of the house a few years ago and this January I lost my regular job delivering pizzas or I'm sure the girls would be interested. I'm not worried about them.

I'm focused on helping President Trump Make America Great Again. See that video. That's me in the red MAGA cap, and I'm holding high a sign about CNN sucking and other important facts. My van's so pretty with big stickers about people trying to ruin America. You know who they are: Muslims, blacks, gays, Jews, liberals – I warn about them all the time on my three Twitter and two Facebook accounts and of course on my incredible van. Like it says in the lower right window on the passenger side:

ZERO TOLERANCE
KILL YOUR ENEMY AND
THOSE WHO ROB YOU
THEN TAKE THEM TO
EVERGLAD FOR GATORS

Don't make a big deal I left off the "es" in Everglades. I often forget the s at ends of words. That doesn't mean I don't know what's right. I attended college in the early nineteen eighties and am plenty smart and you better believe I'm all white. I may look a little brown but that's only because my bastard Filipino father left me when I was a child. And, like I said, my mother booted me but at least she's white like me. I'm a proud white and damn tired of having this country and my life screwed up by those who oppose President Trump.

I'm not a criminal. I'm a patriot. I know you're reading I've been arrested about ten times. I stole a little, but only to get by, and kicked a few asses, trying to survive, and took some drugs, hoping to make my enemies go away. I wasn't trying to kill them. I just sent pipe bombs to Obama and the Clintons and CNN and Eric Holder and George Soros and Robert De Niro and others to warn them to shut up. I'd rather talk and tweet and make my van cool than hurt anyone. My family, instead of sticking up for me, is telling fake news that I need help because I don't understand reality and lack common sense and am disturbed because I know there's nothing wrong with me.

Slaughter in the Synagogue

I bet you haven't heard of Gab.com but you should. This website is committed "to defend free expression and liberty online for all people." Facebook and Twitter are afraid to do that. They deny the truth, which is that most of the world doesn't want white people to survive. I'm not afraid to say and do what must be done. People are damn well going to quit ignoring Robert Bowers. First, I create a dynamite page on Gab.com where I post a photo of "my Glock family" and another of riddled targets at a shooting range and one of a big oven just like those at Auschwitz. It's so important to understand and publicize that "Jews are the children of Satan," I post on Gab. I don't know who else can do anything about them. That's why I didn't vote for Donald Trump. He's surrounded by Jews, and they're the ones bringing in invaders from Central America to kill our people. I can't sit by and watch my people get slaughtered. Screw your optics. I'm standing in front of a big Pittsburgh synagogue, armed with three Glocks and an AR-15 assault rifle, and posting on Gab that I'm going in, and now I'm screaming "all Jews must die" and shooting as many as I can.

Trump Timing

it's only coincidence i'll be sending five thousand troops
to
border
day
before
midterm
elections

FIFTY-THREE

Jair Bolsonaro Seizes Brazil

Brazilians love me and several weeks ago thousands at a rally were carrying me toward victory when a deranged man crept through the masses, lunged, and stabbed me in the abdomen. I grimaced but otherwise remained calm, as people would expect of a former military officer, and soon I realized the wound, though serious, was not fatal. From my hospital bed I spoke confidentially to one of my sons, and he shook my hand and walked downstairs to tell the media: "Today, the cowardly assailant has made my father president of Brazil."

This is what God wants. As a younger man I wasn't so religious but during seven terms in Federal Congress I became increasingly devout and during my presidential campaign evangelical Christians have embraced me because I hate homosexuals and oppose sex education in schools and vow to encourage police to shoot suspected criminals and guarantee I'll shrink bureaucracies and cut taxes and sweep away messy regulations bad for business and thereby create millions of new jobs.

The financial markets began celebrating my victory even before it came, and the Brazilian real is getting stronger versus the dollar as our stock market soars. Brazilians want a strong leader, a man who admires our dictators from last century and who today believes that torture is the right way to deal with leftists responsible for rampant crime and poverty in a potentially great nation blessed with vast natural resources.

I am part of a conservative wave that's sweeping across the United States and much of South America and Europe. People want strong leadership. They yearn for discipline. They demand security. They crave personal wealth. And they cheer my confidence when they learn that years ago I told an obnoxious congresswoman, "I would never rape (her) because (she doesn't) deserve it." They applaud when I say our military dictators failed because they tortured rather than killed. They roar when I say, "If I see two men kissing in the street, I will hit them." They nod when I say many indigenous and African Brazilians are so lazy and inept they can't even procreate. They agree when I say, "My four sons would certainly never fall in love with black women because my sons are very well educated."

President Trump delights me with a congratulatory telephone

call. We agree on many topics and plan, as he tweets, to "work closely together on trade, military, and everything else." The world's headed the right way.

Trump Mobilizes

As brown masses march toward our borders I every day feel more like Abraham Lincoln and Franklin Roosevelt, two other presidents who faced threats that could've destroyed our nation. And like those heroic leaders, I am responding with bravery and vigor. I'm mobilizing our troops for war. At first I thought five thousand soldiers from the regular army would be enough when combined with ICE agents and the National Guard. Then I realized I better call up ten thousand, and after continuing to watch scary Fox News films of endless dirty invaders moving our way I decided we probably need fifteen thousand troops. We need everyone we can get.

We also have to get rid of the crazy law that allows illegal women to sneak into the United States and have babies who automatically become citizens of our country. That's not right. I don't think I have to bother with Congress and amending the Fourteenth Amendment of the Constitution. Some very bright lawyers have told me I can take care of the whole thing with an executive order. We're the only nation in the world that allows aliens to give children eighty-five years of our extraordinary benefits. I know even some Republicans, like Paul Ryan, are saying an executive order isn't enough. Others point out, usually in private, that Canada and Mexico permit the same kind of thing. I doubt that.

Whatever the legal technicalities of anchor babies, I definitely can send more troops and keep arousing all patriotic Americans to defend the borders on November sixth.

Trump on Election Day

I'm up early because I couldn't sleep last night after Sean Hannity shined my butt at an election rally and now my tweeter's hotter than ever telling patriots this Republican candidate's great and that one's wonderful and those others are important and it's vital to get out and vote because my name is really the only one on the ballot.

I know I'm not going to lose the Senate. The economy's way too strong for that. Jobs are up and unemployment's down. Right? Sure, they are. No way I lose the Senate. But the House worries me. I think we'll win it, of course. The fake polls, the same ones that two years ago said I had no chance to win, are claiming the Democrats are probably going to retake the House and then try to impeach me. I'm preventing that disaster by tweeting "law enforcement has been strongly notified to watch closely for ILLEGAL VOTING." Thank God, as long as we hold the Senate, we'll have the power to prevent the crazies from destroying this great nation.

You know they want to roll that caravan of Central American illegals right into our country and register them to vote. My troops at the border won't let them in. We need people who understand and appreciate that I've built the greatest economy ever. I've also scared hell out of Kim Jong Un and broken the horrible nuclear deal with Iran and am now intensifying sanctions and taking away their oil money used to finance terrorism and I've cancelled an intermediate ballistic missile treaty with Russia and continue to be tougher on Putin than anyone and I'm defending our economic rights against the very unfair Chinese and Canadians and Europeans who've so long taken advantage of us.

Don't worry. My tax cuts are fueling the economy and will keep it great forever. The only things that can screw me up, besides illegals, are excessive health care and social security expenditures. We can't afford entitlements. We must instead have a growing military and my powerful leadership. Get out and vote Republican.

Thousand Oaks Nightmare

former marine throws smoke grenades into thousand oaks nightclub
and opens fire
again
compelling
responsible
citizens
to
ask
why
is
anyone
allowed to own extra capacity magazines and other weapons of
mass destruction

Trump Tweets Golden State

shape up california you're burning billions of federal dollars
and
still
can't
fight
deadly
fires
only way i can teach you is cut off funding and demand
you
quit
calling
me
ignorant

My Midterm Victories

Who's Matt Whitaker? I guess I met him a dozen times this fall and said he's a great guy but that doesn't mean we're friends. I do know he believes the Mueller investigation has gone too far and that attorney general Jeff Sessions needed to be removed in favor of someone who'd cut Mueller's budget so low his investigation would run out of gas. I'm confident Matt Whitaker will be a great acting attorney general and get this phony Russia collusion charge out of my life. That'll also be great for the nation.

You've all heard how happy I am about the midterm elections last week. We increased our majority in the Senate. In twenty-one previous midterms the president's party had done that only four times. No Senate like that is ever going to convict me of anything, especially since I've never done anything wrong. I'm just protecting you against fake news.

You don't have to go anywhere for the truth except my daily White House newsletter where I explain that House and Senate candidates who won embraced conservative messages of low taxes, low regulations, low crime, strong borders, and great judges. Candidates who lost ran away from those themes. The country is behind me so I'm warning the House, quit messing with me or I'll unleash the Senate and it's a lot bigger dog.

FIFTY-FOUR

Mohammed bin Salman Swears

i didn't order murder and dismemberment
of
comrade
jamal
khashoggi
but
did
arrest
culprits
who'll be decapitated after receiving fair trail

I'm No Bitch

Who the hell's Congresswoman Tulsi Gabbard? She's a nobody who better quit calling me "Saudi Arabia's bitch" or I'll soon be telling you plenty about this sneaky woman in a hula skirt who wants to be president.

Let's be honest. You love oil and you need it. You want to walk? Better thank my Saudi friends for cutting oil from eight-six bucks a barrel several weeks ago to less than sixty-five today. That wouldn't have happened if I'd cancelled arms sales to our faithful allies. Oil would've skyrocketed and damaged our economy and many others around the world.

Maybe Mohammed bin Salman knew about the murder of Jamal Khashoggi. Maybe he didn't. Why don't we talk about Iran instead?

Franz von Papen to John Roberts

"John Roberts, chief justice of the Supreme Court, I've been waiting for you to speak up."

"Who's calling?"

"This is Franz von Papen."

"I've heard your name but can't quite place your position," Roberts says.

"I was vice chancellor of Germany in June 1934 when I took big risks to give a speech calling for an 'incorruptible judiciary' and reminding the chancellor that 'a press worthy of the name must point out injustices, errors, and abuse. The government must lack confidence in its essential correctness and popularity since, like a weakling, it refuses to endure criticism and labels every dissenting patriot an enemy of the state.'

"Your demand for 'judicial integrity and independence' very much reminds one of my speech. Let me hasten to emphasize I'm not comparing Donald Trump to our chancellor, but some principles are eternal."

"Thank you, Herr von Papen."

Thanksgiving Concertina

I know you troops stationed overseas are excited to hear my voice address you from luxurious Mar-a-Lago where I'm ready to throw up my turkey dinner because of disgraceful judges who tell us how to protect our border. These wimps are often Californians who support sanctuary cities and liberal asylum laws that have allowed millions of illegal aliens to enter our country and hide. I'm changing all that, as you know, and have deployed thousands of your comrades along our southern border to make sure caravans of criminals don't charge into the United States. If things get out of control, I'll sign an executive order and close the Mexican border until order is restored. We're already installing concertina wire like razors all over walls and fences and will soon have the border looking scarier than a prison. Happy Thanksgiving.

Economic Stats

tax cuts increased deficits
while
trade
wars
inflated
steel cutting five gm plants in u.s.

and
fourteen
thousand
jobs

Trump Climate

i read little of climate report from three hundred scientists
and
then
shoved
it
into
dark
place

Yemen Saved?

trump and mohammed bin salman mourn
bipartisan
senate
vote
to
stop
their
slaughter
of
yemenis

Guardian Trump

After ducking big rocks, my brave forces weren't firing tear gas
and rubber bullets at women and children charging my beautiful
concertina-wire border. They were stopping hordes of invaders, mostly
adult males, who would destroy the paradise we European Americans
have created. I made the truth clear. I'll close the whole border with

Mexico. There's plenty of precedent for that. President Lyndon Johnson, bereaved and frightened by the assassination of President John F. Kennedy, sealed the border. President Richard Nixon ordered Operation Intercept to stop the flow of marijuana from Mexico into the United States. They didn't find much pot but that wasn't Nixon's fault since dealers flew the stuff over his militarized border. And President Ronald Reagan shut the doors after our drug agent Enrique Camarena was kidnapped, tortured, and murdered. If necessary, I'll close down everything from the Pacific two thousand miles to the Gulf of Mexico, and I'll keep it blocked as long as necessary. To those who try to enter this country illegally, I say this: you will be stopped; you can apply for asylum here but you won't get it if we determine you're an economic refugee; in that case you'll either have to stay in Mexico, if the Mexicans will let you, or return to your countries, which I know are wracked by murder and chaos.

Russian Greeting

at g20 summit putin thrills
mohammed
bin
salman
with handshakes and smiles

FIFTY-FIVE

Babe Welcomes George

Babe's playing catch with a teammate on the sideline when a tall lean fellow, wearing a first baseman's mitt, jogs onto the infield and says, "Hi, I'm George. Can I play today?"

"Kid, I got first base because I was out pretty late last night and don't feel like pitching or running in the outfield."

"Why don't you DH then?"

Babe stares at him.

"You'd be an incredible designated hitter."

"I guess so. But what the hell's that?"

"All you'd do is hit," says George.

Babe motions for his teammate to warm up with another player. "I'd hit every inning?"

"Not every inning but every time it's your turn to bat."

"And what am I supposed to do when we're in the field?"

"You'd relax on the bench," George says.

"You better not be saying I can't field."

"Not at all, Babe. I'm just trying to keep your bat in the lineup and not tire you out."

Babe waves his glove at George and says, "Why don't you DH since it's such a great job?"

"I'd be honored, Babe, but I confess I'm not much of a hitter compared to guys like you."

"There's no one like me."

"I mean I'm not a major league hitter."

"You ever play any organized ball?"

"Don't you remember me?" asks George.

"Could be. Where'd we meet?"

"I'm George Bush from Yale. You came to our game. I was team captain so had the honor of receiving the manuscript of your autobiography you gave us. We shook hands and had our picture taken together. I treasure that photo, Babe."

"Thanks, kid. When was that?"

"Nineteen forty-eight."

"Jesus, by then cancer had about eaten up my throat and I could barely talk."

George walks to Babe and shakes his hand. "You're the real Babe again, and I'm happy as heck about that."

"You're looking pretty damn good, too. Sorry you couldn't play in the big leagues. What'd you do?"

"Well, before Yale I served as a naval aviator and piloted a bunch of combat missions. One time the Japanese shot my partner and me down and we bailed out. My parachute opened but his didn't. I had an inflatable raft and waited a few hours for a submarine to pick me up."

"I'm proud of you. What'd you do after Yale?"

"I got married and started having kids, six in all, and moved to West Texas and started a couple of oil companies, one drilling on land and the other offshore."

"You make any money?" Babe asks.

"We did pretty well and moved to Houston. Then I served a couple of terms in Congress and would've continued but President Richard Nixon... Remember him?"

"Never heard of him."

"He asked me to run for Senate to help our Republican party, to help him, really, but I lost."

"You go back to the oilfields?"

"I went to the United Nations, Babe."

"Where the hell's that?"

"In New York City, right on the East River. I guess that came a couple years after you moved here. I served as our ambassador to the U.N."

"Damn good, Bill," says Babe.

"George."

"Right, kid. What'd you do next?"

"I was chairman of the Republican National Committee for two years, envoy to China for a couple more, then director of the CIA for two more years."

"CIA?"

"Central Intelligence Agency, finding out what foreign leaders and spies are doing."

"You must've retired after that."

George smiles and says, "I like to keep active, Babe. I ran for president in 1980."

"You win?"

"No, a guy named Ronald Reagan beat me."

"The actor?"

"Yeah."

"I remember him as The Gipper."

"That's him," says George. "He picked me as his vice presidential running partner, and we won both elections and served eight years."

"Sorry you didn't make president, kid."

"I'm not bragging, Babe, but I became president in 1988."

"You didn't go any higher than that, did you?"

"Years later I parachuted from an airplane when I was ninety."

"Damn. I died at fifty-three. Let's play ball."

"I'm at first base and you're DH'ing, right?" asks George.

"I'm DH'ing, all right, but you're pitching for the other team."

Strategic Trump

I know so much more than the generals. They don't understand my tweets: "There is no longer a nuclear threat from North Korea… Kim said very nice things. He wants to get denuclearization during the Trump administration… (I know) we will prove everyone wrong! There is nothing like good dialogue between people who like each other."

Kim and I are almost buddies. I'm sure he wanted to please me recently at his nation's 70th anniversary parade where, for a change, he didn't have any ICBMs on display. The absence of those missiles is a sign of his "commitment to denuclearization."

Kim better not try to fool me. I hear he may still be producing five to eight nuclear bombs a year and now have around fifty they keep moving around to various hidden and fortified storage facilities, some under mountains. If he doesn't behave, I may terrify him by attacking nonnuclear Iran.

Trump Right about Sex

I've combatted Donald Trump since the 2015 day he crawled down an escalator to launch his presidential campaign founded on division and bigotry but right now I'm compelled to say this in his behalf as well as yours. It's no one's damn business when consenting adults get laid in private. Blue nose politicians should have no legal right to threaten Trump with impeachment and imprisonment because he paid two now-overpublicized women to keep quiet. Understandably, he ordered his sacrificial attorney Michael Cohen to hand over a hundred thirty and a hundred fifty grand, respectively. That's no crime unless he used public money, and it's doubtful he did. Of course he lied about it. He had to. He sought the highest office in a land of hypocrites who pretend they're inspired by God to smite those who commit adultery, as long as the adulterer is in the other party. Twenty years ago Bill Clinton had similar difficulties when panty-sniffing Republicans preached until the nation ignored them.

Ultimatum Trump

either fund my wonderful berlin wall
or
i'm
shutting
down
federal
government

James Mattis Writes to Trump

Dear Mr. President,

You have the right to a secretary of defense who, like you, does not understand that "our strength as a nation is inextricably linked to the strength of our unique and comprehensive system of alliances." You have the right, no matter how shortsighted and crude, to disrespect and even insult our traditional European allies without whom "we cannot protect our interests." You have the right, despite the danger, to kowtow to "malign actors" like China and Russia and North Korea who "want to shape a world consistent with their authoritarian model." And I now have the uneasy duty to inform you that my last day as secretary of defense will be February twenty-eighth, 2019. It grieves me, as it does most of the democratic world, that you will probably replace me with a fanatic and warmonger but I believe our nation and others can survive your presidency as long as you do not precipitate a nuclear war.

James N. Mattis

P.S. – If after reading this letter you want
me to leave now, I'd be delighted.

Federal Reserve Trumps Stock Market

my greatest ever stock market and economy would've continued up and
up
if
fed
understood
interest
rates
strong
dollars and trade wars but they're like powerful golfers too tight to putt
even
lefties
like
paul
krugman
say
loosen
up

2019

FIFTY-SIX

John Kelly Out

old soldiers don't walk away
i
fought
to
keep
trump
well
informed
but
he
wanted
appointments
secretary not chief of staff

Pedophiles Delight

vatican
delays
measures
to
stop
priests
molesting
children
in
u.s.

Trump Counterpunches Romney

Oh, Christ, here comes Mr. Holy Pants, Mitt Romney, a freshman senator arriving in the town I own and craving the job I have, and right away he writes a column for the *Washington Post*, complaining I lack the character and knowledge to be president. He believes I don't "demonstrate the essential qualities of honesty and integrity" and am not equal to presidents who "blessed" the country by calling "on the greatness of the American spirit." He then implies I'm the one who divided the country and made everyone angry.

He also complains I made a "steep descent" when I fired Jim Mattis and John Kelly, generals Romney pretends to respect but I know are over the hill. And he claims I'm not providing leadership for our allies or respecting "our enduring commitment to principled conduct in foreign relations." But don't despair. Mitt promises he will support policies he believes "are in the best interest of the country (and) oppose those that are not."

Really, Mitt's just grabbing my coattails when he admits I was right to reduce corporate taxes and cut damaging regulations and to get tough on China for unfair trading and to appoint conservative judges. He says these are "mainstream" Republican policies. If so, why am I the one getting it done? Mitt couldn't because he was a pansy during his 2012 race against President Obama. He should've fought. I tried to help him. But, unlike me, he lacks the character and temperament to become president. And, don't forget, I've got ten times more money than Mitt Romney.

Ocasio-Cortez Visits Trump

From his Oval Office chair Donald Trump rises and winks, smiling as he says, "Thanks for coming, Alexandria."

"It's my duty," says first-term Congresswoman Alexandria Ocasio-Cortez.

"Please, sit down."

"Which chair?"

"Any one you want."

After seating herself, she says, "I'm surprised you invited me."

"I'm not worried you're a socialist, Alexandria. The most important thing is we're a couple of stars from New York City who want the best for America."

"We have very different perspectives."

"That's why I've got to say you Democratic Socialists of America are crazy to blame the free markets for everything from racism to sexism to dirty air. Business built America."

"I know business has done some good things but it's also responsible for global warming, unaffordable health insurance, massive student debts, and a lot more. We've got to get rid of gas guzzlers right now, before they poison the world."

Grinning, Trump asks, "How'd you get here today, Alexandria? You walk? Ride a bicycle? Hang glide? I saw you step out of a chauffeured SUV. I also know you got to most of your campaign rallies thanks to internal combustion engines. This is Washington, D.C., the big leagues. You can't just talk about fantasies. But I'll humor you. How you gonna pay for what you're dreaming about?"

"We can have Medicare and free college for all if we tax the wealthy at seventy percent."

"Had you been drinking before you said that? I know you were a bartender."

Ocasio-Cortez frowns and says, "I'm an elected member of the Congress of the United States and demand to be treated as such."

"You're being treated better than any politician of twenty-nine I've ever heard of. Look where you are and who you're talking to. I've had my staff crunch some numbers about your tax proposal. First, you'd only generate maybe twenty billion a year, and we'd lose a lot more than that because entrepreneurs would be discouraged from starting businesses and creating jobs for people who pay taxes."

"We'd generate a lot more than twenty billion and all of it would be used to create jobs that cleanse the environment and provide a decent living for everyone. I'm not against the rich. I just want them to quit jumping through tax loopholes and pay their share."

Trump gazes at his visitor before saying, "You're a helluva of fine looking woman, Alexandria, slim and feisty."

"Don't objectify me, Mr. President. You've done that to enough women already."

"Calm down. That was high praise but also a warning. Every time I see you on TV you look very stylish. Who's paying for those great outfits?"

"I am. Who's paying for your suits, which are designed to hide your paunch?"

"I can pay for anything I want. I know you can't. You haven't received your first paycheck from Congress but you're already headed for the Best Dressed list."

Using both hands to smooth her lapels, Ocasio-Cortez says, "My supporters expect me to look professional."

"I guess you're not going to tell me how you got that wardrobe, but that's okay. You're a big celebrity and already a popular guest at benefits, and that popularity's going to increase, at least until people learn you can't pay for your fantasies. Until then, you'll make plenty of dough outside the Capitol."

"Anything I make or purchase, including my business attire, will be for the people."

"That's not human nature, Alexandria."

"Either address me as Rep. Ocasio-Cortez or I'm going to start calling you Donald."

"Please, call me Donald."

Don Junior Hunts Reporter

I'm a sharpshooting stud who all over the world has killed many beasts including leopards, elephants, buffaloes, deer, bighorn sheep, foxes, and plenty more. I also know a helluva lot about security and expect you to pay attention when I write, "You know why you can enjoy a day at the zoo? Because walls work." My dad and I understand walls are the only thing that will protect us from being eaten by wild humans.

Dad gives a great speech about border security and immigration the other night and I assume everyone agrees until someone shows me a column written by Ted Hesson in *Politico*. Who's the hell's he? He travels around writing about immigration. So what? You know damn well a lefty's not tough enough to kill big game.

Instead of applauding Dad's patriotic address, Hesson calls some of our facts fake. I decide not to simply shoot this guy on social media, I decide to slay him in person. Not with my guns. I'm a law-abiding guy who only shoots four-legged critters though I may take out a few apes my next trip to Africa. About this Hesson, I find out where he lives and, just like on a safari, I put on my camouflaged hunting outfit and pick a good place where I'll be able to see him but he won't spot me.

When he gets home, I sprint at him and wave the deceitful column in his face.

"You said it's 'not true' there's a crisis at the border. Are you an idiot?"

"Even fewer people are being arrested crossing the border now than under President Obama, and under him – the Deporter in Chief – there were a lot fewer than in a long time."

"You think four hundred thousand illegal aliens trying to sneak in aren't something to worry about?"

"It's not ideal but doesn't warrant the hysteria your father's trying to whip up," Hesson says.

I shake my head and say, "You claimed our southern border isn't a 'pipeline for drugs.' Are you a pink-panties fool?"

"No, I'm immeasurably better informed than you and your father. Read the facts, which no one has refuted. 'Most fentanyl comes from China.' And most drugs that are stopped are intercepted at 'legal ports of entry.' Migrants and their families rarely try to bring in drugs."

I shake my finger at him. "They're drug dealers and many are killers."

"That's a distortion," he says. "Studies reveal that 'undocumented immigrants' only commit about half as many crimes as citizens born in the United States."

"That's crazy. As Dad noted, even the Democrats want a barrier. They prefer steel. He's okay with that."

Hesson adjusts his dorky black glasses. "Democrats didn't say they wanted steel. They 'said they didn't care.' They really don't want a wall, regardless of composition, and they don't want the government shut down while this is being debated."

"Dad's shut lots of agencies down to turn up the heat. He'll also make sure Mexico pays for the wall because of his new trade agreement."

"What you're referring to still hasn't been approved by Congress and it's doubtful to generate several billion extra dollars for our government."

"All the Democrats have to do is give Dad about six billion bucks to build a wall, and he'll let the federal government open up."

"You're not going to get that much because most people understand there's no emergency and a wall wouldn't solve problems that don't exist," Heeson says. "Now get the hell outta here or I'll call the cops."

I raise my right hand, motion to come here, and two secret service agents rush up. "This guy threatened me," I say, pointing at Heeson, who tries to look surprised.

FIFTY-SEVEN

Pompeo Preaches in Cairo

*Highlights from the recent Cairo speech by Secretary of State
Mike Pompeo*

I'm always eager to visit Egypt, a land I know so well, and am especially happy this time because I'm an evangelical Christian arriving soon after the Coptic Church celebrated Christmas here in beautiful Cairo. "We are all children of Abraham: Christians, Muslims, and Jews. In my office, I keep a bible open on my desk to remind me of God and His word and the truth."

You don't hear this worldly truth often in the Middle East but today at esteemed American University, I, a military man by training and instinct, am guaranteeing you that under normal circumstances "America is a force for good in the Middle East." Tragically, several years ago when this region convulsed "from Tunis to Tehran" and even in Egypt, we, your long-time friend, were absent too much because President Barack Obama "gravely misread our history and your historical moment." In this very city, he told you that "radical Islamist terrorism does not stem from an ideology… (and) 9/11 led my country to abandon its ideals…" and your world and ours "needed a new beginning." Oh, how tragic his misjudgments have been.

I can't fathom why President Obama considered American actions in the Middle East to be a principal part of your problems. What was he referring to? Two wars against Iraq? A war that continues in Afghanistan? Military and economic support of dictators in Saudi Arabia and Egypt and elsewhere? All that was essential. Obama should have done more but he "grossly underestimated the tenacity and viciousness of radical Islamism" and thus allowed the rape and murder of thousands of civilians and the birth of a "caliphate across Syria and Iraq" that slaughtered innocents in every direction.

President Obama's timidity continued during the Green Revolution in Tehran when the people of Tehran tried to overthrow the brutal mullahs who have suffocated them for forty years. America offered scant support and this emboldened Iran to "spread its cancerous influence" to Yemen, Iraq, Syria, and Lebanon. Meanwhile, like an ostrich, Obama buried his head in the sand as Hezbollah, Iran's henchmen in Lebanon, amassed more than a hundred thousand rockets and missiles, many aimed at our sacred ally Israel. And what did Obama do when Syrian despot Bashar al-Assad began shooting, bombing, and gassing his fellow Syrians? He criticized Assad but otherwise did nothing, and hundreds of thousands of Syrians have perished and millions fled into exile.

I already knew then what the U.S. president did not. "When America retreats, chaos often follows." But do not despair. "The age of self-inflicted American shame is over." In only two years President Trump has reestablished the United States "as a force for good in this region." We have learned from the mistakes of the Obama administration and our current president stresses that "Muslim-majority nations" must "meet history's great test – to conquer extremism and vanquish the forces of terrorism." Your courageous Egyptian liberator, President Sisi, agrees about this.

America is again ready to help you. When barbaric Assad gassed his people, President Trump "unleashed the fury of the U.S. military not once but twice." Our arms are again blazing in the Middle East, and you should all remember this: "America has always been a liberating force, not an occupying power." We liberated Europe from the Nazis and Kuwait from Saddam Hussein and then Iraq from Saddam. Despite our many military bases in this region, "we've never dreamed of domination." We only build and staff bases when we're invited to do so. We have quite small deployments in Iraq, Saudi Arabia, Bahrain, Kuwait, Qatar, Turkey, and the Emirates. And we're leaving Syria, as you know. President Trump has so ordered since "ninety-nine percent of the territory ISIS once held is liberated." In humanitarian ways our churches and non-profits are helping to ensure that ISIS never returns.

Now let's talk about Iran, my favorite and most frightening subject. As you know, President Trump "withdrew from the failed nuclear deal, with its false promises." Now America has reimposed sanctions that should not have been lifted, and we're cutting "off the revenues (the mullahs) use to spread terror and destruction throughout the world." I guarantee that a majority of the Iranian people agree their government is squandering the nation's wealth and former good name. Almost everyone now understands "we must confront the ayatollahs, not coddle them." Bastions of freedom like Egypt, Oman, Kuwait, and Jordan are helping "in thwarting Iran's efforts to evade sanctions." Today, I haven't said much about Saudi Arabia, but our trusted friends are also countering "Iranian expansion." Our coalition in the Middle East and Europe, including Germany, Britain, and France, has "cut Iranian oil imports to zero" and agreed that doing business with the regime is bad business.

I want the leaders, and the people, of Iran to understand that "America will not retreat until the terror fight is over." All freedom lovers in the Middle East will battle to destroy ISIS and Al Qaeda and radical Islamists who "threaten our security and yours." It's true that President Trump is withdrawing our troops from Syria, but that's what we do. We go home, sometimes. And while so doing we ask "our partners to do more." We will help you with military and economic aid as well as our continued airstrikes.

Forty years in power are far too many for that medieval clan in Tehran, and we will continue the strongest economic sanctions in history until Iran begins "behaving like a normal country" and quits invading, occupying, or tormenting nations like Syria, Lebanon, Iraq, and Yemen. Some blame Saudi Arabia for the humanitarian catastrophe in Yemen. I believe the Iranians are far more responsible. And blame them we shall for as many outrages as we can until we figure out what to do. I surmise that'll be unleashing more sanctions, more rhetoric, and probably a missile and bombing campaign sometime before the 2020 election.

Pelosi v. Trump

I'm back on top in the House and heading for the airport to lead a delegation to Egypt and Afghanistan. My cell phone vibrates in my purse.

"Speaker Pelosi, you can't go overseas," says an urgent aide.

"I can do whatever I want."

"President Trump says you must reschedule 'this public relations event' until the shutdown's over. Either that or fly commercial."

"Bleep him," I say. "Goodbye. Driver, take me to the White House at once."

I can't imagine the home of Lincoln and Roosevelt is inhabited by such a little man. At the gates I power down my window and tell two secret service agents, "I expect you haven't been paid in weeks. I'll fix that. Let me in."

They call inside. Several minutes later an agent says, "I'm sorry, Speaker Pelosi, but President Trump says he's very busy working to secure the border and get eight hundred thousand federal workers back on the payroll."

"Open this gate or I'm plowing through."

"You can't do that, Madame Speaker."

I power up my window and order, "Driver, proceed."

"But…"

"I said, 'Proceed.'"

He eases the big bumper to the gate.

"Floor it," I shout.

After some thirty seconds of burning rubber and thickening smoke the gate breaks down, clanking on pavement, and we shoot to the White House entrance. Secret service agents rush to surround the vehicle. President Trump walks out the front door.

"They'd have shot your ass, Nancy, but I told them not to," he says.

I exit the vehicle and march my slender frame straight up to the president. "You shouldn't cut off people's paychecks."

"Just fund my border wall and everything'll be fine."

"I'll never invite you to give the State of the Union address, and stage a political farce, as long as you're playing politics with the lives of our governmental workers and people fleeing poverty and violence."

"Nancy, look at the polls. Americans are with me."

"Forty-two percent want a wall and fifty-four do not. Did you flunk math?"

"My campaign and my presidency have changed the trend. Soon, most Americans will demand a big beautiful wall."

"That would be obscene and against our principles," I say.

"Why are liberals so afraid of securing the border?"

"In fact, we're arresting most undocumented migrants."

"Not enough," says Trump. "You better leave before I have

you arrested."

"You're a coward and a jackass."

"If you were Joe Biden, I'd pound you."

"Try it."

Lunging, I bury my left shoulder into his soft belly and, like a defender from our hometown San Francisco 49ers, lock my arms around his waist and drive him to the cold White House turf. Instantly, I'm sitting on his belly, a firm leg on each side, and digging fingernails into wrists I pin against my knees.

"You guys do your damn job," he demands. "Guys, where the hell are you?"

Summit Meeting

"Mr. President, may I please have a word with you?" says a young man, standing in the open door frame of the Oval Office.

Trump glances up and immediately rises and walks to shake the visitor's hand. "Dr. King, I wasn't expecting you."

"I visited you last year on this occasion and intend to do so next year, which I trust will be your last in this office.

"Don't bet the farm on that. My base is solid as ever. Happy ninetieth, by the way."

"You're most gracious." King extends an open hand toward a chair and says, "May I come in?"

"Of course. Please have a seat." After his guest is comfortable, Trump returns to the chair behind his desk.

"I come not to rebuke you, Mr. President, at least not entirely, for I know you've suffered an enormous and no doubt painful political setback after exiling nearly a million federal workers in order to force your adversaries in Congress to build a wall odious to everything we should stand for."

"Come on, Dr. King. I handled Nancy Pelosi like she was a baby."

"Evidently a baby who postponed your State of the Union speech."

"I agree with her about that just as I'm sure, in private, she understands I was right to cancel her trip overseas. I'll give my speech when everything's settled."

King pauses before saying, "Your clinical obsession with a wall that'll never be built in the form you want has compelled you to endanger the nation. Airports have fewer traffic controllers, and you're costing the nation billions in tax collections by forcing IRS workers to walk off the job."

"It isn't as bad as my enemies in fake news claim. I had to wake everyone up. There's an emergency at our border. I'm reopening the government for three weeks, but if I don't get my wall, we're off to the races."

"Mr. President, I urge you to accept the billion dollars Democrats are offering to strengthen our already very efficient border patrol."

"You know I've staked my campaign and my reputation on the wall."

"Add some agents and technology, and claim victory."

"We're speaking confidentially, Dr. King?"

"Of course."

"I may do that, as long as I look tough and super successful."

State of the Trump

Look at those Democratic ladies dressed in white flags of surrender during my State of the Union address. They know I've given Americans their best wages in decades and an economy growing almost twice as fast as when I took office. Some say I inherited a good economy. Not as good as the one we've got now. Unemployment is the lowest in half a century and the lowest ever for African Americans and Hispanics. More women are working than any time in our history. Overall, we added three hundred four thousand jobs last month, almost double the number expected. It's an economic miracle. And the only things that can stop it are needless wars and investigations. We have to choose between greatness or gridlock.

You're too smart to try to slow me down. I'm a high energy guy and have led the United States to become the number one producer of oil and natural gas anywhere in the world. We need plenty of fuel for our military, the most powerful on earth by far. We'll stay number one by outspending and out-innovating all other countries. America is winning again each and every day.

With me as your president we're prepared to confront the urgent national crisis on our southern border where my expanded security measures are putting ruthless coyotes and cartels out of business. And I'm sending three thousand more troops to prepare for the onslaught Mexico's causing by trucking Central American and other aliens to weak points on our border. Believe me, I want people to come into our country in the largest numbers ever, but they have to come here legally. Many who enter illegally commit really bad crimes. When my wall is built, and it will be built, those problems are going to stop. Ask our agents at the border.

I'm doing great things all over. Chinese theft of our intellectual property and our jobs has come to an end because my tariffs are working. The Russians are worried I recently withdrew from the Intermediate-Range Nuclear Forces Treaty they were cheating on. I'm at the same time rebuilding America's crumbling infrastructure and bringing down the cost of prescription drugs. I'm on your side against big drug companies. I'm also battling HIV and childhood cancer and working to get nationwide paid family leave. This is all for free people who understand America will never be a socialist country.

You can relax about North Korea and ignore fake reports that Kim Jong Un is continuing to develop more and better nuclear weapons. That's ridiculous. He's not even test-firing missiles or exploding nuclear bombs like he was until I got tough. My relationship with Chairman Kim is a good one. If I hadn't been elected president, in my opinion we would be in a major war with North Korea right now. Instead, Kim and I will hold our second meeting in about three weeks in Vietnam.

I'm also going to clean things up in the Middle East. We've been fighting in Afghanistan and Iraq for almost twenty years. Great nations do not fight endless wars, especially when I lead the most powerful. I know the Taliban is even more tired of war than we are. My counter terrorism efforts will force them to behave in the forty percent of the country they control and deter them from trying to expand until after we leave.

Our most dangerous enemy is the radical regime in Iran. Thank goodness I withdrew from the disastrous Iran nuclear deal. We will not avert our eyes from a nation that chants "Death to America" and is dedicated to the destruction of Israel. The Iranians may not have any nuclear weapons now but I know they'd like to have them. It's my duty to punish them for even wishing.

God bless you, and God bless America.

Trump Denounces Bezos

I'm not only protecting you against invaders I'm battling enemies right here at home. One of the most dangerous is Jeff Bezos, a lousy businessman who needed lots of luck and cheating to amass a fortune of a hundred sixty billion and employ six hundred thousand people. The United States Postal Service subsidizes Bezos and Amazon, losing a buck-fifty a package for the millions delivered every year. That drives many fair retailers out of business and I'm going to stop it. I'm also tired of Amazon not paying its share of taxes on products sold over the internet. As you know, I'm a straight-up guy who always pays what he owes and will prove it when the IRS completes its audit of my finances and I release my tax records. That could be a while yet.

I'm so sorry to hear Jeff Bozo was taken down by *National Enquirer* reporting more accurate than his lobbyist *Amazon Washington Post* newspaper. It deserves a more responsible leader. Bozo's been caught cheating on his wife. Don't accuse me of getting caught. Broads are just making statements for money. I couldn't stop AMI, which runs the *National Enquirer*, from paying Karen McDougal to keep quiet. And she didn't stay silent long, anyway. A smooth operator knows how to avoid getting photographed with his pants down. Bozo not only dropped his drawers, he took a picture of his stuff. I'd never do that and you shouldn't trust anyone who would.

Bozo also released what he calls a blackmail letter from AMI. It's not that at all. AMI, in behalf of the *National Enquirer*, politely and very confidentially informed Bozo it not only had his dick pic but lots of other fun stuff like a photo of married girlfriend Lauren Sanchez sucking a cigar and Bezos in underpants with his dong hanging out. AMI wanted to help Bozo keep this private. He only had to say he has "no knowledge or basis for suggesting AMI's coverage was politically motivated." The *National Enquirer* is a truth seeker, and Bezos should have played ball. Instead, he tried to find out how these fine journalists acquired his pornographic photos. He's a bad dude.

State of Emergency

I'm a gambler. I've made billions from my casinos and know when to double down. I told Kim Jong Un I'd destroy North Korea if he continued testing ballistic missiles and exploding nuclear bombs. And I ordered renegade Iran to continue abiding by terms of our nuclear deal even after I dumped it. Just look at the results. Kim stopped misbehaving and we've already met and developed a very good relationship and will soon have another summit. In Iran my sanctions are making citizens very angry at a corrupt theocratic government I'm trying to overthrow peacefully but am prepared to strike unless they become peace loving and trustworthy like the North Koreans.

Now I'm heating the dice and rolling them on immigration. My base, poorly educated white workers and media studs like Sean Hannity and Rush Limbaugh, insists I keep my promise to build a great wall on our border with Mexico. I'm already doing that. Using incredible abilities as a dealmaker, I got about a billion and a half dollars from Congress when no one else could've gotten any. But we still need a few billion more. And I'll get the money. I'm declaring a state of emergency on the border and authorizing the chiefs of the army, navy, air force, marines, the border patrol, and others to let me know what they need to stop the invasion of drug dealers and killers who're making angel moms out of too many Americans. How can anyone justify letting illegal aliens come here and commit violent crimes? You can't, and after some court battles I'll have my wall.

President's Day

what
would
washington
and
lincoln
think

Beware

fox news flash
alexandria
ocasio
cortez
boyfriend
enjoys congressional email
while
she
plans
socialist
takeover

Trump Media

lying
new
york
times
true
enemy of people I care for

FIFTY-EIGHT

The Big Train

kim jong un's long armored train chugs north into china
then
south
more
than
two
days
almost three thousand miles to sino vietnamese border
where
excited
hosts
greet
him
and
wonder why guy with nuclear weapons travels like that

Trump in Hanoi

People in Hanoi are thrilled I'm here because Kim Jong Un and
I are denuclearizing the Korean Peninsula. How do I know? My gut
tells me. We've already established a great relationship. I'm not in a
rush. As long as there's no testing, I'm happy. Sure, there's other stuff.
We'll talk about some of it the next couple days.

Dining with Kim Jong Un

Chairman Kim and I have dinner Wednesday night in Hanoi
at the Metropole Hotel where outside lights give the place a golden
look I like at night. It's a decent five-star hotel, with rooms starting at
about three hundred thirty, but not a Trump-caliber place. That's okay,
though. I think Chairman Kim will be comfortable negotiating here.
It's an honor to be with him again. Our first summit was a great success
and this one will be even better. We have a very special relationship.

"I hope you're hungry, Chairman Kim," I tell him as we're each seated with two staff members and an interpreter.

"I'm always hungry, President Trump, but would've preferred lots of Vietnamese food rather than what you've dictated," he says.

"Sorry about the late changes, but I had to keep it light after my five-course lunch with Prime Minister Nguyen this afternoon. Otherwise, we'd see who can knock down the most chow."

Kim looks confused during the translation but smiles after further explanation.

"I'm confident I can out-eat the great American president."

"You obviously enjoy food, Chairman Kim."

"I doubt I spend any more time in the kitchen than you, President Trump."

Waiters bring in our chilled shrimp cocktails spiced with fresh lemon and herbs, diced avocado, and Thousand Island dressing. Skillfully using chopsticks, Kim demolishes his shrimp faster than anyone. If I'd been home watching sports or Fox News, I'd have grabbed my shrimp instead of spearing one at a time with a fork.

"The next course is one of my favorites, Chairman Kim. Tender marinated sirloin grilled with sauce. And, in your honor, kimchi fermented inside a pear. Frankly, I think salty cabbage and Korean radishes are hard on the stomach but they beat the alternative."

Chairman Kim, who's already about finished his second shrimp cocktail, puts down his chopsticks. "And what might that alternative be?"

"Starvation," I say, "but nothing personal."

With his right hand Kim picks up the chopsticks and points them at me. "That kind of arrogance prompted the United States to kill countless Koreans and, a generation later, slaughter the Vietnamese, many right here in Hanoi where your B-52 bombers indiscriminately blew people up."

"I'm sorry, Chairman Kim. What I'm really saying is that your country can soon be unbelievably wealthy. And we'll help you. Imagine all those malnourished citizens who could soon be eating sirloin."

Kim ignores me and starts in on his steak, using knife and fork like a pro. Secretary of State Mike Pompeo grins at me while one of Kim's diplomats frowns. Chewing hard and fast Kim devours his sirloin and orders another. I honestly believe I could've kept up if I hadn't eaten such a big lunch. But tonight I barely finish my entrée.

"I'm saving room for dessert, Chairman Kim," I say. "Hot runny centered chocolate cake with chocolate crumble and fresh berries and vanilla ice cream."

I've never seen anyone eat as fast as Kim not even the man himself during our first incredible summit. He downs his dessert and snaps fingers for another and finishes that when I'm half through my first. After burping into a napkin, he stands, nods at this aides, and walks away.

"Chairman Kim, there's still dried persimmon and honey punch."

He spins and in English says, "Send it to my room."

"We sure will. See you at the summit tomorrow."

Inside the Hanoi Summit

We're sitting at a long polished wooden table decorated down the middle by small bouquets of flowers dividing Chairman Kim Jong Un and his staff from me and mine. I sense my brilliance and boldness will soon be needed. Eleven presidents who preceded me had sixty-five years to bring real peace to the Korean Peninsula but they lacked vision and toughness. Thankfully, I've got balls and think my friendly counterpart does, too.

This afternoon I've already been patient at least twenty minutes, feeling him out, before I drop the hammer.

"Let's go all in, Chairman Kim. Let's make this the greatest summit ever."

"That's why I'm here, President Trump. We simply ask that you remove sanctions so we can breathe as we destroy all our nuclear weapons and ballistic missiles."

"We want to remove sanctions and help your country become an economic giant."

"Then please proceed."

"Chairman Kim," I say, "we can't give you what you want without getting something big in return."

"I'm offering you the greatest concession possible: I'm ready to dismantle the Yongbyon nuclear facility, by far our largest."

I cross my arms and examine Kim's face, which is even fatter than in Singapore, and say, "Yongbyon's gotta go, sure, but so do plenty of other places. Secretary of State Mike Pompeo will read part of our list, your list, really."

Mike, who may be heftier than Kim, and both are definitely fatter than I am, names this place and that and other dangerous weapons facilities in North Korea. Kim tries to stay cool but I know he's thinking, "How'd they find out about all those?"

"Chairman Kim," I say, "there really isn't anything in your country we don't know about."

Kim locks his hands into one big fist on the table and says, "We're not asking you to remove sanctions against weapons, President Trump. Our offer is really quite generous. Furthermore, I'm prepared, right now, to sign a promise to forever halt our bomb and missile tests."

"You haven't been testing bombs and missiles, and I'm confident you won't. Please don't. What you're really offering is an aging facility you don't need to keep expanding your nuclear weapons programs. You probably read our press more than I do. I'm not accusing you of building more bombs and missiles but our intelligence agencies say you are."

Even while negotiating I love the two little honeys doing our translating.

"We aren't expanding our nuclear programs. We can hit the United States. That's all we need. Why would we do more?"

"I believe you, Chairman Kim. And I believe President Putin, who's told me the same. But for domestic political reasons I've got to at least consider what my experts are telling me. Your country has a bad record in keeping its promises."

Kim unlinks his hands, making two small fat fists on the table. "And the United States just walked out of a good nuclear deal with Iran and is looking for a pretext to strike there just as it manufactured lies before attacking Iraq in 2003."

"Listen, Chairman Kim, despite what my opponents say, I was against attacking Iraq, and in Iran I was just getting out of the worst deal in history. We're not going to attack Iran."

"Russia, China, England, France, Germany, and others still think it's a good deal and are adhering to its terms, and so is Iran."

"We're here to talk about North Korea," I remind him.

"I'll demolish Yongbyon."

"That's not enough for sanctions relief."

"We can't do everything today, President Trump. But we should be able to declare an end to a war that in fact ended in 1953. I hope you appreciate how difficult it is for me to offer to freeze our missiles and nuclear weapons."

"Okay, but you'll need to go much further. We're here to denuclearize the Korean Peninsula and help your country move into the twenty-first century."

"We'll progress much more rapidly once the United States withdraws its troops from South Korea."

Sometimes I wish I was just a real estate tycoon and reality TV star.

"Chairman Kim, I'm cancelling our working lunch and signing ceremony because we have nothing to sign."

"I agree."

Kim and I stand, and I walk around the shiny long table to shake his hand.

"We'll talk again," I say.

"When?"

"Maybe our staffs should move this along more slowly, step by step, then we'll actually have something to talk about."

"You're right, President Trump, let's proceed cautiously."

Trump Assails Michael Cohen

I'm not going to tell you where I live but Donald Trump and his goons just pulled up in five black beasts from which they jump and Trump motions to encircle my house as he pounds up the walkway to kick my door.

I jerk it open. "The doorbell works fine."

"You're a bum," says the president.

"Can't deny it after ten years cleaning up your garbage."

"No one cares what you say."

"Plenty are interested in my tapes of you and copies of check receipts you wrote to cover what I paid Stormy."

"All people really know is you're a convicted liar. I had no idea the Russians had stolen Crooked Hillary's emails and given them to Wikileaks."

"Maybe, but they definitely understand you're a racist draft-dodging conman."

Trump says, "How the hell'd I ever trust you. You don't even pay your taxes."

"Says a man who avoided paying a billion."

"You don't know that," he says.

"Prove I'm wrong."

"My taxes are confidential until the IRS audit is complete."

"You're free to release your taxes anytime."

"You'd already be in jail if I'd known you were selling sensitive opinions about me and my operation," Trump says.

"I should've gone to the police."

"The FBI came to you, remember? And that led you to a very bad place."

"You'd be going the same way if you weren't president. And you won't be once prosecutors prove you knew in advance about Don Jr. and Jared Kushner meeting with Russians in Trump Tower."

"I didn't know."

"Remember, your own family's going to crack before Congress, just like I did."

"They'll show some loyalty."

"Not if it results in prison time."

"They'll lock you up for years, Michael, and lots of bad dudes in prison don't like snitches."

"Why don't you pardon me? I know you'll do that for Paul Manafort."

Trump says, "Paul's a good man."

"Maybe Mike Pence will pardon you."

"I won't need it."

"I'd bet a hundred grand on that but you wouldn't pay," I say, and close the door.

Nuclear Restoration

i'd be very disappointed in chairman kim if he's already
rebuilding
rocket
site
he
must've
started
right after hanoi but it's very early report so we'll see if
he
thinks
i'm
dumb
he
better not forget someday i'm gonna solve this

North Korea Dry

severe drought in land of kim
food
rations
tightening
but
don't
expect
dear leader to lose much weight

Colonel von Stauffenberg
Discusses Kim Jong Un

A prominent reporter asks what many people have: "Colonel von
Stauffenberg, what should the North Koreans do?"

By that he naturally means what should the military officers do?

"It will likely be up to the colonels," I say. "Generals have usually
lost their youth and vigor while gaining power and prestige. If a

lower-ranking general still has the insight and verve of a colonel, very well. The point is, an unusually brave and ambitious officer, or group of officers, must destroy the man who darkens their world. They must eliminate Kim Jong Un who daily fattens as he grows more unstable and paranoid. Perhaps I shouldn't call him paranoid. His fears, some of them, are quite reasonable. A family in its third generation of bloodletting and incompetence can rightly believe many victims and alarmed observers yearn to eliminate it.

"Despite my near success in blowing up Hitler, I'm afraid a bomb wouldn't work today. It's unlikely any officer would be permitted, as I was in July 1944, to carry an unexamined briefcase into any room occupied by the Dear Leader. And someone might move the briefcase.

"Let us then surmise that the best way to kill Kim is with a gun. Armed men surround him."

"One of his bodyguards should shoot him?" asks the reporter.

"Yes," I say, "but that group is the most fanatical and subservient. I'd wager on a pistol-wielding colonel."

"Kim recently had his half-brother poisoned in a Malaysian airport, Colonel. That might work."

"Poison seems harder to deliver and less lethal than a bullet. However, I'd have no objection to poison being part of the plot. One colonel could douse Kim with poison as another shoots him."

"There's really no excuse for some officers not trying," says the reporter. "You'd lost an eye, a hand, and two fingers on the other hand, yet spearheaded the conspiracy and activated a bomb you placed near Hitler's feet."

"Why the hell didn't I simply shoot him? I had to rush back to Berlin to lead the plot. Also, I confess, I had fantasies of surviving."

"I don't think whoever attacks Kim Jong Un will live, Colonel."

"Sadly, you're correct," I say. "North Korea needs a man willing to receive eternal thanks in the hereafter."

"Someday they'll name a street after him and celebrate each anniversary of his brave act, as in Germany."

"When he arrives here, I'll shake his hand with the three fingers I have left."

The reporter extends his hand.

FIFTY-NINE

Trumpanomics

I'm demanding the biggest budget ever to feed my economic miracle that includes eight billion for my wall and big cuts in Medicare and that stuff. Don't worry about growing federal deficits they'll shrink thanks to incredible growth by corporations stimulated by my tax cuts for big guys who create jobs.

Trump Emergency

who says trump can't have his fake national emergency
forty
seven
democratic
senators
and twelve republicans endangered by bikers for trump

Trump Links

swear
i
didn't
know
illegal
aliens
worked
at
several
of
my
beautiful
courses

Battleground

you
ohio
tank
workers
better
love
my ass because i saved yours

Squeaky Clean President

You know from the beginning I've been shouting and tweeting: "No collusion, No obstruction, complete and total EXONERATON. KEEP AMERICA GREAT!" Phony Republican investigator Robert Mueller finally had to release his report and basically admit this is the most ridiculous thing in history. It's a shame our country and your president had to go through something that began illegally before I was elected. People should've instead been looking at what the Democrats were doing. I still think we'll get Crooked Hillary locked up someday.

My enemies misrepresent everything. They claim in the seventies my dad and I refused to rent to people of color. We settled that in court but without admitting any wrongdoing. They accuse me of many times not paying carpenters, electricians, cooks, and other servants. That was also settled confidentially. And some laugh about Trump University. I didn't get punished for that. I got elected president.

I wasn't doing anything wrong by praising Vladimir Putin while trying to make a deal for Trump Tower Moscow. I bet that'll happen when I retire from politics in January 2025. That's what I do. I make great deals. And I hire wonderful people. Unfortunately, some, like Paul Manafort, did things before I knew them that I only learned about later. Others, like my former dumb lawyer, Michael Cohen, became convicted liars and are going to prison.

I'll never go to prison because I never lie or use politics to make money. And I'll always keep our economy great and our military the best in history. I know you never stopped trusting me and understand

I couldn't have colluded because I'm a patriot and trust Putin when he tells me Russia didn't interfere.

Windbag

i love internal combustion engines and
will
protect
them
against
cancer
causing
windmills

Joe Six Pack Celebrates

By God I knew President Trump was being witch-hunted by a pack of liberal dogs and am so happy the Mueller Report completely clears him of any collusion or obstruction of justice during the presidential campaign. The only people breaking the law were Democrats who spied on him. That's what needs to be investigated. I hope like me you've already glanced at the Mueller Report released by Attorney General William Barr. He's an impartial legal scholar who damn well isn't behaving like the president's defense attorney as many lying liberals claim. Barr only redacted what he had to for national security. The bottom line is President Trump's clean as a whistle and didn't need any Russian help to beat Crooked Hillary by a country mile. Just as I feared, though, the lefties aren't going to accept facts and apologize for their terrible accusations. No siree. They're still claiming the president misbehaved, even if not in a criminal way, and should be impeached. They know that's bull and there's no way sixty-seven senators would vote to convict an innocent man. Democrats also know they don't have anyone who can beat President Trump in 2020. Thank God, he'll be our leader almost six more years.

Democratic Delusion

clinton was moderate likewise
obama
now
dems
lurch
leftward off electoral cliff

SIXTY

Trump Assesses Democratic Candidates

I love democracy or I'd say cancel the 2020 election because all the Democrats are children compared to me and I'm going to win easily. Go ahead. Throw me some names and I'll explain.

Joe Biden – Can't believe this wimp threatened to punch me because of my popularity with women. Look what's happening. Even liberal ladies are complaining he gets too close and touchy and smells their hair. He's also a gaffe-artist and almost eighty but doesn't know his presidential desires have never been more than a fantasy. Who cares his poll numbers have skyrocketed against little Dems? You know surveys that show him beating me have to be fake. I'm shocked even Fox News and Rasmussen got the same results.

Bernie Sanders – Gray Bernie's even a year older than Biden and so senile he wants to turn us into a nation of socialist whiners who give trillions of dollars to poor people for health care and welfare. He even scares liberals. Imagine what the rest of America thinks. Forget those ridiculous polls that have him leading me. Americans aren't going to elect a guy who calls himself a democratic socialist and wants to make college free and increase social security benefits. People know they have to pay for higher education and accept lower social security benefits because we must spend more than seven hundred billion a year to fight terrorists and deter nuclear-armed enemies who're becoming more radical. Bernie doesn't get it. He'd leave us broke and in foreign chains.

Kamala Harris – This is a nasty chick who's always rude and abrasive when she interrogates Republicans during Senate hearings and was really bad the way she treated patriotic Attorney General William Barr who, like you, is sick of the phony Mueller investigation but delighted that it cleared me of collusion and obstruction and everything else. Kamala's also hyper as hell at town hall meetings all over the country, telling her story and saying she intends to win. She's lost half her support during the last month and is sending her subscribers endless emails begging for money.

Elizabeth Warren – Really, I'd love to run against Pocahontas. She's got the appeal of a dorky elementary school teacher and only excites my base when she says I might be in jail by 2020. She knows that's a lie. Let her rant against the rich. Americans like winners and love billionaires like me. Elizabeth's nowhere in the polls and just doesn't have it.

Beto O'Rourke – Get serious. Beto couldn't even beat my good friend Ted Cruz in the U.S. Senate race in Texas last year. And you know how I manhandled Lyin' Ted in the Republican primaries of 2016. Like Kamala Harris, Beto's lost half his support in recent weeks. He should go back to playing in a punk band.

Pete Buttigieg – It doesn't bother me at all that Mayor Pete of South Bend, Indiana is gay, but I bet it bugs you. I'm open-minded. For years my favorite attorney was Roy Cohn, a really smart guy who'd been Senator Joseph McCarthy's man of action, kind of like a much brighter Michael Cohen. I didn't care who Roy slept with. Same with Pete. But I'm bothered he wants to lower medical bills and get rid of student debts. I'm the only guy who's got the answers to our health care problems, and I'll reveal my plans once I've taken care of loudmouth Democrats like Pete Buttigieg who, be honest, you know can't win.

Cory Booker – They say Cory's a social media sensation? Yeah, and I've got fifty million more followers on Twitter. Some people love a complainer and this guy's always speaking solemnly about some exaggerated injustice. Most Americans are tired of that. They've already tuned him out and he's only polling about two percent among the challengers.

Amy Klobuchar – After she drops out of the race, and that won't be long, I may offer her a job in my administration. She should resign from the Senate and start using some of her good Midwest business ideas my supporters would like. Sure, let's increase export opportunities for smaller American companies. We've got to do something about the trade deficit. In this kind of job Amy's bitchy temper and abuse of employees wouldn't be the issue it is in politics.

Tulsi Gabbard – You know it, but I probably can't say it. Tulsi's a babe who should be married to a guy like me. I admire her for serving in the National Guard and Iraq but wish the little honey had learned about the importance of regime change. I know she's going to try to raise hell when I drop the hammer on the mullahs in Iran but not many will hear. She's polling less than one percent now and is weak as hell on social media. But have you seen her in a bikini? Nice.

Julian Castro – I'm not going to lie. Julian gave a helluva keynote speech at the Democratic Convention in 2012 and I'd be a little worried but ninety-nine percent of Democrats are ignoring him. When a guy's getting trounced by a group of knuckleheads, he needs to forget being president. I guess he'll be considered for the presidential ticket if another Crooked Hillary gets the nomination. Otherwise, a woman will caddy for the male I trounce.

My prediction – One of two geezers, Joe Biden or Bernie Sanders, will get the nomination and probably take Kamala Harris as running mate. It really won't matter.

Putin Hosts Kim Jong Un

In Vladivostok, on cold east Russian shore of western Pacific, I greet President Kim, who traveled almost seven hundred miles in armored train. I hope someday he will have airplane so he can go places rapidly. This afternoon, at our summit meeting, flanked by interpreters, I smile and motion for Kim to please sit down.

After amenities and minor business, he says, "We need Russian investments in our factories and infrastructure."

"We'd like to help you, President Kim, and under certain circumstances I think we can."

"I'm sure you can be quite helpful, President Putin, but we can't give up our nuclear weapons."

"I understand that would be mission impossible. They're your only protection against United States."

"Do you think President Trump will be angry?"

"Undoubtedly."

"Will he tighten sanctions?"

"He'll certainly try to do so."

"Will you help him?"

"We have to cooperate, or at least pretend to do so."

"Do you think he'll attack us?"

"Not in foreseeable future. He's too invested in personal diplomacy with you. Besides, he's focusing elsewhere, and after he squanders years on nonnuclear Iran you'll have deterrent he wouldn't dare challenge."

"I hope he's reelected next year," Kim says.

"He will be."

William Barr Declares

i'm attorney general of u.s.
you know
and happy explaining to cbs that
eleven counts of possible obstruction
in mueller report don't matter because
he also said he couldn't say whether or
not president clearly violated law but
my department of justice analyzed and
determined that as matter of law evidence
was deficient and many instances
wouldn't amount to obstruction but
we didn't exonerate the president
you know

Abraham Trump

I love Jon Voight and know you do too. He's a wonderful Academy Award winning actor and has great political insight he often displays especially when he recently said I'm the greatest American president since Abraham Lincoln. Frankly, I agree. Honest Abe and I are two peas in a pod. He freed the slaves and I'm liberating the country from Democrats. Abe was a great wartime commander and I may have to become that, too.

Millions of Americans are in tune with Jon Voight and their support has several times encouraged me to say the economy's going so well in my Great Again America that maybe we'll change things, the Constitution and all that, so I can serve three terms or four or even five. I'd only be ninety, and the nation and the world would benefit from twenty years of my brilliance.

Bashing Biden

Sure, I'd listen to people from another country if they said they had important information about my political enemies. Don't bother moralizing. You wouldn't call the FBI, either. Stakes are too high. I'm not only making us great and guarding against terrorists, I'm fighting a very dangerous guy at home. Actually, Joe Biden would only be dangerous if he beat me in 2020, and you know that's not going to happen.

In Iowa this week I'm learning people don't respect him. All he does is mention my name dozens of times in speeches and slide further into the tank. He's worse than Crooked Hillary. And now he's saying I must be fascinated by him. Irritated is more like it. He claims he opposes everything I'm about and that I'm an existential threat to America and trying to become a dictator.

Really, I wish Biden could win the Democratic nomination. He'd be easy to beat because he's a mental weakling and I like stepping on weaklings, been doing that all my life. Biden can't make Iowa farmers believe they're suffering because of my tariffs against China. People here and everywhere know I'm protecting our trade and agriculture and they keep looking at the great economy I've built and know they can't trust Biden. He spent his career supporting a ban on federal funding of abortions but now, since the Democrats are to the left of Lenin, he's flipping his position. I've always been consistent as well as honest.

SIXTY-ONE

Badass Bolton

I must tell you that we are in great danger because the Iranians are planning to attack American personnel in the Middle East. This I know because I'm very shrewd analyzing intelligence, and that's how I knew Saddam Hussein had weapons of mass destruction and was preparing to start World War III. Every day I give thanks that strong men like George W. Bush, Dick Cheney, and me slaughtered our enemies and crushed the country. We must now be ready to thus strike the Iranians. Look what they did the other day. They sabotaged two oil tankers belonging to our dear friends the Saudis and ordered their proxies, the Houthis of Yemen, to drone strike two oil pumping stations on royal land. What evidence do I have the Iranians are responsible? Just look at my credentials above and don't give me any crap about this being another Gulf of Tonkin frame-up.

The United States always acts in a righteous way. We used to be able to change regimes behind the scenes, and I hope we'll soon regain that ability, but for the time being we must send more B-52 bombers and F-15 fighters and warships including an aircraft carrier to the Middle East, which just hasn't learned the lessons we're teaching so I've ordered a hundred twenty thousand troops to get ready, too. Of course, President Trump is in charge of all this, and now that I've been advising him on national security more than a year he more clearly understands the existential danger posed by the Islamic State.

Weak generals like my predecessor, H.R. McMaster, and James Mattis, the former secretary of defense, didn't understand the threat and had to be replaced. We need men of steel like John Bolton because I love threatening smaller nations and making exciting plans and studying maps and moving our unparalleled military equipment first across maps and then around the globe in order to crush steadily rising threats to U.S. forces. We warned the Iranians and withdrew from the nuclear deal that saps like England, France, Germany, Russia, and China are still backing. We know it's a bad deal and our sanctions are squeezing Iran and forcing oil exports down, down, down, and other nations even our friends better not buy any or we'll slap sanctions on them, too. What we say is the real law of the world. That's why with a happy hand in 2002 I signed our country out of the International Criminal Court so inferiors around the world couldn't someday try to put heroes like Bush, Cheney, Trump, and me in the dock at Nuremberg.

Saudi Strikes

saudis beg u.s. to surgically strike iran
why
don't
heavily
armed
saudis
do
striking

Donald Mellows

Lighten up. I'm not really planning to go to war with Iran. I hope I don't have to. I just want them to think I'm ready. The Iranians know John Bolton and Mike Pompeo want war but are also aware I've got people around me who're doves compared to those two. Nobody's going to push me into war. My brain analyzes all relevant information before I decide what to do. Keep in mind, I've many times said my instinct is to stay out of foreign conflicts. I didn't want to invade Iraq in 2003. Only liberal liars try to deny that.

Nancy Pelosi doesn't need to warn me we have "no authorization to go forward in any way." I'm a dealmaker and ready to talk to the Iranians. Why aren't they anxious to talk to me? They should ask Kim Jong Un about the benefits of getting to know me. I'd just tell the Iranians we can all be friends and business partners if they stick to the nuclear deal I left and quit developing ballistic missiles and threatening nations in the Middle East and don't make too big a deal out of my attempts to starve them and destroy their regime by peaceful means.

Curtains

a fight's the last thing i want
but
if
iran
starts
something
that'll be the official end of
the
whole
damn
country

Trump Heights

"Congratulations, President Trump," says Benjamin Netanyahu, prime minister of Israel, speaking into a hotline. "We've just erected a large sign celebrating Trump Heights where the bloodthirsty Syrians had claimed ownership of the Golan Heights until you said it belongs to my country. Thank you so much."

"You're quite welcome, Bibi. Thank God for you as well as that other defender of liberty in the Middle East, Mohammed bin Salman."

"He's quite wonderful," Netanyahu says. "I couldn't have imagined Israel would ever be so close to Saudi Arabia, but you made it happen."

"Like us, Mohammed's urging the international community to get tough on Iran after its attacks on oil tankers in the Persian Gulf."

"The Gulf of Oman, Mr. President."

"Same thing."

"Pretty much."

"Mohammed doesn't want war, though, and neither do I. You don't want war, either, do you, Bibi?"

"Of course not."

"I knew the liberals were lying that you wanted us to attack Iran just like you'd wanted us to attack Iraq."

"Oh, no. I want peace, Mr. President. I only attack when I have to."

"We've all got to be ready. Iran's getting desperate. Pretty soon they won't be able to sell a drop of oil anywhere in the world."

"That's certainly true, Mr. President."

"One more thing, Bibi. Rather than Trump Heights, which reminds me of Golan, why don't you make a sign that says Trump Tower."

"I will, Mr. President, as long as you promise to soon build some real Trump Towers on our new heights."

On the Brink

From a secret war room, national security advisor John Bolton places his pointer tipped black with an arrow on the wall map, and says, "The Strait of Hormuz is by far the most dangerous place on earth. The Iranians aren't content to spread terror throughout the Middle East and dream about building nuclear weapons. Now they're attacking oil tankers nearby in international waters and, most horrifically, they've just shot down one of our very expensive unmanned drones. This calls from an immediate and devastating attack."

"No way I'm going nuclear on this one, John."

"I'm not talking about nuclear strikes, Mr. President, but I'm urging you to cleanse the Middle East of the bearded mullahs who'll never let their neighbors live in peace."

"I'm no historian, John, but I'm pretty sure Iraq attacked Iran almost forty years ago and we backed Saddam Hussein."

Nodding, Bolton says, "That's why in 2003 I advocated destroying Saddam and his doomsday weapons and bringing democracy to that backward land."

"That's the kind of quagmire I've promised to avoid."

"You're quite right about that, Mr. President. By devastating I simply meant you should launch airstrikes against radar and missile batteries and, while we're at it, hit a few nuclear targets."

Trump turns to several generals in bemedalled uniforms and says, "What do you think, gentlemen?"

"Limited strikes against radar and antiaircraft sites would be the most we could do without risking a major war," says one general.

"In fact, Mr. President," says another general, "we'd be risking a major war with any strike."

Frowning, Trump says, "I can't just let the Iranians hit us without paying a price."

"The sanctions are already ruining their economy," says the first general.

"Stick to military assessments," says Bolton, aiming his pointer at the man.

"Don't point that thing at me, and stay the hell out of military matters," says the general. "Limit yourself to advocating wars you won't be fighting in."

Trump holds up a hand and says, "Easy, guys. Just get me a plan to take out three sites, radar, missiles, that stuff."

"Yes sir," the generals say.

The following day, just before meeting the generals, Trump tells Bolton, "John, wait in your office during my military conference."

"But Mr. President…"

"Don't worry, I'll let you know what happens."

Donald Trump marches to the secret war room and is received by stern generals.

"The initial plan will destroy the targets," says one general, "but after that anyone who tells you he knows what'll happen is lying."

"It's a painful decision," says Trump, "but order the operation to begin."

A general picks up the phone. Trump paces the room. He looks nervous. The generals are impassive. Minutes drag by.

"Gentlemen, how many people would die in this operation?" asks President Trump.

"A hundred and fifty, sir," says a general.

"Okay, call it off. It's not too late, is it?"

"We still have time."

"Great, call it off. The drone was unmanned or I'd have to kick some asses."

SIXTY-TWO

Trump Analyzes First Debate

I'm busy defending freedom and building the greatest economy ever but know you'll be fascinated by my opinions of the communist party's first presidential debate. They have twenty stooges running, and ten are standing on stage tonight. Wait, is Julian Castro standing? He's even shorter than schoolmarm Elizabeth Warren. The guy ought to wear high heels. Now let's be honest, Tulsi Gabbard's the kind of babe I grab, but she brags a lot about serving two tours as a medic in Iraq, and no one's really interested in her as president.

Pocahontas Warren is so phony. She talks about corporations having one goal and that's to earn a profit, as if making money's bad. Listen, if you don't profit you go bankrupt which I've done five times but I did so using all the laws. Warren would drive our country into a permanent depression if we let her spend everything on her fantasy of turning the world into a green heaven. And she claims she'd abandon her private insurance for a universal public option. She's not that dumb, folks.

I know you've heard how Amy Klobuchar abuses her staff members. The fake news lefties won't come out and say it. She's a bitch. I'm not fooled by her smile that's really a snarl when she tries to talk nice. Stay away from her. That'll be easy. She isn't going anywhere.

Now there's Beto O'Rourke confusing himself and everyone else about what he really wants for health care and then, like a dunce, he starts speaking Spanish and alienating the majority of Americans who're sick of undesirables invading from the south. I didn't understand what he said and don't care. I speak English, the language of greatness. So Cory Booker's also a fool ranting in Spanish. Don't they realize they're handing me the heartland.

I'm glad most Americans understand I'm the wall between them and chaos. When my immigration and security plans are complete, we won't have any more tragedies like a father and young daughter drowning in the Rio Grande after being denied asylum. They should've just gone home. Julian Castro says he's proud to be the first candidate to offer a comprehensive immigration plan. I haven't read his plan, and I won't. Why should I? I haven't even read my own plan, but I know Castro basically wants to open up the borders. Look, we either have a country or we don't. I'm surprised Beto and Castro aren't debating this in Spanish.

Dick DeBlasio, that joke of a mayor from New York City, says immigrants aren't the problem. Corporations are. Little Dick, who's probably the biggest pansy in the history of my rough city, should know that without powerful corporations we wouldn't have the wealth to live better than anyone in history while attracting freeloaders from all over the world.

The Democrats are out of control. Amy Klobuchar believes we all share the goal of universal health care. That's nonsense. And Julian Castro says he supports reproductive justice which he thinks is under attack in many places including Missouri, Alabama, and Georgia. Elizabeth Warren jumps in to say everyone must support Roe v. Wade. These people are way out of step with our changing America.

Cory Booker's not going to win many votes from blue collars whites by announcing it's repugnant to profit from law and order by having large private prisons. People want to be protected and don't care whether the bad guys are locked up by bureaucrats or businessmen. Let them compete for the honor.

Now they're moving into foreign policy, and Amy Klobachar – who's going to remember that weird last name? – charges I made the United States unsafe by getting tough with Iran and that I'm conducting foreign policy in a bathrobe while leading us within ten minutes and one tweet of war. In fact, I'm starving and scaring the mullahs so there won't be any war. General Tulsi Gabbard, again stating she served in Iraq at the "height of the war," demands we stand up to "chickenhawks" like John Bolton and Mike Pompeo. I know she's implying I'm a chickenhawk, too. I guarantee you if I hadn't had bone spurs I'd have been a great soldier in Vietnam. The military knows I'm tough.

The Democrats insist on being the party of weakness. Elizabeth Warren wants the federal government to decide what to do with guns she says are a "virus killing our children." Bad people kill children, Elizabeth, not guns. Good guys with guns save lives. Tell that to the children you say ask how you're going to keep them safe. Don't move into Cory Booker's neighborhood. He's proud to be the only presidential candidate who lives in a ghetto where seven people were shot last year. Booker says he wants to "buy back" guns but he really wants to take them away from you. Julian Castro and Amy Klobuchar also talk about common sense gun control and mental health care and a buy buck, but watch out.

My opponents are still the touchy feely party. They want to limit the police, squeeze the wealthy, and restrict my ability to use our military to protect us. Those positions won't help them and neither will their obsession with making everything about me. Some guy up there named John Delaney told the truth. Most Americans are interested in jobs, infrastructure, and health care, and my powerful economy is taking care of the first en route to resolving the other two.

Casting Director Watches Second Debate

Blessed with the insight of a soothsayer and the power of a kingmaker, I have many times selected the best stars for classic roles. I said cast Humphrey Bogart instead of Ronald Reagan in *Casablanca*. I picked John F. Kennedy over Richard Nixon. I decreed that Reagan replace Jimmy Carter and Bill Clinton topple George Bush. I insisted Barack Obama would be a better leading man than John McCain and Mitt Romney. I'm no idealist. I'm a ratings guy always searching for stars who bring box office clout. Admittedly, I said go ahead and cast Donald Trump instead of Hillary Clinton because The Donald puts more fannies in seats. Now, however, I realize we need a more talented actor in the White House. I didn't see any likely replacements in the first Democratic debate so, like a hungry talent scout, I focus on the second cattle call.

I like Bernie Sanders but politics has been Hollywood since the televised days of young JFK, and Bernie at almost seventy-eight looks old, and his demands for universal Medicare and free college tuition and housing for the homeless, though admirable, have become repetitive and many citizens wonder how we'd pay for his dreams. I can't select Bernie for any roles other than someone's cantankerous uncle or a senator from Vermont.

Joe Biden's only a year younger than Bernie and not a skillful contender so why is he leading in these early polls? He's riding the lengthy coattails of Barack Obama who a majority of Americans still wish resided at 1600 Pennsylvania Avenue. Joe never will. He'll be perfect as a retired elder statesman, and there'll be less talk about which women he spooks and the segregationist senators he's proud to have worked with in collegial fashion.

Kamala Harris throws a headlock on Biden, telling him his remarks are hurtful since the long-dead senators opposed busing and Harris was herself bused to school during the early days of integration in Berkeley. It matters not that Biden has a strong positive record on civil rights. The Miami audience is applauding his critic. And split screen images of proactive Harris and passive Joe are unkind to the former vice president, who appears elderly compared to his assailant, who's fifty-four. Let us remember, as well, that The Donald recently turned seventy-three.

Her path to the presidency obstructed by powerful but slowing septuagenarians, Harris decides to attack. She quips that Americans don't want to watch a food fight; they want to know who's going to put food on the table. She earns another big hand when she condemns the existence of private detention facilities for undocumented immigrants and promises on day one as president she'll reinstitute DACA for the dreamers, review asylum cases, get rid of private facilities, and empathize with mothers who take these risks. She rouses the audience again, noting that climate change is an existential crisis, and the greatest threat to the world is Donald Trump.

Democratic opponents keep firing on each other. Pete Buttigieg responds to criticism he mishandled race relations in South Bend where blacks comprise twenty-six percent of the population, but only six percent of the police force, and another unarmed man of color was shot dead by a white officer. He admits he didn't get it done. There should've been more "bias training." Youthful Pete is usually bright but brains aren't the primary component of stardom. I'll still give him a role somewhere, perhaps as mayor of South Bend.

As a supporter of participatory democracy, I thank the other six contestants and offer unwanted advice. To John Hickenlooper, perhaps a new surname would help. To Andrew Yang, please stick to business. For Michael Bennet and Kirsten Gillibrand, why not continue being senators. Eric Swalwell, you're a fine young congressman. And to Marianne Williams, you're a groovy chick from the sixties and I'm going to read some of your popular books about love and inner peace.

Kamala Harris, you still haven't proved you're a national star but, if you can get to the general election, you may be the Democrat with the best chance to beat Donald Trump if he ever loses his immunity to being a louse.

Note: A day after the second debate, Ivanka Trump sat at the table near her father and President Xi Jinping of China during G-20 trade talks in Osaka, Japan.

Putin Buries Liberalism

What great guy is Donald Trump. Finally, United States has president who understands trends of history. As new kind of candidate, Trump "saw changes in American society and took advantage of this." He knows "Western liberalism is dying if not already dead." Reason is simple: liberals "presuppose nothing needs to be done… Migrants can kill and rape with impunity because their rights must be protected." I praise President Trump for "trying to stop immigrants and drugs."

It's absurd, of course, to accuse me of interfering in 2016 presidential election. United States interferes in elections all over world and has many times overthrown, and even killed, political enemies abroad, as well as invaded more countries than I have space to recount. Yes, I know, Russia and other powers throughout history have behaved in similar ways. So don't make big deal of little cyber activity. Play it cool like President Trump at G-20 meeting in Osaka.

When reporters ask him about my alleged interference, he smiles and points at me, saying, "Don't meddle in the election."

Right, we won't meddle in your elections, and you won't meddle in anyone else's, will you?

Freedom of Trump

silicon valley better watch out
either they stop censorship and

bias against conservatives or
they'll face legislation i promised
to fox news and other defenders of
free speech at white house where google
facebook and twitter weren't invited

Trump Counters British Ambassador

Shaking several papers in his hand, President Trump shouts, "What the hell are these?"

"They're quotes just leaked from private diplomatic memos by the British ambassador," says adviser Kellyanne Conway.

"Who's that?"

"Kim Darroch."

"Man or woman?"

"Ambassador Darroch is a man, President Trump. And he gives great parties."

"Tell the secret service to get my beast."

"Where are you going?"

"To the British Embassy, and you're coming."

Trump, Conway, and a security detail exit the White House and enter several beasts that need fifteen minutes to grind through traffic three miles to the elegant four-story manor where Ambassador Kim Darroch works and lives.

Pocketing his tweeter and exiting the vehicle, Trump approaches two guards behind the black wrought iron fence and tells them, "You know who I am. Open up."

"Do you have an appointment, President Trump?" one guard says.

"Tell Kim Darroch his ass is in hot water."

The other guard speaks into a device clipped to his collar.

"Hurry up," says Trump.

A couple minutes later the guard says, "You're in luck. Ambassador Darroch's available."

The gates open and Trump directs Conway and five agents to accompany him. Before they reach the front door, Kim Darroch emerges wearing a fine suit, spots Conway and approaches her, saying,

"Kellyanne, how nice to see you."

They shake hands and chat a moment before she glances at Trump.

"I don't mean to break up your little reunion," says the president, "but I'm here on urgent state business."

"I have an idea what that might be," says Darroch.

Trump holds out his hand and an agent fills it with the leaked comments.

"Let's see," says Trump, "I could start anywhere. You wrote that my Iran policy is 'incoherent.' I'm trying to prevent them from getting nuclear weapons."

"The nuclear deal is still doing that quite well, but your departure imperils everyone in the region."

Trump shakes his head. "I want you to apologize for writing that I 'might be indebted to dodgy Russians.'"

"I still believe that could be the case, Mr. President," says Darroch.

"The Mueller report exonerated me: no collusion and no obstruction."

"Actually, the Mueller report, which still needs more thorough public examination, explicitly did not exonerate you of anything. It merely concluded the government couldn't prove you colluded with the Russians, and I don't believe you did. But the evidence may point to obstruction."

"You must get your talking points from CNN. You claim we'll never 'look competent' and you doubt my 'administration is going to become substantially more normal, less dysfunctional, less clumsy and inept,' and so on. I do things my way, the new way, and career bureaucrats like you are amateurs."

Kim Darroch appears to have been told he's on Mars.

"Mr. President, your accusation of amateurism is most ironic, otherwise you'd know that my task as ambassador is to make confidential assessments about the current administration in the United States. Furthermore, while you were bilking workers of wages, using race to deny rental applications, and misguiding several large businesses into financial disaster, I worked all over the world as a diplomat, served as national security adviser to a prime minister, and was my nation's representative to the European Union."

"That's why I've already tweeted you're a 'very stupid guy.' The European Union's a loser. And you better get your ass out of my country. You won't have any contact with me or the many people in my administration and the State Department."

Ambassador Darroch glances at Kellyanne Conway, who looks away, before he says, "After more than forty years of service, I'll gladly resign my post rather than deal with you."

Motioning toward his beasts, Donald Trump says, "Come on, Kellyanne, this guy's a bozo."

A View from the Philippines

This interview was conducted online with Jose Abeto Zaide, a former Philippine diplomat who during a career of more than forty years served as ambassador to Austria, Germany and France. In this book, our discussion is shortened to keep the focus on Donald Trump and related concerns. Since retirement, Ambassador Zaide cheers from the bleachers writing a column in the Manila Bulletin.

George Thomas Clark – You're a man of tact and insight, qualities that enabled you to flourish in your career. At the same time you must have written some confidential, and at times critical, assessments about leaders in your host countries. Please tell us how you, and ambassadors generally, operate in that regard.

Jose Abeto Zaide – We observe the Queensbury rules and as a rule do not include ad hominem comments on personages, especially heads of state and/or government officials. Dispatches sent in confidence report factually. (Although personal observations not for public consumption may be a little more colorful. In the event, allow for plausible denial.)

We report some alternative approach, which HQ in good judgment generally approves. But it is not rare for our counsel to be overruled; and after some exchanges, HQ prevails. I have had no reason to think otherwise, even during trying times when we were under martial law.

GTC – President Donald Trump, who's so quick to insult people and even quicker to squeal when he's criticized, recently went ballistic when the private diplomatic opinions of Kim Darroch, Great Britain's ambassador to the United States, were leaked. Darroch wrote scathingly of the Trump administration. Do you agree with his appraisal?

JAZ – I do not have the privilege of knowing if the British dispatches were taken out of context. But public disclosure of snippets of some, followed by unexpurgated presidential hyper-reaction, necessitate the recall of Her Majesty's envoy to Washington to restore the privileged relations between the two nations.

Furthermore, it appears that the U.S. president remains in form, neither inhibited nor cramped by the disclosures.

GTC – What caused these leaks, presumably from within the British foreign service? Do you think British adversaries of Darroch, and probably admirers of Trump, scattered this information to force him out even earlier than his projected retirement at the end of 2019?

JAZ – I do not see how exchanges benefit one side to the detriment of the other. Nor do I image the leak would cause the premature retirement of a professional diplomat, who should remain on Her Majesty's Service.

GTC – If you were the Philippine ambassador to the United States now, how would you deal with people like Trump and his national security advisor John Bolton and Secretary of State Mike Pompeo, who presume American superiority in all matters and seem to be eager to start a war with Iran?

JAZ – An envoy is respectful of the Head of State and all high level officials of the country to which he is accredited. If I were privileged to serve in Washington, I would venture to bend the ear of those who would listen. Even those of contrarian opinion, if they would listen to test ours.

But that probably doesn't get the message nearer to the dramatis personae. Perhaps, to send the message through their minders?

However, one must also be sensible to the reach (or the lack of it) of the country you represent.

GTC – In the United States and China and North Korea, and Italy and Poland and Hungary and elsewhere, there are movements lumbering to the right. This also appears to be true in the Philippines, where President Rodrigo Duterte and his henchmen are reportedly gunning down thousands of "drug dealers" without trials or even discussion. Does this trouble you? Or, are reports exaggerated, and is Duterte really a selfless law and order man trying to help the country?

JAZ – Clint Eastwood's "Dirty Harry" got him elected Mayor. The use of force, (or the threat thereof), was his very effective approach. He did not aspire for higher office as President Rodrigo Duterte did successfully.

I am frankly concerned about allegations of extrajudicial resolutions. But the jury hasn't yet ruled on this.

GTC – Can reporters and columnists for major newspapers in the Philippines write frankly about President Duterte and his administration?

JAZ – Reporters and columnists from major dailies are free to write frankly about President Duterte. The *Philippine Inquirer*, a major daily, is one such.

GTC – I know you've written two books about your diplomatic adventures but they're out of print. I hope you'll someday transform them into eternal ebooks so people all over the world can learn more.

JAZ – Thank you. Old stories get better in the retelling.

GTC – Merci beaucoup, Mr. Ambassador.

SIXTY-THREE

Trump Addresses White America

Look at all you fine Americans in the arena tonight and in television land and my online universe. You know I'm no dummy and was aware three of the four congresswomen I tomahawked in tweets the other day were born in the United States. The worst of them, Ilhan Omar of Somalia, really should go back to the cesspool she came from since all she does is criticize the United States and Israel. And she ought to take Alexandria Ocasio-Cortez with her because Cortez, let's shorten her name, isn't merely a socialist, she's a scary brown communist who wants to turn the country I've made great into a Soviet Puerto Rico. Yeah, Cortez is from the Bronx, and look at that place. It'll get even worse with her in Congress. She loves accusing me of racism because I'm guarding our border and humanely treating the not-so-good people who try to sneak in. She's lying, something I never do, when she says our border housing is like a concentration camp. Cortez needs to get online and check out Dachau or an Indian reservation, then she'll know what a concentration camp really is.

Rashida Tlaib is so bad. She was born in Detroit and has helped turn that once great city into a junkyard and shooting gallery. She doesn't say much about that. She'd rather attack Israel for "dehumanization and racist policies" and complain that her "ancestors were killed and uprooted from their land (in order) to create the state of Israel." Too bad Tlaib's ancestors didn't come from a great democratic nation like Israel, which is getting bigger all the time as it expands West Bank settlements and I look the other way and hope you do too. That's the American white way. Ayanna Pressley, who's probably Elvis' older sister, was born in Cincinnati and raised in Chicago before moving to Boston where she's hoodwinked those who should know better. Lots of Jews in Boston think she's their friend and an able public servant. She's not. She's black, female, and a far leftie, and you know what they're like.

I've gotta wait while you folks chant, "Send them back, send them back…"

I understand how you feel. That's how I want you to feel. I want you concentrating on four first-term congresswomen who are dark and dangerous. Don't worry about what they and other aliens say about me. I'm the guy they can't beat, and they know it. In the whole world no one has my star power, not a single person, and our enemies just can't handle that.

Donald Says

i
don't
have
a
racist
bone
in
my
body

At the Ranch

A helicopter churns above hills covered with oaks near Santa Barbara and descends into green pasture and lands a couple hundred yards from where a man watches, mounted on his horse. When whirling blades stop, he rides up and dismounts and takes off his cowboy hat as the door opens and a heavy man in red cap poses at the top of several pull-down steps before he descends and shakes hands with his smiling host who says, "Welcome to my ranch."

"Mr. President, it's an honor to meet you."

"The honor's mine, Mr. President. Please, call me Ron."

"Okay, if you'll call me Donald."

"What do you say I get you some riding boots and a cowboy hat and we go for a ride?"

"I don't ride much anymore but I play a lot of golf. In fact, this place, with the hills and trees and big pond, would make a terrific golf course and resort. Let me know if you ever want to sell it."

"Nancy and I love this place too much to ever sell. Follow me."

They walk to an attractive but modest structure.

"I guess you know, I own one of the most luxurious vacation homes in the world, Mar-a-Lago."

"I've seen pictures of it," says Ron. "Come on in."

They sit at a wooden table polished bright.

"I'm doing a lot of the things you did, making us great again and giving people hope."

"The economy looks good," says Ron.

"And, like you, I'm rebuilding the military, which was really weak when we took over."

Ron nods. "I was plenty tough but after making my point I focused on reducing nuclear arms. You seem to be going the other way."

"The world's so much more dangerous today than in your time," says Donald.

"I found the world less dangerous the less we intervened. When three hundred of our marines were blown up in Lebanon, I asked myself what the hell are we doing there, and I brought them home."

"That would be impossible today, Ron. We'd probably have to invade."

"There'll always be wars if leaders want them."

"I sure don't want war," says Donald. "I don't have a violent bone in my body."

Ron studies him and says, "There's chaos at our southern border."

"I'm making damn sure everyone understands the danger."

"We've had pretty good relations with Mexico since before the Civil War."

"Come on, Ron. Some of the baddest people on earth are invading us."

"Most people aren't like that. Have you heard my final speech as president when I talked about our immigrants?"

"I probably heard it but can't remember everything right now."

"Here's the transcript from thirty years ago. All right if I read a little of it?"

Donald nods. "Sure."

Glancing at his script, Ron says, "America represents something universal in the human spirit. I received a letter not long ago from a man who said, 'You can go to France to live and not become a Frenchman. You can go to live in Germany or Turkey, and you won't become a

German or a Turk.' But then he added, 'Anybody from any corner of the world can come to America to live and become an American.'"

"That was before terrorism," says Donald.

Ron points at his paper and continues, "This I believe is one of the most important sources of America's greatness. We lead the world because unique among nations, we draw our people, our strength, from every country and every corner of the world... Thanks to each wave of new arrivals to this land of opportunity, we're a nation forever young, forever bursting with energy and new ideas, and always on the cutting edge, always leading the world to the next frontier... If we ever closed the door to new Americans, our leadership in the world would soon be lost..."

He puts the script down and says, "I hope you'll seriously consider what I've just said."

"I gotta go," says Donald. "Teeing off this afternoon in Santa Barbara. I may buy the place."

"The whole town?"

"Just the golf course."

Happy Tweeter

Real early this morning after another night alone I reach into my pants, grab my tweeter, and shoot too bad Robert Mueller has to subject himself to sadistic Democrats who blew two years and thirty million bucks on a phony investigation led by a guy even Michael Moore soon admits is a frail old man with a bad memory and no backbone. I guess I should thank the Dems for holding this meeting because now even they've got to shut up and drop the impeachment nonsense. Remember, truth is a force of nature.

Daughter Debates Dad

Our flat screen shows a wide stage containing ten eager presidential candidates.

"Daddy, what's a Hickenlooper?" asks my daughter.

"That's a former governor of Colorado," I say.

"What's he doing in California?"

"They're in Detroit for a debate."

"Why?"

"They're trying to become president of the United States."

"Who's going to win?"

Jabbing my index finger and looking stern, I say, "Melissa, I told you you were going to have to be quiet."

"She gets up from the sofa and walks toward her bedroom, turning to tell me, "I'm going to play video games."

"Come on back, Melissa, I'm sorry. Besides, no video games on weeknights."

She returns. "I still want to know who's going to win."

"Among those here tonight, I like Bernie Sanders and think he has the best chance."

"Which one's he?"

"The one who's talking right now."

Melissa throws hands over eyes and says, "Oh, no. He's older than Grandpa."

"Only a few years. But you may have a point. A lot of people worry about his age."

"Who else do you like?"

"Elizabeth Warren, in the red jacket."

Melissa shakes her head. "She looks like Mrs. Bodkin, my Sunday school teacher. But Mrs. Bodkin's younger."

"Mrs. Bodkin's not running for president, Melissa. And Elizabeth Warren is very healthy and vigorous at age seventy. She's three years younger than President Trump."

"She doesn't look like a president."

"Because we've never had a woman president," I say.

"Elizabeth and Bernie are boring."

"Maybe you'll like some of the candidates tomorrow night."

Opening wide eyes, Melissa says, "You mean there are more candidates?"

"Ten more, among those who qualified."

"Are they really old, too?"

"Well, the leader in the polls, Joe Biden, is only a year younger than Bernie."

"Uuuhhh."

"These are all bright and conscientious people, Melissa."

"They sound silly."

"Only because you're too young to understand the issues."

"I'm voting for President Trump," says Melissa.

"Why, in God's name?"

"He's fun to watch."

"Thankfully, you're way too young to vote."

"I'm old enough to know who's going to win."

Trump Irritated by Democrat Debate

What a ridiculous debate, just like the one the night before. The Democrats don't have anyone like me, but that's not their biggest problem. With their crazy policies, they couldn't beat me if they nominated George Washington.

Right away the candidates start arguing about who'd be better at spending trillions of dollars for health care. What they really want is to take away the private insurance plans millions of you love, and force you to pay the government for the public option. Many of them try to deny it, of course. Kamala Harris and Joe Biden pretend each has the better idea but once the Democrats get started they'd destroy private insurance, restrict the profits of our brilliant pharmaceutical companies, and bankrupt the nation. They can't compete with me. I wrote the book on bankruptcies.

I love it when my opponents talk about immigration. They're conceding the election. Julian Castro says it shouldn't be a crime to enter our nation illegally but he somehow denies favoring open borders. So do a lot of Democrats. Rather than worrying about your jobs and your safety, people like Kamala Harris are complaining about private detention facilities. That's the problem with Democrat politicians, most have always fed at the public trough and envy those of us who create jobs and make money.

Watch the Democrats carefully about busing. In her first debate, Harris bragged about being bused in Berkeley. The rest of the liberals feel the same way. They want to take your kids from the suburbs and bus them into the ghettos and send the ghetto kids to the suburbs you worked so hard to move to. When the suburbs are invaded, you know what would happen. The Democrats call me a racist. I'm the least racial person you'll ever meet. Joe Biden's not often right about anything but he nails it when he points out Harris, as attorney general of California, did nothing to desegregate Los Angeles and San Francisco. On the other hand, I've done more to help blacks than any president in history, using my economic genius to reduce black unemployment to its lowest level ever. The prosperity I'm creating will actually do something about the Democrat complaint that eighty percent of people in prison drop out of high school. I'm going to transform our rat-infested ghettos into chic urban centers. By the way, the next time Julian Castro calls me a racist I'm going to call him Fidel.

Other than tree-hugging nutcase Jay Inslee, the Democrats don't talk much about the supposedly end-of-the-world problem posed by global warming. The environmental restrictions of their proposed green new deal would devastate our economy and bankrupt us even worse than their health care plans. I'll keep air and water clean by wisely spending money generated by the greatest economy in world history. The Democrats don't bother denying unemployment is at record lows while the stock market hits all-time highs. And they can't damage me by noting women earn eighty percent of what men earn for the same work. I'm a pioneer in hiring women executives. I promoted the first elite female executive in the New York construction business, I made my first wife, Ivana, president of the Plaza Hotel, and, as you know, I give huge responsibilities to my sexy daughter Ivanka.

Cory Booker, the failed mayor of disastrous Newark, who's now a senator, brags he'll bring home our troops from Afghanistan as soon as possible and he "will not conduct foreign policy by tweet." First, Cory, clean up your own nest before you try to command the most powerful nation on earth. You'll never be our president. You've only got four million Twitter followers compared to my sixty-two million. That's what counts.

Staying in foreign policy, Joe Biden has to admit he backed the war in Iraq. He alibis that his "mistake was to trust the intelligence reports of President George W. Bush." Biden and Bush should've been smart like me and opposed the war. Ignore those who claim I didn't really speak out against the war. And there's Tulsi Gabbard, still bragging she's a warrior. I probably would've enlisted, too, but my Vietnam bone spurs still hurt.

For some reason, despite my exoneration, boring Booker soon says, "We should start impeachment proceedings immediately." Right, to remove Cory Booker from the United States Senate. Julian "Fidel" Castro says let's "go forward." Incompetent New York Mayor Bill DiBlasio claims it's "obvious Trump has committed crimes worthy of impeachment." I'm a real New Yorker and know it's time to impeach DiBlasio. He and Booker can start a lousy comedy team. Some nobody named Michel Bennet says the "best way to impeach Donald Trump is to beat him in 2020." In other words, it ain't happening.

In closing statements these losers continue with the predictable. Tax hell out of the wealthy for universal health care. Be ready when Trump accuses us of being socialists. Remind people Trump believes in "socialism for the rich." Keep saying that Trump has "torn apart the fabric of this country." Be aware that "warmongering politicians" aren't worried there are thousands of nuclear missiles pointed at us. Trump thinks he's still on reality TV.

That's right, and I've got the highest ranked show in the world.

Trump Visits Elijah Cummings

Donald Trump squeezes his Oval Office phone and calls secret service agents, ordering them to ready several black beasts for an executive motorcade to nearby Baltimore. After entering the city limits they begin passing old buildings marred by broken or boarded windows and piles of trash outside.

"Look how they live," says Trump. "Disgusting. Get me Rep. Elijah Cummings."

The call is placed. Cummings answers.

"This is President Trump. Meet me in your disaster zone in ten minutes."

"I'm dealing with a personal emergency here at home," says

Cummings. "You come here."

Cummings reveals the address and Trump shoots it to his driver who conveys the destination to drivers of other beasts. In a better part of town, they pull behind three police cars parked in front of a three-story brick residence connected to a row of similar residences.

Trump rolls down the window and to an officer says, "You must be busting Cummings. What'd he do?"

"He was robbed."

"You think he's armed?"

"No sir."

"He better not be. We're going in."

Trump and his entourage walk into a first floor room where two detectives are interviewing Elijah Cummings.

"I'm real sorry to see you've been robbed, Rep. Cummings," Trump says.

"I appreciate that, Mr. President."

"I hate to see you and other citizens of Baltimore suffer in a rat and rodent infested hellhole. But that's what happens when you and other liberals don't do anything to create jobs and enforce the laws."

"We're living a lot better here in Baltimore than those poor Central American and Mexican children you've torn from their parents and crammed into concentration camps built for half as many. The children are sitting in their own feces. They can't take a shower. What's that all about?"

"Don't play the brutal bully with me," Trumps says. "The brave men and women of the border patrol should've arrested you when you questioned their humanity and dedication. You and the rest of your gang better keep in mind that the murder rate in Baltimore is higher now than in Guatemala, El Salvador, and Honduras."

"We need more funding for jobs, education, housing, law enforcement, and so much more."

Trump nods to an agent who pulls an electronic tablet from his blazer and summons a 1999 video of formidable young Rep. Cummings saying, "This is a drug infested area. Children I watched grow up are now walking around like zombies."

"I'm glad you used to agree with me and hope we can work together soon," Trump says.

"You must do something for these people."

"I've been president of the whole country only two and a half years. You've represented Baltimore more than twenty years. What have you done?"

"I've done everything possible. Why don't you help us instead of billionaires?"

"Don't worry, Rep. Cummings. I'm going to keep creating unprecedented numbers of jobs for blacks and someday I'll be a hero in Baltimore."

SIXTY-FOUR

Joe Six Pack Demands Better Security

I served three tours in Iraq and two in Afghanistan, belong to the NRA, go to the shooting range every week, hunt many times a year, and know a helluva lot more about security than almost anyone. So I'll explain what we've got to do.

Take that shooting early Sunday morning in the nightlife district in Dayton. The police did a great job, killing the body-armored shooter thirty seconds after he opened fire, but we've got to do better. Not the police, who can't be everywhere, but all of us. We've got to be packing all the time. I'm not saying we should be marching around with assault rifles, like these killers, but we could damn sure be carrying high-caliber handguns with plenty of ammo. Imagine if even half the hundreds of partiers had been armed. At least one would have put a slug in the shooter's head before he murdered more than a couple of people instead of nine who died.

Now look at that Walmart in El Paso where about twelve hours earlier another shooter murdered twenty-two and wounded more than two dozen. Bloodshed wouldn't have been that bad if every employee had been armed and ready to go. Also, lots of shoppers should've had guns on their hips. That's just common sense. I bet they could've kept the body bag total under ten.

A few days before, at the Walmart in Mississippi, armed employees would've helped but the situation was a little trickier since the killer was disgruntled and gunned down two coworkers. If someone's pissed it's easy to start shooting. A police officer shot the shooter but if the victims had been prepared they might've been able to wound or kill the killer before he killed them.

The Gilroy Garlic Festival last week reminds me of the Dayton partiers. All those people having a good time in Gilroy forgot one thing: to bring their guns. If you aren't armed, take it from a warrior that you're not going to stop a guy who's wearing tactical gear and firing an assault rifle. I know two of the three who died were children, so I'm not blaming them. But they must've been there with adults who should've been ready. You get thousands of people in one place, it's a guarantee some will be crazies. I'm surprised only about a dozen people were wounded. There would've been more bloodshed but police closed in and the killer shot himself.

The libtards are saying that President Trump's patriotic speechmaking and defense of the border may have encouraged unstable people to cross the line. That just isn't fair. This stuff was happening long before Trump became president. The guy in Gilroy had been complaining online that hordes of mestizos are invading the country, which is true, but he also didn't like Silicon Valley "twats." To get a better picture of things, go online to 8chan where minutes before he started shooting the guy in El Paso posted three hot pages against immigrants taking our jobs and diluting our European identity. I don't read 8chan that much but just tuned in and learned that about the same time as Dayton someone shot seven people in Chicago. According to the website, which I imagine is a good source, no one's dead yet, but that could change. The anonymous commentator – they all hide their names – posted: "its absolutely fucking happening !!! the FIRE RISES!!!"

That kind of stuff attracts thirty-five thousand visitors every day. Make sure your guns are loaded.

Trump Denounces Racists

white supremacy is an evil ideology
our nation must condemn it with one voice
hate has no place in america or my tweeter

Donald Tweets

i hope fake news will report dayton shooter supported
bernie sanders
elizabeth warren
antifa and
assault rifles

Love in Dayton and El Paso

Donald Trump, clad in a red bathrobe, tiptoes down the long hall of the White House private quarters and knocks on a closed door he tries to open. It's locked.

"Melania, hurry up, almost time to go," he says, placing his lips to the door.

"I'm not going, Donald."

"You have to."

"You do. I don't."

"You promised you'd go."

"I'll be out when I'm ready."

"Do you always have to keep your door locked?"

The president knows the answer. He returns to his bedroom to shower and dress. In the dining room he eats a hearty breakfast by himself. Melania enters in a black dress, long and sleek, and asks, "Will we be safe?"

"Of course. The secret service is great."

"I mean emotionally."

"Melania, we're going to have a historic day."

After huge Air Force One lands in Dayton the Trumps enter a beast and go to a hospital to visit survivors, relatives, and first responders. Fake news has been banned and only members of the presidential media team take pictures and shoot film. In less than two hours the visit is over and the Trumps return to their plane for the flight to El Paso.

Hoping to relax, he gets tense watching Fox News. Dayton Mayor Nan Whaley and Senator Sherrod Brown are being interviewed.

"I told the president that we need action on gun control," Whaley says. "And he said, 'We're going to do something.'"

Mayor Whatley continues, "I told him, 'How about getting an assault weapons ban, something President Obama couldn't do.'"

Trump made no commitment but Mayor Whaley concedes, "The president and Melania said and did the right things in the hospital."

Throwing his cheeseburger onto the plate, Trump shouts, "Get me my goddamn tweeter."

He tweets the nation and world that he'd just had a "warm &

wonderful visit. Tremendous enthusiasm & even Love." Then he had to watch Whaley and Brown "totally misrepresenting what took place inside of the hospital. Their news conference… was a fraud."

Trump orders his social media director, "Tell everyone the truth."

Complying at once, the director tweets, "The president was greeted like a rock star."

That's what counts. Trump seems relieved and devours his cheeseburger. Then he walks to Melania's private room and is allowed to enter. She glances up from her fashion magazine.

"Please don't knock my hand away this time," he says. "When we get to El Paso, it's important we hold hands when we walk down the steps."

Melania resumes looking at photos.

In El Paso, the first lady, guarded by dark sunglasses, complies with her husband's request and they descend to the tarmac and greet dignitaries before they enter a beast and go to a hospital for more visits.

A few hours later, back on Air Force One and flying to Washington, D.C., Trump releases a tweet with an attached video of people smiling in the Dayton hospital and himself gesturing thumbs up and these pretty images are accompanied by rousing music. One wonders what they were celebrating.

Now, in the dark heavens, Donald Trump is happy his difficult duties are completed and he's received more reports confirming that ICE agents earlier today arrested about seven hundred illegal aliens at several companies across Mississippi.

"That's the biggest operation like this in history," says Trump. His social media director and staff members smile and flash thumbs up. Melania's already back in her room.

SIXTY-FIVE

Trump Twists Netanyahu

In their private communications rooms in Washington, D.C. and Jerusalem, Donald Trump and Benjamin Netanyahu stand before movie screens and gaze at each other before breaking into smiles.

"Great to see you, Mr. President. I just wish I could shake your hand."

"We'll soon be shaking hands again, Bibi, but right now I have a serious matter to discuss," says Trump, suddenly stern.

Netanyahu summons a grim expression. "Go ahead, please."

"I'm very unhappy that Israel might give Representatives Ilhan Omar and Rashida Tlaib permission to visit your great democracy."

"We're such special historical allies, Mr. President, that we usually grant elected officials the opportunity to visit and learn about each other's countries."

Standing heavily in his suit, Trump says, "These Muslims aren't coming to Israel to learn. They think they already know everything. Why haven't they scheduled any meetings with Israeli officials? Because they plan to spend all their time with Palestinians, planning boycotts."

"I'm very much aware they aren't friends of Israel, but I don't consider a couple of freshmen congresswomen to be a significant threat."

"They'll be as big a threat as they can and shouldn't be allowed in your country."

Netanyahu pauses several seconds. "I have to consider the political damage throughout the Middle East if I bar them from coming."

"More importantly, Bibi, you have to consider the political damage I'd suffer if they start agitating on the West Bank. And that's exactly what they'd do."

"That wouldn't look good."

"I'm the most powerful and committed friend Israel has ever had, and I know you want me to continue helping you at least five more years."

Netanyahu nods. "That's right, Mr. President."

"We can virtually guarantee my reelection right here, Bibi. We paint them as Muslim terrorists and racists and force the Democrats to support them after you ban them. That way I convince Americans that Omar and Tlaib, as well as Alexandria Ocasio-Cortez, are the face of the Democrat party."

"There's no way you'd lose running against them next year," says Netanyahu.

"So we have an understanding?"

"Of course, I'll not only prohibit them from visiting, I'll denounce them. That should help."

"Thanks so much, Bibi."

My Huge Island

smart people understand greenland's got natural resources
and
great
location
near
arctic
naturally
i
want
to
buy
it
from tiny danes before big russians and chinese move in

Cold Iceland

what's that hot prime minister's name
katrín jakobsdóttir
who
cares
she'll
be
out
of
iceland

when
mike pence arrives i know she'd have
stayed to meet me

Heat

just had hottest july ever
but
don't
worry
republican
gonads still safely frozen
in
ice
melting
fast

Progress

brazilian trump bolsonaro
encourages
fools
to
burn
amazon
until cow farts prevail

Chosen

I am the chosen one. I'm the chosen one to take on the Chinese
and stop them from ripping us off. I'm the one to denuclearize North
Korea and Iran. I'm the one to prevent Russia from expanding. I'm
the one to keep our great economy expanding. I'm the one to protect
your sacred right to bear arms. I'm the one to guarantee that global
warming is a hoax. I'm the one to tell you my behavior has always
been good and stable and is getting better. Isn't it amazing? In every

way, I am the chosen one.

My Network

either fox news jumps
back
in
my
pocket
or
i'll buy my own network
and
deliver
the
truth

SIXTY-SIX

Pitiful Challenge

mark sanford
former south carolina governor
lied he hiked alone on
appalachian trail when really
he screwed wild woman
in argentina i hate guys
who lie to their wives and
challenge me in primaries

Bolton Out

Late on a summer evening at the White House, Donald Trump and John Bolton are speaking unpleasantly as they walk toward each other and by the time they're nose to nose they're almost shouting.

"I'm the president."

"Yes, and I'm the national security adviser with decades of experience in foreign policy, and I'm telling you you shouldn't bring representatives of the Taliban to Camp David under any circumstances especially when we're so close to the eighteenth anniversary of 9/11."

Looking down on Bolton, Trump says, "I'm amazed what a shrimp you are, John. Did you get bullied at school?"

"There you go, resorting to insults when facts and logic fail you. You're caving in to the Taliban just as you caved in to Kim Jong Un and let him continue his nuclear weapons programs."

"I stopped his missile testing," says Trump.

"He's still testing shorter range missiles all the time. Don't you read our intelligence reports or at least remember what you see on Fox News? We needed to attack North Korea long ago and the longer we wait the more dangerous our task."

"You're a loudmouth with no political base."

John Bolton takes a step back and inhales before he says, "And you let Iran get away with attacking our friends' oil tankers and shooting down one of our drones. You should've struck then. You should've struck long before that."

"It's people with small brains like you who always want war because you lack the vision or social skills for great diplomacy. I'm ready to meet President Hassan Rouhani without preconditions."

Bolton steps into Trump's space and says, "When you cancelled the nuclear deal you did the right thing but only if you understood it was the first step to war. The Iranians can't sit on their hands while the United States, and our European lackeys, keep tightening sanctions and cut off all their oil revenue. You had the perfect pretext to attack but you failed."

"I'm tired of your mouth, your abrasive personality, and your desire to start wars every goddamn place on earth."

"I'd be happy to offer you my resignation, Mr. President."

"You can't offer me your registration because I'd already decided to demand it."

Trump's Debate Tweets

What a bunch of pansies.

I don't look as old as Bernie Sanders and Joe Biden, do I? They need my hairdresser.

Tulsi Gabbard's hot but couldn't even qualify for this debate. Ivanka's hotter, anyway.

Kamala Harris is way too old for me.

I agree with Julian Castro that Biden's senile. And I'm sure Joe agrees that Castro's an open-borders smart ass.

Pete Buttigieg's a wimpy kind of guy. Whatever he did in Afghanistan, I could've done better.

Andrew Yang's one smart Asian. I may order my sons to hire him after he drops out.

Beto O'Rourke not only admits it, he brags he wants to break into your homes and steal your assault rifles. Then he'll take the rest of your guns. Other Dems would do the same.

Pocahontas Warren wants to socialize everything you've got.

Cory Booker's to the left of Warren and still living in a ghetto. He'll move when he gets reparations for African Americans.

Amy Klobuchar's got a nasty look, doesn't she?

I'm not watching the rest of this. Time for big bedtime snack.

Land of Netanyahu

I don't care if I lose the election. It doesn't matter if my traitorous enemies frame me for corruption. I care only for Israel. I could have retired years ago. I'm running again only because I've been prime minister ten straight glorious years during which Israel has grown and gotten stronger in order to survive amid, let us be frank, a partially-civilized band of non-nations that explicitly seek the annihilation of Israel.

I'm the only one who can save us. My special relationship with President Trump has already allowed me to officially add the Golan Heights to our nation, and I swear if you give me the mandate, if you reelect me as your leader, I will annex the Jordan Valley. That's right. Without equivocation I will simply decree that one-third of the already occupied and dismembered West Bank is ours. And soon enough we'll build settlements throughout the region everyone will call Judea and Samaria.

Weaklings may protest I'm breaking international law and further oppressing several million Palestinians. None of that matters. What's essential is that I continue as protector of my people, who, when I do some more annexing, will be a minority in greater Israel, a Jewish state nonetheless.

Why Saudi Oil was Attacked

You want to know who is responsible for the drone strikes that blasted the world's largest oil distribution facility and temporarily knocked out half of Saudi Arabia's production. Let's follow the trail. China, Russia, the United States, and European allies bargained arduously with Iran and in 2015 the nations signed the Joint Comprehensive Plan of Action better known as the Iran nuclear deal. Iran agreed to hold its production of nuclear material well below weapons-making levels and their compliance was ten times confirmed by the International Atomic Energy Agency. In exchange, powerful nations, particularly the United States, eased many sanctions that damaged Iran's economy and citizens. Saudi Arabia still pestered the United States to strike Iran. So did Israel. The Saudis and Israelis are forever anxious for Americans to slaughter hundreds of thousands of Arabs, and now Persians, while also spilling much American blood and burning trillions of dollars.

President Barack Obama and his administration, along with the other signatories, ignored the warmongers. Then candidate Donald J. Trump began calling the Iran nuclear deal the worst in history, and that must be pretty damn bad considering people who sign deals with Donald Trump often get fleeced. Furthermore, one wonders how Trump understood the deal's contents since odds he read the entire document are about as long as his someday becoming an honest man. Trump, of course, wasn't content to merely defecate on the deal. He also resumed crippling sanctions and added more, sending economic jackals around the world to threaten nations with dire consequences if they dared buy oil from Iran. Rather than tell Donald J. Trump to shove it, most nations dropped their drawers and bent over, and Iranians began to suffer.

Meanwhile, Saudi Arabia continued to pump and sell ten percent of the world's oil and make billions of dollars a week. Iran decided this wasn't fair, especially from a nation that has used its splendid military hardware, purchased from the United States, to slaughter thousands of Yemenis during their civil war to the south. Now there's been a devastating drone strike probably beyond the technical and economic abilities of the Houthis or any other group in Yemen. So Mike Pompeo, the corpulent, bible-thumping secretary of state, has blamed Iran for the strike. Information has indeed been filtering in that Iranian forces in southern Iraq, perhaps aided by their Shia Iraqi allies, may be responsible for the attack. Iranians probably were involved in the strike. But the person most responsible for turning a manageable situation into an inferno is Donald J. Trump.

Saudi Cathouse

tulsi gabbard tells trump we aren't your prostitutes
and
won't
be
pimped
out
to
saudi
arabia

SIXTY-SEVEN

Environmental Trump

i'm
deleting
california's
auto
emission
standards

Hungry Democrats

we're
humbly
asking
to
be
incredibly
grateful
for your generous donations

Bernie

you're
old
and
ill
please
quit

Memo to Trump

read joe mathews column
in california third of doctors
sixth of medical professionals
fifth of biomedical researchers
forty percent new entrepreneurs
are immigrants

My Kurds

Democrats are going to lie and complain even when I keep my campaign promise to avoid endless foreign wars especially in the Middle East. I'm not afraid to strike the Iranians for blowing up Saudi oil. I'm just being realistic they could do it again.

Now even Republicans are complaining I moved our troops out of harm's way in northeast Syria so Turkey can do some shooting and make a little buffer zone to keep Syrian Kurds from joining Turkish Kurds who want to terrorize our great NATO ally.

Do you want me to fight Turkey? I know you really don't. But what about betraying allies who helped us crush ISIS? I've got the Kurds' back, and if the Turks go too far I'll destroy their economy. And what if the Kurds run into the arms of Bashar al-Assad? That's probably what they'll do and you can't stop it and would protest if I tried and even I couldn't do anything and have anyway promised to stay out of stuff like that.

SIXTY-EIGHT

Whistleblower

you
know
what we used to do
to
traitors

Ukrainian Embrace

We recently learned that three months ago President Donald Trump called Volodymyr Zelensky, president-elect of Ukraine. Highlights of their conversation follow.

"Congratulations on your great victory," Trump tells him. "It's a fantastic achievement the way you came from behind and won easily."

"We worked very hard and are going to drain our swamp. You've been a great teacher for us."

"Very nice of you to say that. We do a lot for Ukraine, much more than European countries are doing. They should be helping you more than they are. All they do is talk. You should really ask them about that. You know how good the United States has been to Ukraine."

Nodding his head so hard Trump may be able to feel it, Zelensky says, "You're absolutely right. Not merely a hundred percent but a thousand percent. The United States is actually a bigger partner for us than the European Union. I'd especially like to thank you for your great support in the area of defense. We're ready to continue to cooperate so we can buy more Javelins and other equipment from the United States for defensive purposes."

"I'd like you to do us a favor," says Trump. "We've been through a lot and Ukraine knows a lot about it. There's this cybersecurity firm CrowdStrike claiming the Russians hacked into your artillery and caused a lot of losses. I want our attorney general, William Barr, to talk to you and find out what kind of people are around you."

"We're going to cooperate in every way, President Trump. I'll make sure I surround myself with the best and most experienced people. I want to emphasize we're great friends and you, Mr. President, have many friends in our country who'll help us continue our strategic partnership. We're recalling our ambassador to the United States and replacing her with an experienced diplomat who will earn your confidence and make sure our two nations grow closer. One of my assistants recently talked to your personal attorney, Rudolph Giuliani, and we hope he can visit our country very soon."

"That's good because there's a lot of talk about Hunter Biden acting shady in Ukraine, and that Joe Biden stopped the prosecution and a lot of people want to find out about that. Whatever you can do with Attorney General Barr would be great. Biden went around bragging he stopped the prosecution so if you can look into it... It sounds horrible to me."

"I assure you I'm bringing in a very strong prosecutor, someone who's a hundred percent my person and will investigate everything."

"You've got a great country, President Zelensky. I know many incredible people in Ukraine and predict you're going to get richer and richer."

"We're working on cooperation and we're buying American oil," says Zelensky, "I hope we can meet soon to discuss more opportunities and get to know each other better. I'd like to thank you very much for your support."

"You're welcome. I'll tell Rudy Giuliani and William Barr to call you. And whenever you want to visit the White House just call and give us a date."

Notes: President Zelensky visited the White House last week.

Donald Understands

this isn't an impeachment it's a coup
designed
to
destroy
democracy
freedom guns god and border wall

Transparency

don't you know how countries do business
watch
me
tell
china
to
investigate
criminal
bidens

Trump Dumps on Dems

Nothing makes me happier than watching Democrats debate each other in front of Americans who undoubtedly think the candidates are incompetent. You know there's NO WAY any of them can beat me and they know it too. That's why they're pushing for the illegal and absurd impeachment of an extraordinarily successful president. That won't work. Next year they're going to have to send a lamb to die in the general election.

Right now it looks like Elizabeth Warren is the least weak candidate emerging from a bad field. I'll rip Pocahontas for her plan to take people's private health insurance and replace it with Medicare for All. How many trillion dollars a year would that cost and who'd pay for it? Warren also wants to cut our revenues by outlawing fracking for oil and natural gas. That disaster would be worsened by her goal of legalizing illegal border crossings and then giving Medicare for All to alien criminals. She also wants you to pay reparations to descendants of slaves. Really, the Democrats are staggering so far left they might as well cancel the election and spare themselves a beating.

Alexandria Ocasio-Cortez and Ilhan Omar, two really bad broads, don't fool us when they announce they're supporting Bernie Sanders. They know damn well Bernie was looking hunched and feeble long before his heart attack and people aren't excited about him like they were four years ago. AOC and Omar and their America-hating gang are just sending a message to Elizabeth Warren that she better continue imitating a commie.

That's what the new Democrats want. They want defeat and know they're going to get it unless a Republican-controlled Senate helps convict me of doing a little routine business with President Zelensky of Ukraine. Damn right I said take a look at Crazy Joe Biden and his unethical son. That's good diplomacy. Get Over It.

SIXTY-NINE

Tulsi Counters Hillary

Hillary Clinton says she should've won presidency in 2016 but lost so close races in Pennsylvania, Michigan, and Wisconsin because communist Jill Stein siphoned off critical votes. Now, Hillary hears Russians are programming computers to boost another dictator-loving witch, Tulsi Gabbard.

Combat-ready Tulsi responds: "You, the queen of warmongers, embodiment of corruption, and personification of the rot that has sickened the Democratic Party for so long, have finally come out from behind the curtain."

Hillary gasps and dashes back into boardroom.

Vigilantes

I'm being lynched by a slobbering gang of Democrats who still won't accept I won a landslide to become commander in chief of the United States and most of the civilized world.

Every day my domestic enemies meet in secret and prepare to release more lies about me. It's like fighting a ghost. Okay, I'm a fighter, too, and always hit back harder than those who attack me, and am proud thirty House members of my Freedom Caucus activated their cell phones and invaded a secure room in the Capitol where traitors were trying to frame me for Ukraine just like they'd tried to string me up for No Collusion, No Obstruction in the Russian farce.

I'm not going to turn over information to this mob even if they do have some slimy subpoenas. They won't get any help from us. What I'll give them is endless counterattacks on Twitter: "Where's the whistleblower? The fake *Washington Post* keeps doing phony stories with zero sources that I'm concerned with impeachment scam. I am not because I did nothing wrong. The witch hunt continues..."

The Democrats are getting more desperate and by Election Day, in little more than a year, they'll be waving white flags.

Baghdadi at the Movies

This is really exciting, like being at a movie I'm directing. I'd rather be on site close to the action, exchanging gunfire, but my generals insist I've got to watch from here as our several helicopters fly in low and fast before landing at a secret location in northwest Syria. About sixty elite soldiers jump out and start blowing away ISIS enemies. There's bearded and bloodthirsty Abu Bakr al-Baghdadi, whimpering as he drags three of his children into a subterranean tunnel. When our dogs close in, Baghdadi activates the suicide vest around his filthy body, mutilating himself and the children. The tunnel caves in but our guys have plenty of DNA and facial recognition equipment that give us certain and immediate and positive identification. It's Baghdadi. We have a very long reach. Monsters like Abu Bakr al-Baghdadi can never sleep safely – we'll pursue them to their brutal end.

I'd like to thank our dear friends whose help made this operation possible – Russia, Turkey, Syria, Iraq and, of course, the Syrian Kurds. I'm sure you want some sensitive information about our intelligence and planning prior to the operation, so here are a few key things we knew and how we knew them before we decapitated ISIS, the most bloody group of terrorists in world history.

Blue Grass

not
my
fault
governor
bevin
couldn't hold serve in kentucky after i lifted him fifteen points
closer
at
end
we
won
five other races and hope mitch mcconnell hangs on next year

Happy Anniversary

today we celebrate forty years
since taking enemy embassy in
tehran and boast faster centrifuges
and more enriched uranium than
under deal donald dumped

SEVENTY

Donald Duck Diplomats

Don't turn on your TV. These hearings are a bore. I don't know why I'm even watching. Can you believe these bums the Democrats are using to smear me? Neither William Taylor nor George Kent, high-ranking but low-IQ diplomats in Ukraine, even talked to me directly about my perfect conversation with President Zelensky. And that incompetent broad, Marie Yovanovitch, who used to be our ambassador there, is the worst. Look at her, pretty damn nasty. While she lies to the world, I'll tweet the truth: "Everywhere she went turned bad. She started off in Somalia, how'd that go?" Then in Ukraine Zelensky "spoke unfavorably" about her. I'm not tolerating that. As president I have the absolute right to appoint ambassadors and fire them when they betray me.

Biden Blast

as more patriots pound trump
for pressuring ukraine to investigate i'm in atlanta
dazzling debaters with vow to
keep punching at domestic violence and news i have
support of only african american
woman ever elected senator not counting kamala
harris standing over there

Joe Six Pack Says

I feel so sorry for President Trump having to listen to all these witnesses lying about Ukraine. Who the hell are Alexander Vindman, Gordon Sondland, and Fiona Hill? They're nobodies in the spotlight only because they're attacking the president for making sure Ukraine quits interfering in our elections like it did in 2016. Barack Obama probably put them up to it so he could help Crooked Hillary win the election. That didn't work because all the Republicans came together to take our country back and now our party's supporting President Trump more than ever.

Pallid Peewees

Born in New Hampshire and raised in Iowa I'm proud as hell the fine folks of my tiny states, second and fourth whitest in America, have such great influence at the start of presidential primaries. We've only got about one point three million citizens in the Granite State but ninety percent are the right color and it's about the same among three million or so in the Hawkeye State. You know the Founding Fathers would've wanted God's chosen people to decide who'll lead our nation. We've got to be careful where we launch our biggest political event in a darkening land where we now only have a couple hundred million whites out of three hundred thirty million citizens. At least fifty million are Latinos, forty million blacks, and almost twenty million Asians. And in horrible places like California, Texas, Florida, and New York they're trying to vote earlier and steal our power.

China Rebuffed

in beleaguered hong kong
ninety
percent
shout
democracy

Danielle Stella for Congress

Like President Trump I'm a truth-telling patriot appalled by Rep. Ilhan Omar, the Somali traitor who I must defeat next November at the Minnesota ballot box. I shouldn't be an unknown trying to beat a darling of the left. Omar shouldn't even be in office. That's why I tweeted, "If it is proven Omar passed sensitive information to Iran... (which is way worse than my shoplifting at Target)... she should be tried for treason and hanged." Predictably, Twitter closed my account forever, proving that liberals and their social media are "terrorists, pedophiles, and rapists." I know you'll remember me now.

Flotus

new biography *free melania*
reports she's expert in clothes
makeup hairstyling jewelry and
party preparations but not as
attuned to cyber bullying

SEVENTY-ONE

Bring It

i didn't
corruptly solicit anything
or obstruct anyone and
can't wait for impeachment
trial in senate where I'll
crush dems

William Barr Barks

you should trust me
as attorney general
when i reveal
administration of barack obama used fbi and intelligence
agencies to spy
on trump and
undermine democracy

Impeached

I know what the deceitful Democrats are going to do and so do you and that's why I'm writing to Nancy Pelosi this whole impeachment is "an unprecedented and unconstitutional abuse." I'm not even being accused of committing any crimes or misdemeanors, nothing. That's because I've never done anything wrong. It's Pelosi and the Democrats who're "violating their oaths of office (and) breaking their allegiance to the Constitution." They're even "declaring open war on American Democracy" and invoking the Founding Fathers as they try to nullify my election and your vote. What a liar Pelosi is, claiming she's praying for me. She's praying for me to disappear.

My enemies' first claim, Abuse of Power, is a "baseless" pile of garbage. We all know "I had a totally innocent conversation with the president of Ukraine." And I had a second conversation that has been "misquoted (and) misrepresented." How dumb is that? There's a transcript of the conversation that proves this is all I said to President

Zelensky: "I'd like you to do us a favor because our country has been through a lot and Ukraine knows a lot about it." That favor was for my country, not me. I never represent the interests of Donald J. Trump. I always "put America's interests first" when I talk to foreign leaders. I simply wanted President Zelensky to investigate the really horrible behavior of Joe Biden and his drug-addicted son Hunter.

How can it be impeachable that I wanted Ukraine to prove that "Biden used his office and a billion dollars of U.S. aid to coerce Ukraine into replacing the prosecutor who was digging" into his corruption? Biden even bragged about this, stating, "'If the prosecutor isn't fired, you're not getting the money.' Well, son of a bitch. He got fired." Now that's criminal.

On the other hand, "President Zelensky has repeatedly declared that I did nothing wrong" and he felt no pressure to investigate the Bidens in order to get four hundred million dollars of military aid to battle Russia in eastern Ukraine. That money was coming all along. There was absolutely "No quid pro quo." Zelensky knows that and so does Vladimir, who would never mess with me.

The second charge, "'Obstruction of Congress,' is preposterous and dangerous." I do executive business the same way every other American president has "throughout our nation's history." The Democrats evidently want to impeach all our presidents "many times over." They need to get over that I beat their queen, Crooked Hillary, in an "Electoral College landslide." But instead of moving on, dark and dangerous opponents like Maxine Waters and Rashida Tlaib have been cursing as they call for my impeachment. I don't care.

I've been firing tweets all day, and now that they're voting I'm not even in Washington, D.C. I'm among red-blooded friends in Battle Creek, Michigan and don't "feel like we're being impeached." In fact, I feel loved more than any president ever. Everyone in this great arena tonight knows in less than three years I've created "seven million new jobs" and "the lowest-ever unemployment rate for African Americans, Hispanic Americans, and Asian Americans" and I've "rebuilt the military" and reformed the VA "for our great veterans" and hired "one hundred seventy new federal judges and two Supreme Court Justices" and made "historic tax and regulation cuts" and been responsible for "a colossal reduction in illegal border crossings" and you can read a lot more from this huge list and understand that I've done an incredible job and nothing wrong and I feel your love.

"Is there a better place in the world to be than at a Trump rally?"

Memo from Strategist

Quit handwringing and moralizing. If Democrats are to win in 2020 they must find a candidate who's more appealing than Trump. That may sound easy but who would that be? Which Dem would you bet your house on? I've been looking but don't see anyone who can win. Politics is show business, and Donald Trump – bloated and obscene – is a solid favorite. I hope no one thinks Joe Biden can win. He can't. If Trump is to be defeated, something unforeseen must come up, something that hurts him in razor-thin races in the Rust Belt. There must be some new outrage that Independents, at least, will not tolerate. Trump supporters didn't care about Mueller and Russia and don't give a damn about Hunter Biden and Ukraine. Get real and batter him on the issues and hope he implodes before the election, before he can start a war in Iran and, now that his buddy Kim Jong Un isn't so cuddly, in North Korea.

2020

SEVENTY-TWO

Trump Strikes Iran

From the start I've said the Iran nuclear deal was the worst in history especially in the hands of terrorists seeking weapons of mass destruction. I can't believe Obama gave them hundreds of billions. Yeah, it was their money we held but they got a windfall they used against their neighbors and us. I had to tear up the deal. And I still know I'll come out ahead. I'm smothering their economy. They're in bad shape. My knockout of General Qassim Soleimani at the Baghdad airport guarantees I can eliminate anyone. I'm not worried they just fired a couple of dozen ballistic missiles from Iran. They didn't want to hit our soldiers at two Iraqi bases. As I write this we haven't released official results but we know what they are: fireworks launched to comfort Iranian viewers.

Holiday Guest

A short man in suit and tie twice taps the frame of the doorway to the Oval Office. "Mr. President, may I please have a word with you?"

"Dr. King, I'm always glad to see you but you really should make an appointment."

"I thought I had one every year on this day."

Trump stands and walks to shake King's hand. "Of course you do. Happy birthday. You look great."

"Not bad for ninety-one."

"You'll always look thirty-nine," says Trump. "Come on in and sit down."

"Please excuse me for standing, Mr. President. I'll be brief."

Smiling, Trump says, "I guess you're here to thank me for creating more jobs for blacks than any president in history."

"You do deserve some credit in that regard, as does your predecessor. But I'm here to talk about your impeachment."

Trump's mouth tightens. "The Democrats are lying."

"I'm afraid, Mr. President, that witnesses are gathering to contradict you."

"Mitch McConnell's not going to let a bunch of traitors overturn my election."

"I presume that means you'll be blocking testimony and burying documents."

"Guys," Trump hollers, "Dr. King is leaving now."

Impeachment Snore

even fewer watching
trial on tv than hearings
last year you know what
that means

Trump Denounces Bolton

John Bolton's a warmonger who couldn't have gotten any job that required Senate confirmation so he begged me to make him national security adviser. People I trust convinced me to bring Bolton in to scare Iran and North Korea but he actually wanted to attack them and plenty of others and would've started World War Six by now if I hadn't fired his ass and saved billions of lives.

Now look what Bolton's doing. He's trying to peddle a nasty and untrue book he wrote really fast, claiming I withheld military aid from Ukraine in exchange for political favors. Really? Let me show the world this video of him saying I'd just had a "warm and cordial" conversation with President Zelensky and appreciated the free and uncorrupt nation he leads. He isn't publishing his lies or a bunch of classified national security secrets. Try that and he'll go to jail while getting his pants sued off by my army of lawyers. Game over.

Fake Trial

this is a trial
ain't
it
so where are the witnesses
probably
gagged

by mcconnell's boxer shorts

Trump News

in my executive newsletter i explain
0 + 0 = 0
zero crimes
zero wrongdoing
zero bipartisan support
dishonest dems threaten constitution

A Perfect Union

i'm creating jobs building walls arresting aliens and killing
terrorists
to
be
innocent
tomorrow
and
win
in
november

Trump Rips Pelosi

Nancy Pelosi is a terrible person who hates our country. That's probably why I didn't shake her sticky hand before my State of the Union speech but maybe I just didn't see her. Either way, she didn't deserve my attention. Remember, last year she tried to keep me from delivering my annual address to the nation and would have done so this year if I didn't have the overwhelming support of our great citizens. Nancy and her deranged Democrat allies need to get real. My approval rating's at its highest ever – forty-nine percent, three points better than faltering Barack Obama at the same stage of his first administration. Go ahead, Nancy, grimace and misbehave while I'm speaking to people who're on their feet and clapping, and after my triumph rip up your copy of my speech. You might as well be tearing up the Constitution, a document all real Americans hold sacred.

I actually feel sorry for the Democrats. They couldn't even count a small number of votes in the Iowa caucus. That proves they're incompetent and also means they really didn't want to know results that had to be bad news. Well, maybe they're happy that Creepy Joe Biden finished fourth and will soon be finished. But look who won, Crazy Bernie Sanders, a raving socialist who looks like he went to school with Karl Marx, and Pete Buttigieg, who mismanaged wonderful little South Bend. I'm producing jobs for blacks while blacks in his community denounce him. Neither stands a chance against me. And look who took third place, unlikable Elizabeth Warren, falling fast as a skydiver.

Give me five more years, baby, at least that many.

SEVENTY-THREE

Trump Conquers New Hampshire

I'm getting ninety percent of the vote in our New Hampshire primary while the Democrats keep struggling to decide which bozo they want. Looks like old Bernie Sanders has about a quarter of the vote, about a point more than little Pete Buttigieg, who should grow up before he tries to tangle with me, and several ahead of Amy Klobuchar. I don't have a nickname for her yet but may start calling her Amy the Weasel since she often screeches at aides in a disgraceful way. I hear Sleepy Joe Biden, the guy who says he'll clean my clock in November, is slipping out of the state before polls close so he can take his dying campaign to Nevada and South Carolina where he's getting weaker and will continue to sink since even hardcore Dems know he can't beat me. No one can. Barack Obama and Bill Clinton didn't get nearly as many votes in New Hampshire at the end of their first terms. Neither did George W. Bush.

I'm really not worried about the presidential election. I'm concerned about your safety. No matter how nice some immigrants may seem, it's certain some will turn out to be snakes who snatch money right out of your pockets to feed their welfare habits. That's why I'm proposing a budget to reduce the thirty-six million freeloaders on food stamps. There's also way too much Medicaid. You know Obamacare still hurts the working people of this nation.

Desperate Democrats are trying to convince you that I want to destroy our social safety net. That's a lie. Here's what I promise: "We're not touching Medicare... We're not touching social security... But we're going to cut waste and fraud." I'm going to whack off about a trillion bucks from entitlements over the next ten years, and I'll do it in ways that won't affect beneficiaries but instead increase bills to doctors, hospitals, and other providers. Don't worry about the details. I'll handle everything.

I believe in being responsible to my country, family, and friends, and am supporting Roger Stone who was falsely convicted of obstruction, lying, and witness tampering as part of the phony Mueller investigation. Dishonest prosecutors recommended Roger get seven to nine years in prison. I'm tweeting up a storm about this "miscarriage of justice" and within hours my Department of Justice overturns the outrageous recommendations. Four of the prosecutors resign in protest. Good riddance. You know damn well after the election I'll pardon Roger Stone, if I have to, as well as Paul Manafort. What about my dumb former lawyer Michael Cohen? I hate traitors. Let him rot.

Coronavirus

in only weeks hard to keep track
ten
twenty
fifty
hundred dead several thousand infected
now
more
than
hundred daily dead fourteen hundred in all
sixty
thousand
infected
don't worry trump says heat will kill virus

Clueless Klobuchar

can you name president
of mexico asked journalist
no replied amy klobuchar
recent graduate of trump
university of international
relations

Here Comes Melania

Oh boy. This is going to be great. I've always yearned to meet her but frankly thought I'd never have a chance. Only rich and brilliant winners like Donald J. Trump get to be with women as pretty as Melania. That injustice changed just minutes ago with the arrival of the best text message I've ever received. I'm not kidding. This is what it says: "CA4 text: Melania Trump 3/18 LA, Tickets $2800> (link) or DonJr & Kimberly in Danville $500 March 3."

I'd like to meet Don Jr. and his hot girlfriend Kimberly and learn about big game hunting and tell him he's already a fine politician with a deep voice but, really, Melania's the one I've got to talk to. I admit I'm pretty worried. I don't own a single suit. Imagine what she'd think. Actually, she probably wouldn't even notice a guy like that. I'll have to buy a real nice suit or maybe rent a tuxedo. I know I'll have to look sharper than ever.

As you see above, this isn't going to be cheap, even leaving the wife at home. That more sign, >, worries hell out of me. If I only pay about three grand, I'll probably be the poorest guy at some unidentified fancy place in Beverly Hills and will be seated far away. I bet only guys donating fifty grand and up will actually get to meet Melania. Let me tell you, I don't care, I'm clicking the link right now and getting my ticket. On the big night I'll work my way to the front, so I better practice what I might say.

I'll shake her hand firmly, but not too hard, and say, "Melania, Mrs. Trump, you're even more beautiful in person."

"Thank you," she'll say, smiling. "Do you live in Beverly Hills?"

"No, I drive a truck in Bakersfield, which isn't too far from here. Have you been there?"

"Not yet."

"President Trump was there last month and told lots of farmers how he's going to help them. He'll get seventy percent of the vote in Kern County."

Even if I get this far, which probably I won't, I know some secret service agent will tell me to move along.

"Hold it, hotshot, I didn't pay three thousand bucks to be given the bum's rush."

The agent, and one or two others, will grab my arms and start to lead me away.

As Melania's smile fades into a frown, I'll tell her, "Your husband may be getting his money from these big donors, but it's working people like me who elected him. He'd never have won Pennsylvania, Michigan, and Wisconsin without us."

I know all these zillionaire Republicans will be looking down on me but I'll still always be glad I met Melania.

What If Trump Won't Leave?

I'm amazed and becoming a little worried several people in recent months have asked me, "General Jones, what would the military do if Donald Trump loses the election in November but claims fraud, or something else, and refuses to leave the White House?"

"I've been a soldier since entering West Point forty years ago," I tell them, "and as a veteran of combat and student of history I often think about General Washington and his brave revolutionaries repelling the Red Coats, and General Grant and our nation crushing the Confederate traitors, and President Roosevelt harnessing our spirit and industrial might to help defeat Nazi Germany and the Empire of Japan. I remember all our other conflicts large and small as I talk to a million dead soldiers and more than that maimed and pray for their families and to all of them I say, 'Thank you fighting for our country. God bless your sacrificing everything for liberty. We will forever honor and benefit from your legacy, and no one will ever take away our freedom.'

"I can't fathom any president of the United States trying to become a dictator. I'm confident that such vile criminal action would never be attempted or even contemplated. Fear not."

"Yes, General Jones, but what if..."

"Any aspiring tyrant would be removed from the White House by the very forces who have heretofore so valiantly protected our right to live as free people."

Greeting Michael Bloomberg

I'm richer, smarter, and tougher than these low-level Democrats and have spent four hundred million dollars to advertise my success while giving speeches and practicing for my first debate I know I'll win right here on this stage in Las Vegas.

"I'd like to talk about who we're running against: a billionaire who calls women 'fat broads' and 'horse-faced lesbians,'" says Elizabeth Warren. 'I'm not talking about Donald Trump. I'm referring to Mayor Bloomberg.'"

Like a New York street fighter who worked hard for sixty billion bucks and won three mayoralty races, I counter, "Elizabeth, you're not fat or exactly horse-faced, but let's be honest, you're a dork."

"That's the kind of humiliating comment that forced many of your female employees to file sexual harassment suits against you."

"I didn't harass anyone," I explain. "I was just joking. They didn't understand humor so I apologized."

"Just how many of those lawsuits were there, Mayor Bloomberg?" she asks.

"I don't know. A lot fewer than Harvey Weinstein and Jeffrey Epstein. We're probably talking something in the Donald Trump range."

Jabbing her finger at me in a way that would've gotten her fired, Warren says, "Let's see what these women really experienced. Release them from the non-disclosure agreements that wealthy jackasses like you and Trump so often use."

"They wanted to move on. I suggest you do the same."

Waving his hand like a drunkard, Bernie Sanders says, "Your stop-and-frisk policing policies targeted blacks and Latinos and allowed the police to throw five million innocent citizens against the wall."

"Don't play dumb, Bernie, though the role is quite natural for you," I say. "You're a native New Yorker, albeit a deserter to Vermont, and know what I was battling – several hundred murders in our city every year. Damn right I targeted those who commit the crimes. The murder rate declined when I was in charge. But I did apologize for some of the excesses. Why don't you talk about the real victims?"

Joe Biden, the ultimate goofball, looks stern as he says, "It doesn't matter whether or not you apologized. Your policy was abhorrent and violated every right people have."

"All of you are letting the Republicans be the party of law and order and prosperity. Bernie and Elizabeth are Communists. But Bernie's a millionaire leftist with three homes."

"Just a minute, Mayor Bloomberg, I only have my modest home in Vermont, a place in Washington D.C. where I work, and essentially a pup tent in the backwoods of Vermont. Senator Warren has far more money than I."

"We're not Communists, Mayor Bloomberg," says Pete Buttigieg. "We're Democrats and you're not. You're a Wall Street crony who also backed the 2003 invasion of Iraq and is still proud of that position."

Frumpy Elizabeth Warren won't shut up, preaching, "Democrats can't win if we nominate a man with a history of evading his taxes, harassing women, and leading racists to redline minorities from getting home loans."

I wish I didn't have to listen to these lightweights, and refuse to look at them. I'm instead looking over the audience and into the future and frowning at what I see.

Bernie in Bakersfield

No, I better not go. I think I'm too busy. But busy doing what? I've been writing about Donald Trump for several years and working to finish my second book about the blowhard from Queens. I can't sit at my computer when Bernie Sanders is just a few miles away and soon to speak. I hustle to my car and drive by expensive suburbs and the state university to Spectrum Amphitheater where I've only attended rock concerts.

A few Trump supporters, clad in red Trump caps and T-shirts bearing their hero's surname above "Keep America Great," are sitting under a tree near the parking lot entrance where a security guard says, "It's full."

Not bad. Most concerts don't fill up the lot a half hour before showtime.

"Let me check it out," I say, and luck into a place just vacated by some picnickers.

I take my folder and step out to join people flowing toward the amphitheater like fans eager to watch their favorite band. Then we reach a long line leading to security entrances. To the left two young men bear signs saying "Socialism is Bad." I'd like to reassure them that Bernie's socialism is the northern European style of wealthy countries making sure everyone has health insurance and a roof overhead, but there's no time. The line moves and soon I'm emptying my pockets.

I sit in the last row of an amphitheater filling fast, and after several stacked rows of photogenic supporters stand on little bleachers stage rear, and some preliminary speakers discuss the perils of living without insurance, Bernie Sanders marches to the microphone before a full house and more standing on the hill curving behind the seats. He's wearing black slacks, a light blue shirt with long sleeves rolled up and an open collar, and soon dons a dark blue baseball cap to shield himself from spring-like sun pumping out seventy-four degrees. Bernie's even hotter, offering not surprises but passion and promises I scribble the essence of on paper braced by my notebook.

"We've got to work together to solve our problems," he declares. "I won't tolerate the obscene level of income disparity in this nation. A few days ago I debated Michael Bloomberg, who's worth sixty-five billion dollars. He says he worked hard for that money, and I'm sure he did. But he's not the only person working hard in America. Democracy means one person one vote, not some multi-billionaire buying elections. We've got to overturn Citizens United, and get rid of voter suppression, and end extreme gerrymandering.

"I want to make sure we get the highest level of voter turnout in the world, not one of the lowest. Our staff and volunteers here in California have knocked on almost a million doors to defeat the most dangerous president in our history. He's a pathological liar, a racist, a homophobe, a xenophobe, and a religious bigot, and those are his better qualities."

That line brings the biggest cheer yet. Bernie, hunched a little and emphasizing points with his right hand, continues, "We're going to win because we're going to bring our people together. If you work forty hours a week, you should not live in poverty. We need a minimum wage of at least fifteen bucks an hour. And we need more unions to improve conditions for workers. We also need affordable housing. We get that by creating good-paying union jobs and understanding the importance of education. I'm fighting so every teacher in America can earn at least sixty thousand dollars a year. We need affordable education. I would cancel all student debt. And we must understand that health care is a right, not a privilege. We've been talking about universal health care more than a hundred years, back to the days of Teddy Roosevelt. When I'm president we will pass single payer Medicare for all. No one will pay more than two hundred dollars per year for prescription drugs."

I draw a breath and hope Bernie does too.

"Climate change is real," he says. "I visited Paradise (CA) where a massive fire destroyed everything. Look at the ongoing fires that are burning up Australia. (More than a billion animals have been killed to date). Scientists say the problem is worse than they thought and if we don't get it together there will be a hundred million climate refugees worldwide. We must take on the greed and lies from the fossil fuel industry. And, of course, we must guarantee that workers who lose jobs receive pay and job training for five years.

"We've got to invest in our young people. We've got to end private prisons. We need to legalize marijuana in all states. Instead of large corporations making all the money, we're going to enable blacks and Latinos to benefit from the sale of pot. They're the ones who've suffered most because of bad laws."

I grab more blank papers in my folder.

"I will end the demonization of undocumented immigrants in this country," Bernie says. "Donald Trump is a fraud. He loves undocumented workers as long as they're the ones he pays low wages to work at his properties. I will help the DACA people (who were brought here as children.) I'll make sure no babies are ripped from their mothers' arms.

"When I'm president our gun policies won't be determined by the NRA. There'll be universal background checks and I'll close the gun show loopholes. The Republicans complain we've got to get government off our backs. They want to outlaw abortions. Don't Republicans understand that women control their bodies, not the government."

Surveying several thousand supporters in red Kern County, Sanders must be happy he leads all primary opponents by at least ten percentage points in recent statewide polling.

"California is the largest state in the nation. The candidate who wins here will likely win the Democratic nomination. Bring your aunts and uncles, people you haven't seen in years... I'm inspired by audiences like this. Look at the diversity. We're ready to take on the military industrial complex and the prison industry and we're taking on the top one percent. They aren't paying their share of taxes. The Democratic and Republican establishments are getting nervous. I've got news for them. They can't stop us when we stand together."

I'm rushing like I do after a good concert but have no idea how Bernie Sanders and the nation would pay for all these wonderful services.

Notes: I stand and stroll to the shade of a tree and ask one of the Trump supporters, a stocky man with a mustache, if I can talk to him. He agrees and we shake hands, and for about ten minutes I mostly listen as he delivers talking points he repeats after departing, just outside the amphitheater where he and a couple of other red shirts are surrounded by the Bernie brigade. Several muscular police officers study the scene. People are outraged by fossil fuels.

"I've been an all oil worker for many years," the man says. "How'd you get here today? Oh, you drove. So what're we going to do with all these cars? How many out of all you have an electric car? Let's see, two. Okay, the rest of you leave your cars in the parking lot and walk home. And take off your shoes because gas is used to make them."

Bernie Sanders is already en route to Nevada where he wins the caucus the next day and then flies to Texas, one of fourteen Super Tuesday prizes on March third. Three days earlier he'll battle Joe Biden in South Carolina.

SEVENTY-FOUR

The New Bernie Sanders

Bernie's in South Carolina trouble. Good old boys and girls down here are worried as hell he's not only Jewish he's a communist. And in this debate his Democratic primary adversaries are plenty heated up, too, lashing from all sides as locals cheer.

Peach-fuzz Pete Buttigieg says, "It's time to stop acting like the presidency is the only office that matters... Democratic candidates not only aren't backing (this radical), they're running from him." He thinks Sanders' presidential candidacy is fated not only to fail but destroy their advantage in the House and squander any chance of retaking the Senate and torpedo Democrats running for governor and state legislative offices across the land.

Sanders is also tomahawked for having backed the NRA in backwoods Vermont. Waving a hot hand at moderators, in the manner of his opponents, he counters, "I've made some bad votes but thirty years ago I lost a race for the only House seat in our state because I wanted to ban assault rifles." He doesn't add but implies he rode the NRA's political train a long time before recently earning a D- rating from the kings of automatic weapons.

When his opponents briefly stop implying Sanders is a devotee of Fidel Castro, he lectures, "The United States has overthrown regimes around the world... (It's all right) for us to acknowledge that Cuba did some things well in education and medical care. They have a hundred percent literacy rate."

Eager Pete says, "A look at the bright side of Castro's Cuba is a bad look for Democrats."

And what about the U.S. commitment to Israel, a right wing country that could be compelled to moderate its behavior by a liberal leader of the United States?

"I'm proud of being Jewish," Sanders says. "I once lived in Israel for some months, and I'm committed to Israel's security. Their problem is the reactionary racist leader Benjamin Netanyahu" and his apartheid policies.

"This feller might as well be criticizing our history of race relations in South Carolina," one local whispers to another. "He better remember the Civil War started right here at Fort Sumter."

Sanders knows. He's not going to win in the land of Strom Thurmond and Lindsey Graham. Joe Biden, a bit more coherent tonight than in previous debates, is widening his lead and will prevail here Saturday.

On Super Tuesday Sanders will win California but leads by less than two points in Texas and North Carolina. If Biden takes those states and others where he's competitive, the Sanders scientific team may replace the current candidate with the more telegenic and less strident Bernie Sanders of 1988, a YouTube sensation, who'd have a better chance against Donald Trump. But what if team Trump replaces the rotund president with dashing young Donald from the same year?

Doctor Pence

I'd like to thank the greatest man on earth, President Donald Trump, for putting me in charge of the battle against the coronavirus. He picked the right guy. Before becoming vice president, as governor of Indiana, I stamped out an HIV epidemic by authorizing needle exchanges in Scott County. I hadn't wanted to permit that immoral act but the virus was spreading and I prayed my way to the right response and kept the number of cases under two hundred.

Now I'm praying warm weather from heaven will strike down the coronavirus. And I'm helping President Trump marshal our vast medical and logistical resources in case God wants to test our ability to stop a virus that in other countries has infected eighty-three thousand people, killed almost three thousand, and at home this week knocked twelve percent off the stock market and burned six trillion dollars of wealth.

Now an American in the United States has died, and, as I stand by President Trump at a hastily-called press conference, he's right to say "this is very serious stuff" but that it's a "hoax" the way the media's criticizing how we're adeptly handling this crisis.

Fancy Letters from Bloomberg

When a guy's worth sixty billion and rapidly spends five hundred million in a presidential primary he's not going to mail you cheap sheets of thin paper. These ads are triple wide and firm. The first two-sided color production says, "Undefeated Mike Bloomberg – He Beat the NRA – He Beat The Coal Lobby – He Beat Big Tobacco – Next Up – Beating Donald Trump."

Given his ineptitude as a debater and lack of warmth on the campaign trail, Bloomberg isn't going to defeat Bernie Sanders or Joe Biden in order to take a swing at fellow New Yorker Trump, but he's bright and tough and keeps firing his mailers.

"My Son Joe Was Shot Six Times," says a lady in a large color photo.

"It takes a lot of courage to take on the gun lobby," the team responds, "and Mike Bloomberg was willing to take on the NRA when others were not."

Bloomberg's right the NRA is a national health threat and returns fire with a fancy mega-pamphlet featuring a diptych cover of candles against a black background and this refrain in white, "We've lit too many candles, mourned too many loved ones."

Open the covers left and right and see twenty horizontal inches of Bloomberg rather awkwardly holding hands, slapping hands, walking, talking privately, and speaking publicly with families of victims.

The next ad on top features a mountain ablaze titled "Fire" and a smog shrouded freeway labeled "Pollution" below. Boxed in the center it says, "Trump's Policies Are Killing California." On the other side Bloomberg poses with Governor Jerry Brown in one photo and with children and adolescents in the other three. Another ad has four folding parts stating "We want" on one side and on the other "Climate Action" or "Quality Healthcare" or "World-Class Schools" or "Gun Safety."

When the ninth-richest man in the world spends his money to try to help, he will be listened to. And when people listen they're often impressed with the ideas but, according to polls, uncomfortable with the messenger.

Super Tuesday at Bernie's

Late Monday morning I get an email titled "Anybody but Bernie Sanders" that tautly announces, "The Political Establishment has made their choice… That is fine. We always knew it. You've always known it. Now it just happens to be clear for everyone to see."

I have no recorded evidence but believe Bernie Sanders, temporarily the Democratic frontrunner and forever a proud socialist, has for a day or two been privately erupting, "See. Look at them. The billionaires are lining up their Joe Biden stooges – Pete Buttigieg and Amy Klobuchar – and offering them cabinet positions in Biden's presumed presidency if they'll get out of the race and support the former vice president. They gather in Dallas on the eve of Super Tuesday to pronounce Biden a savior and me a divider. Until a few days ago, despite three campaigns and numerous primaries over three decades, Biden had never won a single primary. Now that he's taken South Carolina he's suddenly a combination Jack Kennedy and Barack Obama.

"This isn't about Bernie Sanders. This is about the wealthiest one percent preventing you from having affordable medical insurance and polluting the environment and starting unnecessary wars for profit and power while they suck in more money because of low taxes handed to them by the above mentioned stooges and Donald Trump. We're not going to let them stop us. We've got the support of the people. Together we'll stop the oligarchs from oppressing us."

Okay, Bernie, I think I better drive downtown to your Bakersfield headquarters and talk to some of your people. I tried a couple days earlier but was told no one could be interviewed without permission of Anna Bahr, Sanders' media consultant in Los Angeles. She quickly responded to my email and said I could talk to any of the volunteers but staff members would have to be cleared by her. No problem. I figure people donating time are motivated and well-informed.

I introduce myself to a young lady and ask, "Are you worried that Pete Buttigieg and Amy Klobuchar dropped out and endorsed Joe Biden?"

"No, I'm not worried, but a lot of us are hurt," says Riddhi. "Beto O'Rourke also joined them on stage in Texas, but that's only three people. We have millions who've come together from bottom to top to fight for civil rights and labor rights and LGBTQ. It's amazing how dedicated we are. We don't care about Bernie because of what type of grandpa he may be but because of his policies, free Medicare and free college for all."

I dare not ask Riddhi her age lest she ask mine but she volunteers she's twenty-four. People so young generally haven't focused much on health care. Spiraling costs changed that.

"How'd you get involved in the Sanders campaign?" I ask.

"I studied neuroscience at St. Louis University and began to realize that the American Medical Associations and other organizations let people slide through the cracks. Doctors hate billing and all the paperwork. They're frustrated and depressed. They want to concentrate on keeping people healthy. After college I worked one year at Children's Hospital of Philadelphia. We spent hours on the phone trying to get approval from insurance companies. And this was for kids with cerebral palsy.

"We need Medicare for All. Joe Biden doesn't support that. The way things are, people often spend hundreds of thousands of dollars a year and go bankrupt. Sixty million people are uninsured or underinsured. Biden wants to continue and improve the Affordable Care Act. The system isn't working. I know someone who's diabetic and can't get insulin. And I have a reproductive disorder and need regular obstetrics and gynecology treatments. I'm lucky to have Blue Cross through my parents, for the time being, but special care is really expensive. I'm paying five hundred to eight hundred dollars twice a month. That's a lot for most people."

"I had great health insurance for years as a teacher," I say. "Many people don't want to give up the health care they have."

"And lots of people are stuck in jobs just for the health insurance. What Bernie wants isn't radical. He reminds critics that he stood in the front lines for the ACA. We need something better now."

I thank the lady for her time and, after talking to a couple more people, head back to my home office to follow the returns. No realistic person expects Bernie Sanders to conquer the south but as evening arrives the reality of Biden's strength with African Americans and

Sanders' weakness becomes clear as, moving east to west, Obama's vice president takes Virginia, North Carolina, Alabama, Tennessee, Arkansas, and Oklahoma, creating an electoral blockade that Sanders will struggle to penetrate in subsequent primaries in the South. In a little while Biden adds big Texas to his great southern wall. He also takes Massachusetts, routing native daughter Elizabeth Warren, who should withdraw from the primaries forthwith and join Buttigieg and Klobuchar in Democratic harmony. The latter's backing helps Biden win in Minnesota. He also takes Maine by a whisker to cap his stunning turnaround. At least Bernie wins his adopted state of Vermont as well as Colorado and Utah and later as expected earns California.

I know the Bernie brigade must be hurting so I drive back downtown. About thirty volunteers and staffers may feel morose but they're chatting with each other and checking their cellphones while munching pizza and sipping sodas. Siddhi, still battling, orders taken down the sad CNN election returns projected huge on the wall and writes a link on an adjacent marker board.

"Call L.A. and tell people they can vote until ten p.m.," she says. "Everything helps. If Biden gets less than fifteen percent of the vote he doesn't get any delegates."

The gods, as well as the Democratic establishment and a majority of the electorate to date, are against Bernie, and the computer link doesn't work.

A staffer announces, "Hey, we're up in all Central Valley regions. But we'll have to wait until tomorrow to see the percentages and who gets how many delegates."

The legions cheer. Bernie will fight on for a while and ensure people think about health care being a human right that should offer affordable rates and convenient paperwork along with excellent medical service. Many Americans don't want that yet. A nation of warriors can't emulate those effete social democrats of northern Europe, not yet.

Notes: Joe Biden won ten of the fourteen states on Super Tuesday and leads Bernie Sanders in delegates five hundred sixty-six to five hundred one. Elizabeth Warren lags with sixty-one delegates and no longer has a valid place on the electoral stage. She should support the most like-minded candidate, Bernie Sanders, if she's been sincere about her health care proposals.

Big bucks Michael Bloomberg dropped about six hundred million the last two months and captured American Samoa and its five delegates. Wednesday morning he withdrew from the race and endorsed Joe Biden and will likely gear up to beat Donald Trump who tweets "Mini Mike" is a failure, albeit one who has about a hundred times more money than the prevaricator still cowering behind unreleased tax returns.

Big Gun Congressman

Blowhard Congressman Ken Buck removes MR-15 from Capitol wall, assumes battle position, and challenges Joe Biden to come and take it. To that one responds, "Okay, tough guy, when the law changes and assault weapons are illegal, either relinquish yours or we'll take it from you. And you won't fire a shot..."

Scientific Trump

i love science and really get it
amazed doctors ask how do you
know so much it must be natural
ability that tells me i'm doing an
incredible job containing corona
virus and detecting phony advocates
of global warming

Trump Stock Market

when stocks soar it's my market
when
they
drop
two
thousand
points

in a day it's the coronavirus
barack
obama
didn't
prepare
for

SEVENTY-FIVE

Bernie's Last Stand

Look how the political lackeys are marching to the drumbeat.

Kamala Harris says, Joe Biden, it was very hurtful when you opposed busing because I was a little black girl who took buses to better schools but considering the alternatives I've decided to back you for president of the United States.

And Cory Booker runs in to say, Joe, you wouldn't have remotely as much support among blacks if you hadn't been Barack Obama's vice president but that's what you were and you kicked my ass in the primaries so I'm supporting you for president.

Billionaire Michael Bloomberg announces, Joe, you're not nearly as sharp or rich as I am – who the hell is? – but I've still decided to endorse your doddering effort to flatten Donald Trump and become our next president.

Callow Beto O'Rourke tells his viewers, Latinos love you, Joe, and my Texas is very Latino and I'm almost one myself so I'm going to help you become president.

Pesky Pete Buttigieg, who thinks wealthy northern European socialism is the same as poor Cuban communism, claims I'll ruin the Democratic Party.

Joe, says abrasive Amy Klobuchar, I'm at this stage what America needs, a real smart woman, even if it's only as your vice president.

I guess Andrew Yang isn't really interested in change since he's jumping on the shaky Biden train.

Elizabeth Warren, who we now see never was a progressive, is also waiting to climb on Joe Biden's back.

I wonder who these people are, other than a bunch of political opportunists salivating to run for president in 2024. They know Joe Biden. He's a man who's slipping fast mentally and who supported the war in Iraq I opposed and backed the banker-friendly bankruptcy bill I fought and used to talk about cutting social security, an atrocity I'd never permit.

And what's the result of all this? I've got to win Michigan, where I topped Hillary Clinton in 2016, but blacks and other voters gang up to help Biden win by seventeen percentage points and twenty delegates, and it looks about the same in redneck Missouri and is even worse in backwoods Mississippi. The powerbrokers prevail even in liberal green Washington where I'm in a dead heat. At least I win a two-delegate advantage in North Dakota. But let's be frank. The overall numbers don't look good. I'm down by about a hundred fifty delegates and liable to get whacked next week in Florida and the week after that in Georgia.

Joe Biden's probably got the nomination about wrapped up. I'm not going to admit this, though. I'm going to fight on and debate him in Phoenix in a few days and ask if he's really going to veto a Medicare for All bill if it's passed in Congress. I'm going to keep denouncing the wealthy who rob the poor. And I'm going to fight for you but too many of you are voting against yourselves.

Trump Attacks Coronavirus

Stated and unstated highlights from President Trump's solemn address to the nation

I don't remember saying the coronavirus would soon be down to two cases or maybe one in the United States. That's just natural optimism based on my having already marshaled "the full power of the federal government and the private sector to protect the American people." I'm leading the "most aggressive and comprehensive effort to confront a foreign virus in modern history."

You know how tough I am about defending our homeland. "At the very start of the outbreak, we instituted sweeping travel restrictions on China and put in place the first federally mandated quarantine in over fifty years." And because of my "early intense action, we have seen dramatically fewer cases of the virus in the United States than are now present in Europe." These same Europeans, who neglect to pay their share of NATO and allow their continent to be overrun by aliens, "failed to take the same precautions and restrict travel from China and other hotspots."

Therefore, "I have decided to take several strong... actions to protect the health... of all Americans. To keep new cases from entering our shores, we will be suspending all travel from Europe to the United

States for the next thirty days." This restriction will not apply to the United Kingdom. The rates of infection and mortality are a little higher there than here but they are our historical brothers. Over in Asia, another troubled continent, we're keeping an eye on the Chinese and South Koreans, "and as their situation improves we will reevaluate the restrictions and warnings that are currently in place."

I'm also "cutting massive amounts of red tape to make antiviral therapies available in record time… (And) testing and testing capabilities are expanding rapidly day by day. We are moving very quickly." My politically motivated critics don't want to admit that. They should acknowledge that for "the vast majority of Americans the risk is very, very low." If you're not really old, I think you've got it made.

Don't worry if you get the virus and have to stay home from work. "I will soon take unprecedented emergency action to provide financial relief." Thanks to the economic policies I've "put into place the last three years, we have the greatest economy anywhere in the world by far." We're rich and ready because I cut funding to some of Obama's disease security programs. I also slashed about eighty percent of the budget for The Centers for Disease Control and Prevention. Some say those moves look dumb now. Others say they looked dumb even then. Let them talk. We all know who's got the greatest brain in the world.

Pandemic Irritates Joe Six Pack

I still think liberals may be scheming with the Chinese to blame the coronavirus on President Trump but since he seems to be taking it pretty serious now I guess I better try to do the same. But I'm only going so far.

No way am I staying home when a kickass movie's playing or professional wrestling comes to town or a great country concert plays here or I'm invited to a party where I know there'll be some single babes or even married ones looking for someone new. I guess I don't mind they're closing some schools since I'm not a student and my three kids and ex-old-lady live in another state.

What pisses me off is those panicking lefties who're buying up all the good stuff at the markets. Everywhere I go they don't have any toilet paper or kleenex or hand sanitizer. How the hell's that supposed to work? I can't even find rice and beans, which are about the only things I can cook, and I can't afford fast food three times a day. They don't even have water anymore. I knew I should've installed that water filter instead of giving it to a buddy for his birthday.

"Ma'am," I say to a pretty little checker, "shouldn't you guys be limiting people to how much they can buy. I've seen videos of three fat ladies fighting over toilet paper and lots of people huffing out the market pushing one overflowing cart and pulling another."

"You're right, sir. From now on we're limiting each customer to five gallons of water. Didn't you see the signs we posted."

"Only saw all those empty shelves."

"Keep checking back every day," she says.

"Like that's all I've got to do."

I've got plenty of responsibilities pounding nails on construction sites and running errands for my old father who always wants more water. A couple of weeks ago, when it was still available, I couldn't just walk into his assisted living facility because they started keeping the door locked. Next time I visited they took my name and temperature before they let me in. He just called a little while ago and said now they're not letting anyone in but that I can drop off water with aides if I can find it. That may be a spell.

On the Ball

i've got coronavirus
under
tremendous
control
and am working to
pardon
michael
flynn

Biden Sanders Debate

joe's lucid tonight but silent when bernie asks
why
give
tax
breaks
to
billionaires
but not minimum wage of fifteen an hour

Trump Concedes

guess coronavirus isn't under control and will last more than
two
weeks
more
like
four
months
destroying
many
jobs

Bernie Announces

Don't try to talk to me unless you're wearing a surgical mask. I wouldn't hear you then and don't want to now. I don't care I lost Florida by forty points and also got hosed in Illinois and Arizona and now trail Joe Biden by three hundred delegates. That's irrelevant. What do you mean what am I going to do? I'm the leader of a movement who's fighting the most horrific health threat this century and battling to keep our national economy from collapsing. I'm working to save lives and jobs and homes. What the hell are you going to do? Whatever Joe Biden does won't be as much as I could've done.

SEVENTY-SIX

Cruising with Joe Six Pack

"I don't get it," I tell a waitress. "If it's safe to go into a restaurant and pick up food, why can't I sit here and chat a while?"

"You should be ashamed," she says. "Quarantining is our only tool to shut down the coronavirus. If we let customers sit around here, instead of going right home, they'd give the virus to each other and to me and my coworkers."

"I'm getting the hell out of the country for a while."

"It'll be about the same everywhere else," she says.

I just shake my head and rush home to the computer and buy a great exotic cruise. Smartest thing I've ever done. I don't have to watch Anthony Fauci and Donald Trump contradict each other about what should be done. I'm with a giant shipload of swingers like myself and we're drinking and sunbathing every day and drinking and dancing every night and I'll be polite and say most people who arrived alone aren't sleeping alone. Everyone's relaxed in a paradise of endless supplies and opportunities.

Coronavirus Count

month ago south korea
had four hundred cases
now has nine thousand

month ago iran had six
deaths now has sixteen
hundred

last week Italy had a
couple thousand deaths
now has five thousand

Spanish Influenza Review

As you grumble quarantined in carpeted homes equipped with flat screens and computers, and wait in lines outside markets to learn there's no more toilet paper or hand sanitizer, remember a far deadlier pandemic.

Good morning Spanish influenza says entering healthy young adult hearts pumping lungs fatally full of fluid by that evening or next. Eighty million perish worldwide most in frenetic ninety days, twenty million in October 1918 India, about seven hundred thousand in U.S. In oilfields outside Bakersfield filthy makeshift hospitals hold tough young immigrants prior to death. City schools close three months while in nearby Taft undertaker struggles to bury legion and dig extra graves.

What It Is

watching people die
italian
doctors
warn
it isn't the flu
it's
like
chronic
pneumonia
coming your way

Trump to the Rescue

Come on. Admit it. You're happy Dr. Anthony Fauci, the celebrity expert about pandemics, isn't on stage with me today. He's a little guy, just a squirt, and I think people are getting irritated he always talks about medicine and ignores human pain caused by the shutdown that's starting to ruin my great economy.

Fauci wouldn't understand what a guy on Fox News said an hour ago and I'm already repeating, we can't let the cure be way worse than the problem. I keep explaining we lose thousands and thousands in car accidents every year, and we lose even more to flu. It doesn't help when fussy little Fauci says there's a "false equivalency" between autos and the coronavirus, and "we must face the fact that coronavirus is more deadly than the flu."

Fauci and other liberal health officials are probably wrong about that, especially when you factor in countless suicides that will soon come if we don't stop this panicky destruction of jobs and wealth. I'm going to save those people and order everything back to normal by Easter.

Easter Sunday

pack those churches
long
as
trump and clan in
middle
of
congregation

Asking China

how
many
infections
and
deaths
do you really have

Disappearing Biden

where the hell's joe
while
trump
digs
graves

SEVENTY-SEVEN

I Surrender

I'd like to apologize to President Trump though I realize he's too great and busy to notice or care what people like me think. I'm now in the minority. The majority of Americans, according to recent polls, believe the president is doing a fine job managing the coronavirus pandemic. I guess the majority is impressed by a man who a month ago said the United States had only fifteen infected people and would soon have zero or no more than one or two. Today, as morbidity skyrockets, the United States leads the world with about a hundred thousand reported cases including one thousand five hundred deaths. I suppose the majority is impressed that Trump, a climate-change denier, announced he's inherently bright and coherent in scientific matters, doctors and other professionals having told him so. Evidently the majority is heartened the commander in chief thinks in a couple of weeks we'll walk out of the quarantine and return to workplaces and churches and bars and ballgames and everything will be fine, or at least better than it would be if the economy is shut down any longer. One must conclude the masses like a strutting bullshit artist who's rude to media members asking difficult but appropriate questions. I don't know why I'm surprised. Historically, most people kiss the ass of a leader just before he unloads in their faces.

Letter to Jeff Bezos

Dear Jeff,

I hope this letter finds you in good health and want to tell you I've bought Amazon literary products for years. However, despite my love of the Kindle reader, which stores hundreds of electronic books and permits instant adjustment of lighting and type size and the spontaneous display of millions of books in your inventory, I'm becoming disenchanted with you. For years I'd heard but didn't dwell on reports that Amazon's employees were forced to work too hard at repetitive physical tasks and subjected to more stress than necessary. You've become the richest man on earth but even during this pandemic you're gouging customers who need essentials like hand soap, toilet paper, and beans.

Several times I lined up at six-forty-five a.m., prior to a seven-to-nine o'clock grace period for seniors, but couldn't find anything I needed so decided to see what Amazon offered online. I bought a ten-pack of TP for fifteen bucks. There was no shipping charge but I'd have to wait up to seven weeks. Faster shipping would've cost thirty-five for three weeks. Really, Jeff, do you need those extra dollars on both the product and shipping? This morning a study of Amazon TP offerings suggests you've eased prices a little.

That leads to hand sanitizer, which Amazon vigorously advertises. I selected a two-pack, about five ounces for three dollars each. With a shipping and handling fee of ten bucks and tax, I paid more than seventeen for two small plastic bottles slated to arrive in five to eight weeks. You don't think that's reasonable, do you?

I love pinto beans and don't know what I'm going to do when I run out because I don't eat much meat and beans are my primary source of protein and the damn grocery shelves are still barren. I'll have to stretch the pension check to afford Bezos beans. I'm leaving out brand names but here's a two-pound package for fifteen dollars plus six for shipment that would arrive in about three weeks. I know, buy more and pay less. Here's a seven-pound bag for forty bucks, pretty steep even with free shipping that may be slow.

Wait. What's this? A twenty-pound bag for sixty-five bucks and free shipping scheduled to arrive next week. That's a good deal, Jeff, and I just bought it.

Sincerely,

GTC

Solemn Trump

okay
this isn't a hoax
stay home easter

and all of april
and pray a quarter
million of us don't
die

Memo to China

i'll apologize if i'm wrong
but multiple reports indicate
you're still under reporting
infections and deaths and
again lying as you did early
this year that doesn't prove
you're better it proves you're
dictators

Question for China

is it true crematoriums in wuhan
have
been
more
active
recently

Enlightened Governor

I'm jumping on board right quick with other Republican governors
and shutting down lots of stuff in my state since I learned some "game
changing" information about the coronavirus. "We didn't know until
the last twenty-four hours" that this ungodly virus "is now transmitting
before people see signs." Liberals are saying they knew all along. I
doubt that.

They're jealous I'm the good ole boy who in 2018 ran the coolest
campaign TV ad in history, blowing up government spending, gripping
a rifle "no one's taking away," starting a chain saw that's "ready to rip

up some regulations," and riding in my "big truck in case I need to round up some criminal illegals and take 'em home myself."

I'm the guy Georgia wanted instead of wild liberal Stacey Abrams who might've stolen the close election if I hadn't thrown out thousands of voter registrations that didn't match driver's license and social security information. Watch my campaign ad again and you'll see that no virus or bad guys are gonna get over on Brian Kemp.

Corona Carrier

I fly to Guam and march onto the aircraft carrier USS Theodore Roosevelt and over the radio tell almost five thousand crew members this is Navy Secretary Thomas Modly and I'm tired of your complaining about the coronavirus spreading on board and infecting more than one hundred seventy of you who have a mission and your mission is what matters and your naïve and stupid captain, Brett Crozier, should not have been whining, particularly in a memo to at least twenty officials he begged to remove most of you from this infectious hotbox and into quarantine on shore. Naturally, his memo was leaked – that's why he sent it to so many people – and I'm here now ordering you to toughen up and forget the captain you applauded as he left the ship after I fired him. Now the irresponsible captain has coronavirus and plenty of you do too but that doesn't matter because this great ship has nuclear weapons and lots of bombs and planes and other dangerous stuff and we can't just abandon ship and leave it naked.

SEVENTY-EIGHT

Bernie Out

i believe in medicare for all
and a minimum wage of
fifteen an hour and
sacrificing to beat climate
change but i scare voters
who want joe biden a
decent man who's faltering
but better than trump

Points by Joe Six Pack

Liberals and other weaklings are destroying our country with this extreme and shortsighted lockdown. First, remember most people aren't dying of the coronavirus, they're dying with the coronavirus. I bet you didn't know the difference. Look, I feel sorry for thousands of senior citizens here and in other countries. But let's get real. They were about to die of old age anyway and most had preexisting conditions like cancer, diabetes, or heart disease. It was just a coincidence they had the coronavirus. Liberals don't admit that.

Second, I need to remind you the cure is worse than the disease. We've already lost several million jobs and more than a quarter of the stock market. Imagine all the depression, suicides, and homelessness. Third, these highfalutin scientific models and fatality projections are too severe talking about millions of deaths worldwide and hundreds of thousands in the United States. Face it, the coronavirus just pushes people where they're already headed.

Light

a few weeks ago
we'd have said
it's inconceivable
in one day seventeen
hundred die in u.s.

six hundred in italy
same in France
four hundred in spain
now we call that
improvement

Fauci Under Watters

Quit paying so much attention to what Dr. Anthony Fauci says about the coronavirus. Get your information from clever commentator Jesse Watters of fair and balanced Fox News. He on air asks Fauci, could you have done anything differently than a full-scale national shutdown, like letting those forty-five and under work and have everyone wear masks?

Since the coronavirus transmissibility is efficient enough, we could not take the chance of letting people get infected without serious consequences, says Fauci. The young would have spread the disease to those most vulnerable, the elderly and those with pre-existing conditions.

Could you have concentrated on the hotspots and spared the whole country of an economic shutdown?

The only way to cut off the virus was and is with physical separation, says Fauci.

I have a very high regard for you, Dr. Fauci, Jesse Watters says, sharpening his sword, but some people are very angry with you... Your advice to the president to shut everything down has cost a lot of people their jobs and businesses. What would you say to those people?

That's very unfortunate, Fauci says, and a consequence you have to balance when trying to save as many lives as possible. That's why we're looking for ways to safely reopen the country. We felt and still feel that our approach was right. Maybe there could've been other approaches but that was the choice we made based on the information we had. One can always second guess. Right now, even though many people are still dying, our data indicate we will soon see a radical drop in the numbers of deaths because fewer people are getting infected.

Thank you, Dr. Fauci, says Jesse Watters.

Retweet

I didn't write it. I'm just passing it along. Our great Republican candidate for Congress, DeAnna Lorraine, who got two percent of the vote against Nancy Pelosi, tweeted that irritating Anthony Fauci shouldn't claim I caused loss of lives by not listening to medical experts. In fact, Lorraine noted, Fauci on February twenty-ninth told the American public at large there was nothing to worry about. "Time to #FireFauci."

And I've got this message for governors: when I say it's time for people to go back to work, they will. The only thing I want to hear from state capitals is yes sir.

The Laboratory

as chinese suddenly revise deaths up thirteen hundred
trump
announces
he's
more
and
more hearing coronavirus somehow got out of sino lab
researchers
say
that's
not
scientifically
valid but trump knows blaming external foe good politics

Executive Hysteria

liberate michigan minnesota and virginia
trump
demands
get
back

to
living and working safely states have to ramp
up
testing
gov
cuomo
responds
we can't do it without federal help while gov
inslee
says
trump's
ranting
may provoke violence and death

Crisis Management

trump tweets
he's always right
on ventilators on testing
on when nation should return to work
so he must've known u.s. would have
twice as many deaths as any other country

SEVENTY-NINE

Tiger Trump

scaremongers force patriots to stay
home
and
destroy
our
economy

Joe Six Pack Chants

usa usa usa
we're
still
number
one
and
widening
lead
in
coronavirus
deaths

Sociological Doctors

same doctors who say coronavirus similar to flu
warn
suicides
domestic
violence
child
molestation
on
rise during lockdown and nation must open up

National Review Reports

coronavirus killed a hundred italian doctors
and
thirty
employees
of
nyc
police
when have you seen figures like that

States' Rights

i love incredible people of georgia and
disagree strongly with gov brian kemp
reopening great beauty and tattoo parlors
and other places a little too soon but i told
him he has to do what he thinks is right

Doctor Gonzo

my big scientific brain just saved the world let's
inject
pour
inhale
disinfectants into your system to kill coronavirus

EIGHTY

Biden Returns to Spotlight

Hey, remember me? I'm the guy who won a bunch of Democratic primaries and earned the opportunity to run against Donald Trump. I ought to be the most visible person in the country, jetting around and bashing the worst president in our history. Instead, like you, I'm stuck at home, hiding from this damn coronavirus. I've been plenty busy, though. I've got a crackerjack media room set up in my basement, and sometimes my wife joins me when I'm doing interviews and making videos. That's helpful because she's a doctor of education, you know.

On the whole, though, the basement isn't an exciting place, and it sickens me that Trump gets all that free air time during daily briefings – bullshit sessions – about the coronavirus. We need a president who can tell the truth. We had one in Barack Obama, and he's finally stepped behind me a hundred percent along with those formidable politicians I dusted in the primaries, people like Bernie Sanders and Kamala Harris and Amy Klobuchar and plenty of others, most of whom would love to be my vice presidential running mate.

Under the circumstances, I'm operating well and cranking out two or three emails a day. In one of my favorites I assure people I stand for "empathy, kindness, compassion, generosity, equal rights for all," and lots of other good stuff. And my message is resonating. We're bringing in a fair amount of money, seventy percent from online donations. Donald Trump will be difficult to beat but recent polls show me leading him in battleground states Pennsylvania, Wisconsin, and Florida, and only trailing by a point in North Carolina.

I was an obscure frontrunner until the media rediscovered me for the most outrageous reason: a former staffer of mine, Tara Reade, who I swear liked me, has accused me of grabbing her in 1993, forcing her against a wall, and jamming my fingers inside her. That's a lie. Why did she wait twenty-seven years before saying anything publicly? I was a prominent senator. Then for eight years I was vice president of the United States. Her timing's damn strange. And now she's reminding everyone that a lot of women have complained about my affectionate behavior. Okay, I've sometimes caressed or kissed or hugged or sniffed women in ways that made them uncomfortable. But I did all this in public, and I'm real sorry some took it the wrong way. I'm just a friendly guy. I wasn't trying to hide anything. Now, on the other hand, you look at the twenty or more women who've complained about Donald Trump and there are some real problems.

Georgia Justice

georgia prosecutors declined
to charge white man and son in pickup truck who in hot
daylight pursued unarmed
black male jogger and fired
in self defense

Canada Bans

after another slaughter
canada decrees ar-15s not needed
to down deer so effective immediately
citizens can no longer buy sell or use
assault weapons
meanwhile in fortress America
nra announces some politicians exploiting
pandemic to close gun stores and deny
citizens sacred second amendment rights of
self defense

Trump Corona

Dr. Anthony Fauci and the coronavirus taskforce have done a great job but their duties are meant to be temporary before our agencies like FEMA begin to take over as certain brave governors reopen businesses, relax social distancing, and we daily watch more than a thousand deaths. We may have lost more than twice as many people as any nation on earth but we've also done more testing, and don't complain the testing came late. That's fake news.

Don't Forget

whatever it is
it
is
obama's
fault

Corona Coordination

trump says
open up we have
met the moment and we have prevailed
fauci says
open too soon
and we'll trigger more suffering and death

Scandalous

donald
declares
obamagate
makes
watergate
look
small
time

EIGHTY-ONE

Online Doctor

She needs to see her doctor and for days has been anxious for their meeting tomorrow. Thank goodness. There's the text confirmation from his office. All she needs to do is reply yes. But this text is highlighted in drab green and states: Due to COVID-19 precautions, we will email you a link tomorrow to access your tele-appointment. She calls to protest but is told the doctor won't be able to talk to her today and no patients are allowed inside the office.

That seems inhuman. She can't go to work because she no longer has a job and she can't be comforted by her husband since she booted him for infidelity and he's already engaged. She can't go to the mall to shop and talk. She can't eat out. She can't go to a bar or nightclub for companionship. She can't visit friends because they're locked in and scared as she is. In the whole world all she can do is click the link in the morning.

The link works and possibilities appear. There's the handsome young doctor about her age. He's married but maybe he's unhappy. She hopes he is, not because she's cruel. She just knows they would be a great couple.

"Hello, Marilyn, how are you?"

"Very sad."

"What's the matter?"

"I'm so alone."

"This is a difficult period," he says. "Are you taking your medications?"

"Yes, but they're not helping nearly as much. I need a higher dosage."

"You know I can't give you any more."

"Why not?"

"They're potentially dangerous. Keep in mind, every year several of our patients overdose on prescription medications and die."

"I can't take much more isolation, Doctor."

He says, "We definitely have to restart the economy soon or we'll destroy what's taken three hundred years to build. On the other hand, the pace of death still hasn't slowed in the United States and if we open up too soon we could ignite a second wave even worse than our first pandemic."

"That's what's going to happen," she says. "It's inevitable. I've got a choice to either die of loneliness in my apartment or have my lungs destroyed by the virus."

"Marilyn, you're young and strong and odds are overwhelming you'd survive even if you contract the virus."

"That's not what my mind's telling me. I feel the worst cough I've had and it keeps getting worse and I choke and there's no one here and I'll die alone on the floor."

"We need to get you back in group therapy once we get this virus under control. You're less obsessive when you spend time with people."

"I can't wait that long, Doctor."

"I've got other patients waiting, Marilyn. We'll talk again next month."

"I told you I can't wait."

"You'll have to."

"I have to talk to you today, after work."

Shaking his head, the doctor says, "You know that's not possible. I only see patients in my office."

She unbuttons and takes off her blouse and removes her bra and says, "Doctor, I need you right now."

"Marilyn, put your blouse on immediately."

She unzips her pants and steps out of them.

"Get dressed immediately or I'm terminating this session."

"Do it and get your ass over here."

Political Lesson

hey biden democracy means more
than one candidate the other one's
trump and if some african americans
support him they're still black despite
your dumb ass statement and others
may stay home from polls to spite you

Church of Trump

we need prayer i pray
five times a day and
know we must reopen
our churches today
and am baffled some
worshipers aren't
jumping right in

Trump Unmasked

i wasn't making fun of
biden and his wife for
wearing masks why would
i ever do that i just
don't like wearing them
especially in public

Murder in Minneapolis

Derek Chauvin is a rough hombre. Look at his history. He has almost twenty years as a police officer. Twelve to eighteen times, depending on the source, the Minneapolis Police Department investigates him for using excessive force. He shoots Ira Toles, unarmed and black, in 2008. Three years later he's placed on leave for the "inappropriate police shooting of Leroy Martinez, an Alaskan American native." I doubt we have tapes of those incidents. But we've got clear video and audio proving that alarmed civilians warn Chauvin he's killing George Floyd and to take his knee off the man's neck. Derek Chauvin is having so much fun, while two other officers pin Floyd's legs and body and another stands guard, he keeps his knee buried in the back of Floyd's neck for almost nine minutes, the final three when Flood stops saying, "I can't breathe," and lies dead quiet, his face in the gutter.

Parts of Minneapolis erupt in flames, and a police station is abandoned before protestors torch it. Unrest spreads around the nation.

The four police officers are fired and finally, four days after the murder, the Minneapolis Police Department arrests Derek Chauvin. His wife also terminates him, filing for divorce. She knows he isn't going to walk away from this crime. His violence is too sustained, too cold, too public. He's going down for third degree murder and manslaughter and maybe more. Arguments by his defense attorneys won't be effective. Everyone knows what they're going to say. George Floyd, according to the initial autopsy, didn't die of asphyxiation. He had coronary artery disease. He had hypertensive heart disease. He may have been intoxicated. He served several years in prison. He was a large and imposing man who'd just tried to pass a counterfeit twenty dollar bill at a deli. None of that matters because George Floyd would today be alive if Derek Chauvin hadn't shoved a fascist knee into his neck and ignored Floyd's pleas for life.

Minnesota Trump

terrible crime
bad stuff i called
george floyd's
family about our
national tragedy
i won't let it get
worse when the
looting starts the
shooting starts

Sacred Trump

i'm a god fearing man bible in hand
solemnly
standing
outside
church
where
criminals

fail

to keep me from being photographed

What People Think

I'm sick of three months lockup getting worse watching Derek Chauvin drive his knee into the neck of George Floyd till he dies and the nation rumbles. I should get out but where would I go other than the market or pharmacy or on an aimless drive around dreary Bakersfield? People I've invited over say it's too dangerous even if we sit twelve feet apart in my living room and wear masks. I need to make some adventurous friends like the eighty percent who don't wear masks where I buy food. That may not happen. I want something stimulating now so call an outgoing guy I've known a long time. He lives near Seattle and just got back from Tucson where he and golfing buddies flew in a commercial plane about half full.

"What are people saying about George Floyd in Tucson and Seattle?" I ask.

"Everyone I've talked to, and I mean every one, thinks it's murder," he says. "I know a lot of conservative guys. They all say that cop's a killer. Cops here think the same. Derek Chauvin isn't what they stand for. His life is basically over. I doubt he'll ever get out. And I don't know how they'll protect him in prison, even if they put him in a white collar country club."

"How bad are the riots in your area?"

"There's no problem where we are, thirty miles from downtown. But I guarantee you, our guns are loaded and we'll kill anyone who tries to loot our family homes. The protestors' anger is justified, but they, like Martin Luther King, should be marching peacefully. A majority of those breaking windows and setting fires and looting businesses aren't there for social justice. They're there to raise hell and see how much stuff they can steal."

EIGHTY-TWO

Letter from Hell

Dear President Trump,

I must correct you for saying I'm happy in heaven looking down at recent economic numbers you like but are still wretched. In fact I'm buried looking into darkness and you remind me of the guys who put me here.

Sincerely,

George Floyd

Downstairs

i wasn't scared or
worried about security
i just decided to inspect
my bunker late one night

Don't Shout

trump's favorite new words
defund
the
police

Emerald City

rioters in seattle better beware or
i may dominate with my military
the mayor and governor better shut
up or they'll be hiding in bunkers

Bare Faces

may be coincidence we're fat and uneducated
but
we
hate
wearing
masks
and don't shop at stores that require them

Tips from Atlanta

don't get intoxicated in car and block fast food
lane after failing field sobriety test don't fight
police officer trying to handcuff you don't take
his taser gun don't run and don't turn and fire
taser at officer you may be shot no matter what
your color

911

when armed intruder
aims
at
you
call a defunder

Beware Kim Yo Jong

You know I'll likely outlive and succeed my obese brother so I must
warn mongrel dogs in South Korea to quit contaminating our skies
with lying leaflets. Our military is as ever ready for the next action.
You don't know what that will be because we don't either but we all
know how powerful is our resentful nation.

Golan Heights

it's official
israel
seals
theft
by
naming
slice
trump heights

EIGHTY-THREE

Trump Assails Bolton and Supreme Court

I achieved a lot for this great nation, winning the election to save us from Hillary Clinton and then appointing two fine conservatives to the Supreme Court. We'd have a five to four majority there most of the time but chief justice John Roberts is playing like an Earl Warren moderate and screwing up my plans, and all that really does is make me damn determined to win in November so I can add at least two more conservative judges and get this country squared away.

Yesterday Roberts cast the deciding vote and wrote the opinion that blocked my wishes to get the DACA illegals out of our country. I don't care they were children when their sneaky parents brought them here and they've been raised as Americans and are now adults. We're a nation of laws or should be but evidently can't be until I pack the Supreme Court. We need more dependable judges. A few days ago, Roberts and Neil Gorsuch, a guy I nominated and trusted, joined the four liberal justices to rule that gender identity and sexual orientation can't be used as reasons to fire people. This country is starting to get very brown and gay and weird, and I'm the only guy who can save us.

John Bolton, the sloppy mustache who served as my national security advisor until I fired his ass, is one sick puppy trying to sell his book of lies and classified information. Before I hired him and during his time as my employee, Bolton often spoke publicly about what a great job I was doing. Now, to make a few millions bucks, he claims I saw conspiracies everywhere and used undelivered military aid to try to club Ukraine into investigating corrupt Joe Biden and his drug-addicted son, and begged President Xi Jinping of China to buy lots of soybeans and wheat to help me win in 2020 and to go right ahead building concentration camps to control its Muslim Uighur minority.

If John Bolton, the warmonger who gets along with no one, really believes I'm bad why didn't he testify at my impeachment trial?

Tulsa Race Riot

It's unlikely Donald Trump will mention this tragedy when he comes to Tulsa tomorrow, ninety-nine years later, so we'll open his speech this way.

It's May thirtieth, 1921 and I'm a teenage shoeshiner entering a large downtown Tulsa building, anxious to use the "colored" restroom on the top floor. I hurry into the elevator, trip, and to avoid falling grasp the arm of a teenage white girl whose screams send me running out. Next day I'm arrested and jailed atop the courthouse and hundreds of white citizens, enraged by street talk and inflammatory newspaper stories, mass outside and threaten to storm the jail and serve justice. Black citizens, though less numerous, arm themselves and rush to support a sheriff who promises nothing will happen. Since there've been numerous recent lynchings in Oklahoma, most blacks are skeptical.

Fearing a "negro uprising" whites hurry home for guns and get more in the local armory, and respective mobs confront each other within hours. Both swear others fire first. Moot point. Someone generally shoots when mobs collide. Whites have more firepower, take the offensive, and realize this is their cherished opportunity to burn Greenwood, the Black Wall Street, one of most affluent African American neighborhoods in America. Many homes and businesses soon glow. Police abandon civic duty and either shoot or detain blacks.

By morning on June first few residents are free to protect Greenwood. While whites loot and burn homes, some golden World War One biplanes, cockpits open to the wind, hold pilots who hurl incendiaries and pump bullets into houses engulfed by flames. On the ground more fire is applied. Twelve hundred houses and thirty-five blocks burn. Under embers most victims are black, perhaps three hundred. National Guard units race in from Oklahoma City, disarm whites, send them home, and herd blacks into internment centers. No charges are filed against me, and I'm hustled out of town and never go near Tulsa again.

The local economy soon tanks so white employers sign papers for release of workers who must wear green tags, like stars later borne by European Jews. The Red Cross offers tents and food for several thousand displaced blacks anxious to rebuild. Whites quickly craft strict building codes designed to preclude recovery and steal abandoned land. A black attorney counters with a legal challenge that succeeds. But there's no financial compensation. The grand jury declares blacks brought this on themselves, and no white ever goes to prison.

The riot is rarely discussed in Oklahoma schools and later most people don't know. Some now learn in a painting of a golden biplane titled *Tulsa Race Riot of 1921* by Curtis James. Somewhere there must also be a painting of a neighborhood later reconstructed.

Triumph in Tulsa

No need to mention there are a helluva lot of empty seats in the upper deck of the Tulsa arena but I do hint by saying some bad people attacked our town tonight. Or, I'm thinking, maybe some tough Tulsans believe Democrat propaganda this county has the highest number of coronavirus cases in Oklahoma and it's dangerous to congregate in an arena with several thousand MAGA supporters, most of them bravely unmasked like me. You've got to be unmasked to chant USA, USA, USA.

It's great to be in front of so many people after a hundred days pigeonholed in the White House. My supporters energize me and I thrill them by beginning our campaign in their state. The silent majority we represent is stronger than ever. And everyone here knows I'm the biggest star in the world. I'm dynamic and clever and my fans clap and cheer when I mention the China Virus and remind them I turned us into the dominant energy superpower in the world.

In order to stay on top we've got to be tough with radical leftist cities like New York, San Francisco, and Seattle. Look at Seattle, six downtown blocks occupied by anarchists. I've told Governor Inslee, call me, I'll help, it'll take less than an hour. He hasn't called. He's a weakling. Remember what Democrats would do to our country. And don't forget what they'll do to your homes once they defund the police. Imagine a lady's home alone while her husband is away working. She hears someone breaking in and calls nine-one-one, and she gets a recording, "Sorry, this number is no longer in service."

All over the United States the radicals are dragging down statutes of great heroes like Robert E. Lee and Jefferson Davis. That's a disgrace. And in Portland these sick people toppled statues of George Washington and Thomas Jefferson and got away with it. But I guarantee you it ain't happening with the Jefferson Memorial or Washington Monument in

Washington, D.C. We've got those places surrounded by some very strong people.

Look around at all this trouble caused by liberals and remember: if Joe Biden is elected he will surrender our country to mobsters who want to double or triple your taxes and destroy your wealth. I just know that won't happen.

The Trump Virus

people mock me by wearing
masks so unnecessary since
i've got coronavirus under
control i'm not worried by
reports new cases are highest
since april that's gotta be
fake news

Sacred Pence

pray the coronavirus task force will brief you more often
pray we won't have many days of forty thousand new cases
pray being unmasked in crowds will somehow become okay
pray that by reopening we keep getting some jobs back
pray that by reclosing a while we won't lose many regained jobs
pray people understand our great testing reveals more cases
pray we'll all continue to pray for families and health care workers
pray that with god's grace we'll do our part to heal our sacred land

Afghan Trump

no one told me russians
might be putting bounties
on our soldiers in afghanistan
can't trust our intel but let me
call putin for the truth

Summoning God

gov newsom's closing businesses again
load
your
guns and pray dear god save the usa

Mount Rushmore

as we huddle beneath great men on
this afternoon before the fourth of july
i promise to defeat those who hate our
history and values which will forever be
celebrated when i build the national
garden of heroes

Trump Worsens Pandemic

Donald Trump doesn't talk much about the coronavirus deaths except to claim he saved millions of lives by sealing off China from the United States. Like much of what he says, that is a lie, and the Associated Press calls his efforts to stop the advance a sieve.

Trump has recently worsened the pandemic by summoning unmasked followers to rallies in Oklahoma, Arizona, and at Mt. Rushmore. These people are his victims yet often say that wearing masks is a "hoax." Isn't that ironic? The hoax is the lying fat man who stands next to the beautiful lady on the White House terrace, pretending he gives a damn about either your liberty or your life.

Mask Monitor

a month ago
twenty percent
wore masks
at the market
two weeks ago
half the people
wore masks
last night
eighty percent
prompting this rhetorical question
will authorities really open schools soon

EIGHTY-FOUR

Privacy

guess
you'll
see
my
tax returns
but
not
before
november

Hidden Face

president trump
puts on public
mask first
time way too
late and also
dons diapers

Trump and Fauci in Private

Hooded and handcuffed, Dr. Anthony Fauci is hustled into a dimly lit interior White House room where President Trump dismisses two secret service agents and rips off the little man's hood, saying, "We're gonna talk."

"Okay, fine, Mr. President. But how about removing these handcuffs?"

"Things are going the wrong way fast."

"I'm thankful you finally acknowledge that," says Fauci. "We need to shut down lots of places that have reopened and keep closed lots of others."

"I'm talking about my polling numbers and reelection prospects."

"This shouldn't be a political consideration, Mr. President. Florida, Texas, Arizona, and others have been recording one-day highs for infections."

"Only because we're testing more than anyone else in the world."

Tensing, Fauci says, "The European Union is testing as much as we are and their new cases are declining while ours go up. We had thirty-one thousand new cases in a day recently versus four thousand in the EU."

"I don't trust European statistics."

"You should try to learn from them. Despite horrific casualties in the early stages of the pandemic, countries like Spain, Italy, France, and Belgium have dramatically reduced new infections and deaths."

Chin out, Trump says, "I'm doing a great job."

"No, you aren't and neither are the lackey governors who opened restaurants and bars and other nonessential businesses to please you and your constituents. Our data indicate rates of infection are also increasing."

"We're going to get this country rolling again. Next month the kids will be back in school and this virus will either disappear or turn into something like the flu and we learn to deal with it."

"We're learning," Fauci says, "but we're not going to be doing much in classrooms. Lots of districts are planning to distance learn and others will run classes in two sessions, one day on and one day off. We'll have a disaster if we don't proceed patiently."

"I'll cut off federal funding for districts that don't start school again," he says, and puts the hood back over Fauci's head.

Reaching into his pocket, Trump presses an electronic button and two agents appear. He jerks his neck and says, "Get him out of here."

Freddy Reviews Daughter's Book

Certainly I've already read my daughter Mary Trump's book *Too Much and Never Enough*. And I'm proud it's the bestselling book in the nation. No matter what Donald says, he knows this deal's a winner, though not for him.

I admire Mary's years of study in clinical psychology and her careful analysis of my father Fred Trump. He was a government-subsidized builder of ghastly high rise apartments, a racist landlord, a rough rent collector, and a cold and authoritarian bastard at work as well as in our large home in Queens.

I must, however, disagree with Mary's oft-stated conviction that my father and Donald destroyed me and in effect shoved me into the grave at age forty-two. They probably could've tried harder to help me but during my long earthly decline I usually understood there was something intrinsically wrong with me. Mary is a clinical psychologist, not a psychiatrist and therefore not an expert in psychopharmacology. She attributes everything to relationships and emotions, and they're quite important, but psychologists often fail to perceive what every psychiatrist knows: many chronic mental problems begin with chemical imbalances in the brain.

I had a great financial opportunity working for Trump Management. In my mid-twenties, though, I told my father I'd rather fly than build and maintain apartments. I'd already served in the Air Force Reserves and earned a great job as a commercial pilot for Trans World Airlines, flying the prestigious Boston to Los Angeles route and soon was offered training in the new 747s. But I turned the big jets down. I didn't want more responsibilities and a longer commute to the airport. I wanted to get away from my wife and two infants and relax on my small boat with buddies who liked to drink and smoke.

"You're going a little heavy there, aren't you, Freddy?" they sometimes said.

"No, you pick up the pace."

I was going too fast, all right, and in a few months TWA told me to either resign and keep my pilot's license or they'd fire me and I'd lose the license. I chose the former and right away got a job with a small airline and then another but those opportunities only lasted about a month. I could fly, no doubt, but discovered that heavy drinking at night left me groggy the next day. Aviation officials wouldn't tolerate that. I needed a job. You know who I called. He took me back but soon after Donald, eight years my junior, graduated from college and joined the firm, our father, in front of employees, shouted, "Donald's ten times more valuable than you."

That would humiliate anyone but, as I've confessed, my serious drinking and chain smoking predated the worst family problems. I knew I couldn't compete with Donald in the real estate business. It didn't matter whether he possessed technical and management skills. He was a leader and visionary and my father adored him. Frankly, if I'd been my father I'd have chosen Donald, too. I just had so much anxiety. While Dad and Donald planned major deals, ethical or not, I liked to slip away for a smoke and a drink, lots of them. My wife left me. That hurt but probably not as much as having two kids and a woman bugging me when I was hungover and depressed.

My father and Donald weren't sympathetic but why should they have been? When a middle-aged guy's back living with his parents and loaded and ill much of the time and can't do even a maintenance job, he's going to be treated like dirt. I was in a frail and frightening state the final time I went to the hospital. My mom and dad didn't come with me. Donald went to the movies. They got the call soon enough.

I'm sorry I couldn't do better for my kids. Almost twenty years later my father died of Alzheimer's, and I'm certain Donald and my youngest brother and two sisters manipulated him into rewriting his will and virtually disinheriting my two kids. Donald, uncharacteristically modest, claimed my grandparents' estate was only worth about thirty million dollars. In fact, it was worth at least ten times that. Mary and her brother Fred III challenged the will and Donald promptly cut off health insurance for Fred's chronically ill son. A couple of years later my kids settled for a lot less than I would've gotten but if I'd lived Donald probably would've devised ways to acquire my inheritance.

The Masked Man

More authoritative than ever, President Trump dons the sleek black eye mask of The Lone Ranger and steps behind microphones to announce wearing masks is a good idea after all since the China Virus is going to get worse before it gets better.

"Mr. President," says a reporter masked over nose and mouth, "you're not stopping the spread of the virus like that."

"You must be an agent of Dr. Anthony Fauci, who, you'll notice, didn't make the cut for this press conference, and neither did any other so-called medical experts. I'm up here alone, fighting the virus and traitors trying to destroy our country."

Kayleigh McEnany, whose babe-factor and Harvard law degree motivated Trump to name her White House press secretary, rushes to the podium and hands her boss an appropriate black mask he at once puts on.

"This is what a real commander in chief looks like," Trump huffs through his mask.

"Mr. President," says a masked female reporter, "people around this nation are worried their civil liberties are imperiled by you and the faceless, camouflaged storm troops you're sending into various American cities. Innocent people are being grabbed on the streets and hauled away without explanation."

"How do you know they were innocent? Our nation is in chaos. Last weekend sixty-three people were shot in Chicago. Several died. Fourteen people were shot outside a funeral home. And the mourners returned fire. That's crazy. A lot of our cities are far worse than Afghanistan."

"Mr. President," shouts a female reporter, "the people of Portland, my hometown, are outraged by the fascist behavior of your storm troops."

"It's outrageous criminals in the South are attacking our cultural heritage, pulling down statues of Confederate heroes, but it's even worse that thugs in Portland are jerking down statues of Washington and Jefferson."

"They did own slaves, Mr. President," a male voice announces.

"We can't judge our heroes of more than two hundred years ago by the standards of today," Trump says. "They're still the greatest Americans ever, along with Abraham Lincoln and myself. I'm also ready to make the toughest decisions and am preparing plans to send help to New York, Philadelphia, Detroit, Baltimore, Oakland, and, of course, the Obama-stronghold of Chicago. Notice all these liberal cities are run by Democrats. And if Joe Biden gets in, the whole country will go to hell."

"Will you respect the election results in November?" asks a female reporter.

"Let's wait and see. I can't say yes when I know the Democrats are trying to register millions of fake voters, like they did in 2016. No way I'm telling you today I'll accept some farce. I'll let you know."

"Joe Biden promises the police and military will be ready to remove

you from the White House if you lose the election and refuse to leave,"
says a male reporter.

"Biden's brain is dead and it doesn't matter what he claims. The
generals love me and will do what I say."

Conventional Trump

kinda tired and slumping
today but got enough
energy to say florida
won't accept big
gop convention either
so will return to north
carolina for some kind
of politically correct
corona gathering

Scientific Trump

i'm promoting lots of
vaccine efforts and
if one works before
november i'll win

Defender of Democracy

china virus hitting us hard despite my great efforts
we
better
postpone
election
until
we
can
safely
vote

instead of mailing in most fraudulent ballots in history

Solitary Trump

nobody likes me
must
be
my personality

Newsletter Trump

like I've always said
partiots
wear
face
masks

Rushmore Trump

"I really think I belong on Mt. Rushmore, don't you," Trump tells me. "I'm ten times the president Ronald Reagan was."

"Most Americans would disagree with that," I say. "Besides, Reagan isn't on Mt. Rushmore."

"I'm at least as great as Lincoln, and I've done much more for blacks."

"Again, Mr. President, a majority of our citizens would take exception to that, especially blacks."

"It bugs me so many blacks don't understand what I've achieved for them economically. My face on Mt. Rushmore would remind everyone."

"Your face might serve as quite a different reminder."

"Listen, I love our great historical heroes, including those in the Confederacy, but I don't think guys like Washington and Jefferson are any better than I am. I forgive them for owning slaves, but let's remember I've never owned any."

"The latter point is very much in your favor, Mr. President. But experts insist that structural difficulties preclude carving any more faces onto Mt. Rushmore."

"Okay, then we can replace Teddy Roosevelt's face with mine. Nobody really remembers what he did. I sure as hell don't."

Clever Fellow

don't you love my nicknames for enemies
lyin' ted
little marco
cheatin' obama
crazy bernie
crooked hillary
sleepy joe
phony kamala
and now I've got another great one
fat donald

Trump Denounces Kamala Harris

We all know Joe Biden hasn't been thinking straight in years but even in his crazy condition I expected him to pick someone better than Kamala Harris as his vice presidential running mate. She's the nastiest and most liberal of all U.S. Senators. It was disgraceful how she insulted Brett Kavanaugh during his Senate confirmation hearing for the Supreme Court. For political reasons, Harris tried to frame a good man. And during a presidential primary debate she was very disrespectful to her colleague and former friend, Joe Biden, virtually calling him a lover of segregationists because he'd been cordial to southern Senators who opposed busing. I've got great sources and guarantee Sleepy Joe was pissed at the betrayal but now he's desperate because of my great handling of the coronavirus pandemic and knows he's got to try something wild to get close enough to try to steal the election with phony mail-in ballots.

If Joe still had any judgment, he'd know Kamala Harris can't help him. In the Democrat primary she couldn't attract supporters or much money and dropped out before voting began so people wouldn't see her in the tank. She wouldn't have even taken her home state of California. Our country won't back Crazy Joe and Phony Kamala. They hate our way of life and are weak on crime. I don't care Harris was attorney general of San Francisco and then of California. She put pot smokers in jail and turned murderers loose.

Postmaster Trump

I'm not going to let Democrats use the United States Postal Service to steal the election. We all know they're claiming the China Virus is so dangerous that people can't safely go to the polls. Listen, I already offered to postpone the election until my scientists develop a vaccine, and that won't be long, but the Dems don't want that. They want a phony election. That's why so many of them, unlike Republicans, plan to vote by mail.

Straight out I'm telling our enemies I won't give them the money necessary to have universal mail-in voting. That recipe for fraud won't happen because I'm going to limit overtime pay and slow down deliveries of ballots so they'll arrive too late to be counted. We're also studying a variety of executive actions to force people to vote at the polls in November.

I've got a fine team helping me ensure we get a fair election. Postmaster General Louis DeJoy is a big-time Trump backer and can be trusted to stamp out corruption and at the same time be very efficient and assure Americans that the "United States Postal Service can handle election mail."

EIGHTY-FIVE

Democratic Convention Highlights

bill clinton says
you know what
trump will do
blame bully belittle

barack obama says
trump had no interest
in putting in the work
result is a hundred
seventy thousand dead
millions of jobs lost and
our worst impulses released

joe biden says
i will draw on best
of us not the worst
i'll be an ally of
light not darkness

USPS

it's a hoax
cries trump
don't vote
especially to restore
funds and services
my guy cut from
post office

by more than
hundred votes
house of reps
including two dozen
from his party

tells fat donald
to shove it

Republicans Open Convention

howdy
i'm matt badass gaetz
patriotic congressman from florida
standing in a room empty as joe biden's head
to warn that democrats want to take your guns
empty the prisons lock you in your homes and
invite central american gangs to live next door
don't bother calling police in democrat-run cities
they're already being defunded and disbanded

Trump Accepts Nomination

How about this backdrop? The White House lit up at night, baby. While Joe Biden hides in his basement, I'm addressing you in front of the world's greatest home, where I've lived four years and will reside four more maybe even eight. Thanks to my gorgeous daughter Ivanka for introducing me. Isn't she fantastic? I've got great genes and always marry babes, and look at the results.

I accept your enthusiastic nomination to continue as president and proudly tell you, in response to the China Virus, I have enabled us to test far more people during the pandemic than any other nation. Don't worry we've also had many more deaths than any other country. We're working on three very promising vaccines that would normally take years to develop but under my guidance they'll be ready by the end of the year if not sooner. It's time for us to go back to work and back to school. We need to fill our offices, classrooms, stadiums, arenas, and churches, and we need to do so with people like those in this vast and wonderful crowd tonight – without masks and rubbing shoulders. That's how you crush the coronavirus.

I know more about security than anyone in the world and have made us much safer. I got out of the Iran nuclear deal that was so unfair to our country. International inspectors visited Iranian facilities many times and verified compliance but that doesn't matter. Using my art of breaking deals, I've now got us in a situation where we don't have anyone checking up on Iran and that's why I need to win the election and kick ass there and elsewhere in the Middle East. You know Sleepy Joe doesn't have the energy to start a war.

You probably see my splendid border wall on TV all the time. We're building ten miles a week and have three hundred miles sealing off the Mexican hordes. Our southern border has never been so secure. Soon, those sanctuary cities the Democrats love will have a lot fewer illegal aliens. We have to be on guard.

The Democrats have the most extreme set of proposals in our history. They want to hike your taxes four trillion dollars. You'd be broke while Joe Biden pursues his agenda of Made in China. My agenda is Made in the U.S.A. I'm going to force the Chinese to play fair by wrapping a lot more tough tariffs around their necks.

Look at all the ways we're better than our Democrat adversaries. We believe all children, born and unborn, have a right to life. The liberals have no problem stopping a baby's heart in the ninth month of gestation. It's just as frightening that if Biden becomes president he'll demolish our suburbs and release criminals into your neighborhoods. He'll take away your guns. Joe Biden is the Trojan Horse for Marxism. He'll also defund the police and make every city like Democrat-run and riot-torn Portland.

Let's be honest. The overwhelming majority of police desperately want to do a good job for you, but they're afraid to act. We can never allow mob rule that's ruining liberal cities all over the country. If you want to be led by the party of anarchists, rioters, looters, and flag burners, vote for Joe Biden and the Democrats. As long as I'm president we will protect the flag and ensure law and order and your right to prosper in the greatest nation ever. God bless you, even those few wearing masks.

As I pose with my beautiful wife and five wonderful children and my grandchildren, we watch spectacular fireworks spell TRUMP over and behind the Washington Monument. Imagine how you'd feel if that had been your name lighting the sky.

Mailer Advocates All-Black Police Forces

Highlights follow from my recent phone conversation with Norman Mailer, twice a Pulitzer Prize winner who passed from this physical earth in 2007.

"Damn it, Norman," I say, "I spent too much time piddling online this morning and lost energy and still hadn't written anything by early afternoon when I decided to read in bed and returned to your Playboy interview from 1968 and was again bored and irritated by verbal flatulence which you sometimes offer instead of substantive commentary."

"Why continue reading it then? I haven't time to field complaints from all my critics in perpetuity. At this stage I generally accept rebukes only from my many wives and children."

"I'm glad I persevered because you finally said something in classic Mailer style."

He laughs. "And what was that?"

"I'm assuming you still follow current events?"

"No one more vigorously devours information than I."

Deepening my voice, I tell him, "You said, 'Part of the New York City police force works in Harlem. It's a hopeless job for any white policeman. He doesn't have a prayer of being a good cop; he's too hated because of all the bad cops who've been there and also because of all the bad Negro cops who've worked in Harlem. (The white cop's) hated because he comes from outside and is a symbol of oppression."

"And what did I next tell Mr. Playboy?"

"You said, 'Suppose the existential fact were recognized that Harlem is more separated from New York City than East Berlin from West Berlin… Suppose, then, that Harlem had its own police force and was offered its fair share of the funds that run the New York Police Department. Suppose they even used part of that money for other purposes and had a volunteer police force, just like the Hasidic Jews in Crown Heights, Brooklyn, a few years ago… The advantage of having an all-Negro professional and volunteer police force in Harlem is that every time something ugly happened, the Negroes would have to recognize one particular complexity in life, which is that their own people can be bad but that police brutality might be something that comes out of being a policeman. And they'd have to face the fact that whitey ain't the only devil in town.'"

I hear Mailer clapping.

"I probably shouldn't applaud my own words," he says, "but I know you'll keep this confidential."

"I respect that you're the shiest and most private of men."

Try This

    s

      t

        o

         p

          resisting

           a

            r

             r

              e

               s

                t

Trump Blasts Biden

As race tightens Sleepy Joe Biden gets so scared he leaves his basement and hurries to Pennsylvania to denounce rioters and criminals in Democrat-controlled cities around nation. Notice he and other Dems didn't say much at their convention. They sympathize with the bad guys.

I always back law and order and worry about patriots like Kyle Rittenhouse, who's only seventeen. He bravely carried his assault rifle across state line into Kenosha, Wisconsin and probably would've died if he hadn't shot and killed two attackers and wounded another. That's how you defend freedom. I'm not going to criticize young Rittenhouse until my people provide more information. He's got enough problems in jail.

EIGHTY-SIX

Operation Warp Speed

thank god president trump
who's been corona slow
now speed of light ordering
federal government to tell
states be prepared to distribute
safe and effective vaccine by
november first and not worry
date politically motivated

Trump Alert

the
radical
left
hates
you

Virus on Tape

I'm the leader. I can't be jumping all over the place. That's what I told Bob Woodward months ago during recorded interviews. I knew the coronavirus was more dangerous than first suspected and often transmitted by air. I did a great job fighting it or we'd have two million more deaths. I didn't want to create a panic by wearing a mask and rushing personal protective equipment out there and shutting everything down. I had to take care of you by saving my beautiful economy. I knew the virus would disappear. And I still think it will. I'll soon get it with a great vaccine, anyway. Just relax. And don't wear those masks so damn much. They make you look weak.

Soaring in Michigan

We're not afraid in Michigan. We're thrilled to be jammed into this wonderful airplane hangar, and behind me you're inspired by the beauty and power of Air Force One which you'll never forget seeing today. You're not going to ruin this experience by wearing masks. You've already forgotten what I told Bob Woodward months ago. With me as your president, we don't run from the coronavirus. We embrace life.

Seeing at least five thousand of you today tells me "this is not the crowd of a person who comes in second place." We're going to win Michigan, which is a really critical state. You're much too proud and independent to follow state guidelines that meetings should be limited to a hundred timid people. Look at us. We don't need negative rules that are ruining our nation. Tell the governor, Gretchen Whitmer, to quit playing politics and open up your state. I wish you had "a governor who knew what the hell she was doing."

Thankfully, I'm an expert in all critical areas and guarantee things are getting better now. You know that because, like me, you feel healthy and happy.

Trump Weapons

bob woodward fascinated
when i tell him i've built
super-secret weapons
system that you and putin
and xi have never seen or
heard about because it's
so incredible

My Nobel

Everyone said it couldn't be done but thanks to my brain the United Arab Emirates and Israel now have normal diplomatic relations that should inspire Palestinians to cooperate since I'm nominated for the Nobel Peace Prize and Bahrain also normalizes with Israel and more

Arab states will soon follow.

Where's Kamala

i know
kamala's
out there
but i keep
looking and
still know
not where

EIGHTY-SEVEN

Ferocity

outraged by allegations he called dead american soldiers losers
the donald vows to get vicious
as wildfires envelop nation

State of Emergency

in
vegas
trump
performs
for
another
unprotected
crowd
later vows to smash shooter of two cops in compton
biden
meanwhile
says
trump
climate
change
denial
disastrous

The Real Problem

criminals
not freedom fighters
howl for blood of ambushed cops

The Golden State

california
great to be here
quit worrying about
all that smoke it'll
start getting cooler
just you watch

Town Trump Hall

a lot of people don't like masks
says the donald

who

waiters touching theirs before
they serve my food

Painful Polling

not politically correct to note
police killed thirty unarmed
black men last year while
blacks killed about seven
thousand other blacks and
many voters are confused
why former is more alarming
than latter

In Barr We Trust

i william barr attorney general for these united states must hereby
declare coronavirus lockdown
greatest intrusion on civil liberties in our history other than slavery

EIGHTY-EIGHT

Justice Quickly

solemn mitch mcconnell says
we're all saddened by passing of liberal supreme court justice ruth
bader ginsberg
but promises senate will
rush to vote on president trump's replacement who will not be
merrick garland

Words of Graham

Hold your voices. Naturally, I've reviewed my video from four
years ago and know I said it was the "last year of a lame duck president
and if Republican candidates Donald Trump or Ted Cruz get to be
president they ask the Senate not to vote on a Supreme Court nominee
by President Obama. So if a vacancy occurs in the last year of their first
term, guess what? You will use their words against them.

"And I want you to use my words against me. If there's a Republican
president in 2016 and a vacancy occurs in the last year of the first term,
you can say Lindsay Graham said, 'Let's let the next president make
that nomination. You could use my words against me, and you'd be
absolutely right. We're setting a precedent.'"

Now that isn't exactly what I meant. The rule applies only when
the Senate and White House are held by separate parties.

Meet Amy

Amy Coney Barrett's pretty. Two years ago I couldn't tell during
the interview because she had some pink eye infection and wore dark
glasses and we just didn't connect and I wanted Brett Kavanaugh,
anyway. Being farsighted, I told her supporters to relax, I'd soon have
the best spot for her – replacing radical Ruth Bader Ginsberg. I'm
always right on big issues.

Listen, we've got to hurry and get Amy through Senate confirmation hearings and wrap this up a couple of weeks before the election.
That way we'll have six conservatives to three libs on the Supreme

Court and my evangelical base is going to be thrilled I've given them a religious woman. I can't swear she talks in tongues but she belongs to a Pentecostal group, People of Praise, that believes husbands should be in charge at home. I bet Amy exercises plenty of authority, too. She and her attorney husband Jesse Barrett have seven children, two adopted from Haiti, which is a tough place.

Everyone knows Amy is talented. She finished first in her class at Notre Dame Law School and a few times won professor of the year there. She teaches a lot of heavy classes and commutes almost two hours each way to Chicago to serve on the United States Court of Appeals. Her work as a judge has been phenomenal. She's against Obamacare, wants to "hollow out Roe v. Wade" so states can make it tough to get abortions, and believes felons should be able to carry guns as long as they're nonviolent. I don't get into technical stuff but aides tell me Amy "looks strictly at the text of the Constitution" and tries to figure out the original intent of the framers, and those were some really smart guys.

Today I'm the sharpest guy around and would like to present the imminent Supreme Court Justice Amy Coney Barrett.

Trust Me

Have I ever lied to you? I'm the most honest man in the world and guarantee new vaccines I'm working on are safe and effective and will soon be available probably before election day. I've just got to keep kicking lazy scientists and CDC bureaucrats so they stop slowing things down.

I'm cranking everything up because I'm the only man who can save the country from riots and poverty, and must use all measures to stay in office and continue to explain I can't commit to a peaceful transfer of power. That would be crazy. If I lose I won't really lose because the only way Sleepy Joe gets more votes is if millions of ballots are delivered to illegal aliens. That's voter fraud on an unprecedented level and, as my life proves, I'm against all liars and thieves.

The A Team

some
traitor
tweeted
putin 2020 trump

IRS Trumps

don't try to tax me
least not more than
seven hundred last
two years even that's
too much usually don't
pay at all but scream
like hell i do

EIGHTY-NINE

Stand Back and Stand By

Donald Trump is not only the greatest president, economist, and strategic thinker we've ever had, he's by far the finest debater. Trump would have hogtied Abraham Lincoln every time he opened his bearded mouth. Joe Biden, no Lincoln even before senility eroded Crazy Joe's modest gifts, is in even bigger trouble tonight.

"People have rights," declares the challenger. "We should wait on nominating a new justice for the Supreme Court. He wants someone to help him get rid of the Affordable Care Act. That could cost twenty million Americans their health insurance."

"You're a socialist, Joe, and your policies would eliminate health insurance for a hundred eighty million Americans."

Shaking his head, Biden says, "You'd also wipe out protection for pre-existing conditions. And…"

"You've already had forty-seven years as a senator and vice president and you've never come up with anything."

"President Obama and I led the creation of the Affordable Care Act. It…"

"It's a disaster, Joe, just like you and Obama."

"President Trump," says bespectacled moderator Chris Wallace, "you have never come up with a comprehensive health plan."

"Chris, you're already starting to irritate me as much as Joe, who just barely beat ancient Bernie Sanders. If Pocahontas Warren hadn't quit, Joe would've lost. He got lucky."

"Vice President Biden, if Judge Amy Coney Barrett is confirmed to the Supreme Court, will you end the filibuster?" asks Chris Wallace. "And will you pack the Supreme Court?"

Biden responds, "I'm a veteran of legislating in the Senate and for eight years served as chairman of the Senate Judiciary Committee. Furthermore…"

"He won't answer the question," says Trump. "Answer the question, Joe. It's obvious he'll pack the court with six new radicals to outvote the six to three majority I've brilliantly put together."

"You're a clown," says Biden. "Two hundred thousand people have died from the coronavirus, forty thousand daily are being infected. And you panicked. You said President Xi of China was doing a great job."

"If we'd listened to you we'd have had two million deaths by now. You said I was xenophobic when I cut off flights to and from China. Many Democrats admit that President Trump did a great job. We're close to a vaccine and fewer are dying. You never could've done that, Joe. You don't have it in you."

"President Trump," says Chris Wallace, "your statements about the coronavirus are at odds with expert opinions from your administration. Some of your people say the vaccine won't be ready for widespread use until the summer of 2021."

"I've got my military all set to distribute the vaccines and make everything right."

Shaking his head as he laughs, Biden says, "Do you believe him, after all the lies he's told you. He's just not smart enough."

"Don't ever use the word smart with me," says Trump. "You were the lowest student at a college you can't name, and you've still done nothing in Washington."

In the manner of a harried schoolmaster, Chris Wallace says, "President Trump, you've questioned the benefits of masks. You've been holding large rallies where people are packed in and most aren't wearing masks."

"I've got huge outdoor rallies, tens of thousands waiting to see me. Joe would hold rallies, too, but doesn't dare because no one would show up. Masks are okay once in a while. I've got one right here in my coat. See? Joe's usually got a giant mask covering his face."

"I'd like to respond, Chris…"

"My economy's doing great. We had the greatest economy in the history of the world before the coronavirus, and I'm bringing us back. But we've got to open up. Alcohol and divorce and depression are all getting worse because people like Joe want to shut everything down."

"Why does he so strongly want to open up," says Biden. "One in six small businesses are gone. We're in trouble."

Chris Wallace checks his notes and says, "President Trump, you only paid seven hundred fifty dollars a year in federal taxes in two recent years."

"I paid millions of dollars, millions…"

"Quit lying, man," Biden says. "Pay your taxes and acknowledge that President Obama and I inherited the worst recession in decades and still left you with a booming economy. You're screwing all of us. You let China develop the 'art of the steal.'"

"Don't tell me about other countries. Your son got three million dollars from Moscow."

"That's a lie by a dishonest president who's been disastrous for blacks."

"Tell us about your 'super predator' bill that targeted blacks, who I've helped more than anyone."

Biden points at Trump. "That's not what we did. We…"

"You and your radical left have turned Portland and Seattle and Detroit and many other cities into riot zones. You're afraid to even say 'law and order.'"

Trump waits a second. "It's devastating, but Joe didn't say it, did he? Why not? Come on, Joe, say 'law and order.'"

"Law and order," says Biden. "Okay?"

"Name one law enforcement group that has embraced you," Trump orders.

Biden doesn't respond.

Chris Wallace says, "Vice President Biden, you never called for the National Guard to help deal with a hundred nights of demonstrations and riots in Portland. "

"You're right, Chris," says Trump. "Somebody's got to do something about antifa, and we know Joe can't stop them, if he even wants to. His leftist radicals are much more dangerous than my supporters."

"All right," says Chris Wallace. "I'd like to ask each of you, 'Why should voters elect you?'"

"There's never been an administration that's done so much in three and a half years. We rebuilt the military, which Obama and Joe left in tatters, we improved the VA, I appointed an unprecedented three hundred federal judges, also three great Supreme Court justices. Obama and Joe left with more than one hundred twenty open judges. "

"Donald Trump is Putin's puppy," Biden says. "He's also made our nation more divided and violent. He calls the military losers. My son got the Bronze Star in…"

"Your son got thrown out of the army and was given tens of millions of dollars by foreign governments. Why?"

"Quit interrupting me. And don't ever refer to my late son, Beau, that way. He was an honorable soldier, public servant, and man."

"I was talking about Hunter, who's so scandalous."

"You can't open your mouth without another lie popping out…"

Chris Wallace says, "President Trump, I want you to quit interrupting."

"Him, too."

"You're interrupting a lot more than he is. You agreed to the format of two minutes of uninterrupted talking by both candidates. Now, let's move to climate change. Forest fires are raging throughout the West, and you, President Trump, took the United States out of the Paris climate accord. Are you willing to state that human activity is to blame for environmental catastrophes?"

"Human activity, to an extent. We have to do everything to keep the environment healthy, but California doesn't keep its forests clean, creating massive fire hazards. That's a lack of management. I'm all for healthy living. I like electric cars but what they're doing in California is ridiculous. They'd destroy the auto industry and our economy. And Joe's Green New Deal would cost a hundred trillion dollars and we could never pay for that."

"I don't support the Green New Deal. I support the Biden plan."

Chris Wallace adjusts his glasses and says, "Now, let's deal with election integrity."

"There's no evidence whatever of corruption of mail-in ballots," says Biden. "Donald Trump cannot stop you from voting. You can determine what this nation will look like."

Unclenching his teeth, Trump says, "It's a disaster sending millions of ballots all over the country. They found some in a creek. This is fraud. We might not know the results for months. It's a fraud, and it's a shame."

"In 2018 thirty-one million voted with mail-in ballots," says Chris Wallace.

"I'm urging my voters to be poll watchers," says Trump. "And if I see tens of thousands of mishandled ballots, I'm not going along with it. Eighty million ballots will overwhelm the post office."

"You've done everything you can to screw up the post office," Biden says.

"Don't interrupt. I just want a fair election. You asked about the Proud Boys, Chris. To them I say, 'Stand back and stand by.'"

Get Well Soon

I dial the special number direct to a White House communications officer who promptly rings the Oval Office phone of the president.

"President Trump, this is Tom Clark."

"I'd rather hear from Tom Jones. He's a star."

"That he is. More importantly, I can tell by your feistiness you're feeling okay. And I assume Melania's also well."

"We're doing great. If it weren't for political considerations, I'd go out and play eighteen holes today. The First Lady's probably in our private gym now."

I say, "That's good news. Even though you're seventy-four and a tad overweight, I've from the start been optimistic about both of you making a quick and complete recovery."

"Piece of cake so far. I know it could get a little worse, about like a bad cold, maybe bronchitis, but my doctors tell me I'd have a ninety-percent chance of recovering even without medical treatment. And believe me, I've got the finest medical team in the world."

"Follow their orders. Remember, British Prime Minister Boris Johnson, who's almost twenty years younger than you, spent several days in the hospital, two in the intensive care unit, so the coronavirus can be dangerous."

"Boris called me just a little while ago, thanking me for my support when he was ill and wishing me the best."

"I guess you'll be back on the campaign trail in a couple of weeks."

Exhaling in exasperation, the president says, "You're kidding, right. I'll be on the virtual campaign trail in a day or two, packing 'em in on TV and Zoom. I'm not going to let the Democrats steal this election."

"They have no desire to steal anything. But I didn't call to talk about politics. In addition to saying get well, I wanted to tell you I've always felt the greatest day in the life of any president is the day he leaves office. I hope you view it that way, too."

"I'll let you know how I feel in January 2025 or maybe January 2029."

"I hope you're joking about the latter. A better bet for departure would be January 2021. But regardless of when your day comes, it will signal a return to the life you had before you walked into the morass of politics. You've got a wonderful family, there's a TV and public speaking career waiting for you, and as a private citizen you can play as much golf as you want. Most people would prefer that to power."

President Trump pauses a few seconds before saying, "I sacrificed because I'm a patriot who wanted to help his people."

"History will have to judge how you did."

"After studying my extraordinary record, history will be kind."

"Give my best to Melania and Hope Hicks, too."

"Will do."

On the Mend

Don't worry. I'm already feeling great Sunday and tweeting up a storm from my makeshift executive office in Walter Reed National Military Medical Center. Look at my latest tweet, just seconds ago, "US election poll: Trump BEATING Biden despite being in hospital with covid." This comes from an important British monthly publication whose name I've forgotten and you wouldn't remember anyway. Thirty minutes earlier I posted, "I really appreciate all of the fans and supporters outside of the hospital. The fact is, they really love our Country and are seeing how we are MAKING IT GREATER THAN EVER BEFORE!" An hour ago I urged, "Get Ready to Vote. Visit vote.donaldjtrump.com for information about voting in your state." You can't get into this super site unless you give us your name, address, email, and date of birth. We're doing things the right way by shooing away phony voters.

The doctors, nurses, and staff are doing a super job for me here at Walter Reed. I wasn't feeling so well Friday afternoon and my aides panicked a little and wouldn't listen to my guarantees I was fine and preferred to continue working from home but they insisted and, as you saw, I walked smoothly from the White House, across the grass, and into my helicopter and came here for some high-powered experimental cocktails to suppress the virus and intravenous Remdesivir that will get me out of here soon.

I'm sure you heard fake news trying to make me sound sicker than I was. I didn't want to worry you and wouldn't have but my chief of staff Mark Meadows and young doctor Sean Conley got confused and let enough slip so the media knew I twice had to take a little oxygen Friday before being hospitalized. No big deal. I haven't needed any since.

Don't let the media mislead you about the timeline. I had some extremely minor symptoms Thursday evening, took a test late that night, and, along with the first lady, received news we were positive for the coronavirus about one a.m. Friday. No way I traveled to political events Wednesday and Thursday, knowing I was infected or had symptoms. And I still believe we had a beautiful ceremony in the Rose Garden last Saturday to introduce future Supreme Court Justice Amy Coney Barrett. A few people who were there – Kellyanne Conway, Chris Christie, a couple of Republican senators, my campaign manager, and some others did test positive but that's probably a coincidence. Anyway, they're all a lot younger than I am and will beat this just as I am and Judge Barrett already did last summer.

I feel like making a video so you can see how healthy I am and by the time you get it I'll be riding in a beast outside Walter Reed, waving to my dedicated supporters. You won't be watching Sleepy Joe on the news tonight. You'll be watching me.

Calling Home

Excited as a Little Leaguer who just hit the winning grand slam, President Trump dances into his office at Walter Reed, strokes the screen for his cell phone contacts, and touches: Melania.

"Can't wait," he says to a couple of secret service agents pressing their backs against the far wall.

The phone keeps ringing.

"Would've expected a quick answer after this triumph," he says.

There's an automated response: "Good day. This is Melania. Please leave a brief message at the beep."

"Hello, my little princess, I bet you're still watching replays of my great comeback ride around the hospital. I thrilled my admirers on the streets and no doubt all around the country. Call me as soon as you can."

In less than a minute his screen shows the magic word and Trump says, "Hello. Wasn't I great?"

"Donald, are an idiot?"

"Relax. I wore a big heavy mask. It was uncomfortable as hell but I photographed pretty well."

"I'm talking about your health. And the health of the secret service agents."

"Melania, they wore tons of protective equipment. A couple of them are here right now. Guys, say hi to Melania."

They smile. One waves. The other raises his voice and says, "Hi, Mrs. Trump."

"No, I mean come on over and talk to her."

Almost in unison they say, "That's all right."

"Of course they're not going to get near you," she says. "Everyone who does gets infected."

"You're watching too much fake news, Melania."

"The fake news, Donald, is coming out of your pie hole. Stay away from Barron until I say so or I may start making speeches for Biden."

Triumphant Return

Timidly, Dr. Sean Conley approaches President Trump at Walter Reed, stands at attention, holds a tight salute, and says, "Sir, you really should stay a few more days. Your progress here has been remarkable."

"It certainly has," says Trump. "You have a dynamite team, and you've been treating a rare specimen. I feel better than I did twenty years ago."

"That's exceptional for any man of seventy-four, Mr. President, especially one who's recently been diagnosed with the coronavirus and had some difficulty breathing."

"I feel like an Olympic athlete."

Dr. Conley looks worried before smiling as he says, "You're not quite out of the woods yet, Mr. President."

"I'm already out of the woods, and this afternoon I'm out of here. I'm going to show strength to the nation."

Boosted by an unprecedented combination of antiviral cocktails and steroids, President Trump marches to his helicopter and returns to the White House where, striding across the lawn, he flashes thumbs up and fist pumps for cameras before shooting up steps to the balcony where he rips off his mask, shoving it into his coat pocket, and juts his chin as he announces, "I'm a leader and going back to work. Don't be afraid of the coronavirus. It's far less lethal than the flu. Don't let it control your life. Go out and live. Live like your commander in chief. And quit talking about those infected around me. They'll soon be just fine."

NINETY

Felonious Woman

joe's
kickin'
my
ass
so
guess
i
better
investigate
hillary

Vice Presidential Debate

I, faithful Vice President Mike Pence, have always been unflappable and remain so tonight when upon my lovely white hair lands the blackest of flies and one likely sent by agents of Senator Kamala Harris. The ruse does not work. I ignore Harris and the fly and their litany of coronavirus horrors and counter that our administration is charging toward what will surely be a barrage of safe and effective vaccines in record time. Contrast that to sixty million infections and twelve thousand fatalities inflicted by the swine flu on the watch of Barack Obama and Joe Biden. They know only luck prevented the swine flu from being even more dangerous than the coronavirus and killing millions. Now, rather than help the nation in this critical time, Biden and radical Senator Harris are undermining our efforts to develop vaccines.

I can see Kamala Harris smirking at me through the two clear barriers between us but her histrionics add to millions who already dislike her. She's also untrustworthy. Until recently she and Joe Biden said they were against fracking. Now they swear they won't ban fracking. Polling rather than conviction dictated their policy change.

As a man of principle, I respond openly to moderator Susan Page's question about whether I believe climate change is an existential threat. I reply climate is changing but we need better forest management than we have in liberal wastelands like California. Don't tell me about hurricanes. There were as many a hundred years ago as today. We should be more worried about how Joe Biden and Kamala Harris are going to raises our taxes and destroy the economy.

This is the most important election in our nation's history. Unless we win, we'll lose our freedom and our affluence. I must therefore ask Senator Harris if she and Biden would pack the Supreme Court after Judge Amy Coney Barrett is confirmed. Harris refuses to answer, just as Biden refused to answer President Trump last week during their first debate. It would be quite easy to say no, if that were true. It's obvious they're planning to pack.

The moderator wants to know what I, as vice president, would do if we lost the election. Would I concede in gentlemanly fashion? Or would I resist, as President Trump has promised to do if he detects fraud. I'm not yet the commander in chief so I don't have to address the question, I have only to say we're going to win because we've rebuilt the military, cut taxes, and appointed conservative judges at all levels. All Joe Biden and Kamala Harris have done is waste four years trying to impeach a great and noble president.

What to Say

to
terrorists
planning
to
kidnap
michigan gov gretchen whitmer
i
hope
president
trump
won't
tweet stand back and stand by

Breakdown Trump

I'm getting better fast but didn't claim even to Sean Hannity that I've tested negative for the coronavirus. I know there was damn little of the virus in my system. There may have been none. I didn't get into details with the doctors because Crazy Joe Biden as much as admitted he's scared to meet me in person and instead wants a virtual debate next week in Miami or anywhere else he can hide, and I said no, that's not what debating is about. Biden in a separate city would probably have answers beamed into his ears and senile brain. I'm not going for that.

I'm ready to roll and could stage campaign rallies this weekend but have decided not to worry my great supporters and will hold off a little while and get ready to soon give speeches and debate in person but everyone knows Joe doesn't want another beating like I gave him in our first battle and he quickly scheduled a town hall excuse for himself. It's like I'm a great heavyweight champion trying to get a scared challenger into the ring.

I hope you watched Mike Pence the other night. He inspired me the way he annihilated that monster Kamala Harris. She's incompetent like Michigan Governor Gretchen Whitmer who blames me that militias want to liberate her locked down and paranoid state.

Paradise

stock market way up economy
ready
to
go
through
roof
my secret health care will be
better
and
cheaper
than
obamacare

don't let sleepy joe ruin it

Joe Says

you may remember i got in trouble
when
we
were
running
against
the
senator
who was a mormon the governor

The Comeback Kid

People really don't talk enough about my spirit and determination but that's changing because I destroyed my coronavirus and charged out of the hospital and am already standing on a White House balcony before several hundred packed but mostly-masked supporters and removing my mask to tell everyone I'm not contagious. I'm not exactly saying I've tested negative for the coronavirus but I guarantee I'm not contagious like when bad things happened a little while last week. Then the virus vanished from my healthy body and it's disappearing from our nation.

My doctor now says I've tested negative on consecutive days and I'm ready to go. I feel powerful and immune here in Orlando and want to give big kisses to you unmasked followers. The next day I want to do the same in Johnstown, Pennsylvania. I'm trying to save you from a guy who's shot. Imagine if you lose. In addition to being senile and corrupt, Joe Biden wants to ban fracking and destroy your economies. Come on, suburban women, please try to like me, at least for a little while. Remember, I saved your damn neighborhoods from thugs.

Democracy in Georgia

three weeks before the election
and they're making us wait hours
before we vote hoping we'll just go
home but we won't do that we've
been waiting an awful long time

NINETY-ONE

Joe Six Pack Studies Judge Barrett

I got laid off again last week because liberals are still scared of the phony coronavirus but at least that gives me a chance to stay home and watch the Senate confirmation hearings of Amy Coney Barrett who's impressive so I forgive her for saying the virus really "is infectious" and smoking causes cancer. Other than on those issues, I think we can trust her.

She's pro-life and refuses to say if Roe v. Wade has been correctly handled in courts. You know she's against unlimited abortions as well as those who marry people of the same sex. She also makes it clear she's no climate change fanatic because this issue is "very contentious and a matter of public debate." She'll help us figure it out.

Diplomatically – don't say deceptively – she tells Dem senators she's "not on a mission to destroy" Obamacare. But she's criticized Supreme Court decisions that upheld most of the legislation. My buddies and I are confident she'll help President Trump get rid of the whole thing. No way we believe twenty million of us will lose our health insurance. Amy and The Donald won't let that happen.

I hope Dems like it when Amy says the Voting Rights Act is "a triumph in the civil rights movement." She proves her love for democracy when she testifies, "I certainly hope all members of the judiciary committee have more confidence in my integrity than to think I would allow myself to be used as a pawn to decide this election for the American people."

I'm pretty clear how Amy will vote on most Supreme Court cases but, given her restraint, not sure how she feels about a president pardoning himself.

Towns

trump appears at different town hall on
different network at same time as biden
woman in audience tells trump he's
handsome when he smiles which he'll
do more when his nightmare ends and

biden's begins

Predator

i'm tired
of this campaign being about coronavirus and me
let's
make
it
about
hunter
biden

What God Wants

God Himself told the great Las Vegas pastor Denise Goulet that I'm the apple of His eye and He's going to give me a second term. The Almighty knows if I weren't in command of our coronavirus battle Dr. Anthony Fauci and his gang of epidemic idiots would've killed a million of us. Don't worry, I've buried Fauci and promoted radiologist Scott Atlas who's tweeting, "Masks Work? NO?" In this great crowd today we don't have to take off our masks because we're not wearing them we're kissing Hunter Biden the only Biden I can beat.

Projected

how many iranians will trump
hit
if
he
wins

Foxy News

on morning of second debate
fair and balanced fox news
banner headlines hunter biden
then says pressure builds for
debate moderator to address
growing scandal

okay joe did you sell influence
to ukraine

NINETY-TWO

Obama Opens Fire

Highlights from President Barack Obama's speech in Philadelphia

Damn, I don't know why I've spent four years denying myself the right of self-defense and the joy of counterstriking Donald Trump. The quaint old custom of saying little about presidential successors no longer applies because, quite simply, our liberty is threatened. I never thought Trump would embrace my vision but I did hope for the sake of the country he might take the job seriously. Unfortunately, he hasn't shown any interest in helping anybody but himself and his friends.

He doesn't understand that behavior matters. Sadly, he does know rather too well that our democracy won't work when our leader lies to us every day. We can't keep track of all his lies. And they exhaust us. That's what he wants us to be, tired and too distracted to remember he inherited a strong economy and ignored the coronavirus pandemic.

Does he really expect to forever hide his malice and incompetence? Clearly, he does. Turns out he has a secret Chinese bank account. If I'd done that Fox News would've called me Beijing Barry. I better be careful offering Trump a nickname like that. He may use it. He's desperate. His ratings are down. His polls are grim. My colleagues Joe Biden and Kamala Harris stand ready to defend democracy.

Kennedy and Nixon Debate

i may cry says my wife standing in front of our giant tv
as I enter the living room and see black and white images
of young john f kennedy and richard nixon debating sixty
years ago

what's wrong i ask

these men are articulate and well-mannered i doubt they'd
get elected today

Polls Tighten

Going negative stinks but it works. Last year Donald Trump refused to forward military aid to beleaguered Ukraine until President Volodymyr Zelensky opened an investigation of Hunter Biden that failed to damage Joe's son but got Trump impeached. Now, bizarrely, still-unsubstantiated allegations against Hunter Biden are helping Trump crawl back into the race, boosted by an announcement, the morning after an almost-civilized debate performance, that Sudan is normalizing relations with Israel, as the United Arab Emirates and Bahrain had recently done. Is that sudden pain from stomach to head a sign he'll connive his way to four more years.

Ballot Burial

scheming
with
usps
lackey
louis
dejoy
trump slows mail delivery of ballots

Bang the Drum

at huge rallies law and order are on my lips as
new supreme court lines up and
surging coronavirus fades in rearview mirror

Beware

biden says soul of nation is at stake
that's right
and if he wins china will own us

Kavanuagh in Robe

Remember my Senate judiciary hearing for the Supreme Court and the way Democrats including Kamala Harris attacked my honor and made me cry. I got treated badly as Clarence Thomas years earlier. Don't respond that Ken Starr and I sniffed Bill Clinton's privates and got him impeached. He really did have sex. I didn't have sex with girls or women or even try to for years after high school. Now, I'm even more responsible and, if necessary, ready to examine this election to determine if Democrats have broken any laws.

Trump Family Newsletter

This is our most crucial deadline. I'm up against fake news and the radical left and the DC swamp and Deep State and Hollywood elites. If we're to win big again we can't afford any patriots sitting on sidelines. I've slashed taxes, rebuilt our military, killed terrorist leaders, and secured our border. I've also nominated and seen confirmed three conservative Supreme Court judges.

I must be reelected and it's looking like I will be. Dems and their pollsters don't understand what's going on as well as Trafalgar Group pollsters who increase weighting of my shy voters and see me winning unexpected places.

Battle for Penn State

don't ignore me
i'm holding multiple
rallies in many states
including pennsylvania
our key to beating sleepy
joe

Down Goes Trump

It's election night at the White House and, after studying more great returns, I tweet "Big Victory!" and walk around patting shoulders and shaking hands until a staffer shouts the race is getting close in Pennsylvania. Hardworking people in the state where I attended business school know Sleepy Joe Biden wants to ban fracking. No way they'll let him destroy their jobs.

Phony vote counters now say Biden's also tightening the race in Georgia. A little later once-faithful Fox News stuns me by projecting Biden will win Arizona. That's ridiculous. There are still hundreds of thousands of ballots to count. Arizonans aren't worried I sometimes insult the memory of John McCain. I insulted him when he was alive, too.

You wouldn't expect any sane person to believe Wisconsin and Michigan are suddenly slipping away and I've got to win those two shitholes as well as Pennsylvania and Georgia or my beautiful presidency would fall into the feeble hands of Joe Biden, who even Barack Obama wouldn't support until he had to.

Early Wednesday morning I appear on TV, saying we want all fair ballots to be counted and all fake ballots discarded. This election is a fraud. We better stop counting votes in states where I trail. We've got to be alert until the Supreme Court makes a decision.

Friday night Joe's already giving what amounts to a victory speech, never mentioning my name as he rants about the coronavirus and global warming and other liberal obsessions that motivated an unprecedented seventy-one million legal voters to mark Donald J. Trump on their ballots. I've had my election observers investigating this for a few days already and know BAD things happened because we weren't allowed up close. Twitter has joined the conspiracy by blocking many of my messages.

I don't care what Old Joe says Saturday night at another low-energy farce. My team and I are cranking out millions of emails to save our democracy. I'm sure you'll help when you read rousing subjects like "Fight Back" and "Defend the Election" and "Shocking News" and "Dems Plan to Steal Election." We've got everything organized into money machines like the Election Defense Task Force and the Official Election Defense Fund. I sign some of these and so do my son Eric and Team Trump and plenty of others offering you this great deal: "Contribute Any Amount Immediately to stand with the President to Defend the integrity of our Election." And we'll throw in ten dollars for every one you send us.

This election is far from over. I'm firing tweets like a machine-gunner and shouting into phones and filing court cases traitors throw out and bringing various state election officials to the White House. Just as I'd warned, our enemies are trying to rob us. Protect democracy. Defend freedom. Stand back and stand by.

EPILOGUE

Warlord Trump

Jabbing his cellphone keys with a fat index finger, Donald J. Trump keeps making errors before he shoves the device at Ivanka and orders, "Here, take dictation. This wouldn't be necessary if the cowardly attorney general of Georgia had found the votes I told him to."

"Dad, even with Georgia, you'd still be well short of Biden."

"Then we'd do the same in Pennsylvania and lots of other states where we won by landslides. You ready?"

Ivanka nods, listens, and tweets the "'Surrender Caucus' within the Republican Party will go down in infamy as weak and ineffective."

"I'm going keep fighting for our freedom," declares Trump.

Ivanka and silent aides nod.

"Here, get these: 'Even Mexico uses voter I.D. – Rigged Election! – Mike Pence didn't have the courage to do what should have been done to protect our Country and our Constitution."

"I don't think the vice president has the power to do that, Dad," Ivanka says.

"He's got the power to do whatever the hell I tell him," Trump says, thrusting his arm at a White House window. "Look at those brave Americans outside. They love me and won't allow liars and traitors to steal our election. This is about them, not me. I'm going to join the protest."

Surrounded by secret service agents, Donald J. Trump walks outside the White House, across the lawn, and through a gate he's motioned to open. A few thousand followers, comprised primarily of the unkempt and undereducated, roar they do love him and he's the greatest president in history and they're appalled by the election hoax.

"Let's march to the Capitol where right now they're trying to vote to certify the most outrageous election theft in history. We've got to be strong. We've got to be tough. We've got to scare hell out of them in order to take what we've earned. I'm coming with you, of course."

Followers cheer as Trump points toward the Capitol and shouts, "Forward march."

"Mr. President, we can't allow you to go," says a secret service agent.

"They need my leadership."

"Sir, the nation and the world need you safe back inside the White House."

"I'm a warrior."

"This way, Mr. President," says the agent, extending a palms-up toward Trump's beloved residence.

The president returns to his command post and orders two cheeseburgers and a plate of fries and several sodas he places on the table and digs into a chair to watch Fox News.

When his legions reach the perimeter of the Capitol, he stands and cheers. Ivanka and Mark Meadows, White House chief of staff, try unsuccessfully to smile.

In minutes Trumpers are battling outnumbered police, who use shields too much and sticks not enough.

"We're kicking their asses," Trump shouts.

He rushes close to the big screen as his followers begin to break through the defenders and dash inside the Capitol.

"Mr. President, I don't think this is a good idea," says Meadows.

"It's a great idea that's inevitable when people are fighting for their freedom. Get me some popcorn…"

Lots of oblique faces, ragged beards, and bad teeth run through halls and various august rooms and a few lurch into the office of Nancy Pelosi, and Trump yells, "Gotcha."

Emboldened patriots start pounding the door to the House of Representatives chamber where several armed agents point revolvers at danger while other agents whisk politicians out the back way to safe rooms that must remain secret.

"This is great," says Trump, back in his soft chair and devouring the second cheeseburger. "What's for dessert?"

"Mr. President, you've got to stop this," says Meadows.

"I can't stop people passionate about their democratic rights."

"He's right, Dad," says Ivanka.

"I'm the president and will be at least four more years."

Mark Meadows walks to Trump and shows him this text: "Mark, this is sinful and crazy. When I get out of this safe room, I may convene the cabinet and invoke the 25th Amendment."

Trump bounds up and says, "I told you Pence was a traitor and a weakling."

"Dad, they mean it."

Trump tries to call Secretary of State Mike Pompeo and Secretary of Treasury Steve Mnuchin and General Mark Milley, Chairman of the Joint Chiefs of Staff. "Pick up, goddamn it. I'm going to order General Milley to mobilize the armed forces and march on Washington."

Ivanka, in tears, walks to her father and embraces him. "Dad, you've got to go on TV and put a stop to this."

"Hell no."

"If you don't do as she says, Mr. President, I think the vice president and your cabinet will remove you from office."

Trump throws his final chunk of cheeseburger at the wall and says, "Okay, I'll do it for freedom."

He picks a pretty spot outside and, being an award-winning entertainer, tells the nation and world, "We won the election but it was stolen. We won by a landslide. It was fraudulent. But go home, and go home in peace."

After finishing he grimly smiles at Ivanka and Meadows.

"They won't invoke the 25th Amendment now, will they?"

"I don't know, Mr. President," says Meadows, "but I wouldn't bet my house either way."

Sources

"Mailer Advocates All-Black Police Forces" – Norman Mailer interview with Playboy Magazine in 1968.

"Spanish Influenza Review" – This information came from a lecture by Garth Millam to the Kern County Historical Society on January 21, 2012.

"Murder in Minneapolis" – Some notes about Derek Chauvin's work history come from a May 2020 Reddit post "confirmed by Minneapolis Police Department spokesperson John Elder."

www.ingramcontent.com/pod-product-compliance
Lightning Source LLC
Chambersburg PA
CBHW071330020726
47502CB00001B/44